# THE DIABOLIST

BOOKS BY LAYTON GREEN

<u>THE DOMINIC GREY SERIES</u>

*THE SUMMONER*
*THE EGYPTIAN*
*THE DIABOLIST*

---

*HEMINGWAY'S GHOST: A NOVELLA*

# THE DIABOLIST

## LAYTON GREEN

THOMAS & MERCER

Published by Thomas & Mercer
PO Box 400818
Las Vegas, NV 89140

ISBN-13: 9781611099843
ISBN-10: 1611099846

*Satan's successes are the greatest when he appears*
*with the name of God on his lips.*

—Mahatma Gandhi

# THE DIABOLIST

**1**

# MISSION DISTRICT, SAN FRANCISCO
# SEPTEMBER 21

They called themselves the House of Lucifer. Thirty minutes before midnight High Priest Matthias Gregory swung wide the doors to Red Abbey, and one by one the members filed inside.

The interior was a Gothic-inspired mockery of its Catholic counterpart: The crimson walls and vaulted ceiling hovered over the aisles with garish menace, pentagrams served as stained glass windows, an inverted crucifix hung on the wall behind the pulpit. Guttered candles lit the interior with a red glow, and Matthias had to admit the architects had achieved the desired effect: He felt as if he were walking straight into the mouth of Hell.

Recognized by the government as an official nonprofit religious organization since 1966, Matthias had shepherded the House of Lucifer into hundreds of chapters worldwide. In the sixties and seventies, America had been fascinated by the House and other occult pseudo religions that had sprung up, like demented cornstalks, out of a collective repressed subconscious. Now demons and warlocks and vampires were regular occurrences in popular novels and films, and the popularity of the occult had leeched its power to shock.

Which made it all the easier, in Matthias's mind, to carry out the business of the House.

Two armed guards frisked everyone at the door. The House of Lucifer received plenty of hate mail, the majority of it from fundamentalist

Christians, but the most recent death threat had been different and more than a little unnerving. Matthias had found the letter on the pulpit six days earlier, after he had unlocked the church in the morning. This disturbed him because he had closed up the night before, and there had been no letter.

Matthias glanced at the clock above the front entrance, his eyes resting on the two naked succubi forming the hands.

Twenty minutes until midnight.

Incense wafting into the cathedral added to the gloom, swirling in scarlet motes above the aisles. Matthias waved a hand, his lieutenant struck a kettle gong, and the congregation began intoning the words to one of the Satanic psalms.

Matthias concentrated on the words, determined to let the ritual chanting clear his mind and strengthen his resolve. Despite his attempts to scoff the threat away, a lump of nervous dread had settled in his stomach.

The letter had arrived not as an anonymous e-mail, or a crude letter bomb, or a phone call in a muffled voice. Instead, he'd found the letter on the pulpit, inside an envelope sealed with red wax, a single word handwritten in capital letters on the face of the envelope.

*HERETIC.*

Matthias had opened the envelope with a frown and read the words, scrawled in black ink, that appeared below his own name.

*You will renounce your false religion and declare yourself a HERE-TIC, or you will die at the hand of the one true God on the sixth midnight hence.*

The letter was unsigned.

The next night Matthias told his congregation about the letter, and in a show of righteous fury he announced a special worship service on the night of his threatened demise. Tonight was that night. Just in case, he had tightened security for the service.

A quarter to midnight. It was time to begin.

Matthias held the letter up, shaking it in his fist. "One more childish letter from the narrow-minded," he shouted, as the members smirked and clapped. "One more act of hate from those who preach love."

The high priest made a good living from the generous tithing of the congregation, but this job was not just about the money. Nor was it about the Devil. Matthias did not actually believe in Lucifer or any other supernatural being; he did not believe in anything outside the Darwinist reality of his own existence. What he did believe in was satisfying his natural carnal desires, and he despised any person, government, religion, or institution that stood in his way.

His members hailed from all walks of life. Plenty came from the margins of society, but there were also businessmen, professionals, politicians, and even a few celebrities. Some joined for the novelty, some joined for the secret orgies, but most joined because they believed in the mission of the House, which was the ridicule and disruption of mainstream religion.

His eyes slid to the clock. Eleven fifty.

Matthias continued his speech, analogizing the death threat to prophecies from other religions that had failed to come true, especially some of the pseudo-Christian cults whose response to failed prophecy was to change the words of the sacred texts and issue new versions.

The vigorous nods of the congregation energized him. As the gong announced the stroke of midnight, Matthias ripped the letter in half with a triumphant shout. Instead of the cheers he expected, the members in the front row reared in alarm. Some flung outstretched fingers in the direction of the pulpit. Even Oak, Matthias's right-hand man and virtual cofounder of the House, looked stunned, and Oak wasn't stunned by much of anything. The lump in Matthias's stomach expanded, tightening his chest with the grip of fear.

He spun to see what had caused the stir. Not three feet behind him stood a black-robed figure, face hidden within a cowl. Just like on the day he had received the letter, Matthias had been first inside the locked building. There was nowhere behind him to hide, and it was impossible for someone to have slipped unnoticed down the constricted aisles.

Before Matthias had a chance to react, the figure flicked one of its wrists and whispered a single word.

*"Burn."*

And burn Matthias did. The flames sprouted as soon as the word was spoken, and Matthias looked down in disbelief as the fire licked and tumbled across his robe. Disbelief turned to horror when he felt the assault of heat against his face, smelled the nauseating stench of his burning flesh, heard the dull whoosh of the flames, saw the hair on the back of his hands curl and wither into blackened wisps.

As Matthias fell to the floor in agony, batting at the flames with the screams of his congregation ringing in his ears, the figure in the black robe disappeared, winking out of existence as impossibly as it had arrived. With his last coherent thought, Matthias wondered if he had been wrong all this time, and if Lucifer himself had not come to reclaim his house.

**2**

# GEORGETOWN UNIVERSITY, WASHINGTON, DC

Viktor Radek waited in the front row while Professor Johannes Holzman, whom Viktor had once mentored at Charles University in Prague, made the introduction. The room was cavernous; Phenomenology of Religion 101 was quite the popular course, and hundreds of chittering students filled the amphitheater.

"It is my pleasure to announce," Professor Holzman said from the podium, "the most respected religious phenomenologist of our time, the world's foremost expert on cults, the man who taught me everything I know but very little of what he knows . . . ladies and gentlemen, I give you our very special guest lecturer, Professor Viktor Radek."

There was the usual applause, but as Viktor rose to his nearly seven-foot height and stepped to the lectern in his somber black suit, he sensed an apprehensive curiosity in the room, as if the students were observing a fascinating but dangerous species from behind the glass.

Without dispensing a greeting, Viktor said in his clipped Czech accent, "If I were to ask you, from a phenomenological perspective, whether human sacrifice was evil, what would be your answer?"

A murmur rippled through the students. Viktor called on a redheaded girl in the second row. "No," she said, even as her pinkish face wrinkled in displeasure. "There's no absolute good and evil."

Viktor chided the incorrect response, then called on a young man wearing a Notre Dame sweatshirt. "Isn't something as terrible as that," the young man said, "always wrong? It shouldn't matter from which perspective you're studying it."

Viktor saw Professor Holzman wince. It was early in the semester, but that should have been covered on day one. More likely the student hadn't been coming to class. "You might wish to reread the class description," Viktor said. "Perhaps you thought this was Ethics 101."

The class chuckled, and in the back left corner a skinny, goateed African-American student raised his hand. "The answer depends on whether the culture where the sacrifice took place believed it was evil. Or perhaps they believed it was evil, but necessary and justifiably so."

The room quieted as Viktor stepped to the edge of the stage, dark brow tightening, blacksmith shoulders hunched. "Human sacrifice," he boomed, "was perceived on rare occasion—and sometimes not so rare—as necessary for the greater good in many ancient cultures, to appease malevolent spirits and keep the village safe. It was used for other reasons as well, including"— Viktor turned to face the student in the Notre Dame sweatshirt—"as a test of faith."

Viktor's gaze withdrew from the room, to a time when he had stood amid a mesmerized crowd of worshippers in the African bush, rather than college students in an air-conditioned auditorium. His attention returned to the present with even more intensity. "And in certain Yoruba ceremonies, the sacrifice was tortured first, the flesh stripped from the body while the victim was kept conscious with potions from the *babalawo*, in order to increase the pain quotient and gain the attention of the spirit world."

A collective gasp issued forth.

"I use this example not to shock but to illustrate the lengths to which you must go to remove emotion from the study of religious phenomenology. In order to understand—to truly comprehend—you must step outside of your milieu and put yourself wholly in the mind of the believer. Your modern-day subject might believe in the existence of angels and demons that walk among us, in ghosts and djinn and mystics, Satanic possession, or multidimensional planes of existence. You'll find your own beliefs challenged; you'll find yourself drawn into a new world that frightens and excites you. You might find yourself ensconced in a remote Siberian village with shamans claiming they have the power to walk in dreams, studying witchcraft and warding off vampires with gypsies in the Carpathian Mountains, visiting a temple in India where thousands of free-roaming rats are revered as reincarnated ancestors, or investigating ascetics and faith healers with powers of the mind that defy science."

By now the students were leaning forward in their seats, and when Viktor stopped speaking a falling feather could have broken the silence.

"But if you decide that religious phenomenology is for you," he said without breaking into a smile, "then for the next eight or so years you will find yourself trapped in a dusty library."

The class chuckled again, and Viktor paced the stage, his looming presence filling the room. "Yet the proper religious phenomenologist must go further still. What is evil? How does the term *evil* apply not just to one particular act but to the larger ethos of the worshipper? From where does the idea of evil derive in that belief system? Is it merely illusory? How does the adherent reconcile the existence of evil, if applicable, to the belief in an omnipotent God?" Viktor folded his arms. "Perhaps the hardest lesson of all is to realize that you, as the dutiful scholar, might have learned nothing about the true nature of good and evil. And that for each investigation you must clear your mind and start anew."

The goateed young man raised his hand again. "I'm cool with all of that. But whether you're religious or in a cult or not, you still have a viewpoint, right? That's just human nature. I suppose one can be one's very own phenomenological study."

Viktor's lips turned upward for the first time.

The young man continued, "So what do *you* think, after all you've seen and studied? Is evil real, or is it just perspective, a state of mind?"

The class tittered, and Viktor let the question hang in the air.

"An inquiry," he said finally, "you must make for yourself. But I shall guarantee all of you one thing."

Viktor waited until the anticipation in the room became palpable, not just for theatrics, but because it was the most important lesson he could teach them.

"If you do continue to become a religious phenomenologist," Viktor said, "you'll be given the opportunity to decide."

After class ended, Viktor retired to Professor Holzman's office. He had once reminded Viktor of himself, back when Viktor was a full-time professor at Charles University and Professor Holzman was simply Jan, an eager PhD student who received the best marks in Viktor's class. Jan had shown great academic promise, which he fulfilled, but the drive for fieldwork had never manifested. He needed to put down his Belgian beer and get his hands dirty.

Viktor didn't understand this: Religious phenomenology was simply anthropology of the mind, and were it up to him, extensive fieldwork would be mandatory. That was what drove Viktor to his career in the first place: The traditional study of religion was too dogmatic and dry, philosophy too remote and theoretical. But religious phenomenology, that shadowy borderland where subjective belief is paramount, that realm of cults and miracles and unexplained phenomena, this Viktor could sink into like a beautiful opera of mysterious origin.

Viktor uncorked the bottle of Absinthe Suisse Couvet on Professor Holzman's desk, preparing the absinthe—Viktor's preferred drink—with a practiced hand. As he laid the slotted spoon above the glass he remembered his own youth, his privileged upbringing in a Czech family that was once minor Bohemian royalty. He had wanted for nothing, had not even had to choose a profession, though his family had urged him to join the family business and become an "important" politician.

*Important?* he had thought. Governors and senators come and go; kings and empires rise and fall. Something else had interested him, something more. The secrets of the universe, of life and death, of God and before: The timeless truths, if there were any, had driven young Viktor.

# THE DIABOLIST

They drove him still. He sensed that the secrets lay just under the surface of the ice, floating away whenever the ice was tapped. The trick was to approach the ice from the proper angle, not to shatter but to peer beneath.

His cell buzzed, breaking his reverie. The caller was Jacques Bertrand, his Interpol contact. Viktor's investigations occupied the bulk of his time now. He consulted with police agencies worldwide, and sometimes private clients, on the pathology of dangerous cults. Swirling his absinthe before he answered, he noticed that Jacques had called from his office number, even though it was after one a.m. in Lyon.

"It's very late, Jacques."

"*Oui*, thank you for answering. We have need of your assistance. You're available?"

"That depends."

Viktor felt the familiar tingle at the prospect of a new case. Most often the case would involve a cult familiar to Viktor, but the tingling was for the sect, religion, or secret society that he had yet to investigate. Or, better yet, one undiscovered: potential bearers of the hidden knowledge that Viktor craved.

"There was a murder in Paris this morning," Jacques said. "Elements are involved that . . . require your expertise."

Interpol called him for one of two reasons: either the case involved Viktor's specialty as well as multinational criminal issues, which was rare, or else the local police in some jurisdiction had requested information from Interpol that suggested the need for Viktor's involvement, and Interpol would recommend him.

Strange, however, that Jacques had called him so quickly. The link must be obvious.

"If possible," Jacques said, "we would like you to go to San Francisco first. There was a similar murder there. It is closer to you than Paris, and there were witnesses."

"Similar? Who was murdered in San Francisco?"

"A man named Matthias Gregory. He was—"

"High priest of the House of Lucifer," Viktor murmured. That was indeed news. The House was the world's largest official Satanic religion. "And the connection to the Paris murder?"

"There are several, *oui*, which we can discuss after you view the crime scene. But the most obvious connection is the identity of the victim, Monsieur Xavier Marcel."

Viktor was lifting his glass to take another sip, and he eased the absinthe down. Xavier Marcel, also known as the Black Cleric, was both a wanted criminal and the underground leader of L'église de la Bête, or the Church of the Beast, Europe's most infamous and dangerous Satanic cult.

News indeed.

# 3

## MANHATTAN

The long shadows of dusk greeted Dominic Grey as he stepped out of the teen homeless shelter and into the twilight world of Washington Heights. After a few months of teaching jujitsu in a makeshift gym, Grey now had seven semiregular students. Most of the troubled kids tried his class once and never came back.

That pained him. He understood the martial arts were not for everyone, but he wanted to help each wary face that came through his door. Most of the kids yearned for knowledge and structure but weren't ready to accept Grey's strict code of honor.

Grey's step was especially heavy that evening. One of his favorite students, a fourteen-year-old Latino gang member named Frankie, had cursed another student in class. Grey showed him the door, and Frankie had cursed Grey on his way out. Though thin and wiry, Frankie was scrappy, smart, and didn't know how to quit. He reminded Grey of himself.

Frankie was also very proud, and Grey doubted he would come back. But that was the way it had to be. Grey had studied the martial arts since he was five, some of that time under one of the top Japanese jujitsu masters in the world. Grey's own *shihan* had insisted that respect came before all else; no one should learn how to harm another human being before learning how to value one.

Like the kids he now taught, Grey had also once been homeless. His father was a lifelong Marine who had mentally and physically abused Grey and his mother throughout Grey's childhood. Mortally afraid his skinny, introspective son would fail to become a *real* man, he'd trained Grey to fight since he could crawl.

When his father was assigned to Tokyo soon after Grey's tenth birthday, he forced Grey to study Japanese jujitsu, one of the most brutal and effective martial arts in the world, designed to use an attacker's own energy to exploit the weaknesses of the human body: joints, pressure points, organs, digits, soft tissue. Zen-Zekai, the style of jujitsu taught at Grey's school, was particularly violent. Barely a day went by that Grey came home without blood on his *gi*.

Grey's mother died of stomach cancer when Grey was fifteen, and on the first anniversary of her death Grey's father came home drunk yet again, reached for his nail-studded belt one too many times. Grey had never quite forgiven himself for beating his own father that night, but he wasn't sure he would do anything differently if given the chance, and that pained him even more.

After leaving his father crumpled on the floor, vowing to kill Grey as he walked out the door, Grey took to the backstreets of Tokyo, staying alive by fighting in underground street fights. Already a black belt in Zen-zekai, Grey thrived on Tokyo's human cockfight circuit. But the underbellies of Japan's throbbing neon cities were dangerous for a teenage boy, no matter how tough. He drifted to other cities and countries, yearning for a place to call home, grasping onto his fierce personal ethos as a lifeline. For to compromise his ethics, to mute that quiet inner voice, was to lose the one thing he could claim as his own.

Grey left the trash- and graffiti-strewn streets of Washington Heights and approached his building, an abandoned high school converted into lofts, on the edge of gentrifying Hudson Heights.

# THE DIABOLIST

"Hey, Teach!"

A shirtless teen was leaning against the steps of his building. *Frankie.* Two men in gang colors sat on the steps beside him, eyeing Grey like he had just kicked their dog.

The streets were empty, a single streetlight illuminating the concrete steps. Grey kept an eye on all three. "Frankie," Grey said evenly as he approached. "I'd like to see you in class again, despite what happened tonight. You have real talent."

"I dunno, Teach. I no think I need you no more."

Grey noticed the other two shift ever so slightly. Dressed in tank tops and baggy pants, they had prison tats on their necks and forearms, and the hardened eyes of street thugs. One was bald; the other had a Mohawk.

Grey kept his demeanor as relaxed as possible as he approached. Five more feet and it wouldn't matter what they had stuck in the waistbands of those pants. It took three seconds for the average man to draw, enable, and point a gun, not to mention aim and hit. And three seconds was an eternity in close quarters.

"Hey Teach," Frankie said softly. "You know wha' we do about *gente* disrespect us?"

The two thugs rose and pulled switchblades as Frankie began to grin. Grey was on them before Frankie's grin reached the corners of his lips. No one pulling a knife expects to be rushed, especially not when it's three against one. Grey approached in a blur, halfway there before the blades were out, and he snapped a vicious side kick into the kneecap of the bald gang member, whose eyes told Grey he wasn't expecting a low strike. Grey heard the crunch of a broken patella.

The thug with the Mohawk managed to raise his knife and lunge at Grey. Again Grey did the unexpected and stepped into the amateur thrust, fluid as a snake, sliding to the side of the knife and brush blocking the arm at the elbow. Grey turned the soft block into a strike, hitting the exposed throat with the hardened web of one hand while smacking the center of the lower back, the vulnerable *ming men* point, with the other. The gang member fell to the pavement and grabbed at his throat, choking violently.

Grey kicked the knives away and moved towards Frankie, who had backed against the door at the top of the steps, now brandishing his own knife.

Frankie was shaking and waving the knife around. "*¿Qué hiciste, qué hiciste?* You kill him!"

Grey stopped advancing and put his hands out, palms up. "Put the knife down, Frankie. They'll both live. I'll call for help as soon as you drop the weapon."

Frankie glanced at his two friends moaning on the ground. "*Hijo de puta madre,*" Frankie said. "You know wha' this does to me?"

"It doesn't have to do anything," Grey said. "Leave the gang and train with me. I'll protect you."

Frankie's eyes were wild, and he kept waving the knife in front of him as he lurched down the side of the steps, as far from Grey as he could get. When he reached the bottom he backed into the street.

"What's out there for you, Frankie? I've been there, right where you're standing."

"You no know *shit*," Frankie said, then turned and fled into the night.

Grey watched him go as the adrenaline seeped away, feeling a sadness for the world descend and settle into the pockets of his bones.

Frankie was wrong.

Grey did know.

After the police and ambulance left, Grey trudged to his fifth-floor loft. There had been a warrant out for the two men with Frankie. Both gang members, ex-cons, wanted for an assortment of violent crimes. Fair or not, the two older ones had chosen their path. Frankie was still young enough to decide.

Grey's studio loft had exposed brick walls, a stained concrete floor, and a shoji screen separating his sleeping area. The furniture consisted of a platform bed and a tatami mat, along with a few chairs he had picked up at an estate sale. The built-in bookshelves contained a selection of novels, philosophical works, and travel and language guides. The latest *Time Out New York*, earmarked at the cheap eats and off-Broadway sections, had been tossed on the bed.

Sick of hotels, he had rented the studio for a year. His job with Viktor required frequent travel, and Grey supposed New York was as good a base as any.

He showered, poured himself a cold sake, and was pleased to see he had a voice mail from Viktor. When he had long spells between cases he grew restless. He had worked on a couple of small investigations in the last few months, but nothing major since the tragic case involving the Egyptian biotech company. Tragic, and incredible. Stretching the limits of his beliefs was quickly becoming part of the job description.

In his message Viktor said there was a new case requiring immediate attention, and that Grey should check his e-mail for travel details. Grey logged on and found a plane ticket to San Francisco leaving at six a.m. the next morning, along with a hotel reservation for three nights at the Fairmont. He was to meet Viktor in the hotel lobby at two p.m. tomorrow.

Grey stared at the empty street below his window as he finished the sake, wondering where Frankie would sleep that night, wondering what the new case with Viktor would be like, wondering how renting a half-furnished loft in a forgotten corner of a city of ten million people, without a friend or barely even an acquaintance, was that much different from braving the streets of Tokyo when he was a teenager, alone and unsure.

He pushed away from the window and started packing, happy to be working again.

## INNER SANCTUM OF L'ÉGLISE DE LA BÊTE, PARIS CATACOMBS

Dante's black duster swept around his ankles as he strode through the gloom, the steady drip of sewer water his constant companion, the pentagram tattoo splayed across his shaved head catching the occasional drop.

Most of the members of L'église de la Bête chose to enter the catacombs through one of the secured hidden routes, but Dante preferred to walk in plain view of the homeless, thieves, murderers, and worse who occupied the levels near the surface streets. He enjoyed the way they scattered or looked down as he approached, careful not to meet his gaze. And there was always the chance that someone new had arrived in the underworld, someone unfamiliar with Dante and his knives.

He left the rat- and filth-infested sewers behind, descending into a section of the catacombs of which polite society was unaware, and to which most of impolite society dared not go.

Dante had been a member of L'église de la Bête for more than a decade. For most of that time, he had been the right-hand man of Xavier Marcel, the Black Cleric. Dante had not feared Xavier, but he had respected Xavier's capacity for cruelty and devotion to cause.

Dante felt no remorse about his new allegiance to the Magus. The Magus had given Xavier a choice, and Xavier had chosen to stand against him. Dante was a weapon, not a politician, and while L'église de la Bête was his church, he had only one true ethos, and that was pain. He would worship and follow whoever granted him the most access to it. For the present that was L'église de la Bête, and the Magus.

*Pain.* Suffering had already polluted Dante's soul by the time he entered prison at the tender age of eighteen, but during his decade of incarceration, his internal torment transformed from an emotion into a calling.

Dante's slight lisp had not gone over well in prison, until he disemboweled someone with a shiv for mimicking it. He participated in so many fights that pain became irrelevant, and he became known as someone who would never quit during a fight, no matter how much injury he suffered. It made him a feared man.

In prison he met two men who would define the rest of his life. The first, a Filipino man also in prison for killing a child molester, became Dante's only and last friend. The Filipino was an expert knife fighter in the *eskrima* tradition and taught Dante everything he knew, practicing with smuggled kitchen knives and wooden shunts. Dante devoted himself to training, turning his trim, iron body into a sort of knife itself. He mastered the art of throwing knives under the tutelage of an ex-soldier in the French Foreign Legion, who taught him how to weight the hilt with liquid mercury to make the weapon fly more true.

The second man who would define Dante's life was avoided by the other inmates. One of the rare few who, like Dante, belonged to no gang and yet no one dared touch. Dante learned he was from Paris, a member of a Satanic church called L'église de la Bête. Dante, immune to the terrible rumors of what befell someone who meddled with a member of L'église de la Bête, cornered the man in the yard one day. His name was Xavier Marcel, and instead of fighting, Xavier told Dante about his religion. Dante learned that this religion also valued pain and decided to accept a rare invitation.

When Dante left prison he followed Xavier to Paris, inked a very special tattoo on his head, filed his incisors to a sharp point, and dedicated himself to his two religions.

Pain and L'église de la Bête.

The Magus appreciated Dante's service; in fact, Dante suspected his new leader actually understood his motives, which had never been the case with Xavier. Xavier had used Dante to stay in power, and Dante had allowed him to do so because it was expedient.

The Magus was different.

The Magus knew.

As he entered the final tunnel, Dante heard the guttural intonations of the Black Mass, inhaled the first whiff of burning flesh that saturated the air in the cathedral of L'église de la Bête. He left the tunnel and entered the cavernous underground grotto, saw the crush of members gathered around the lantern-lit pedestal. He decided to wait in the background.

Xavier had placed great emphasis on the Black Mass, believing it channeled just as much spiritual power as the Christian ritual it mocked. The Black Mass had been performed by Satanists for century upon century, and participation was required. Everyone important would be in attendance.

Dante could tell the ritual neared its conclusion. The reversed Ten Commandments would have already been recited, the unclean host from the sacrifice ingested and imbibed. He saw some of the more devout members walking backwards on their hands and feet, crablike, towards the effigy of the Beast at the base of the huge inverted cross.

The Mass ended, but before the orgy could begin, Dante made his presence known. He waded through the crowd, the worshippers scrambling out of his way when they recognized him. Dante had been known to whip out his knives for anyone who failed to move fast enough, and by the time he was halfway to the platform the path was clear.

A veil of silence dropped as Dante climbed the stepladder and stood upon the wooden platform, his black coat and tattooed head a wreath of darkness within the halo of dim light. He spoke in harsh, raspy French, and with the lisp that had always plagued him.

"I know many of you are having trouble accepting the rule of the Magus."

# THE DIABOLIST

Shouts of agreement rose from the crowd, as well as several cries of blasphemy from those outside Dante's line of view.

"I hear some believe it was I who did this thing," Dante said.

A voice from the crowd: "Who else could do this? Who is this new prophet, and where is he?"

"Trust me, my brothers and sisters, it was not I."

Dante sensed the presence behind him even before he saw the shocked faces of the worshippers. Without turning he knew what they were seeing: the huge cross now aflame, the figure in the black robe on the dais a few steps above Dante, looking down on the crowd. Fear was not an emotion Dante experienced—he was not sure that he experienced emotion at all anymore—but Dante could sense the awe and terror ricocheting through the cavern.

What Dante did feel was the heat from the burning cross a few feet behind him. He hoped the Magus hurried his speech.

Someone cried out, "It's the Angel of Death, the Beast himself."

A voice behind Dante boomed forth, somehow amplified to ring throughout the cavern. "I, too, have heard the rumors, and have come to set your hearts and minds at ease. It was I who deposed Xavier, but I am neither angel nor beast."

Dante recognized the next voice as Margaux Fournier, the oldest female member. "Then who are you?"

"I am the Magus. I came because Xavier refused to recognize the one true God. I remain because I do."

"Then you're our enemy." The firmness in Margaux's voice surprised Dante.

"Enemy? I'm your new prophet. Keep your symbology and your chants, practice your religion how you will. But know that your theology is primitive. I ask you: Would you worship a beast, a discarded fallen angel, or would you worship a *god*?"

A ripple of noise scuttled through the crowd. "Why should the God of Abraham have sole claim to that title?" the voice behind Dante continued.

"Why waste your time mocking an inferior religion? Be free of that yoke, and worship the one who came first, the one your Satan was searching for when he rebelled."

The crowd murmured and then quieted, until the licking of the flames behind Dante was the only thing he could hear. Sweat poured down his neck and back, the heat almost unbearable.

"You have a new mission," the voice said, "a departure from the black cross alone. A mission worthy of the One who sent me."

Another undulation of noise from the crowd.

"Dante will appoint your new leader, and he will instruct you further. Heed his words and know them as my will."

Dante again had a sensation, this time that the presence behind him was gone. Unwilling to show weakness, yet knowing he had to leave the platform before the intense heat overcame him, Dante raised one of his knives. The crowd followed his every movement, wondering who among them had been chosen. Framed by the hellish glow of the flames, Dante pointed his knife at a man in front named Luc Morel-Renard, leader of France's fastest growing far-right movement and a rising political voice among the disenchanted.

Luc raised his fist, and Dante stepped off the platform.

Grey slid his lean six-foot-one frame into an aisle seat in the rear of the plane. Whether restaurant, train, or plane, Grey preferred no one had his back. The seats next to him were empty, and he kicked off his boots and rubbed his week's worth of dark stubble. The day might be a long one and he hadn't fallen asleep until after three a.m. He was dozing before the plane took off, in a state of half awareness cultivated in his missions with Marine Force Recon.

Grey's attempt to exorcise the ghost of his father by joining the Marines, to follow the same path yet prove he was different, had been a disaster. He soon found himself in a dusty Iraqi city brimming with misery, lying on a terra-cotta rooftop a mile from the targets, seeing a human outline in his scope and realizing he did not even know the sex, could not snuff out a faceless life. He already struggled with the violence that kept a constant vigil, like a diseased candle, deep inside. He had closed his eyes and let the weapon lie loose in his grasp.

Back at base a colonel put an arm around Grey and told him that someone as talented as he in the art of inflicting pain and suffering could still help his country. That Grey could teach hand-to-hand combat to new Recon soldiers, or enjoy a court-martial.

Grey left with a clean record and never looked back.

After flirting with the CIA, who loved his profile but loathed his internal moral compass, he stumbled upon an opening in Diplomatic Security. He thought the mix of travel and security work would be a good fit, but after tossing his badge at the feet of the United States ambassador to Zimbabwe, again for disobeying orders, he realized that no government position, no job where he was forced to compromise his principles for any reasons other than his own, would ever be a good fit for Dominic Grey.

In Zimbabwe he had been staffed on a case with Viktor that still caused Grey to lie awake at night. After the case, Viktor offered him a job. The work hit the right notes: travel, intellectual stimulation, using his skills to help those in need.

Working with Viktor was a lonely lifestyle, but Grey had always been an island, and work was not to blame for those demons. And there was one thing he could say for sure about Viktor's cases: They were never boring.

He nodded off. When he woke, a blond woman had claimed the seat next to him. He thought he had fallen asleep after boarding had finished, but he wasn't certain. Maybe she had switched seats.

It wasn't like him not to wake up. In the middle row beside him, a businessman sprawled across all three seats, lightly snoring. The plane had the quiet hum of midflight.

The woman was watching the running script on the bottom of the overhead monitor, and Grey caught the tail end of a news report about the murder of a Satanic church leader in San Francisco. There weren't many details, but he had the strong suspicion he was about to learn a lot more about that murder.

The news switched to sports and then to the upcoming election, both of which Grey ignored. He had never played sports, because his father insisted he train in his spare time. And politics just disgusted him.

A tall man in his fifties appeared on-screen, giving a video conference to a group of reporters gathered in London. He was a dapper man with silver-streaked, coiffed dark hair. The caption read *Order of New Enlightenment Worldwide Headquarters*.

Grey had heard of the Order and its clever Iranian-American leader, Simon Azar. The "church," one of those New Age self-help nightmares, was very young, but Simon's few taped speeches had already become a social-media phenomenon.

# THE DIABOLIST

The Order was reputedly based in London, but Simon appeared only on the Web, from an undisclosed location. The mystique seemed to fuel the growth. Grey had read somewhere that Simon planned to unveil the location of the brand-new headquarters after he gained a million followers. He found it ridiculous that the reporters were pandering to this guy. The Internet had crowned another jester as king.

A reporter was speaking. Grey decided to use his headphones. "Congratulations on your success, Pastor."

Simon was wearing a silver shirt and a crisp black suit with no tie. He clasped his hands in front of him. "Thank you" he said, "but I prefer not to be called pastor." He had the smooth voice of an orator and a smile that showcased perfect white teeth. Grey didn't trust anyone with perfect white teeth. "A pastor implies a traditional religion, and our Order is anything but traditional."

"What title do you prefer?"

"How about my name?" Simon said mildly. "I've no need for a title. And it isn't my success; it's the success of our members worldwide, united in their desire to usher in a new way of thinking for a modern world."

*Another day, another demagogue,* Grey thought. Whether politics or religion or business, it was always the ones with something to prove, the ones who burned from within to dominate others, who clamored loudest to be heard.

It was something Grey particularly enjoyed about his new profession: taking down those who sought to control others for their own gain. Grey's mother had died in extreme pain after electing not to seek medical attention, following the advice of her fist-shaking pastor. Praying every second of the day while the cancer ravaged her from within.

Another reporter said, "Is the Order of New Enlightenment a religion?"

"Call it what you will," Simon said. "What we worship is creation. And we believe God enjoys what He has created, rather than the logical fallacy that defines the rest of the world's religions."

"Would you care to expound?"

"Why would a Supreme Being go to the trouble to create us, this world and everything in it, this physical *universe,* to be concerned only with the realm of the spirit? To deny worldly pleasures, to act against every principle of nature and biology? Worshippers of every creed should ask themselves whether their theology actually makes sense, or whether it was invented to fit the religion neatly inside the particular political and social agenda of the time. We live in a radically different era, and it's time we espoused a theology that relates to today's world."

Despite his own feelings, Grey could see why this church was gaining popularity. The man had a hypnotic voice, as well as a sharp intelligence conveyed in a down-to-earth manner.

"Your followers have been accused of having some rather . . . open . . . views on sexual behavior. Would you like to say something about these radical claims?"

"More radical than a record of rampant child molestation? Or of archaic subjugation of women's rights? Or of arranged marriages, polygamy? Our policy of embracing our natural sexuality in a responsible manner rather pales in comparison, wouldn't you say?"

The reporter faded into the background, and another stepped forward. "You've been hard to pin down on who or what it is that you worship."

"I'm sorry, was that a question?"

The reporter waved a hand. "Do you worship a Supreme Being, or are you just espousing a philosophy, a way of life?"

"Perhaps it would put your mind at ease if I tell you that we worship the same God as everyone else, if by God you mean a force or entity that created and governs the universe."

Another smile, this time accompanied by most of the reporters. Grey wondered if Viktor had seen this guy.

A slender blond woman stepped forward, all high heels and confidence. She reminded Grey of Veronica Brown, the ambitious investigative journalist who had followed Grey on his previous case. She had pursued him in other ways as well, and though clever and beautiful, they were two ships sailing in different directions. Veronica was searching for worldwide fame and fortune, while Grey was searching for a coffee shop where someone knew his name. "What about the criticism that your Order has attracted many, well, fringe elements?"

Simon gave a patient nod. "Is it possible these fringe elements have not yet been spoken to, or been denied access elsewhere? Your statement implies that, should these 'fringe elements' all of a sudden join, for example, the Catholic Church, that Rome and the Papacy should be questioned? Did Jesus not wash the feet of the prostitute? Why was your question not: What is it about my Order that *is* speaking to these 'fringe elements'? We have new followers of all types, all races and cultures and nationalities. We embrace them all."

"But isn't it true that the meetings of the top leaders are conducted in secret? Is that not indicative of a cult?"

"I urge you to name a single religion where this is not the case," Simon said.

The blond reporter opened and then closed her mouth, and Grey smiled to himself. Veronica would have found a clever response.

There were a few more exchanges, then the news switched to a suicide blast in Karachi. Grey removed the headphones. The woman next to him, a tawnier blond than the reporter, said, "He's not what he seems."

He started, surprised she had spoken. When he turned his head towards her, the first thing he noticed was the luminosity of her green eyes, which enhanced the mystery of her statement.

After her eyes he noticed creamy skin and an oval face so symmetrical and compelling Grey couldn't stop staring at it. She was wearing a fitted white blouse, and when she shifted he could see the contours of a trim and compact body. She was not elongated like a model, but well proportioned, an everything-in-the-right-place kind of woman.

"Sorry?" Grey said. "Who, Simon Azar?"

She bit into her lower lip, then glanced down the aisle. "It's important that you believe me."

Her accent sounded like a mix between Spanish and a Slavic language. Grey's guess was Romanian. "Do I know you?"

"I know how this sounds. Just remember what I said, because you'll hear things that will make you doubt."

Grey chuckled. "Okay. Did Viktor send you? Is he on this flight?"

The intensity of her stare never wavered. She took his hand in both of hers and held it, while Grey sat there dumbly. "I have to return," she said, then rose and walked down the aisle, passing through the curtain to first class.

At this point Grey imagined Viktor lounging with a bottle of absinthe in the front of the plane, having a good laugh at Grey's expense.

Except Viktor didn't joke.

Grey's next thought was that she left off "to my seat" in her statement. Why hadn't she said she had to return to her seat? After ten minutes passed, and then twenty, Grey frowned and rose. He walked to first class, checking every seat and restroom along the way. When he didn't find her, he stood by the door to the cabin with folded arms.

A flight attendant approached, and Grey said, "Excuse me, did you see a woman come through first class a few minutes ago? Dark blond hair, white blouse, very attractive?"

"Sorry, no."

"She was sitting next to me and walked up here maybe fifteen minutes ago."

Her head cocked. "Honey, I've been here the whole flight, and no passenger except you has come through that curtain."

"I just saw her come up here," Grey said. "You had to have seen her."

She patted his hand. "Did you fall asleep, have a bad dream?" She giggled. "Or maybe that was a good dream. How about some coffee?"

"I was awake," Grey muttered, although his voice lacked conviction.

He returned to his seat and engaged a male flight attendant standing in the rear of the plane, just behind his seat. Grey asked the same questions.

# THE DIABOLIST

"I can tell you no one's come back here in the last twenty minutes except a seven-year-old boy."

Grey mumbled his thanks and leaned towards the businessman across the aisle, the only other potential witness to a conversation Grey was starting to wonder if he had ever had.

The businessman was still snoring, face buried into a courtesy pillow.

# 6

## SAN FRANCISCO

Grey relished the crisp San Francisco air, a welcome respite from the asphalt-choked swelter of New York in late summer. After dropping off his backpack at the hotel, he had time for a quick run and a shower before meeting Viktor. Grey worked in his jogs whenever possible, his way of clearing the thoughts crowding his head.

The strange encounter with the girl presided over his run. Before deplaning, Grey had worked his way to the front of the flight and had waited outside the gate as the passengers and then the crew left.

No sign of the girl. He could accept the fact that she had tricked him, but why?

Now clad in cargo pants, boots, sweater, and a black Windbreaker, Grey felt underdressed and out of place in the posh hotel. When Grey met Viktor under the canopied entrance to the Fairmont, country flags snapping in the wind, the sweep of San Francisco on the hills below, he felt relief at seeing a friendly face, as if he had been at sea for months and had just spotted land.

Grey knew he was one of those men both blessed and cursed to live on the hinterlands of society, able to see the machinations of his era in their true light, yet unable to erase the part of himself that wanted to be embraced by them. He was also well aware of his isolating dichotomies: a born fighter who abhorred violence, a wanderer who yearned for a place to call home, someone trying to accomplish the Sisyphean task of creating a future while still erasing the past.

# THE DIABOLIST

Viktor clasped him on the shoulder. "It's good to see you, Grey. Come. We have some time before we meet with the detective."

Grey felt silly telling Viktor about the girl, so he made idle chitchat as he followed Viktor downhill to an upscale French coffee bar just off Union Square. A chill seeped through his Windbreaker as they walked. He always underestimated the city's stiff breeze.

Viktor wore his familiar dark suit, looking the part of the stodgy professor, but Grey knew better. Viktor carried a *kris*, a curved dagger from Indonesia, underneath that suit, and he knew Viktor had traveled to as many of the world's unsavory places as Grey himself, which was saying something. He also knew Viktor had an unhealthy fondness for absinthe, and that he had not just an encyclopedic knowledge of the world's religions and sects, but more firsthand experience with pathological cult behavior than perhaps anyone alive.

No, a stodgy professor he was not.

The café, full of polished brass and exposed brick, was across the street from the red-and-green pagoda heralding the entrance to Chinatown. Grey inhaled the aroma of fresh pastries and gourmet coffee. Knowing the best places around the world to eat and drink was another of Viktor's talents. Grey had stayed with Viktor in Prague for a week after the insanity of the biotech case, and had dined in more fine restaurants in one week than the rest of his life combined.

Viktor stirred his cappuccino and relayed what he knew about the murder of Matthias Gregory, high priest of the House of Lucifer. Grey had not yet worked on a case involving a Satanic cult and found himself both wary and intrigued.

"Judging from the identity of the other victim," Viktor continued, "which we shall discuss in a moment, and the fact that the murder was committed at midnight on September 21, a day of feast and sacrifice on the Luciferian calendar, it appears someone has a vendetta against Satanists."

The word brought a chill to Grey, despite his personal lack of faith. His devout mother had possessed a very real belief in God and Satan, and had tried to impress upon Grey the seriousness of their existence. As much as Grey had loved and respected his mother, the circumstances of her terrible death—the failure of her faith after her refusal to seek medical care—had undone any convictions she might have imparted.

"Given the note to the victim," Grey said, "I assume we're talking some kind of religious zealot, maybe a fundamentalist Christian?"

"The obvious answer," Viktor agreed. "And burning to death is a traditional punishment for heretics."

Grey sipped his coffee. "You don't sound convinced."

"I hesitate to speculate too much at this stage, but fundamentalists are not exactly known for such exotic circumstances." He checked his watch. "We're to meet with Detective Chin at the House of Lucifer at four. I'd like to educate you on the cult aspects before we arrive. I assume you have little familiarity with Satanism?"

"I wasn't even allowed to listen to Ozzy Osbourne."

A waiter arrived to check on them; Grey had never been in a coffee bar with servers. Viktor continued, "Many misconceptions about the Satanic cults have endured over the centuries, and some truths as well. The reality is, as usual, far more complex."

"You mentioned cults, as in plural—I didn't realize there was more than one type of Satanic cult."

"There haven't been quite as many Satanic cults, schisms, and heresies over the years as their Christian counterparts, but the number would shock you. Hundreds, if not thousands. Most, of course, were eradicated by the Catholic Church or angry mobs. But plenty exist today, the House of Lucifer being the largest and most well-known."

Grey cupped his coffee mug in his hands. "I've always taken this for granted, and maybe it's an ignorant question, but are Satan and Lucifer the same . . . being?"

"It's an astute inquiry. While Satan and Lucifer are used interchangeably today, historically there was a difference. Many names have been used for the

Christian Devil, though the concept itself is derivative of an ancient Persian deity."

"You're talking about Zoroastrianism?"

"I see you've been doing some reading in your downtime," Viktor said.

"This is my profession now, and I don't like being in the dark. I may never have your knowledge, but I don't need to swim in ignorance."

Viktor gave a crisp nod of approval. "The evolution of the Devil from Zoroastrianism is a story for another day. But Christianity's and Zoroastrianism's version of the Devil, as well as the original Jewish concept of a Satan—which simply means *adversary* in Hebrew—all beg the same question: From where did evil arise?"

"Assuming a belief in God," Grey said slowly, "then either it came from God, which makes evil a part of God's nature, or it came from somewhere else. Thus the concept of the Devil."

Viktor opened the palm of his left hand. "But if the Devil is responsible for evil, then who or what is responsible for the creation of the Devil?

Grey contemplated the question. "On the one hand you have a Devil created by God, which means that even if evil stems from the free will of man or from the Devil, God is ultimately responsible."

Viktor stirred his cappuccino. "And on the other hand?"

"If God is not ultimately responsible for evil, the only other logical explanation is that the Devil is equal to, or was at least created separately from—and by whom?—God."

"Good," Viktor said. "You've just outlined the problem of evil, otherwise known as the dilemma of theodicy: Either God is responsible for evil, or someone else is and God is not omnipotent. Theologians have bent over backwards for centuries trying to resolve this issue."

"I imagine God's a hard guy to figure out," Grey said.

"Back to your original question: The figure of Satan gained strength as monotheism came into being, as a convenient way to explain the presence of evil. If there's a Bible in your hotel room, study the two differing accounts of

King David's ordering of a divine census, a practice forbidden in the Torah. In Second Samuel, God becomes angry with His people and incites David to take the census, then sends a plague to punish the people of Israel, killing seventy thousand. Yet in the parallel account in First Chronicles, written centuries later, it's Satan, not God, who persuades David to take the census and invoke the wrath of God. It's a stunning theological change."

"What about the story of Genesis?" Grey said. "Didn't Satan tempt Eve from the beginning?"

"In the original Hebrew Bible, there was no connection between Satan and the serpent in the garden. The link to Satan was added centuries later, likely deriving from creation stories from other cultures, notably Babylonian. Satan wasn't even an important figure in the Old Testament."

"And Lucifer?"

"Mentioned only once in the Bible," Viktor said, "and not in reference to the Devil. The idea of a Lucifer, or Morning Star, cast out of heaven for his role as the leader of an angelic rebellion against God gained currency much later in history, helped not in small part by Dante and Milton."

Grey shifted in his seat. He knew better than to ask Viktor a theological question before breakfast. "So what do I need to know about the House of Lucifer, and the high priest who was murdered?"

"First: the misconception that the House of Lucifer worships Lucifer."

"You've got me," Grey said. "I admit to that misconception."

"Most of the Satanic cults that arose in the sixties and seventies were products of a fashionable obsession with the occult. Novelties, if you will. Anton LaVey pioneered the modern Satanic movement, and his Church of Satan still exists and thrives today, sharing a similar ideology to the House of Lucifer. I once met both Anton and Matthias Gregory, when I was just out of university."

Somehow Grey wasn't surprised that Viktor had personally known two of the world's most renowned Satanists. He also knew Viktor well enough to know that if he wanted to elaborate on his past, then he would.

"Had you spoken to Matthias recently?"

"Not in thirty years," Viktor said. "While Matthias understood he would never be a national hero, he was a man of intelligence and resolve. Anton was a man of appetite. What Anton and Matthias shared in common was purpose: Modern Satanism was a backlash against traditional religion, which they viewed as a holdover from the Dark Ages."

"So the House of Lucifer's not really representative of a religion?"

"Religion is simply veneration of a person, ideal, or thing. Despite lacking a traditional deity, the Church of Scientology is a religion, Confucianism is a religion, Falun Gong is a religion. As we saw in Egypt, the worship of science or an unexplained facet of nature can evolve into a religion. And there are even stranger religions than these."

Coming from Viktor, Grey had zero doubts as to the veracity of that last statement. "I had no idea that Satanists, well, don't worship Satan."

"I said the Church of Satan and the House of Lucifer don't worship Satan," Viktor said.

"Implying that there are cults who actually worship the Devil."

"Oh yes."

Grey came to an uneasy conclusion. "Which means that fundamentalist Christians are not the only obvious suspects, because to some of the other Satanic cults, the true believers, Matthias Gregory was a heretic as well."

"Precisely."

Grey stared into the porcelain bottom of his mug, rubbing his thumbs along the top.

Viktor checked his watch again and pushed away from the table. "It's time to view the crime scene."

# 7

## MISSION DISTRICT, SAN FRANCISCO

Grey absorbed his surroundings as the taxi passed through Union Square and delved into the chaos along Mission. The rough blocks came first, makeshift produce stands spilling into garbage-strewn alleys, panhandlers and trinket sellers on the corners, thrift shops and massage parlors, throngs of mestizo faces crowding narrow streets. Then came the bubble of gentrification between the BART stops, the hipsters and street artists, stylish restaurants flanked by lofts, townhomes adorned with colorful murals of *Día de los Muertos*. The omnipresent homeless eyed the tourists like prey, the violence lurking on the edges all too apparent to Grey.

They entered an area of the Mission full of tiny chapels, warehouses, and homes in various stages of decline. The taxi dropped them off in front of the House of Lucifer, wedged between an abandoned theater and a line of grimy Victorians. Wires hung low over the street, the sun a smudge of weak light behind layers of fog.

A stocky Hispanic policewoman stood in front of the church, a narrow iron structure with an arched entranceway anchored by spiked columns. Red and orange stained glass windows lent the archway an ominous feel.

The policewoman eyed Grey and Viktor as they approached. She had her back to the entrance, watching the street, but her body language was strained, as if she knew she had to hold that position but was trying to stand as far from the door as possible.

# THE DIABOLIST

Viktor flashed his Interpol badge and introduced himself and Grey. The officer, long hair tied in a ponytail and skin soft and unlined, struck Grey as either a rookie or someone who had never left her desk.

"Where's the detective?" Grey asked.

"Couldn't come," she said with a smirk. Grey and Viktor exchanged a glance. Her tone implied *you may care who murdered this piece of trash, but we sure don't.*

"I specifically asked for the investigating detective," Viktor said.

She snorted. "You're lucky you got me." Her eyes slid to the door and she muttered, *"Que suerte." What luck.*

Viktor folded his arms. "I assume you're at least familiar with the details of the case?"

"Yeah, I was briefed." She shrugged. "What'cha wanna know?"

"Why don't we go inside and discuss?"

She tried to keep a stoic cop face, but Grey saw the slight widening of her eyes, the extra swallow. She unlocked the door, and they stepped inside. Grey whistled as the policewoman crossed herself and muttered in Spanish.

Grey took in the stained glass windows allowing a blood-colored light to filter into the church, the garish red paint, the gargoyles skulking on the walls, the inverted cross that served as the altarpiece. Viktor had once told Grey it was nearly impossible to step out of one's own religious milieu, that the beliefs and superstitions we know as a child take roots deep inside us. The House of Lucifer bothered Grey on a subconscious level he could attribute only to the whispered nighttime prayers of his mother, to the residue of a childhood faith that had wormed its way into the nooks and crannies of his being.

Viktor didn't seem put off in the slightest by the interior. While the policewoman waited by the door and tried to avoid looking at anything, Viktor canvassed the church with a practiced eye. They had read the police report, and the first thing Grey did was inspect the pulpit. Nothing but solid wood and a microphone wire.

Viktor moved to join him. "According to the police report," Viktor boomed from behind the pulpit and in front of the altar, "the figure appeared roughly in this spot."

The policewoman's hollow laughter echoed through the chapel. "Yeah, and then flames sprouted from his ass and burned the vic to a crisp, right before the figure disappeared. The only thing solid about that report is the date."

"What'd the autopsy show?" Grey said.

"Nothing unusual, besides the burns."

"And the burns?"

"My guess is fuel and a spark," the officer said.

Viktor's face clouded, and she said, "What'd you expect? Hellfire? We sent some samples to forensics, it'll take a few days."

Grey's eyes traveled from the blackened floorboards in front of the pulpit to the first row of pews, ten feet of empty space away. "Any suspects?"

Her lips compressed into another smirk. "No suspects in a suicide."

Viktor's eyes stopped roaming the church. "Suicide?"

"What the hell you think happened? *Dios.* He soaked himself in lighter fluid and became a living torch in front of his congregation, God knows why. Unless all the witnesses are lying and they conspired to burn him to death. And if that happened, well"—she swept her arms around the chapel in disgust—"if you play with fire, sometimes you get burnt."

"Did you bring the documents I requested?" Viktor said, no emotion registering on his face.

She took a folded piece of paper from her shirt pocket. "Witness list and a copy of the membership records. Knock yourself out."

"Have you started talking to witnesses?" Grey asked.

"Yeah, I made a few phone calls," she said.

Grey rolled his eyes. He knew from experience that police reports did not capture looks, body language, human emotion. Phone calls meant no real investigation had occurred.

"They repeated the same bullshit's in the police report," she continued. "Some figure appeared out of nowhere in a Harry Potter costume, Matthias Gregory burst into flame, and the figure disappeared."

"Doesn't sound much like much of a suicide," Grey said, "if everyone saw another figure. Any of the witnesses have a record? Arsonists?"

"Of course there were records, with this crowd. Nothing major from the ones we know about, no arson. And although I find it hard to believe, plenty of normal citizens were here that night. Doctors, lawyers, a few local politicians." Her eyes slid to the cross. "No, forget that *mierda*. No one's normal who comes in here and does whatever it is they do in front of this twisted *basura*." She crossed herself again and started speaking rapidly, her Spanish accent more pronounced. "I jus' don't get it, I've seen plenty of lowlifes on the job, but this? There's rules, you know, like making sure the child molesters don't live long in the joint. *Hijo de tu puta madre.* You just don't *do* this."

Viktor said, "Did Matthias have any enemies of which you're aware?"

"You mean, besides the whole city?"

"I mean concrete enemies, verified threats."

"It's been months since the last threat," she said. "Besides, it makes no sense. The Bible thumpers and these people hate each other, so no way an entire building full of devil worshippers is gonna lie and cover for one of them."

"Not unless someone was undercover," Grey said, "pretending to be a believer to get close to Matthias."

"And then what? Someone incinerated Gregory from across the room without anyone noticing? I think they got together and decided to tell the world a fish story. Or maybe they all took drugs that night. I don't know, and you want the truth, I don't give a shit."

Grey's eyes swept the chapel again. Even if someone was working from the inside, the greater mystery was how Matthias had burned to death, and who or what had been seen by all the witnesses. He supposed the other people in the room could have been working in concert, there was no mysterious figure, and Matthias Gregory had been burned alive by his own congregation.

Yet somehow he couldn't see an entire roomful of people in modern-day San Francisco, even Satanists, all coming to the conclusion that their spiritual leader was on the wrong path and burning him alive for it.

Then again, stranger things had happened.

"So I hear you're some kind of cult expert," the policewoman said to Viktor. "You sure look like you've seen this stuff before. How do you deal with it, poking your nose into devil worship all the time? What's it they say about staring into the abyss too long?"

"The House of Lucifer does not practice devil worship," Viktor said as he walked down one side of the room and inspected one of the gargoyles. "And, no," he said to the policewoman, "I don't believe even the author of that statement would want to spend much time observing those congregations that do."

The policewoman shuffled her feet and didn't ask any more questions.

Grey and Viktor ran through a couple of mundane offices in the back of the building. Gregory's study was lined with bookshelves full of tomes on philosophy and the occult. While Viktor pored over the titles, Grey inspected the room. Thirty minutes later they left the House of Lucifer and walked to the waiting taxi with no further information. The policewoman hurried to her car with a relieved bounce in her step.

Viktor turned to Grey. "We need to talk to an actual witness."

"That," Grey said, "and it's time I heard about the other murder."

Grey and Viktor returned to the hotel for a late lunch, ordering room service. While Viktor prepared his absinthe, Grey took in the view outside the window of Viktor's suite. Throngs of tourists filled the streets as the late afternoon sun cast Nob Hill into shadow.

San Francisco spoke to him, the draping of the hills over the night-blue Pacific, the mellow sky, the grungy bars and cafés. A city that would rather be interesting than boast of having the highest skyscraper. Still, he preferred the gritty realities of the five boroughs.

"L'église de la Bête," Viktor said. "The Church of the Beast."

# THE DIABOLIST

Grey turned to face Viktor, hand cupping the back of his neck as he leaned against the window. "Pleasant name for a church. The other victim, I assume?"

"It happened the same night Matthias died," Viktor said. "His name was Xavier Marcel, and he was called the Black Cleric, the chief priest of L'église de la Bête. The church is shrouded in secrecy and, unlike Matthias, Xavier wasn't a public figure."

Grey waited as Viktor swirled his absinthe. He seemed distracted, but he shook off whatever was absorbing his attention and focused on Grey. "Xavier was wanted in France for two kidnappings, teenage twin girls from middle-class Parisian homes. Neither was ever seen again." Viktor crossed his legs, smoothing his tie over his shirt. "It's rumored that entrance to L'église de la Bête is restricted to those who take part in ritual sacrifice."

"We're not talking animals, are we?" Grey said.

Viktor gave a slow shake of his head.

"Jesus." He had not really believed Viktor when they had first met in Harare, and sat around a conference table while Viktor coolly informed Grey and his superior that there were cults around the world that still partook in human sacrifice.

Had not really believed him until Grey saw it with his own eyes in the caves beneath Great Zimbabwe, after Grey's view of reality had been deconstructed forever.

"Unlike the House of Lucifer," Viktor said, "L'église de la Bête practices actual devil worship. The practitioners worship Satan and deny God, believing that through the veneration of the Devil they will be granted worldly power."

Grey saw a familiar gleam in Viktor's eye, one which Grey knew signaled Viktor possessed an interest in the subject of an investigation beyond mere detective work.

Grey liked and respected Viktor. But he also knew Viktor had a private agenda, an *urge*, which drove him around the world to investigate cults on the extreme end of human behavior, searching for hidden knowledge.

"So we're dealing with people who say their Hail Marys to Satan," Grey said. "And since you've already told me human sacrifice is involved, I know we're not talking about bored teens who've listened to too much heavy metal."

"Bored teens sometimes perpetrate acts of unspeakable evil," Viktor said. "But no, L'église de la Bête is not an isolated cult, but rather an organized collection of Satanists headquartered in Paris, with small chapters across western Europe and reputedly in the States. They're rumored to have infiltrated certain levels of polite society, including government, and are believed responsible for a whole host of kidnappings and murders."

"You helped with the Parisian investigation, didn't you?"

Viktor nodded, once.

"And?" Grey said.

"The lead witness was found butchered in a rough neighborhood in Paris."

Grey grimaced. "Any other links between the murders? Besides the fact that both victims were leaders of Satanic cults? Was Xavier killed in the same way?"

"Xavier was found alone in his Parisian flat, cause of death uncertain. The time of death was also estimated to be midnight."

Viktor showed Grey a series of pictures of a compact, middle-aged man sprawled on a carpeted floor, muscular limbs askew and tinged an unnatural shade of blue. One of the close-ups evidenced extreme dilation of the pupils.

"Poisoned?" Grey said.

"Most likely. A toxicology report is pending. The neighbors saw him enter his flat around nine p.m., and never saw him leave. No one remembers anyone else suspicious entering the building. Jacques tells me the neighbors were aghast when they found out the true identity of their bourgeois neighbor."

Grey's breath whistled between his teeth. "Any other similarities?"

"Monsieur Xavier Marcel also received a letter. Except for his name, it was exactly the same as the one delivered to Matthias Gregory, declaring Xavier a heretic and announcing his death in six days' time."

"I guess that settles that. And kills my theory that Matthias was killed by a rival Satanic church, or even someone in his own organization, for not being a true believer. Kind of hard to argue, from what you're telling me, that this Black Cleric wasn't a true believer."

"Indeed," Viktor murmured.

"That brings us back to someone who's trying to put a serious dent in the world's Satanic cults. So far they're doing a pretty good job."

Viktor steepled his fingers, and Grey sensed there was something Viktor wasn't telling him, some angle Grey wasn't seeing.

"It's useless to speculate further at this juncture," Viktor said. Grey pursed his lips but said nothing.

Viktor pulled out the witness list and the membership ledger, and started comparing names on the two lists. He found one and marked it with an asterisk, then marked another.

Grey leaned over. "What're you looking for?"

"The oldest and newest members present the night of the murder. I find that gives the broadest range of insight into cult activity."

Grey filed away the information, and Viktor put his finger on the name Douglas Oakenfeld. There was an address next to the name.

"Oldest first," Viktor said.

8

The fog deepened, the waning sun a penumbra of ambient light as Grey and Viktor took a taxi to Haight-Ashbury. Cocooned in mist, they sped through the blighted streets of the Tenderloin district, past Buena Vista Park and into the Haight, the low gray buildings wraithlike as the taxi glided through the fog.

The earthy smell of marijuana seeped into the taxi. As Grey watched through the window he wondered wryly if there were more shops in the Haight selling Tibetan wares than in the entire Himalayas. They turned right just past a vinyl record store, gathering stares from a group of dreadlocked white kids lounging on collapsed cardboard boxes. Two blocks later the taxi arrived at the address for Douglas Oakenfeld, member of the House of Lucifer since 1966, the year of its founding.

The first thing Grey thought was that Douglas Oakenfeld was doing nothing to conceal his religious persuasion. A spiked iron fence fronted the property, the ironwork on the gate crafted into the image of a man with bat wings and the horned head of a goat, the man sitting cross-legged and grasping a snake in each hand. Behind the gate a yard full of sticks and scraggly grass sloped upward to a large Victorian. Ebony drapes obscured the windows, and every inch of wood had been painted black, including the porch, peaked roof, turret, wide stone steps, and gutters. A reverse pentagram hung above the doorway.

There was no buzzer, so Grey checked the gate. Unlocked. They stepped inside, closing the gate behind them. Worn stone steps led to the front door, but as they started up the path the door opened and a huge mottled dog burst into the yard. It looked like a cross between a pit bull and a rottweiler, and it came straight at Grey without a sound, scrabbling on the steps as it built speed.

There might have been time to open the gate and back out, but Grey wasn't going to chance a monster pit bull snapping his leg in half from behind. He moved ahead of Viktor, yanking off his Windbreaker and pulling it taut by the sleeves. He shoved the tightened center of the nylon coat into the back of the dog's mouth as it lunged.

The dog whipped its head back and forth with incredible strength, but Grey kept shoving, moving the dog's weight to its rear as he lowered and swept the dog's hind legs with his right foot. The dog yelped and crashed to its side. Grey leapt on top of the animal and held its massive throat at bay with the jacket, kneeling on the dog's rib cage to keep it pinned.

A man in a skullcap and biker's leathers rushed out of the house waving a baseball bat, long gray hair flying as he yelled at Grey not to hurt his dog. Viktor stepped between Grey and the man, Viktor's nearly seven-foot frame towering over the shorter but thicker man. Grey could tell by the way the man held the bat that he wasn't a real fighter, so he decided to hold his position and not incapacitate the dog if he didn't have to.

The man stopped five feet away, the bat still raised above his head with both hands. "What're you doing in my fucking yard?"

"We're with Interpol," Viktor said, pulling out his identification.

"I don't care who you're with, you let go of my goddamn dog."

Grey had been soothing the dog with soft words. The dog kept growling, but Grey felt the tension leave its body, and the growls lost their edge. Some dogs would never have stopped fighting, but dogs tended to mirror the personality of their owners, and this dog, like the bully who owned him, had no interest in facing off against someone who could fight back.

Grey rose, keeping one hand wrapped around the dog's collar. "Maybe you should think twice before loosing your animal on strangers. The gate was unlocked and we didn't see a buzzer."

"Christ," the man muttered, pulling at his beard. He had mean eyes and a gimpy left leg. "What the hell do you want? I already talked to the cops about Matty, and I don't see a warrant in your hands. And what the hell does Interpol have to do with any of this?"

"Douglas Oakenfeld?" Viktor said.

The man hesitated as if he didn't want to give his name, then realized he just had. "Just Oak."

"Local police answers to Interpol under international law," Viktor said, which Grey knew was stretching the truth. Local police were obligated to heed an Interpol request for information, but Interpol itself had no jurisdiction on the ground. "I can contact SFPD and we can discuss matters in the police station, or you can answer a few questions for me right now."

The man's small eyes flittered from Viktor to Grey, with the wariness of someone used to dealing with liars and criminals. "Why don't you ask your questions, and I'll let you know if I feel like answering them. And if you don't let go of my dog I'll—"

He cut off as Grey let go of the dog. The dog scampered behind his owner and growled from behind his leg, but Grey knew the dog no longer sensed fear and wouldn't attack again. Grey moved to stand a few feet in front of Oak. He didn't like people who used their animals as weapons, and he didn't like this man, period. "It's better to answer the questions."

Oak tried to stare Grey down, but after a few seconds he looked away and cursed. Viktor pulled a sheet of paper from his suit pocket. "The membership records state that you've been a member of the House of Lucifer since 1966. After the death of Matthias, you're the longest-standing member."

"So?"

"Why don't you tell us what happened the night Matthias died?" Viktor said.

Oak sniffed. "Like I told the cop on the phone, we all saw the same thing. Right at midnight Matty was in the middle of a sermon, and next thing we knew he was a living inferno. It was crazy shit. I wish I could say I'd dropped a hit that night, but I hadn't. Some people are saying they saw a figure in black robes right before Matthias lit up, but I didn't see a thing. *They* probably dropped a hit. Lots of us do before we meet."

Grey said, "You're saying you didn't see anyone else besides Matthias?"

"What do you think, the Devil came and got him? Matty was a charismatic man, had a lot of devoted followers. I suppose some people need to think he didn't kill himself."

Viktor stepped forward, his looming height causing Oak to crane his neck upward to meet his gaze. "Do you have any idea why Matthias might have had cause to commit suicide?"

"Nope."

"Any other recent death threats, enemies you didn't disclose to the police?"

"If I didn't tell the cops, why would I tell you?"

It was Viktor's turn to lock stares, again causing Oak to look away.

"Look man," Oak said, "there's nothing to tell. Just the usual crap from the Tammy Fayes."

"Anyone in particular?" Viktor said.

"They're always anonymous." He tapped the bat against his right palm, causing Grey's hands to tense. The moment Oak reared back to swing, Grey would strike him in the throat and strip the bat, using it to fend off the dog as necessary. "Not many people are stupid enough to insult us to our face," Oak said.

"Had Matthias been depressed or moody, any change in behavior?"

"Nope."

"Surely," Viktor said, "as long as you've known the man, you have some speculation as to why he might've taken his own life, if that's your theory?"

"These things happen, people crack."

Grey said, "Why would he crack?"

Oak threw his hands up. "Life, man. I don't know, maybe he dropped one too many bad hits, fried his circuits. The man's done a lot of heavy shit."

"I suppose you didn't notice Matthias start the fire?" Viktor said.

"You suppose right."

"Did anyone try to help him?"

"Seriously, what do you think? Of course we ran up there, took our shirts off and tried to beat the fire down, but he was already cooked. He must've soaked himself in lighter fluid, because that fire was hot as Honduras, and we had a helluva time getting the fire out."

"But you didn't see how it started?" Viktor said.

"It's not hard to figure out. He was behind the pulpit, and he lit a match."

Oak's diction was odd to Grey, like a cross between an aging Berkeley hippie and a biker thug. Grey also thought Oak didn't seem very upset about the death of his church's founder.

Viktor said, "How long had you known Matthias?"

"Nearly fifty years. Since the beginning, man. We started this thing together."

"You're the lead bishop," Viktor said.

"That's right."

"Is this your only employment?"

Oak lifted his head towards his house. "I do all right, if that's what you're asking. The House has some generous members. And I got this place back when the Haight was no-man's-land."

"Have you assumed Matthias's duties?" Viktor said.

"I'm too old to handle all this shit. I'll do it until we find someone else."

"Did you remain close friends during all those years?"

"What kind of question is that? Goddamn, show some respect."

Viktor's lips creased. "Forgive me, but you don't sound too distraught."

"Are we done here?"

"Perhaps it's because you didn't share the same theology?"

Oak pointed the bat at Viktor, and Grey stepped forward. Oak hesitated, then took a step back. "It's time you got off my property."

"That ring on your right index finger, the image of which has no doubt been branded somewhere on your body," Viktor said. "That's a symbol of allegiance to Lucifer."

Grey followed Oak's eyes downward, glimpsing a square-faced silver ring with an engraved image of a dragon intertwined around a black cross.

"I'm with the House of *Lucifer*, man. What the hell you think I'm gonna wear?"

"I think you're going to wear a ring that aligns with the tenets of your religion," Viktor said, "rather than a ring symbolizing a secret initiation rite involving the Black Mass, blood sacrifice, and swearing lifelong allegiance to Satan, under the aegis of L'église de la Bête."

Oak ran a hand over his hair and tried to look nonchalant, but Grey saw the shock in his eyes. "I don't know what you're smoking. I picked this ring up at a pawnshop, liked the way it looked. I'm sorry Matty's dead, but I don't know what else I can tell you." He shook the bat at them. "And don't you dare come back here and tell me I'm not grieving enough for my friend."

Viktor dismissed him with a thin smile. "We'll be in touch."

Through a split in the shades, Oak watched his two visitors walk towards the center of Haight-Ashbury. Oak was intelligent, but he was also larger and angrier than most people, and after he graduated from Cal Poly he decided he would rather deal drugs and join a biker gang than waste away behind a desk. It was California in the sixties, and his decision had seemed almost normal, an alternative career path. He met Matthias a few years later, and it was a natural fit.

The House of Lucifer stood for anarchy and personal freedom, two things Oak valued above all else. Most of the public thought the members of the House bit off the heads of chickens and sacrificed babies, and that suited him just fine, even though the sacrifice of living creatures was taboo under House doctrine.

Oak prided himself on being a badass, and he had wanted to swing his baseball bat at that skinny asshole's head. But something in the guy's hard green eyes told Oak that taking a swing would have been a very bad idea, and that was a feeling Oak hated above all else. He was the one who made *other* people feel that way.

That was fine. He had something special for those two. Some*one*, that was.

He grabbed a Coors Light and a shot of Jäger, working up his courage for the phone call, still on edge after the craziness of the last few weeks. As the alcohol loosened his mind, he thought about how it had all come to this.

# THE DIABOLIST

To most of the members, the House of Lucifer was a fad, an alternative lifestyle, a way to protest anaesthetized suburban living and conformist religion and politics.

To others, the House of Lucifer was a gateway drug.

As the years went by, Oak yearned for something real, something other than intellectual back-patting and Dungeons & Dragons occult bullshit. He searched the Internet for organizations more in alignment with his true desires, tried a few things here and there, found a few cults that went a step or two further down the Left-Hand Path. But none had the ring of authenticity.

Then, just last year, he found the Church of the Beast. No, that wasn't true. The Church found *him*. He had heard about the Church and was intrigued, but he knew membership was by invite only, and there was zero information out there. He hadn't even realized the Church had a presence in the United States. Now, of course, he knew they had a chapter in every major American city.

Oak's invite had been a letter slipped under his door, sealed with a symbol he hadn't recognized. The same symbol that was on the ring the giant dude had noticed. That had stunned Oak; no one outside the Church of the Beast was supposed to know about that symbol.

The letter contained a date, a time, and an address. At midnight on the date in the letter, Oak had approached a Russian Hill mansion set behind an ivy-covered wall. He was terrified by what he might find, but feverish with curiosity. He wanted what he assumed everyone wanted: evidence of something secret, something real, something *else*.

He had not been disappointed. The San Francisco chapter of the Church of the Beast, fifty members strong, had heard his plea, knew his background, and extended a rare invitation. At that first ceremony, he had participated in the Black Mass as it was meant to be done, not symbolically like in the House of Lucifer. He had watched the sacrifice of the goat and drunk its blood and cavorted, naked and unrestrained, around the basement of the mansion. It had been a bacchanal worthy of the true Dark Prince, ending with an orgy that left Oak giddy with sated desire, trembling for more.

He had found his church.

Was he evil? he briefly wondered. Yet how could satisfying his natural desires, even taken to the extremes offered by the Church of the Beast, be evil? And how was the worship of Satan worse than the veneration of a God who allowed the Holocaust and who, if most Christians were to be believed, condemned billions of His own creation to eternal damnation? Who didn't feel some affinity with Satan, the rebellious teenager kicked out of his parents' basement, doomed forever?

Oak enjoyed the notoriety that came with his position in the House of Lucifer, and saw no reason to give it up. Matty, the old fool, had no idea anything had changed.

Then *everything* changed.

Oak was asked to attend a different kind of ceremony, an initiation for a woman who had been attending the Church of the Beast a few weeks longer than Oak. Oak knew what this meant; he knew the requirement for membership was to make the final cut on the throat of the sacrifice. He also knew why they had brought him along slowly, because he was familiar with fringe-group psychology: Like any perversion, sexual or violent or otherwise, acceptance and addiction required a gradual approach.

Only it wasn't an addiction, he told himself, and it wasn't a perversion. Satan reflected the true nature of humanity, and it was intellectually dishonest to believe otherwise. It was weak.

He wanted to be part of the Church of the Beast more than he wanted to be in alignment with his artificial, socialized Western morality. He would see for himself what the real Prince of Darkness was about.

Oak didn't remember much from that night, due to both intoxication and denial. They had brought in a homeless man, a drain on society, and performed the Black Mass while the homeless man hung upside down from the cross. Then the new initiate had completed her task. There was no torture, just a swift kill. A simple offering. The ultimate act of love and devotion to his new Prince, Oak told himself, far cleaner than the wholesale slaughter in which organized religion had engaged over the centuries.

# THE DIABOLIST

Oak had almost vomited when they passed around the cup filled with warm blood, but he managed to let the liquid trickle into his mouth. After the sacrifice, there was an orgy that helped Oak forget what he had just seen and done, and when it was finished Oak stumbled out of the basement and into the moonlit night, gibbering with spent emotion, his frail humanity conquered.

After that night, Oak stopped wondering whether he was evil. Not because he had come to any conclusion, but because he no longer cared.

The next night, the same night on which Matty received the letter, a man named Dante approached Oak in the shadows on the street outside Oak's house. He shuddered as he formed a mental picture of Dante: lean and hard as redwood bark, swathed in black clothing, nose and lips and ears filled with piercings, incisors filed to points, and that awful and powerful tattoo covering his shaved head, a red pentagram stuffed with the severed head of a goat.

Oak knew the rumors: that Dante was a master with his hidden knives, the right-hand man to the Black Cleric himself, enforcer of an already terrifying organization. He couldn't wait to see Dante slice Dominic Grey into little pieces and offer his lifeblood in ritual to the Beast.

Yet even Dante no longer struck the most fear into Oak's charred heart. That night, Dante had told him of someone else, a man who had transcended his human shell and become something more, a man who would one day lead his followers into the mainstream and finally allow their religion to take its rightful place in the world. Oak loved the idea of a revolution, but he had not really believed what Dante had said about the man's powers.

Oak wanted to be part of this new thing, and he was petrified of saying no to Dante. Dante outlined the plan, telling Oak the Magus would appear at midnight six days later, just as the letter had read.

*This* would be his initiation, Dante had said, not just into the Church of the Beast, but into the new organization that would subsume both the House of Lucifer and the Church of the Beast. And Oak would be at the vanguard, might even be invited into the Inner Council.

Oak had played his part, still not expecting anything to happen. Then the clock struck midnight and the Magus appeared just as Dante said he would, materializing in front of hundreds of witnesses, burning poor Matty alive with a whisper.

After that, Oak didn't just have a church.

He had faith.

Oak held the phone in his hand before he dialed, remembering for a moment his bland Sacramento childhood, his poor pious mother, who, were she alive, would be devastated by his choices in life. He loved her still, but she was weak and had understood nothing.

Dante answered the phone with his throaty, heavily accented English. Oak felt a shiver of fear sweep through his body. He composed himself, then spoke in the gruffest voice he could muster. "I just had some visitors."

# 10

The taxi dropped Grey and Viktor in Pacific Heights, on the street outside the home of the next witness, John Sebastian Reynolds III, Esquire. A foghorn moaned, and lights from the Marina District twinkled below.

Grey shoved his hands in his pockets, the air thin and cool, seeping through his ripped coat. "Oak's a liar, though not sure I make him for a murderer. Doesn't have the nerve. I could see him paying someone else, but that's about it. And that still doesn't explain what happened."

"No," Viktor said.

"What's your theory?"

Viktor paused on the sidewalk, oblivious to the chill. "I believe there's a power struggle happening, and Matthias and Xavier were on the wrong side. I'm just not sure who's behind it or why. Given the involvement of both the House and L'église de la Bête, it would seem that someone's trying to win the hearts and minds of Satanists."

"What a prize."

They approached the house, a fancy Georgian with a lamp-lit walkway. Grey pressed the doorbell twice before a dead bolt clicked. The door opened a few inches, stopped by a chain.

A man's ruddy, clean-shaven face appeared in the crack. Grey thought him to be in his forties, once handsome, now saddled by the mushy skin and bulging veins of an alcoholic.

His voice was slurred but under control. "Do I know you?"

Viktor produced his identification. "John Sebastian? We're investigating the death of Matthias Gregory. We'd like to ask you a few questions."

He looked at the ID and then up at Viktor. "Interpol?"

"We're assigned to local police," Viktor said, handing him a card.

John released a deep, resigned sigh, then unhooked the chain. "Come in. Anything I can get you officers, or detectives, or I suppose you call yourself agents?"

Grey and Viktor exchanged a look. A far cry, Grey thought, from the greeting they had received from Oak and his hellhound.

John led them into a study filled with creamy leather furniture. A bay window overlooked the city. Both Grey and Viktor refused his offer of a drink, and he refilled the tumbler in his hand with a generous pour of Scotch, his trim haircut and tidy fingernails marking him as a professional even without the esquire.

"What can I tell you?"

"Have you spoken to the police?" Viktor said.

"I gave a written statement at the scene, but no one's contacted me about it. I'm no criminal attorney, but any fool can see the murder of the city's leading Satanist is not exactly public priority *numero uno*."

"Why don't you take us through your version of events?" Grey said.

"Sure. It was my third ceremony. *Third*. And this madness happens. I don't know how much you know about the House, but we don't actually worship Lucifer, Beelzebub, Satan"—he waved his glass at them—"whatever you want to call that archaic nonsense. The House is antireligion, a protest against the creationists and jihadists of the world. Hell, I'm not even political, I just have too much time at night on my hands since my divorce." He eyed one of the bookshelves, filled with the gold-lettered spines of legal volumes. "My professors were right, you know, all those years ago. The law is a terrible mistress. She steals all your time and leeches the fun out of life, leaves you sterile and analytical. I suppose when I joined the House I was trying to rekindle an intellectual passion of some sort, any kind of passion." He directed a sardonic chuckle at his glass. "I guess I chose poorly. Oh well, it was fun while it lasted. On to Zen Buddhism."

"The ceremony?" Viktor said.

"I was pretty intoxicated that night, so I'll never make a decent witness in court if that's what you're after. Then again, I'm intoxicated most nights, and I hold it together fairly well. That's to say, I know what I saw."

As if to prove his point, he took a long drink and regarded them both with a steady eye. "I arrived towards the end, maybe fifteen minutes before midnight, and I sat in front with the other new members. I had a great view of Matthias, because he was all alone at the pulpit. It's not a huge church, probably holds a couple hundred people. No organ or choir loft or anything like that, though why am I blabbering? I'm sure you've seen it."

"We have," Viktor said.

"My point is, there's nowhere for anyone to hide up there, and I had an unobstructed view." One side of his mouth lifted in a sardonic grin. "At the proverbial stroke of midnight, a figure in a black-and-silver robe appeared behind Matthias. Then Matthias burst into flames"—he snapped his fingers— "just like that. Everyone started screaming, someone called the police, we tried to put out the flames, and that was that." He gave a little shudder. "The poor bastard burned to death right there beside the pulpit."

"And the robed figure?" Grey asked.

"I took my eyes off him when Matthias became a living torch, so I can't say for sure what happened. But when I looked back he was gone."

Grey noticed Viktor staring at the witness with an intensity not present before. "You said the robe was black and silver," Viktor said.

"That's right."

Grey wasn't sure what Viktor was getting at, but the police report had mentioned only a black robe.

"I should clarify. The robe was black, but there were silver stars on it."

"You're absolutely sure of that?" Viktor said.

"They were definitely silver, and there weren't that many of them, I'd guess about—"

"There were seven," Viktor said, and it wasn't a question.

Grey joined John as he turned to stare at Viktor. "If you say so. It was too chaotic, and I can't say for sure. I'm a trial lawyer, so I know how easy it is to appeal to memory."

Viktor's face relaxed a fraction. "Was there anything else distinguishing about the robe or the figure?"

John Sebastian cocked his head as he thought. "Just the stars."

"Have you heard any rumors from the other practitioners," Viktor said, "perhaps relating to other Satanic organizations?"

The man laughed, too loudly. "You think this was some sort of take out? By a rival Satanist?" He downed his drink and poured another. "I know how to pick them, don't I? Religions and wives, my fortes." He took a cloth off the bar and patted the sheen of sweat on his brow. "I can't think of anything like that, though everyone knew Matthias and Oak weren't getting along. Sorry, Oak's the lead bishop, he's been with Matthias longer than anyone."

"We just met him," Grey said. "Helluva guy."

"Not exactly the brains of the organization, though he might surprise you. I think he was an engineer or something back in the day, before he sampled California's finest pharmaceuticals for thirty years. Or at least that's the rumor. Never spoke to the man myself."

Viktor said, "Do you know what may have caused the rift?"

"There were rumors Oak had different ideas about the direction the church should go. Advocated a more direct approach to fulfilling the church's goals, if you know what I mean, while Matthias was pretty much a pacifist. This is all hearsay from the other newbies, but I think if Oak had his way, the House would fight back a lot harder against the fundies, as we call them."

"Perhaps become more like a true Satanic cult," Viktor said quietly.

"I don't really know about any of that. I've been a member for a month, and all I had to do was memorize some tenets and pay a small fee. Oak didn't kill him, though. I can tell you that. He was there the night it happened, a few seats down from me, right in front of Matthias. That was a bit odd, come to think of it, because he usually sits by himself on the far left. But not always."

# THE DIABOLIST

Viktor leaned forward. "What do you think happened?"

John took his time answering, contemplating the question with a shrewd narrowing of his eyes. Grey thought he was a probably a good attorney.

"I haven't thought about much else, these last few days. I don't believe in God or the supernatural, so that's out, at least for me." He looked down at his Scotch as he swirled it. "I suppose one way or the other, Matthias left us with a parting gift to think about, something to test our faith, or lack thereof. I don't know, gentlemen. What I know is that I'm going to get stinking, roaring drunk tonight, and probably every night for a while."

# 11

It was late by the time Grey and Viktor filed into Viktor's suite. Viktor returned to his absinthe, and Grey unwound with an Anchor Steam, feet propped on the marble-topped coffee table.

Grey again wondered about Viktor's home, his family, his past. Since Grey preferred not to answer reciprocal questions, he avoided such topics, but the human need for connection was strong, and the lack of personal information between the two of them at times bordered on awkwardness. In their short time together they had discussed everything from philosophy to literature to where to get the best sushi in Tokyo, yet Grey didn't know where Viktor had grown up, or if he had ever had a family.

As Viktor sank deeper into his emerald brew, Grey had the sudden urge to question him about his past, even if it meant answering questions himself.

"Viktor, have you ever been married?"

Viktor's dark eyes burned beneath torpid eyelids, as if the absinthe could not reach that deep. "No," he said, though his response was slow and distracted, oozing a tale untold.

Grey wanted to inquire further, but instead he took a swig of beer. "Do you want to tell me about the stars on the robe?"

Viktor's gaze shifted to the window. "The silver stars are a classic sign of a magus. A magician."

"I take it you don't mean the David Copperfield type?"

"No."

# THE DIABOLIST

"So whoever or whatever the robes were attached to," Grey said, "it involved the occult?"

Viktor waved a hand. "The *occult* is an extremely broad term, and simply signifies supernatural or mystical beliefs and practices. The occult has thousands of branches and subsets, and a magus is but one type of practitioner of the occult."

"Then why were you so surprised when the silver stars were mentioned?"

"Because magicians, at least real magicians, have no connection to Satanists. The popular American conception that gullible teenagers are drawn into Satanism through the occult is an urban myth. Someone who reads *Harry Potter*, plays role-playing games, or dabbles with tarot and palm reading is no more likely to start worshipping the Devil than anyone else."

Grey said, "You have to admit it gets confusing when neither the House of Lucifer nor the Church of Satan actually worships the Devil."

"They're not helping to alleviate popular misconceptions, but that's rather the point."

"So is there anything to it?" Grey said, kicking his feet down and leaning forward, elbows on his thighs. "The practice of magic?"

"That depends on who you ask. I think you know by now that the line between belief and nonbelief, magic and reality, can be a thin one. And one which we do not yet fully understand."

Grey gave a compressed smile, the memories of his last few cases with Viktor lingering in the back of his mind like a spider's abandoned web, gumming up his secular worldview. "Like I've always done, I'll try to keep an open mind."

The answer seemed to satisfy Viktor, and he stroked his glass as if caressing the arm of a lover. "Though a robe with seven silver stars is a classic accoutrement, it affords no particular insight into the magician's specialty. I'll have to find some way to narrow down the branch of magic with which we might be dealing."

"Specialties? Branches?" Grey waved his hands. "What is it that magicians . . . believe? What do they think makes magic work?"

"Unlike priests, who look to a spiritual entity or entities as a source of power, magicians look to the cosmos, to the ineffable powers of the universe."

"That sounds New Age," Grey said.

"The New Age movement is a modern one; the roots of true magical study extend for thousands, perhaps tens of thousands, of years. Magicians spend decades, an entire lifetime, practicing and honing their beliefs."

Grey drained the last of his beer, cupping the empty bottle in his hands. "I still don't understand what they do."

"A collection of works on the history and practice of magic could fill the Library of Alexandria. But generally speaking, the typical magus believes in the universe as the source of all mystery and power—thus the stars on the robes—and believes that he or she can access this power through various rituals and practices."

"Going with the flow," Grey said, "does this universal power have a name or personality? Is it good, evil, doesn't care?"

"Most magicians believe the universe is an incredibly vast and complicated entity that can never be fully understood by man. And that understanding even a part of the universe is worthy of a lifetime of study, and can grant access to a whole new realm of power and comprehension. Of course, different magicians gravitate towards different aspects of the universal power."

"Does it work?" Grey said bluntly. "Or are you going to tell me that depends on the definition of *work*, and the perceived effect on the mind of the believer?"

"To be frank, I'm not as convinced in the possibilities of advanced magical study as I am in, say, the effect of mental persuasion offered by the Yoruba *babalawos*. But there are legions of brilliant and long-practicing magicians who would vehemently disagree. I do believe in unexplained powers of the universe, whether they're termed science, magic, or faith. I'm just unconvinced that the complicated spells and rituals of the magus unlock them."

"Something tells me we're going to have the chance to find out on this case," Grey said.

"Perhaps," Viktor murmured.

# THE DIABOLIST

"So why would Oak lie?" Grey said. "Unless he's protecting someone."

"That's the only conclusion I can draw."

Grey ran a hand through his hair and left it cupping the back of his neck. "From what you're telling me, magicians and Satanists are about as similar as Christianity and Shinto. So what's the connection between these murders and a practitioner of magic?"

"That," Viktor said, standing in a brusque manner that Grey knew meant the discussion was finished for the night, "is our job to uncover."

Grey returned to his room, exhausted. He pulled off his boots and shirt, then washed his face. He moved into the bedroom, stripped to his boxers, and crawled into bed. He felt a hand brush his cheek, and he scrambled to get out of the bed, adrenaline spiking, a thousand scenarios running through his mind. He panicked as he got tangled in the sheets, knowing it was unlike him either to panic or get tangled, but he heard a soothing voice and the same hand, warm and soft, returned to stroke his face. Then he noticed the mass of dark blond hair, the exotic face both round and defined, the voluptuous lips. Before he could speak, before he could ask her how she had gotten into his room and how he had failed to notice her in his bed, before he even knew her name, the woman from the plane wrapped her bare arms around his neck and pulled him close, the covers falling off her chest. She pressed his face into her hair and he felt weak from the sensual power of her scent, and when their lips brushed desire coursed through him in shuddering waves, leaving him weightless. He sank with her into the sheets, groaning as she moved along his body, feeling the erotic swirl of her tongue, warm and insistent. She dug her nails into his back as he stripped off the rest of their clothes.

He rose with her, her full breasts pressing against his chest, his desire arcing to an unbearable level. As he lightly bit her neck she moaned and moved her head downward, kissing his chest as her hands massaged the ridged muscles in his stomach. Then he looked down over her shoulder and saw not the smooth curvature of her back, but scaly skin and a jagged reptilian ridge where her spine should be. Stomach recoiling, Grey tried to push her away, but somehow she was too heavy. He was suffocating under her weight, unable to catch his breath.

He shot up in bed, panting, realizing it had all been a dream. The bead of sweat dripping off his brow evidenced the intensity of the nightmare. Despite the gruesome ending, his whole body was flush with desire, tingling at the memory of her touch.

He was parched and went to the bathroom for some water. This time he saw her in the mirror when he flicked on the light, standing behind him with the same expression she'd had on the plane, that exquisite face pleading for help.

She was gone before his eyes adjusted to the light, a lingering effect of the dream, a living ghost to torment his lonely nights. He checked behind the shower curtain as if he were a child, then splashed his face with water and hovered over the sink. As water dripped off his chin, he peered up at his unshaven face and tousled dark hair and sleep-filled eyes, at his scars and the edges of the tattoos covering his back and triceps.

He returned to bed and succumbed to the drone of late-night television, his pulse slowly returning to normal. The memory of the dream faded as the entropy of deepest night arrived, and he felt as if he were the only person awake on earth. Yet the one thing he failed to shake was the feeling of her cottony lips merging with his own, soft hair feathering his chest as he pulled her close.

Viktor had been eager for Grey to leave, not because Viktor was tired but because two things called for his full attention: his absinthe and the past. Two things in which he never indulged too deeply while Grey, or anyone else, bore witness.

First the absinthe. Loosening the collar of his dress shirt, he sank into the sofa, imbibing until the cool liquid fire stoked his mind and prepared the way for the coming journey. This particular cubbyhole of memory, dank and secret, was more personal than most.

Grey had asked why a practitioner of magic might be involved with these murders, and Viktor had been less than forthcoming in his response. As Viktor had said, he did not yet understand the connection, but what he had withheld was that there was one area of magic that did indeed concern the study and invocation of the powers of darkness.

It was not a likely scenario, but Viktor had to admit it was the only one that made sense at this point. Yet before Viktor drew this to Grey's or anyone else's attention, he had to be sure.

Because Viktor himself had once dabbled in this type of magic, and he preferred that chapter of his life to remain buried.

The absinthe swirled under Viktor's practiced hand, rocking gently in the glass. When she stilled, drawing Viktor's gaze into her murky depths, he began to remember.

Viktor Radek had come of age under the long shadow of the Iron Curtain, and during his childhood he saw his beloved Czechoslovakia sink further and further into the stultified embrace of Communism. Minor Bohemian nobility under the Austro-Hungarian Empire, Viktor's family had transitioned to successful merchants and bankers when the Czechoslovak Republic was formed in 1918. The arrival of Communism reduced the Radeks from royalty to simply filthy rich.

Viktor loved every single statue, castle, and Gothic cathedral in his country. He loved the beauty and culture of Prague, he loved the medieval villages tucked away like treasure chests in the forests, he loved the Czech Republic's weird quirks, literary prowess, and strange fascination with death.

But his countrymen were suffering. The Czechs took the occupation harder than most, as they did not even have religion to sustain them. It fascinated him to this day, that a country whose buildings and landscape dripped with mystique could remain one of the most secular cultures on earth.

Viktor, on the other hand, had always questioned the *why*, had asked his parents about the nature of God when he was five years old. But the religious pessimism of his birth country influenced Viktor's worldview from the beginning, making him who he was today: someone who yearned for answers, but for whom blind faith would never suffice.

What Viktor sought was cold, haughty, adamantine-hard proof. He had witnessed enough seeming impossibilities and inexplicable occurrences in his profession to know that at least some of the answers were out there.

Or had he? He wondered if it was even possible, from the tragically challenged vantage point of humanity, to do more than chip away at eternal truth and divine mystery, to discover if a puppet master cackled as he pulled the strings.

But there was the rub, he thought with a languid draping of his arms over the sofa, the absinthe working its way into his marrow. The universe was a machine, beautiful and complex beyond imagining, but still a machine. And machines have builders, operators, repairers.

They have designers.

So he would search, and study, and bear witness, until he had overturned every secret-laden stone on earth, until he had done everything in his power to uncover the why. Dark or light, good or evil, right or wrong, it was knowledge that was paramount. *Truth*.

Oh, he could hear them now, the philosophers and existentialists clamoring in their beer halls, shouting to the monks at the next table over that truth was a fable, a personal lens. Well, Viktor was also a philosopher, one of the best in the world, and he was here to tell them that truth existed somewhere, whether they liked it or not.

It was just deep, deep in the cave.

Viktor had trod the cobblestone streets of Prague as a young teen, exploring the remnants of the religious traditions that lay hidden in the nooks and crannies of Old Town, always looking over his shoulder for the *Státní bezpečnost*, the Communist party's dreaded enforcers. Before he had entered high school, he'd studied with the underground Jews and Catholics, had sought the wisdom of the kabbalists, the Trappist monks, and the secret societies that littered the underbelly of Prague. His parents, worried that Viktor would draw the attention of the *Státní*, sent him to boarding school.

Switzerland felt like a sterile compound compared to Prague, but Viktor had gained something very important: intellectual freedom. He devoured religious and philosophic books with a hunger that baffled his teachers.

Viktor did exceedingly well in school, choosing Oxford because it had arguably the finest library in the world. Yet he soon discovered the library was no longer where he wished to be. Once Viktor decided to pursue religious phenomenology in graduate school he would return to the scrolls and dusty rooms he loved so well, but the cultural awakening of 1960s England spoke to his burgeoning youthful passions, and at Oxford he discovered something even more exciting than the riddles of the universe: He discovered how to live.

The Oxford girls loved this enigmatic, cultured visitor from Bohemia, tall and darkly handsome. Viktor never dove into the deep end of the countercultural revolution, standing on the sidelines with a cool air and his brooding intelligence while hordes of his generation threw themselves into drugs, free love, and Beatlemania. That just made him even more intriguing to the fairer sex. He could barely believe the freedom at his fingertips on this strange, freewheeling little island, and he didn't think life could get any better.

Then he met Darius and Eve.

He found a kindred mind in Darius Ghassomian, an Iranian-American Viktor had met in an introductory World Religions class. Darius and Viktor always received top marks in their classes, and were considered perhaps the two most intelligent students at an already elite university. Both were also wildly ambitious.

Darius was similarly obsessed with religion and philosophy, yet he introduced Viktor to something far more interesting, something that was experiencing a revival in the universities and other mainstays of the countercultural revolution.

He introduced Viktor to the occult, and together they plunged headfirst into those dark and seductive waters.

During orientation Darius had met a girl named Eve, who had dabbled in witchcraft and the occult and was impressed by his knowledge. Eve's shyness bordered on disability, yet she had an otherworldly beauty behind the thrift-store skirts and turtlenecks. When Viktor first met her Eve reminded him of the American actress Faye Dunaway, mysterious, withdrawn, her face possessed of a ghostly symmetry. Darius, awkward and thin as a javelin, knew Eve was drawn to him not out of attraction, but because she did not feel threatened.

Viktor felt an instant connection to Eve and thought she felt the same. To Viktor's chagrin, it was obvious that Darius was hopelessly in love with Eve. Viktor did not have great experience in such matters, so he decided to ignore the situation—a ridiculous idea, he soon realized—because Viktor thought he had everything of which he could dream: personal and intellectual freedom, a vibrant social life, and two very close friends with whom to share his experiences.

Neither Viktor nor Darius was sure if Eve shared their obsession with life's more esoteric questions, or just enjoyed having someplace she belonged. Neither bothered to ask. She seemed excited about the new adventure they had planned for next year, when they returned from summer break. They had sampled a wide variety of the occult; exploring witchcraft, ancient goddesses and fertility cults with Eve; the kabbalah, secret societies and Eastern mysticism with Viktor; and introduced by Darius to the rich and enigmatic world of magic.

All of these things were interesting, but it was time to broaden their horizons. To journey to a place only the intrepid dared venture, Darius told them, to plunge into the darkness and rise back out with the keys to knowledge and power grasped firmly in hand. Eve and Viktor agreed at once to Darius's plan, and Viktor spent the entire summer in anticipation of the coming year.

For Viktor, Eve, and Darius had decided to become black magicians.

Viktor didn't know when he had drifted off, but he woke from his stupor just before four a.m. After drinking a glass of water, he tried to sleep, but his mind was too steeped in the past to relax. He went to his laptop and Googled the press conference for the Order of New Enlightenment.

Earlier in the day Grey had asked Viktor if he had heard of a charismatic New Age preacher named Simon Azar. He had heard of him, but hadn't had a chance to hear him speak. Cults and charismatic religious figures abounded, coming and going every day by the hundreds, around the world. Viktor became interested when they turned from populism to criminal behavior, or if there was another compelling reason.

A link to Simon's first press conference appeared, as well as to another broadcast that had aired earlier that night. Viktor clicked on the former.

Seconds into the video, Viktor's mouth fell open, shoulders hunching as his body coiled into a spring of tension.

The face staring back at him from the screen was the face of the man who had just featured in Viktor's absinthe-fueled journey to the past.

A man who had once been his best friend.

# 13

## LONDON, ENGLAND

Dante went deep, deep into the heart of London's East End, to a neighborhood on the cusp of gentrification that housed the First Temple of New Enlightenment. Today it was a striking but modest building, a six-story cylindrical glass tower that would one day have sixty-six stories, and six hundred and sixty-six rooms. A house that would serve as the beating black heart of revitalized East London, a turning point in the religious history of the city that had long stood at the crossroads of the world.

It just wasn't going to be the religion everyone thought it was.

Dante was impressed not just by the favor the Magus curried with their dark God, but also by his genius. Why shove something unpalatable down people's throats in the beginning when you could introduce it gently, one doctrine at a time, building the new religion on the backs of the failed ones? Bait and switch was the essence of the phenomenal growth of many modern religious organizations, especially the ones that used pseudo-Christian ties as the bait.

The Magus took this tactic to a whole new level. And when the time was right, when enough people were assimilated, when mind-sets and prejudices had gradually shifted, when the traditional conception of God had weakened beyond repair, then more and more of the truth could be revealed.

As with the catacombs, Dante liked to pass through the dodgiest parts of East London on the way to the temple, absorbing the stares of the denizens of London's worst neighborhoods. Even with his long black overcoat concealing his knives, street thugs had a sixth sense when someone higher in the hierarchy of the jungle entered their realm, and they almost always looked the other way when Dante passed.

Almost. Before the First Temple broke ground, a crew of local toughs had challenged him on the street. Out came Dante's knives, two of them flowing through the air and finding their victims' hearts before anyone knew what was happening. And the last three Dante dispatched from close range, his blades spinning and striking so fast and with such skill that it must have looked to the bystanders like the neighborhood thugs had been gutted by a tornado.

Dante delivered his message to the crowd while standing amid the bodies, flanked by three other members of L'église de la Bête. *This is our territory now, and there will be no more questions.*

The message got through just fine.

He skirted the edge of Hackney and walked past block after block of crumbling, soot-covered tenements, then entered an even rougher area of abandoned buildings and black-market warehouses. Faces peered out of broken windows, thieves and gang members slinked between the graffiti-covered buildings. He was deep inside the wilderness of East London, a place as far removed from Piccadilly and Buckingham Palace as were the farthest outposts of the once-mighty British Empire.

He ducked through a hidden underpass, then came to a canal full of sludgy green water that would lead him to his destination.

East London reminded Dante of his childhood in Montreal, not because the culture was similar but because the poverty looked the same. The same trash-strewn streets and dilapidated tenements, the same drawn faces passing by, bodies and souls forever dampened from eking out an existence on the edge of society.

Despite his environs and a lifelong lisp, Dante had been a buoyant child, full of energy from his undersize feet to his long brown curls. His parents were kind and gentle, and that mattered far more than environment. When Dante told his father how the kids at school made fun of him for his lisp, his father had convinced Dante they were only jealous of Dante's unique way of speaking. As Dante grew older and confronted his father with the truth, his father told Dante that in his mind, he *had* spoken the truth.

But environment did matter, and it mattered most when Dante was thirteen, and a burglar, pistol in hand, entered Dante's house the night of Christmas Eve. Dante's father heard the noise and confronted the intruder. The intruder shot both his parents and disappeared, leaving Dante to deal with a screaming younger sister and two parents with their lifeblood pumping onto the frayed carpet.

His parents died before the paramedics arrived, and Dante lost most of his soul that night. He couldn't take the sight of a gun from that moment forward. The pain from his loss, unbearable, began its dominion over Dante, growing stronger when Dante and his sister were placed in an institution. Not only had Dante lost his beloved parents, he now had to endure a wretched shadow existence in a state-sponsored kennel.

He preferred the institution to foster care, as he enjoyed the constant fighting that helped him expel his rage, but his sister, the only piece of himself he had left, was not faring so well. When she turned fifteen, Dante told the governess they were ready to move to a home. It was a choice Dante would forever regret.

Late one night, six months after they were placed in foster care, Dante held his sister's jaw and forced her to tell him about the bruises on her thighs, the ones he had glimpsed when she slipped into her bedclothes. It took her all night, but as the sun slipped above the horizon and she told him everything, Dante didn't hesitate. With his foster parents still in bed, he went to the kitchen, grabbed the butcher knife, and counted the fifty-two slashes he made into the spongy middle-aged flesh of the bastard who was raping his sister. When the wife intervened, he murdered her, too.

Dante went to juvenile prison without a shred of remorse, holding on to an even tinier piece of his soul for the visits from his sister. When his sister killed herself a year later, unable to cope with a life in foster care without Dante, the last sliver of Dante's soul slipped away, and pain became his only emotion, his only master, his only desire.

Dante padded through the underground entrance to the First Temple, making his way to the sixth floor. He stepped into the antechamber where the Inner Council met. The antechamber was an empty hexagonal room with ebony walls, as well as six armchairs crafted from the same dark wood. The rounded ceiling, painted by a master artist to resemble a star-filled galaxy, gave an illusion of depth to the room. A black-painted skylight allowed a splinter of light to slip through. It was a beautiful room and gave the effect of floating through the boundless void.

The sigil-inscribed door to the inner sanctum loomed opposite Dante. As far as Dante knew, the inner sanctum was for the Magus and his consorts alone, to commune with the Beast.

No, not the Beast, the Magus taught. Like the Old Testament God, Dante's newfound deity dealt out both life and death. The Magus called him by another name but allowed him to be addressed as the Beast or even Satan, the adversary. Lucifer was not appropriate, because the Magus's dark deity was not an angel.

He was a god.

The door to the inner sanctum swung wide. The Magus stepped into the room in his silver-starred robe, his presence commanding yet wise. "Thank you for coming. We have much to cover."

"Before we begin," Dante said, hating the sound of his lisp since his father had died, "I received a phone call from San Francisco."

"Dissension in the ranks?"

Dante gave a raspy chuckle. "Oak would never dare. He received a visit from two men associated with Interpol. He found the visit troubling."

"In what manner?"

"There was a tall one," Dante said, "an expert on religion. He might become a problem. His name is—"

"Viktor Radek."

The Magus's eyes, the color of barely steeped tea, glowed with what Dante thought looked most akin to eagerness. It surprised Dante, because the Magus rarely showed emotion.

"Then you know of him and the investigation," Dante said.

"Oh yes."

"And this doesn't worry you?" Dante said. "Interpol's channels of communication can be bothersome."

The Magus's face regained its trademark equanimity, of someone in firm control of every situation. "I've anticipated his interest. You need not concern yourself with him."

"And the other?" Dante said. "His name is Dominic Grey."

"His partner."

"Oak seemed to find him formidable," Dante said.

"He'll come to London or Paris, soon. I leave him to you."

Dante ran his thumbs along the edges of his knives.

**G**rey woke with the bizarre dream of the woman still lingering in his mind. The disappearance on the plane, those troubling images from the dream . . . it all left him unsettled and on edge.

He met Viktor at the same café. Grey stifled a yawn as he ordered a cup of coffee. He found Viktor in a secluded corner, legs crossed and head bowed in thought, an empty cappuccino on the table alongside a fresh one.

Still shaking off the dream, Grey said, "So what's on tap for today? More witnesses, an arson expert, do a little checking into Oak's activities over the last few months?"

"All good ideas," Viktor said in a distracted voice. He finally looked up, and Grey was startled by what he saw. Though clean-shaven and dressed in his familiar black suit, his eyes betrayed a sleepless night. His broad face and dark brow, always intense, seemed locked in a duel with some unseen entity. Grey knew how tight a rein Viktor kept on his emotions, and knew he could magnify whatever manifested on Viktor's face by twenty.

"Viktor? Everything all right?"

He composed himself. "Forgive me. I was pondering the preacher you requested I look into. Last night I viewed his press appearances."

"Simon Azar?" Grey said.

"Yes, though that's not the name I know him by."

"You know of him?" Grey said. "From a previous investigation?"

Viktor's massive head moved side to side. "He was once my best friend."

# THE DIABOLIST

At Viktor's request, Grey and Viktor returned to the hotel before discussing Simon Azar any further. Viktor uncorked his absinthe with a distracted air, though it was not yet ten a.m. Grey sat on the couch with a fresh cup of coffee, waiting for Viktor to continue. Nothing could have surprised Grey more than what he had heard in the café. Viktor and Simon did look to be about the same age, late fifties, but that was the only similarity Grey could fathom.

And not on any of their cases had Grey seen Viktor this unnerved.

"His real name is Darius Ghassomian," Viktor said, sitting in a chair across from Grey. "He's from New York, though he moved to London during high school. His parents were both Iranian. We once were very close, when I was a student at Oxford. I haven't heard from him since university, though for some time I heard rumors of his whereabouts and activities."

"Rumors?" Grey said.

Viktor gripped his glass between his palms, hovering over it like some giant, dark bird of prey. "Do you remember we discussed two types of Satanic cults?"

"Sure."

"The House of Lucifer and LaVey's Church of Satan are examples of symbolic Satanism, for obvious reasons. Adherents of L'église de la Bête and its ilk are known as theistic Satanists, because they actually worship the Devil. There is a third type, however, far more rare and whose roots are planted deep in history, even before the Gnostics. It originated in ancient Persia, where the concept of the Devil arose."

"Zoroastrianism again." Grey whistled. "And your friend's Iranian."

"He's indeed Iranian, but he had no love for Zoroaster, and we did not part ways as friends."

Whatever this third type of devil worship entailed, Grey had the uncomfortable suspicion that Viktor had more than a surface knowledge. "What happened?"

"Remember when I said the origin of the Devil was a story for another day?" Viktor said. "Unfortunately that day has arrived."

LAYTON GREEN

"It always does."

Viktor swirled his absinthe into a tiny whirlpool inside the glass. "What even most theologians fail to realize is that the concept of the Devil as an antagonist to God *predated* Christian thought."

"I'd think the idea of an evil deity would be timeless. Universal."

"Not exactly," Viktor said. "Pantheistic belief in multiple deities, both good and evil, was, of course, widespread in ancient times, as were pseudo-monotheistic beliefs in religions such as Hinduism, where a multitude of avatars represent different facets of one Supreme Being. But not until the Abrahamic concept of pure monotheism arose did we encounter a single omnipotent god and the problem of evil."

"Which led to the need for horns and a pitchfork," Grey said, though he had to digest Viktor's words before responding. Viktor's encyclopedic knowledge of religions and cults amazed Grey, but during these lectures he often felt as if he were a student in one of Viktor's classes, struggling to keep everything in context.

"That's right. As I said, the dilemma of theodicy troubled monotheistic theologians from the beginning, but long before the Christian era the Zoroastrians were dealing with the issue in a novel manner."

"Dualism," Grey said, recalling his readings on Zoroastrianism. "The belief in an equal and rival deity to God."

Viktor rose and started to pace, reinforcing his professorial demeanor. "A logical solution to the problem of evil. The Zoroastrians believe there are twin forces at work in the universe, Ahura Mazda and Angra Mainyu, also known as Ahriman. Zoroaster and his followers worshipped Ahura Mazda as the benevolent creator-God, while Ahriman and his legion of daevas, or demons, represented the forces of darkness."

"It does simplify things."

"The concept of dualism threatened the fabric of the early Christian Church," Viktor said. "The Gnostics, the gravest danger to the Catholic Church in history, lifted the dualistic elements of their theology from the belief in Ahriman. As did many other heresies."

76

# THE DIABOLIST

"To be honest," Grey said, leaning back on the sofa, "it's easier for me to conceive of some evil god up there causing mayhem than to believe in a Supreme Being who I have to hold responsible for genocide and child prostitution."

"And many learned minds in history would agree. Had the Catholic Church not been so politically powerful, popular dualistic heresies such as Manichaeism, Catharism, Bogomilism, Albigensianism, and Marcionism would likely have endured to this day. Saint Augustine was a Manichaean for nine years."

"Saint Augustine was in a cult?" Grey said. "I've never even heard of the Manichaeans."

"That's because cults, heresies, and alternative beliefs were not just frowned upon by the Catholic Church. They were annihilated."

"It all sounds so . . . cosmic. The idea of an evil God."

Viktor stopped pacing, his lips curling upward. "Who truly believes in his own evil, Grey? The perspective of those on the inside of a cult, even a monstrous one like L'église de la Bête, would surprise you."

"I think I've got a handle on the history, and I see where this is leading, but how does this connect up to Darius or the murders?"

Viktor stood in front of the window, staring off into space again. Grey had the suspicion he was deciding how much to tell him. "I seek knowledge above all else, and I hope you understand that. When I was a student at Oxford, at the beginning of my journey, I was a practitioner of magic. Darius and I and . . . a girl . . . explored it together."

Grey had a hard time imagining Viktor either as a young, carefree college student or as a romantic, but he could see by his wistful, faraway gaze that he had once been both. Yet Grey also saw a sadness, a great loss, lurking in those memories. He wondered if this was the girl Viktor had thought of when Grey asked him about marriage.

"There is a subset of black magicians," Viktor said, "whose practitioners believe that magic derives not just from the laws of the universe but from an entity or entities who control the darker forces. These magicians are called Diabolists."

Grey held a finger up. "When I was reading about Zoroastrianism I read about a priestly caste called magi. They were magicians of course, which is where we got the name, and also the Three Magi from the Bible. Did Ahriman have his magi as well?"

"The magi who worshipped Ahriman were reputed to have instructed King Solomon in the dark arts, including the summoning of demons. We know almost nothing about Ahriman's followers, except they were feared throughout the ancient world. And there's almost no mention of Ahriman in historical records except for the writings of Rudolf Steiner, a prominent philosopher and Goethe scholar from the early 1900s."

"Don't know him, either," Grey said.

Viktor pushed away from the window to prepare more absinthe, speaking as he fitted the slotted spoon and sugar cube above the glass. "He started a movement he termed anthroposophy, which combined elements of Nietzsche, Goethe, European transcendentalism, and theosophy. He gained a sizable following, but his cosmology was bizarre. He viewed three figures as central to human evolution and spiritual development: Christ, Lucifer, and Ahriman. He believed an 'Ahrimanic influence' has been at work since the middle of the fifteenth century, and that Ahriman would incarnate sometime during the third millennium, just as Christ once did."

"The third millennium being now? 'Bizarre' would be an understatement."

"I mention it solely out of lack of reference points," Viktor said.

"Another guess," Grey said, rising to stretch his legs. "Your old pal was a Diabolist."

Viktor's lips pursed. "Correct."

Grey placed his empty coffee cup in the kitchen, returning to face Viktor. "And so were you."

"I dabbled," Viktor said evenly, "but no."

Grey had long known that Viktor's interest in religion and cults went far beyond mere law enforcement. On more than one occasion he had questioned whether Viktor's decision making was geared towards helping the victims or satisfying his own curiosities.

# THE DIABOLIST

"So what does this mean for us?" Grey said.

"Darius—Simon—was brilliant, but awkward and terribly reserved. A social outcast. It's hard to believe this was the same person I saw on the Internet, yet I'm sure of it. And magicians, especially Diabolists, shun the limelight."

"Maybe your old pal had a change of heart along the way," Grey said. "Decided he'd rather have a Porsche and some nubile young followers."

Viktor did not look convinced.

"So a Diabolist," Grey reasoned, "could have motive to call both Matthias Gregory *and* Xavier Marcel a heretic."

"Possibly, yes."

"Of course it could all be a coincidence, the Diabolist's robe, the emergence of Simon close in time to the murders."

"Of course," Viktor said.

"I don't believe very much in coincidence," Grey said.

They stared at each other, Viktor in silent acquiescence.

"The immediate question," Grey said, checking his watch, "is whether it stops here. Are we solving murders or preventing them?"

"I received a call from my Interpol contact this morning. Jacques said another letter has been delivered, to a society of magicians in York. One of the oldest in the world."

"I didn't know there were societies of magicians," Grey said.

"There are many."

"Well, today's a day of enlightenment," Grey said. "Another six-day deadline?"

"Yes, but three days have already passed."

"So we go to York?" Grey said.

"I do, but not yet," Viktor said, his gaze disappearing into his glass. "There're a few things I need to investigate in San Francisco, based on this new information."

Grey didn't even bother asking. "And my job?"

"I need you to look into Xavier's death."

Grey nodded, slowly. "That makes sense."

"Good. I'll purchase a ticket to Paris for this evening. We've no time to waste."

Grey said his good-bye and moved to leave, then paused with the door half-closed. "Just one more thing."

"Yes?" Viktor said.

"I understand why you didn't mention the Diabolist angle sooner. Keeping things to yourself is fine, Viktor, we all have our secrets. Just make sure it never impacts an investigation I'm working on."

# 15

## PARIS

From a booth in the corner, Luc Morel-Renard watched the crowd gather at the working-class bar in the eighteenth arrondissement. The neighborhood was home to Sacré Coeur, but also to some of the worst neighborhoods in metro Paris, and for some time Luc had seethed as North African and other immigrants overran his childhood home, bringing unemployment, crime, and gangs.

Luc had been a rising star in the far right Unité Radicale, but when that organization disbanded after the failed Chirac assassination, Luc, gifted in both oration and the ideology of hate, had been approached by a member of L'église de la Bête. Though shocked at first by the group's depravity and the requirements for membership, Luc realized that both his carnal and political ambitions could be furthered by joining the underground society.

Luc had never been comfortable with Xavier's leadership, which was too blunt for his taste. Xavier's misguided Arceneau kidnappings had almost exposed them, and if the press got a whiff of Luc's affiliation with L'église de la Bête, even his own radical followers would shun him. His church helped his political career from the inside out, not the outside in.

As a fight broke out in the corner, Luc pondered his good fortune. Xavier was dead. Luc was now in charge of the direction of the church, and the only person he had to answer to was far more closely aligned with his own goals. In fact, Luc had come to realize the beauty and power of the Magus's vision, and counted himself a loyal disciple. The Magus had promised to help Luc's political career and more. *Much* more.

The fight in the corner ended, a rare silence encasing the crowd as the bartender cranked the volume on the television. Simon Azar was speaking again, and every union man, biker, anarchist, Satanist, and local thug was listening. Luc watched in awe as Simon, sitting in a high-backed chair, spoke with a potent cocktail of intelligence, charisma, and self-effacing wisdom, his humanist message somehow managing to please intellectuals, blue-collar types, and social outcasts all at the same time. Religious leaders had already denounced him, but everyone else, the vast swaths of humanity swimming in the murky waters of agnosticism, clung to his life raft of hope. As Hitler said and proved, the power of the spoken word had started the greatest religious and political avalanches in history.

Luc listened to the translator.

"This morning I logged on to the Internet, and do you know what the three top news stories of the week were?" Simon ticked them off on his fingers. "One: another earthquake in Haiti. Two: Severe flooding in Brazil destroyed thousands of homes and millions of dollars' worth of crops. Three: An Italian man living in an upper-class neighborhood, less than a mile from Vatican City, kidnapped and dismembered two local schoolchildren."

Simon paused to reflect on the gravity of the events. "Do you know what these three atrocities have in common? They happened, you see, in three of the most devoutly Catholic countries on the planet, and all in the same week. How many tens of thousands of people in those countries, how many millions, had prayed just that week for peace and prosperity? How far did it get them, how did it help the poor souls who died in those events? To think that God would kill our children or allow such atrocities to occur, under any theological system, is beyond ludicrous. We are not a rational species; rather, we rationalize. We do what we must to fit God within the framework we know."

The crowd murmured in approval.

"And what if such tragedies were to occur in the countries of the godless, where original sin brings them hobbled into the world, and eternal damnation finishes the job? What kind of being creates humans so terribly flawed, and then condemns the majority to everlasting punishment?"

Simon clasped his hands and leaned forward in his chair. "Who then, I ask you, is the evil one? Ah, you say, but Hell is not literal, eternal damnation a myth. What then, I must ask, is the meaning of Christ's sacrifice? From what is there to be saved?" He opened his palms. "I understand that many of you don't believe in the concept of Hell or eternal damnation, but why cling to an ethos that includes such anachronistic concepts? Why not be free thinkers, free beings? What is there to fear except a life unlived?"

A look of infinite sadness lengthened Simon's face. "Isn't it time we redefined our concept of God? That we cast not us in His image, but His in ours? Our pleasure, our pain, all the aching beauty of our love and loss and longing: these hallmarks of human existence are all that we know. All that we have. Isn't it time," he said softly, "that we look for universal solutions to our problems, rather than unattainable ideals that divide our nations, our cities, our villages?"

Despite his knowledge of the speaker's true identity, Luc found himself drawn into the speech. It was, quite simply, the God that everyone wanted, whether they admitted it or not. Wise, caring, devoted, fair, and just a little bit flawed. It was a modern God, a stay-at-home-dad God, a God more in line with the complexities of the world.

Luc could only smile.

Since becoming a member of L'église de la Bête, Luc had agreed with the wisdom of the old adage that the greatest trick the Devil ever pulled was convincing the world he didn't exist. But there was a reason for this trick, the Magus taught, and it wasn't to spend eternity playing second fiddle.

On the contrary: When the time was right, when the tipping point had been reached and the balance of faith had shifted, the curtain would be yanked away and the illusion revealed to the crowd, shining and terrible beyond imagination.

His cell phone vibrated. When Luc saw the number he swallowed.

Dante.

Luc had done things in life that would make the Marquis de Sade blush, but talking to Dante made him feel ill and unbalanced. Looking at Dante was like looking at someone without a soul, a human cavity where nothing existed except those empty eyes and that horrific tattoo. The Magus might have his gifts from the Beast, but Dante was someone Luc would rather die than cross.

He excused himself from his friends, wading through the stench of the patrons and into the street. *"Oui?"*

"A man named Dominic Grey is coming to ask questions. There is someone he should meet."

The phone call ended as abruptly as it began, and Luc was left standing in the street with a silent cell phone clamped to his ear.

# 16

**G**rey spent the flight to Paris half expecting the girl to pop up beside him, and he felt both relieved and disappointed as he stepped into the bright lights and cosmopolitan bustle of Charles de Gaulle Airport. He couldn't shake her from his mind, and he realized he and Viktor had never finished discussing her strange appearance.

It wasn't just the girl that made him uneasy. This case had just begun and he already felt a twinge in his gut, a knot of tension he hadn't felt since Zimbabwe. Working with Viktor had challenged his perception of reality before, and Grey had the unsettling feeling that it would happen again on this case.

Or, he thought as he cleared security and the image of the girl flitted across his mind, maybe it already had.

Viktor had given him three things before he left: the address of Xavier's flat, a phone number for Viktor's Interpol contact, and the address of an ex–investigative journalist named Gustave Rouillard who had once researched the Church of the Beast. Apparently the Church was almost impossible to find, secretive and dangerous in the extreme, but Viktor said this man might help if Grey mentioned Viktor's name. Grey had asked for a phone number, but Viktor said that after Gustave's last encounter with the Church, which had left him crippled and homebound, he stayed off the grid.

Lovely.

After leaving his backpack at an airport hotel, Grey took a train into Paris. He always felt a little uncomfortable in the City of Lights, as if he were a peasant invited to the lord's ball, always saying the wrong things and stumbling into the furniture.

His first visit had been his favorite. He had loved the disheveled charm of the Left Bank, the grandeur of Champs-Élysées, the bakeries and street food that turned the entire city into an aromatic café. The underground fight circuit had been a joke, and after Grey trounced the city's top fighters in a dingy gym, he gathered his winnings and treated himself to a solid meal, then took a bottle of wine to a bridge over the Seine and, under an amber moon, gazed at the sublime majesty of Notre Dame.

There would be no enchanted lights on this trip. He decided to start with the former residence of Xavier Marcel, known to most as the Black Cleric, known to his neighbors as Jean-Paul Babin. Grey called Jacques, the Interpol contact, and arranged to have an officer meet him at Xavier's flat.

Following Jacques's directions, Grey took the metro to the ninth arrondissement. He walked a few streets south of the Havre-Caumartin stop, to a flat on a street full of handsome ash-colored buildings. A man in a suit was leaning against the wall of Xavier's building, with the rigid stance and active eyes of a police officer. There was something else, however, that Grey normally didn't see in the eyes of a policeman.

Fear.

Grey opened the Interpol liaison identification Viktor had procured for him a few months ago, feeling strange as he used the ID for the first time.

The officer inspected the ID. *"Parlez-vous Francais?"*

*"Non, pardon,"* Grey said. *"Parlez-vous Anglais?"*

The officer gave a half smile as he unlocked the door for Grey. *"Non."*

The officer signaled with a wave of his hands that Grey was free to roam. Grey stepped into the flat expecting to see walls encrusted with blood, or pentagrams chalked into the floor. Instead, he saw the home of a meticulous man. Everything was in order, the floors polished, the furniture carefully arranged, the spines on the bookshelves aligned by size.

He moved through the spacious living room and into the study, feeling a little chill as he saw the title of the book that lay closed and bookmarked on

# THE DIABOLIST

the desk: *Le Livre de Lucifer*. As if this were a typical upper-middle-class home, except the Book of Lucifer had replaced the Bible in the study.

A bookshelf had been built into the wall behind the desk. Grey always felt a bookshelf was the best judge of personality, and the Black Cleric's bookshelf did not disappoint. Grey spoke Spanish and recognized enough Latin cognates to figure out most of the titles. Again, the books were well organized, classics on one shelf, history and philosophy on another, religious books from a surprising variety of faiths on a third, and then the shelves Grey expected to find: tome after tome on magic, the occult, and Satanism, some with shiny new bindings and some looking old enough to crumble into dust if touched.

Grey riffled through the desk and found nothing of interest, then moved into the wood-floored bedroom, where the police report indicated that Xavier had died. The room looked innocuous: a queen-size bed along the wall, a mahogany armoire that matched the headboard, and a bedside table topped with a lamp and an alarm clock. A bathroom off the bedroom contained the expected items: soap, a collection of men's skin-care products, a shaving kit, two toothbrushes, and a portion of the counter allocated to Xavier's girlfriend: makeup, deodorant, feminine hygiene products, a cone-shaped bottle of perfume.

He opened the closet door, then grimaced. A curved knife with a jeweled handle hung on the wall. Grey knew the reputation of the Black Cleric, and he knew the purpose of this knife.

There was nothing else of interest. After he left, the detective locked the door and hurried to his car. Grey knocked on the door of the neighboring flat. A few moments later an older man in a suit opened the door, his eyes going at once from Grey to Xavier's flat.

He swallowed. *"Oui?"*

Grey flashed his badge and said, *"Parlez-vous Anglais?"*

"Yes. I have already spoken to the police."

"I understand," Grey said. "You were here the night of Xavier's death?"

"Yes."

"Did you see anything unusual?"

"No."

"Did anyone enter with Xavier?"

The man's eyes slinked to Xavier's flat. "I did not see him enter."

Grey pursed his lips, the man's extra blink giving away his lie. "Was there someone with him?"

"*Pardon?*" the man said, as if he did not understand the question.

"I understand you had no love for your neighbor, but anything you can tell me might help the next person."

"*Que alors?* No love? My neighbor was a *monster*. I have already contacted my estate agent, I will not stay in this house."

"Did you see anyone enter the house at any time that day?" Grey said.

"There was a woman, but there was always a woman. Even before I knew what he was, I knew he had a"—he waved his hands—"how do you say . . . voracious . . . appetite."

"What'd she look like?"

"She was wearing a coat and a hat. I did not see her face."

"When did she arrive?" Grey said.

"I don't remember."

"But you didn't see Xavier enter?"

"Why would I? I do not spy on my neighbors."

"You saw the girl," Grey said.

"I was walking my dog."

He tried to close the door, and Grey stopped the door with his hand. "Was she thin, tall, white, black? Blond hair, dark hair?"

"I can't remember."

"Try harder."

His face sagged, and his eyes flicked to Xavier's flat again. He took a step back. "I am sorry, monsieur. There's nothing more."

Grey removed his hand and the man shut the door. Grey stood alone as a stiff breeze swept the street.

# 17

Viktor left the Fairmont and strode towards Polk Street to meet Zador Kerekes, the Hungarian owner of a used and rare bookstore specializing in the occult. Worry for Grey fluttered through him as he walked, turning into tendrils of fear that snaked up and constricted his chest.

L'église de la Bête was a frightening cult. Viktor had investigated them once before, when twin girls from a wealthy Paris suburb had been the victims of ritual murder, but Viktor had been unable to penetrate the cult. It was one of the few failures of his career, and he considered himself lucky to have survived that investigation with his life.

Grey was a formidable adversary, but L'église de la Bête was based in Paris, and they didn't play by the same rules as everyone else. Not to mention whichever faction had murdered the Black Cleric. That had shocked Viktor. He didn't know anyone in the underworld who dared raise a hand against Xavier.

He walked down California Street and through the quiet chic of Nob Hill, the wind whipping through the streets like a heat-starved missile, racing beneath the fabric of his suit. Viktor had visited Zador before, both to conduct research for an investigation and to find select works for his personal library. Zador himself was a magician, rumored to be a rare Ipsissimus of the Hermetic Order of the Golden Dawn, a storied group of sorcerers that claimed Bram Stoker, W. B. Yeats, and Algernon Blackwood as members. Though the

Order had officially dissolved a century ago, many claimed that Samuel Mac-Gregor Mathers had disbanded the original Order to escape the public eye, and that its work continued unabated in secret.

Viktor neither knew nor cared about that rumor, but he did know that Zador, for all his eccentricities, had his finger on the pulse of the occult community. If, as Viktor thought, someone had recruited Oak in San Francisco to work against Matthias, then Zador was a good place to start asking questions.

Darius's recent emergence as Simon Azar pooled and gummed in Viktor's mind like the muddy waters of a swamp channel. Nothing made sense. Though Darius had possessed a superior intellect, he had never been handsome or charismatic. To achieve what Viktor had seen on that video, he must have gone to charm school and undergone a physical metamorphosis when he reached adulthood.

Still, he was an angle that had to be investigated. Viktor got an acrid taste in his mouth. There were few things in life he wanted to do less than contact Darius Ghassomian.

As he turned onto Polk that thought tugged at him, pulling him down into the rabbit hole of memory. He let them come, the memories he shunned above all others. He let them come because he needed to see clearly in the present.

Becoming black magicians possessed a powerful allure to the three young adepts, but first they had to be scholars. They started with the modern canon, Eliphas Levi's *Doctrine and Ritual* and *History of Magic*, the Necronomicon and the Lovecraftians, Blackwood and Dion Fortune, everything Aleister Crowley had ever written or said. Then they moved further back, to Blavatsky and the theosophists, to Francis Barrett and MacGregor Mathers. They studied the late alchemists Isaac Newton and Comte Saint Germain, and then braved the wicked intelligence of Arthur Dee, Cornelius Agrippa, Abramelin the Mage, and the other Renaissance occultists. Then they delved deeper still, like moles into a secret mountain, seeking out ancient books and even more ancient masters, back in time to when myth and reality blurred and were one, when King Solomon and the Witch of Endor looked to the star-filled sky for answers, when Hermes Trismegistus and the Egyptians built the Pyramids and tapped into things unknown.

They grew in confidence, moving from minor arcana to more complicated spells and rituals, eventually braving the great grimoires themselves. It was hard to say whether everything worked as planned, because most real magic did not have overt results. But there was one thing Viktor could say for certain about every dark incantation performed by the light of the moon: It was thrilling. They were dancing with the hidden forces of the universe, snapping the shackles of human convention, exploring the deepest levels of reality and consciousness.

There were gatherings with other occultists and budding magicians, there were parties and drugs and sex, but above all else, there was a great tittering excitement at probing the waters of the unknown.

It was the happiest time of Viktor's life, buzzing with the discoveries of youth, adrift in the sort of foggy, romantic mystique that dissolves with the responsibilities of adulthood. It was all so fresh, vibrant, *alive*.

Though Viktor enjoyed the occult, he wasn't consumed by it, as was Darius. The three of them seemed to Viktor like the famous puppet shows of Czech culture, marionettes poking their noses into the bizarre and stumbling around the stage of life, fools all the while. Their own quest for magic had produced no real answers, and they knew no more than the puppets.

Eve, Viktor knew, enjoyed the occult on a surface level, like a role-playing game. She participated because it quenched a thirst deep inside, an empty place that had never been filled by her absent salesman father or her codeine-addicted mother. She enjoyed the drug-induced rituals most of all, though after the first few Viktor decided those were not for him. It was not until many years later, when the Juju nightmares first appeared in London, that he would turn to absinthe to help numb the memory of the monstrosities he had witnessed.

While Viktor sought answers and Eve sought solace, Darius sought power. Unlike Viktor, who conducted himself with a cool, if somewhat remote, confidence, Darius came from a poor family and was ill at ease with the world. Painfully thin and frail, he had never had a girlfriend, and had never enjoyed the finer things in life unless Viktor paid his way. Viktor knew that being a magician gave Darius a sense of control he had never before experienced. Goethe's *Faust* was Darius's favorite play, and he used to tell Viktor that if he ever had the chance, he would call the Devil and worry later about how to escape the consequences.

There was only one thing Darius craved more than power, and that was Eve. It was becoming harder and harder for Viktor to hide the electricity flowing between Eve and himself, and Viktor knew how much it hurt Darius when Eve looked right through him.

Viktor had fallen just as hard as Darius. He had mistaken Eve's introspection for shyness, her sensitivity for weakness. Now he knew her for who she was: an intelligent, highly emotional, complex human being, whose beauty was matched only by her empathy. And Eve, he knew, found comfort in Viktor's solidity, probably saw her father in Viktor's remoteness—though Viktor was someone she could reach. And he was a striking figure on campus, handsome and foreign and brilliant, towering above the other students.

Viktor and Eve had started seeing each other in secret, though Viktor knew Darius loathed their obvious chemistry, and loathed their pity even more. But he also knew Darius would never disrupt the trio, because it would mean losing touch with Eve.

Instead, Darius found solace in the one thing at which he excelled even more than Viktor: the practice of magic. Darius had the gift. His dexterity was extraordinary, his stamina already a thing of legend, and most important of all, he had the one thing Viktor had never been able to achieve through the application of his powerful will: faith.

Viktor knew that if magic did, in fact, work, even if it was just some unexplained function of the universe, then Viktor had to at least believe in it to see the results. This, above all else, was what drove and tormented Viktor

# THE DIABOLIST

Radek. He had a burning desire to know, yet he himself believed in nothing. He wanted, he *craved*, that faith-supplanting proof.

Darius, on the other hand, had an abundance of faith, so much so that it drove him to believe that true magic lay at the intersection of the magician's esoteric skill set and a higher, mysterious power. Darius had never claimed a religion or moral alignment, but he came to believe that it was the so-called forces of darkness that responded most to human entreaty and practical magic.

After that year's All Hallows' Eve party, something changed in Darius. He talked to Viktor less and less, grew sullen and angry. The three almost split when Darius demanded that, for the sake of their magical development, they follow Aleister Crowley and explore sex magic as a group. Perhaps the most notorious black magician to have ever lived, dubbed by a British tabloid in 1923 as the "Wickedest Man in the World," Darius idolized Crowley and his infamous motto, "Do what thou wilt."

Eve threatened to never speak to Darius if he ever again mentioned such a revolting thing. Darius had been crushed and started using prostitutes for his magical experiments.

By this time Darius and Viktor knew a rift was inevitable. Neither, however, could have guessed just how deep and terrible the circumstances of that rift would prove to be.

Viktor's reverie with the past broke when the muscular sprawl of the Pacific appeared in the distance. He realized he had walked too far and berated himself for losing concentration. It was unlike him.

Despite the chill, his body felt hot beneath his suit, a warm flush from the intensity of the memories. He straightened his tie and strode towards the bookshop, a denizen of the present once more.

He found Zador's Rare Books halfway down a side street off Polk, the narrow entrance almost unnoticeable, the incline so steep the cars had to park angled against the curb.

A bell tinkled as Viktor entered the shop.

Grey grabbed a *croque-monsieur* on the street, walking as he pondered the morning's events. It was good to get a visual of the crime scene, but he doubted he was going to discover anything of interest unless he found one of the members of the Church of the Beast. Even if he found one, he knew they weren't going to be sipping cappuccino and discussing the case. But he would deal with that when the time came.

Grey followed the directions he had printed to the house of the journalist Viktor said might help. Gustave's apartment was in a shabby section of Saint-Denis, one of those edgy urban areas populated by artists, a host of people on the fringe of society, and die-hard cityphiles who didn't make much money but wanted to live in town.

According to Viktor, Gustave had investigated the Arceneau kidnappings, running an exposé on the twin girls who had turned up in pieces in a sewer. Gustave had exposed a few reputed members of the Church of the Beast, but despite a lengthy investigation and a huge public outcry, no arrests were made.

For his troubles, Gustave had received a visit from two men in goat masks who had left him impaled through his anus on a Judas Cradle. His neighbors rescued him before he died, but the horrific torture had left him crippled.

Grey approached Gustave's building, the weathered stone streaked with grime. The building was on the corner of a hectic intersection, and judging by the seedy bars and package stores, the area might be busier at night. The perfect place for someone uncomfortable in isolation, Grey thought. Someone forced to live a life of fear.

After following another resident inside the building, using his Interpol badge to allay suspicion, Grey climbed to the fourth floor. He knocked and knocked on Gustave's solid metal door, obviously a special install, with no answer. No sounds emanated from the apartment.

He called and knocked even louder, then took out his lockpick. He had the door open in seconds, surprised neither the dead bolt nor the chain had been set. As soon as the door opened, the stench of death poured out of the room and settled onto Grey like a shroud. He covered his mouth and nose with his sleeve, then crouched and moved inside.

In the center of the high-ceilinged room a man hung upside down from a wooden beam, slash marks on his neck and wrists, blood coagulating beneath him in a sea of flies. Grey guessed the body was a few days old.

He searched the apartment, finding nothing of interest except an empty laptop case and a few pictures identifying the man hanging in the center of the room as Gustave Rouillard. Grey snapped a picture of the body on his cell phone, sending it to Viktor with a short text.

Gustave's investigation had taken place years ago. Why kill him after all this time?

There were only three reasons Grey could think of. Either Gustave had reignited his investigation, which was unlikely, or someone had tapped into Gustave's e-mail and seen the message from Viktor, which Grey also found unlikely. Judging from the state of the body, Gustave had died before Viktor had contacted him.

It was option three that Grey found most reasonable.

Gustave was a loose end, and the Church of the Beast was under new management.

Grey backed out of the apartment and into the street, eyes scouring every vehicle, storefront, and face. He cobbled together enough French to make an anonymous call to the emergency police operator before he slipped away. He wasn't in the mood for questions. The French police hadn't helped Gustave before, and they sure as hell couldn't help him now.

As the afternoon faded he decided to return to Xavier's flat. Losing Gustave had been a body blow to the Paris investigation. Grey had no other leads, he didn't speak the language, and he knew from experience that trying to deal with a feared and deadly cult made it difficult to pry information out of witnesses.

Nevertheless, his best option right now was finding someone who could provide more color on Xavier's murder. Perhaps another neighbor would be more forthcoming. He knew it was a long shot, but Viktor had yet to respond, and Grey was itching to do something.

He noticed the man following him as soon as he entered the metro. As Grey descended the long escalator, his eyes had flicked over his shoulder, observing the street for any unusual activity before making a change in environment. The sandy-haired man in the brown pullover was fifty feet behind him, his step a little too purposeful, his gaze a bit too sure.

Grey took his time buying his ticket, checking the metro map and then using the crowded restroom. When he left the restroom the man was still there, standing next to a magazine stand in the corner. Grey moved through the turnstile and down to the platform, the man in the pullover trailing behind.

Grey would put good money on who had sent the flat-faced man, and he wasn't going to waste an opportunity. He took the metro back to Havre-Caumartin, then stepped into a surface elevator just as it was closing, making it look as natural as possible. After hurrying outside, he ducked into a pharmacy with a good view of the metro.

The man in the pullover came bounding out of the metro entrance, looking both ways before darting in the direction of Xavier's flat. Grey's suspicion that the man had guessed where Grey was headed was confirmed when Grey followed him to Xavier's street.

The man loitered near Xavier's flat, then found a bench and pretended to read a magazine. Grey ensconced himself in a small park, the autumnal trees still providing plenty of cover. Eventually the man checked his watch and made a call on his cell, waving his free hand in agitation.

When dusk settled, the man finally left the bench. Grey followed him through the posh neighborhood to a less desirable area of the city filled with the metallic screech of shopkeepers pulling down roll-up doors. Darkness made Grey's job easy, and he debated taking the man to a deserted alley for a private chat. He decided the man might lead him someplace more interesting. There was also the possibility of not being able to communicate with his captive.

They were now in an isolated section of the city, filled with warehouses and automotive repair shops. The streets were eerily quiet and smelled like motor oil. The lights of Paris twinkled above, providing just enough ambient light for Grey to follow his quarry from a distance.

The man ducked into a shuttered warehouse, and Grey waited long minutes before approaching the padlocked door. He didn't hear any sounds from inside and was surprised not to see any light seeping underneath the door. Grey hovered over the padlock, fingers twitching as he worked his metal filing.

He eased the door open as slowly as he could, relieved when it didn't squeak. Moonlight filtered in, and Grey's eyes widened at the closet-size space, empty except for a worn manhole cover set into the floor. Grey lifted the cover, eyes widening even farther when he lifted the cover and saw an iron ladder descending into darkness.

He listened, hearing nothing except the faint drip of water. Then he sent Viktor a text with his location, used a pen-size flashlight to light the way, and stepped onto the first rung.

# 19

Zador's shop contained the same claustrophobic aisles as Viktor remembered, piles of used and rare books stacked not just on the shelves but on the floor between rows, on top of the shelves, and on every available counter space.

An elderly man with an oversize head and a shock of white hair emerged from one of the aisles. Viktor had no idea of Zador's true age, but he knew he was older than he looked, which was about seventy. Others claimed Zador had studied magic with Crowley and Blackwood, but that was impossible, unless Zador had run into a certain strange elixir somewhere along the way. Zador gave Viktor a nod of acknowledgment, then headed back into the stacks, his uneven gait a mixture of mental energy and creaking limbs.

Viktor followed. Zador was shelving books from a cart, and he spoke without looking at Viktor. "There is something in particular you look for? Last time it was the, yes, the *Liber Iezirah* second edition. Most rare indeed. You would like something else in the kabbalist canon?"

Viktor had to concentrate to understand Zador's thick Hungarian accent, which sounded like he was softly gargling while he spoke. For anyone besides Zador, Viktor would have been shocked that he remembered his last purchase, more than two years ago. "I'm here for something else this time," Viktor said. "I'm looking for information."

"I'm a seller of books, not information."

"One might argue they're one and the same," Viktor said wryly.

"Information from people isn't to be trusted."

"Do books not have authors?" Viktor said.

"Once something is written it becomes a truth of its own, a self-contained, immutable work presented to the eyes of the reader without inflection, to interpret as you will."

"Be that as it may," Viktor said, "I'm not looking for a book."

Viktor saw a grin lift the corners of Zador's mouth, though he still faced the stacks. "One is always looking for a book."

"I'm investigating the death of Matthias Gregory," Viktor said. "I assume you know who he was."

"I do."

"I also assume you know who Xavier Marcel was," Viktor said.

"I do."

"Have you heard anything about these deaths in the occult community?"

"Anything?" Zador said.

Viktor gritted his teeth. Zador's obtuseness was a thing of legend. "Potentially useful information. Rumor. Fact. Anything in between."

"Oh no, I wouldn't know anything about that."

"Have you had any strange visitors recently?" Viktor said.

Zador stopped shelving, revealing a wandering gaze that always made Viktor uncomfortable. Viktor knew Zador didn't see well, but it was more than that, the way his eyes never focused on Viktor but remained in constant motion. Not motion as if he were looking around the room, but as if he were mentally absent, his gaze focused on other realms or planes invisible to the human eye.

No one, at least that Viktor was aware, knew the story of Zador's past. The shop had been there as long as anyone could remember, and the rumor was that he had arrived from Budapest the day after the previous owner had died and assumed ownership the next day. Another rumor was that Zador and the previous owners were part of a secret society, a sect of magicians that kept watch in various bookstores over a repository of hidden knowledge, doling out the rarest texts only to those they deemed worthy, to further their own mysterious agenda.

"Most who enter my door are strange," Zador said, the delivery implying the inclusion of Viktor.

"Have you ever met a man named Douglas Oakenfeld?"

"The name is unfamiliar."

"Do you know who Simon Azar is?" Viktor said.

"Neither."

Viktor took a stab in the dark. "His real name is Darius Ghassomian."

"Ah, Darius."

Viktor's next question was halfway out of his mouth before he cut it off. "You know Darius?"

"He was here a year ago, perhaps two. I am not so good with time."

"What was he doing in San Francisco?" Viktor said. Zador shrugged, and Viktor did his best to stay calm. "What was he doing in *here*?"

"Looking for a book, of course. I told you, everyone is always looking for a book, whether they know it or not. And this book was rare, very rare indeed."

Viktor leaned forward. "Which book was it?"

"Ah," he said, his eyes focusing on Viktor. "You should have said you wish to discuss a book."

A customer had entered the store during their conversation, a somber man with clipped dark hair and an exaggerated Roman nose. Zador waited until he left, then flipped the sign on the door to CLOSED. "Come," he said to Viktor. "We shall go to the back."

# 20

**G**rey counted eighteen rungs before he landed in a rounded tunnel extending in two directions. The darkness was broken only by the shallow beam from his pocket flashlight, the plop of dripping water, and a pervasive stench.

He hated to use the light, but he had no choice. The passage to the left sloped downward, and on instinct he chose to follow the passage heading down, checking his cell before he started walking.

No signal.

After a few hundred yards the tunnel leveled out and Grey arrived at a locked iron gate. The gate was rusty, but the lock was not, piquing his interest. He picked the simple lock in no time, then passed through the gate into a different sort of tunnel, a rough-hewn, rock-walled passage that confirmed Grey's suspicions.

Grey had visited the Parisian catacombs as a tourist, many years before. He didn't remember much, but he knew the section open to the public was only a small portion of the catacombs crisscrossing beneath the city, a two-hundred-mile network of narrow tunnels and caverns, many of them lined with human bones. After overcrowded cemeteries in the eighteenth century started to contaminate the city's water supply with decomposing human rot, the deceased were moved to stone quarries beneath Paris, where the bones were dropped into pits and set into the walls.

The tunnel tightened as Grey walked. The top of his hair brushed the ceiling, and he could touch the pitted rock walls on either side. The cooler underground air chilled his sweat, raising the gooseflesh on his exposed forearms. After a time the tunnel spilled into a small cavern whose walls were covered with bones, the glow from his penlight reflecting off the dull white surfaces.

He had entered the catacombs proper, but it wasn't like the polished tourist area he remembered: This section was rougher, disheveled, bones and skulls strewn on the floor and sticking out of the walls at weird angles. Alone in the underground cavern with the skeletal remains, his penlight casting distorted shadows on the walls, the gooseflesh spread from his forearms to the rest of his body.

Tunnels branched in five directions, all of them lined with bones. As he considered the situation, he saw the light of a torch bobbing in the distance down one of the tunnels. The light disappeared as quickly as it had come, and Grey guessed that someone was following a cross-tunnel up ahead.

He pointed his flashlight at his feet, padding down the tunnel towards where he had seen the light. This might be his only chance for information, and he could still turn around if needed.

The tunnel intersected with another a hundred yards down. To his right, Grey saw the faint flicker of a torch. Grey switched off his own light and moved forward as fast as he could. The pounding of his heart outpaced his footsteps, and he tried to avoid crunching on loose bones. The stale air stagnated in his mouth as he worked to control his breathing.

Though Grey could see the light up ahead, he was wading through darkness and had to keep his hands in front of him to ensure he didn't run into a wall. Whenever the tunnel took a slight turn, Grey recoiled as his hands brushed one of the knobby skeletal remains poking out of the walls.

He had no idea if anyone else was in the tunnels behind him, or how many entrances to the catacombs were scattered across Paris. Grey knew he was pushing his luck, but he was gaining ground, pressing forward among the bones and the darkness, the only sound the faint hiss and pop of the torch a hundred feet ahead. As he got within fifty feet of the man another light source, a broader and richer glow, entered his field of vision at the far end of the tunnel. At the same time, he heard a sound that sent a tingling flushing through his nerve endings: the murmur of voices speaking in unison in a foreign language.

Not just speaking, but intoning.

Chanting.

The chanting didn't have the lilting cadence of French, but rather an older, rougher, more guttural inflection. Grey was good with languages, but he didn't recognize this one. What he knew was that it set him on edge.

The bad news was that an unknown number of people waited up ahead, most likely members of L'église de la Bête who would not be amused by Grey's decision to crash their party. The good news was that Grey had drawn close enough that the noise of the chanting drowned his footsteps.

Though Grey could theoretically retrace his steps and outrun any pursuers, there might be shortcuts within the tunnel network , a warning system, or traps of which he was unaware. Further, Grey had seen at least five passageways branching off, making it likely that someone would appear behind him.

His target, buried within a black cloak, was twenty feet ahead. Grey tried to gauge how far it was to the end of the tunnel, estimating a hundred yards. When Grey passed a small alcove on his left he decided to act. He knew he wouldn't get another chance to talk to a member of the Church of the Beast.

As he sprinted forward, Grey could see the mouth of a large cavern up ahead, probably one of the central grottos used to collect the bones before they were distributed to the smaller tunnels. Tonight, Grey knew, the cavern served a different purpose.

Or, he thought grimly, perhaps it didn't.

Grey caught the man just as the backs of more black-garbed figures materialized inside the cavern. A sinister red glow emanated from the mouth of the grotto, but Grey wasn't close enough to make out the source.

Grey's hand reached around the man's face and clamped over his mouth. He yanked him backwards and switched to a blood choke, trapping the two sides of the man's neck between Grey's left biceps and forearm. He reinforced the choke by grabbing the biceps of his right arm with his left, then placing his right hand on top of the man's head. The effect was of a python wrapping its prey. A proper blood choke, cutting off the oxygen from both sides, rendered someone unconscious far faster than a strangle. Grey dragged the man backwards to keep him off-balance, the man's futile gasps and struggles only expending more oxygen. Six seconds later he was unconscious.

Grey picked up the man's cloth-wrapped torch and dragged him into the alcove. Seconds after they were secured, he saw the flickering shadows of approaching torches. Grey extinguished his torch and held his breath until the torches passed, shaky at how close he had come to being discovered.

Underneath the polyester black cloak, Grey recognized the sandy hair and brown pullover of the man who had followed him. The man was dressed in slacks and a dress shirt beneath the pullover. After searching the man and failing to find identification, Grey took a long curved knife he found tucked into the robe and laid it on the ground next to him.

He had released the choke a few seconds after he felt his captive go limp, causing no permanent damage. The man was already stirring. As soon as his eyes fluttered Grey slapped him across the face, hard enough to stun him and cause him to moan in pain. The slap also brought a sense of dominance to the situation, as did the fact that Grey was sitting on top of the man's chest, knees pinning his arms, feet tucked under his buttocks.

The man wriggled and got nowhere, then glared at Grey, who was holding the knife against his throat with one hand, a fistful of hair in the other.

Grey waited for the ceremony to begin in earnest. Three more torches passed in the next few minutes, and each time he pressed the knife against his captive's throat, his own stare boring into the man's unblinking gaze.

After another few minutes the chanting ceased, and Grey could just make out a single voice intoning in the same harsh tongue as the chanting. The crowd answered in repetition each time the speaker paused, and Grey knew the ceremony had started. He eased the knife an inch off the man's throat.

His captive spit his words out. *"Savez-vous ce que vous faites?"*

Grey noticed an expensive watch and trimmed fingernails, and his hand was grasping a head of coiffed hair. "Speak English."

"Do you know what you are doing?" The man said in educated British English, with only a slight French accent. "When they find you they will tear out your eyes and eat your heart."

Grey slapped him again, this time so hard the whites of his captive's eyes showed and he went limp in Grey's grasp. He shook him, and the man whimpered.

"You should be worrying about your own health," Grey said.

Grey felt strange interrogating the man with the archaic chanting in the background, like it was background music for some cheap horror film. But he had already seen enough of the Church of the Beast's handiwork to know its horrors were all too real.

"I'll make this quick," Grey said. "Trust me, you don't want to know what happens if you don't answer my questions."

The man sneered. "What makes you think—"

Grey pressed his thumb into the hollow of the man's throat until he coughed and gagged, releasing the pressure only after the man's eyes bulged in pain. Grey despised torture and thought it immoral, especially on an institutional level. But Grey was not an institution, and had long ago accepted that in rare situations he was going to do what he thought he had to do.

"*Trust* me." Grey didn't waste his time asking why the man had followed him from the metro. "Who killed the Black Cleric?"

The man said nothing, and Grey kept the knife against his throat while pressing a finger into the pressure point just below his ear, digging underneath the jawbone. Press hard enough, and the pain was excruciating.

Grey knew that if the man didn't have full faith in Grey's intentions, he would refuse to talk or hold out for a much longer time than Grey had. For this to work, the man had to look into Grey's eyes and know he would carry out his threats.

Which wasn't a problem.

The man arced in Grey's grip, causing his neck to press into the edge of the knife. Grey released the pressure point and again took him by his hair. "Who. Killed. Xavier."

The man's breath came in short heaves from the pain. When he caught his breath he gave a mocking laugh. "But that is the wrong question."

"Enlighten me," Grey said."

Grey pressed the knife deeper, drawing blood, and the man hurried his words. Victims saying anything to relieve the pain was the principal drawback to torture, which was why Grey preferred a hard and fast approach, to try and get as much of a gut reaction as possible. "We have a new leader," the man said, "one with the blessing of the Beast. Xavier refused to step aside. He was no longer in favor."

"I don't suppose this prophet wears a black robe with silver stars?" Grey could see the surprise of recognition in the man's eyes. "He killed Xavier?"

"He destroys anyone who stands against him."

"I hate to put a dent in your hero-worship," Grey said, "but your new prophet was in San Francisco the night Xavier died."

The man's condescending smirk, as if he knew that already and the six-thousand-mile difference between the two cities didn't affect his response, sent a chill down Grey's spine.

"Where do I find him?" Grey said, and the man didn't answer. "Is he here tonight?" Grey pressed his thumb into the man's throat again, harder than before. The man gagged and still didn't respond.

Grey set the knife down, again taking the man by the hair. "I'm going to say this once. I know the kind of man you are; I saw your Church's work in Gustave's apartment. But you know nothing about me." Grey placed the thumb of his free hand on the man's eyeball, nudging the bottom of the pupil just enough to make him squirm. "Look at me. *Look* at me. If you don't tell me his name and where to find him, right now, you're going to lose an eye."

Grey pressed harder into the eye, feeling the eyeball try to slip away from the pressure. The man's screams were drowned by the noise from the ceremony.

# THE DIABOLIST

"Wait!" His trapped hands clawed at the air as he tried to free his eye from Grey's grip. "I don't know his name, and I swear I don't know where he is, or if he comes tonight. No one does. He comes and goes as he wishes."

"What do you mean?" Grey said. "Where does he live?"

"I mean it does not *matter* where he is. He has the power of the Beast."

Grey knew the man was telling the truth, or at least thought he was, but sensed he wasn't telling all of it. Grey increased the pressure on the eye even more, and the man convulsed in pain.

Grey's voice was harsh. "I don't want to hear about magic. You know something about where to find him. You have the count of three to tell me, or you lose an eye and we move to the next. One."

The man jerked and bucked, but couldn't break the hold.

"Two."

A gong sounded in the background, above the chanting. "*Oui*, stop!" the man said, and Grey released a tiny bit of pressure.

Pain rattled through his voice. "It is you who now has the choice." His eyes flicked towards the cavern. "That was the signal to begin the sacrifice. Do you torture me, or save the girl? She has seconds to live."

"You obviously don't know me very well," Grey said evenly. Any trace amount of sympathy he possessed for the man had just left the room, but Grey didn't want him to know that his statement about a sacrifice, uttered with the composure of truth, had gotten to Grey.

"And you misjudged the timing," Grey continued. "She has seconds, but you don't. Three," he said, increasing the pressure to an unbearable level, feeling the eyeball start to separate from the socket.

"London!" he screamed. "Dante's in London serving the Magus. I have no idea where or why. That's all I know, I swear by La Bête."

Grey jerked him up by his hair, striking his temple with his free elbow. The man went limp. Grey picked up the knife and the cloth-wrapped torch and sprang to his feet, donning the man's black cloak before racing into the passage.

# 21

Zador led Viktor to a nest of rooms in the rear, an area somewhat more orderly than the front room, stuffed with books from every conceivable genre of magic and the occult. Entire shelves were devoted to thematic subjects such as Egyptian, Babylonian, and Druidic magic, as well as rows of rarer specialties like Shamanism, Necromancy, Geomancy, and Numeromancy. There were plenty of one-offs as well, esoteric titles that made Viktor shake his head, such as *Variants of Subtropical Lycanthropy*.

Many of the books were secured behind glass cases. Viktor's fingers twitched at the sight of it all, and he would have given a small fortune to spend a day alone in these rooms. Zador led him past the glass cases to a study in the very back of the store. The study contained two musty leather chairs, a floor lamp, and an antique writing desk.

Zador pulled a chain on the floor lamp, filling the room with mellow light. "He was on a journey, that one."

"Darius?" Viktor said.

"*Perdurabo*. The Great Beast."

Viktor frowned. "Crowley? What does he have to do with this?"

"We discuss the world of magic, do we not? If we discuss magic in the modern era, we discuss Aleister."

Viktor wasn't quite sure when they had started talking about magic, but he would play along. It was true that Aleister Crowley was the most infamous black magician of the twentieth century. A rival of Yeats in the Golden

# THE DIABOLIST

Dawn magical society, a prolific author of occult texts, and the founder of his own magical society as well as the infamous Abbey of Thelema, Crowley was reviled for his publicized use of sexual and drug-induced rituals. Believed by many to possess potent supernatural powers, Crowley was feared even more than he was loathed. "To be honest," Viktor said, "I never understood why a true magician would seek fame and fortune."

"Aleister was an egotist, yes, but he kept his secret magic, his true ambition, to himself."

Viktor's eyes narrowed. "Then how do you know about it?"

"One's innermost secrets are revealed through one's choice of books."

Viktor snapped his fingers. "The San Francisco visit."

Viktor had studied Crowley's life in detail, and he knew there was speculation that he had been searching for someone or something in San Francisco, though no one had ever figured out who or what.

"The San Francisco visit was well before his death," Viktor said, "not long after the turn of the century. Did your predecessor know him?"

"You were very much alike," Zador said, ignoring the question. "He was large in body and spirit, full of life and himself. And, yes, full of power."

"I long ago learned the foolishness of being full of myself," Viktor said.

"Of course you did, of course. That was Aleister's undoing, you know. He sought to become a god on earth, as does someone else. As perhaps do you. As perhaps do we all."

"Someone else?" Viktor said. "Who? Darius?"

Zador's gaze stopped wandering, fixating for a rare moment on Viktor. "I shall tell you what I told him: I've never touched it, and I never will. That book should never have been made."

Viktor wanted to throttle the old man. "Does this book have a name?"

"All books have a name," Zador said, amused. "It is called the Ahriman Grimoire."

Viktor worked hard not to reveal his shock at the mention of Ahriman. "I've never heard of that book. And I'm aware of all the major grimoires."

"Are you?"

Viktor couldn't imagine a grimoire existing that was both unknown to himself and so important that both Crowley and Darius would have gone to such lengths to search it out. Surely it would have come across Viktor's radar at some point in his studies.

"What is it?" Viktor said. "What did you tell him?" Viktor was letting his excitement get the better of him. He forced himself to regain his stoic facade. "What can you tell me about this grimoire?"

Zador's eyes started roving again, and Viktor had the disconcerting feeling that Zador was talking to someone else, in another place and time. "A codex, made in the time of the monks. There is only one copy in existence, if it in fact still exists. It is said the grimoire forbids the reader from making another. The power is not just in the content of the words, but in the making."

"Which was?" Viktor said.

"Legend says the scroll was authored with a pen dipped in the still-warm blood of virgins, dripping from their bodies during prolonged torture. The victims were sacrificed at the end of the ritual, the edge of the codex bound and covered with leather soaked in their blood."

It sounded outlandish, but Viktor had heard of plenty of similar grotesqueries performed during human history, especially during the Middle Ages. The more disturbing fact was that Zador had memorized the process.

Viktor said, "When was it written? Ahriman hasn't been worshipped for two thousand years."

"The grimoire was allegedly written in Avestan."

Viktor caught his breath. Avestan was a variation of Old Persian, and the sacred language of the Zoroasters. Spoken, he knew, from roughly seventh to fourth century BCE, and transcribed a century or two after Christ.

"Would you care to see a book on the subject?" Zador said. "This book is not so rare as the Ahriman Grimoire, but rare indeed. I believe there are"—his head moved side to side as if mentally making calculations—"yes, six copies in existence outside of the Vatican." Zador's eyes gleamed, and Viktor wondered why he had become so helpful all of a sudden. He had the unsettling feeling that he was being led down a path, that this whole visit had been a hand of tarot stacked and dealt by Zador.

"I would," Viktor said.

Zador disappeared, then returned cradling a thin book with a binding so aged it resembled peeling sandpaper. There were a few areas of water damage, and several gouges in the cover, but the book was otherwise intact.

After setting the book on the table, he handed Viktor a pair of disposable latex gloves and a pen-shaped device Viktor knew was used to turn the pages of rare books. The title, written vertically on the side in Latin, was *The Ahriman Heresy*.

"When was this written?" Viktor said.

"In 1551."

A muscle in Viktor's neck twitched in anticipation as he eyed the piece of living history on the table. "The price?"

Zador's oversize head wobbled back and forth. "Ah, but this book is not for sale. You may explore its contents in this room alone."

"You haven't heard my offer," Viktor said.

"The purpose of this shop is to preserve and spread knowledge, not just to sell wares."

"If you were interested in spreading knowledge, you'd open the back rooms to public browsing."

"Ah," Zador said, "but not all knowledge was meant for everyone."

"*Do prdele.* Why then, pray tell, was I chosen to receive such sacred knowledge?"

"As you know, the practice of magic requires balance. One of the darkness has read this book recently, and so shall one of the light."

Viktor stifled his chuckle, amused both by Zador's melodrama and the content of his words. The day Viktor represented the light was a sad day for the forces of goodness. Maybe Zador was talking about something else again, or maybe he was just addled.

"Sometimes we do not choose which side we represent," Zador said with a grin. "And sometimes, we're forced to switch sides in the middle of the contest."

Viktor put the gloves on. "I'll take a look, but why have I never heard of this work or the Ahriman Grimoire?"

"The Vatican took great pains to destroy all evidence of the Ahriman Grimoire and the short-lived heresy it spawned. Including the book you now hold in your hands, which is but a history treatise detailing the heresy."

That made sense to Viktor. History's victors tended to do the telling, and over the centuries, the Catholic Church made the Nazis seem like concerned librarians when it came to disposing of books with which it disagreed. What the Church did not want known, they destroyed or kept for themselves, making the Vatican the largest rare bookstore on earth. Unfortunately, membership was required.

Viktor said, "Why did Crowley and Darius want this grimoire so much?"

"I haven't read this book."

"But you know."

Zador didn't answer, his gaze floating over Viktor and around the room.

"Did Crowley read *The Ahriman Heresy* here?" Viktor said.

"He had his own copy."

That comment set Viktor's fingers tapping. "Then the grimoire must be mentioned in *The Ahriman Heresy*, and he was here looking for it." Viktor decided to ask a blunt question. "Do you know where the grimoire is now?"

"Not here," Zador said, and Viktor knew that was the most direct answer he was going to get.

"Darius was looking for it, too, wasn't he?" Again no response, and Viktor said, "Did you send him anywhere?"

"Soon you will know as much as I."

Zador left the room with a half bow, closing the door on the way out. At first Viktor thought Zador meant the answer lay within the copy of *The Ahriman Heresy*, but he realized if that were the case, then Crowley wouldn't have come to the bookshop searching for the grimoire.

# THE DIABOLIST

*Darius was following Crowley,* he mused to himself. *Crowley might have learned about the grimoire from* The Ahriman Heresy, *or from another source, and then begun his search. Where did* Crowley *look next, that's the question.*

That something like the Ahriman Grimoire had survived did not surprise Viktor. No matter how great the persecution, powerful ideas and hidden knowledge have a way of staying alive, secrets buried in the cracks of history, waiting to be uncovered like vine-covered ruins in the jungle.

Wishing he had his absinthe, Viktor settled into the chair to read. When he finished he closed the book and sat in silence, his elbows on the table, fingers steepled against his mouth.

# 22

*lone in the catacombs,* Grey's mind shouted at him, with God knew how many members of the Church of the Beast in that cavern and a maze of tunnels in every direction. But if there was an innocent girl bound to a rock slab in that tomb of horrors, then he had to do something, or at least try.

He sprinted down the passage. As he closed in on the mouth of the huge cavern and saw what lay inside, he started to shake. Not from fear, though part of him was afraid, but from an emotion that had always been more powerful than fear for Grey, one that shuddered him to his core as he took in the scene.

Anger.

Dozens of black-cloaked worshippers lined the walls and filled the center of the cavern, surrounding a wooden contraption in the middle, a fifteen-foot-high hangman's tower that supported a table-size platform four feet off the ground. A silver bowl rested in the middle of the platform, and on each corner sat an enormous gas lantern, together casting a reddish glow throughout the cavern.

Hanging upside down above the platform, feet tied to a rope suspended from the top of the wooden tower, long blond hair swaying underneath her, was a naked young woman.

She had cuts on her neck and wrists, her outstretched fingertips dangling above the huge bowl. Blood dripped from her wounds into the basin, her blood-streaked hair and face giving her a ghoulish appearance. Grey could see

114

her swaying a few inches back and forth, fingers wriggling, probably too weakened by blood loss to do much more than attempt a feeble struggle.

*Rage.*

She was alive, and Grey clung to that fact with a desperate hope. A priest in a black cassock stood on the platform beside the girl, holding a red goblet in one hand and a curved knife in the other, identical to the one Grey had taken from his captive. Grey noticed everyone holding a goblet. His eyes flicked to the bowl, and his soul shrank from the implication.

Grey edged into the cavern, still behind the other cult members. Either no one had noticed him, or no one thought twice about another black-cloaked arrival. Just inside the cavern, placed on ledges on either side of the entrance, Grey saw two smaller lanterns, similar to the ones on the platform. He also saw a basin of water, probably to extinguish the torches. Looking around the cavern, he saw three other entrances, each illuminated by lanterns.

The priest on the platform bent to dip his goblet into the silver bowl beneath the girl, bringing it up streaked with crimson. The chanting from the crowd continued, the same monotone words issuing forth in that guttural language, causing Grey to scream to himself in silence.

*Stop chanting, you depraved lunatics, stop chanting and take your knives, your cloaks, and your bloodstained hands and go watch a horror movie or role-play in a nightclub. Do not, do not, do* not *do what it looks like you're about to do.*

The priest raised the goblet and drank, lips stained red with blood. Grey swallowed. He could not, would not, stand and watch in dismay while this girl's life drained away, blood and spirit quenched by these animals.

There were too many, and he knew his chances of survival were almost nil, hers even lower. He had no idea how he was going to get her out of the catacombs, he had no idea about much of anything, save for one thing: The people in this room were about to find out what it was like to go to war.

*You think you have a taste for violence? Let's see just how deep that appetite runs.*

After slipping his knife inside his cloak, he grabbed the two lanterns off the ledges beside him. He broke the glass on the bottoms, with the butt of his torch. Each lantern was filled with a deep basin of highly flammable lamp oil, which Grey splashed on the backs of the robes of the men next to him. As heads turned he tossed the remaining oil as far as he could into the crowd, in a path towards the platform, and then in a circular spray.

Shouts and confused cries interrupted the chanting, but Grey had already brushed his torch against the backs of the thin polyester cloaks of the men next to him, causing a leaping flame that ignited the cloaks like living torches and spread quickly in the crowded space. Grey then broke the glass on the top half of the lanterns, still burning from the residual fuel on the wicks, and threw these firebombs-in-waiting into the crowd. They met with the burning robes and exploded in sharp cracks.

Dozens were on fire or trying to shrug out of their cloaks, the entire cavern in chaos. Grey burst through the first line, knife in one hand and torch in the other, setting more worshippers alight as he waded towards the center of the room and sprang onto the platform. One man in the room had been aware enough, from his heightened vantage point, to notice the source of the confusion, and Grey's blood curdled when he saw what the priest on the platform was doing: standing beside the girl, looking right at Grey with a maniacal grin, curved knife pressing into her throat.

Her eyes bulged in fear, but before Grey could move, before he could plead or bargain for her life, the priest ran his knife across her throat, and the girl's head jerked. Grey knew it had been a death stroke.

The priest came at Grey, knife raised and eyes burning. He died on his third step, blow parried and insides gutted before he even knew what was happening. Grey took him by his hair and slung him off the platform, then went to the girl and lifted her chin. She was already limp, eyes lifeless.

Grey overturned the basin of blood in a rage, then killed the first six men who climbed onto the platform, wielding the knife as an extension of his own prodigiously talented hands, stalking and feinting and slicing from all angles, a whirlwind of violence and terror.

The men below hesitated, no one wanting to be the next to step onto the platform. Grey stood alone above the fray, shivering with rage, covered in blood.

# THE DIABOLIST

"Dominic Grey!"

The shout came from his left, from the middle of the crowd. The stench of burning flesh filled the room, and greasy smoke filled the cavern, giving the air a surreal glow.

"Dominic Grey," a powerfully built man in the middle called out again, a lit torch in his raised hand. "You can't fight us all." He swept his arms in a circle, roaring, *"Lui brûler!"*

*Burn him.*

Torches ignited around the room, knives appeared in the hands of the worshippers not rolling on the ground. There were still dozens, if not hundreds, on their feet. They surged towards the platform, shrieking and thrusting with their torches and knives.

Grey had already spun into motion, knowing his death was imminent if he didn't get off the platform in the next few seconds. He picked up the first lantern and made a path of fire.

He did the same thing as before, this time with all four lanterns on the ledge, smashing them and spreading the lamp oil. He concentrated on the area leading towards his chosen exit, the entrance opposite the passage by which he had entered.

Most of the worshippers still hadn't had the sense to shuck their cloaks, and when Grey ran his torch in a line along the front row, and threw the top halves of the larger lanterns into the fray, it seemed as if the whole room had burst into flame. Now that the main light source had been extinguished, the burning cloaks and sputtering torches illuminated the room with a truly hellish glow.

Grey sprang off the ledge, slicing his way through the panicked crowd, torching more oil-soaked cloaks as he went. He killed those few who confronted him, but he knew once they regrouped, the sheer numbers would overwhelm him.

He barely made it to the passageway, feeling the crush of people surging towards his back. Torch aloft, he sprinted into the darkened passage, praying he had chosen correctly. Since he had seen so few people enter the same way he had come in, he was guessing it was a back route. But he had no idea, and the passage he had chosen might lead to a locked gate, or an impenetrable maze, or worse. His fears were realized when he came to an intersection of four identical tunnels, breath ragged from the fight, his pursuers just behind him.

He gritted his teeth and went right, hoping for sheer luck. His spirits rose when he came to another intersection and found a passage branching off without bones set into the walls. His hope slithered away at the next intersection. Bones riddled the other three passages, shards of the damnable things covering the floor and set into the walls.

He had gone deeper into the catacombs.

If he had to, he would find a narrow tunnel and make his stand, taking out as many of them as he could. He could hear them shouting just behind them, and he knew that eventually he was going to make a wrong turn, or double back on himself, or be cut off from the front.

His luck ran out even sooner than expected. He blew through the next crossroads, choosing one of five tunnels, and thirty feet later he saw torches bobbing in the darkness ahead. Someone noticed him, cried out, and ran towards him. Grey fled back to the intersection, chose another passage, and a few seconds later the same thing happened. This time he plowed forward, thinking he might be able to break through enemy lines. He met four of the worshippers head-on. The tunnel was only wide enough for them to fight two abreast, and Grey dropped the torch to free his other hand.

He killed the first so fast he never knew what happened, then used his sagging body as a shield while he parried and sliced through the second. The third stepped forward, and Grey ducked behind his overhead slash, cutting through an Achilles' tendon and then stabbing him in the back. The fourth, a woman who moved with some actual skill, stabbed Grey in his knife arm before he could maneuver in the narrow tunnel. He dropped the knife and went right back at her, sliding just to the left as she thrust at his midsection. He latched on to her wrist as it came past, and his other forearm came forward like a whip, snapping her extended arm at the elbow. She screamed and dropped to the floor.

# THE DIABOLIST

The fight had cost him. He picked up the knife in his right hand, his left hand throbbing from the triceps wound. The adrenaline drowned the pain for now, but he had lost a fighting arm and knew it was a matter of time before he lost too much blood.

More torches appeared behind him, this time a dozen instead of four. He sprinted to the next intersection and could already see lights down two of the four exit tunnels. He was running out of options. He peered down the two clear tunnels, trying in vain to discern which one might be better.

"This way."

He flung his body away from the voice. It had come from his left, down one of the unlit tunnels. The voice had been a whisper, yet he saw no one around him. And it had been a woman's voice.

A familiar woman's voice.

He had no reason to trust the voice, but neither did he have a choice. He ran down the tunnel to the left, cursing when he came to the next intersection. Torches appeared behind him, and in all three of the other directions, drawing nearer. He'd been tricked, and he had nowhere to go.

He spun, trying to decide what to do, and then he saw her, ten feet ahead of him down the tunnel to his right, blond hair spilling to her chest, the same woman from the plane. She was dressed in dark clothing, but she wasn't wearing a cloak. He could only assume she had been present at the ceremony and was leading him straight to the enemy.

"Come, before he sees us," she said.

"Who?" Grey said.

*"Hurry."*

She stepped into the darkness to her left. He was out of time and options. He approached with his knife raised, on edge for an ambush. When he came to the spot where she had disappeared, his mouth dropped.

It was a narrow side passage, barely large enough to squeeze through, free both of bones and of telltale torchlight in the distance.

The girl was nowhere in sight.

Grey grimaced and raced down the passage. A hundred feet later the tunnel widened and showed no sign of ending, though he now heard shouts behind him.

He ran until his legs cramped, exhausted to the point of delirium. He guessed he had covered at least two more miles down the passage, as fast as he could, with a knife wound on top of everything else that had happened. But the shouts fell farther and farther behind, and his new fear was that this was a dead end, or a passage to their home base, a last ruse before the slaughter.

A light appeared in the distance, not the golden glow of torchlight but a stronger, steadier flood of light. Grey knew he was about to discover his fate.

**D**arius lay on his back on the cushion-strewn floor, flesh melting into the creamy Persian carpet while he gasped for breath, tingling from the currents of sexual energy coursing through him. The woman beside him was near catatonic, halfway to the ethereal plane, her pale body covered in a sheen of sweat from the ritual. He dipped a finger through the sweat pooling on her stomach and ran it across his tongue, the taste a heady mixture of salt and perfumed oils.

The woman's supple curves glinted in the candlelight. Darius felt himself hardening again. His own stamina continued to surprise him, and one partner alone could rarely satisfy. Often availing himself of multiple partners of both sexes, as well as pleasure-enhancing narcotics, he had sampled everything in his pursuit to unlock the spiritual power of orgasm, from sadomasochism to bestiality to consumption of the semen and menses.

Tonight's session had been ritualistic, though it had not been carried out for the purpose of a specific spell. Darius was performing sex magic on a nightly basis now and would continue to do so until the night of the Unveiling, to keep the magical currents as potent as possible.

He shuddered and moved outside of the diagrammed pyramid, rising for a glass of water. He would let her sleep. They had combined their physical and cosmic energies for three hours without interruption.

After pouring a glass of water he sat in front of the computer in the next room, scanning the Internet for relevant hits. As he did so, his mind drifted to the same place it always did after sex, no matter who his partner or partners had been.

It drifted to Eve.

Darius was self-aware enough to understand two defining facts about his life: Ahriman had changed him, made him someone new and better. And he was still in love with Eve.

He could accept both of those things.

Unfortunately, thinking of Eve also made him think of Viktor, which inevitably made him think of the night he had once tried everything to forget.

It had been All Hallows' Eve, their senior year at Oxford. Darius, Viktor, and Eve had attended a costume party. Eve had left shortly after midnight. After another beer with Darius, Viktor left to study for a midterm.

An hour later Darius also left the party, deciding to pass by Eve's flat. It was a few blocks out of his way, but he was restless and thought he might see if she was still awake and wanted to share a nightcap.

Darius saw how Eve looked at Viktor, but Viktor swore they were just friends. Besides, Viktor was leaving England after graduation, and Darius, well, he planned to go wherever Eve was going. He knew Eve enjoyed his company, and with time, once his body matured and he proved to her how much he loved her, her defenses would crumble. He had never known he could love someone as much as this, so much so that separation, even for half a day, was a physical pain.

Darius constructed his entire existence around opportunities to be near Eve. He rescheduled his classes to align with hers, he made sure he ran into her when she stopped for morning coffee at her favorite French bakery, he memorized every facet of her daily routine. Every other girl had become an inferior version of Eve, every choice Darius made—from the clothes he wore to the things he said to the internal thoughts he pursued—was predicated on Eve's tastes.

# THE DIABOLIST

When he neared her ground-floor flat he noticed a dim light in the bedroom. The view inside was hidden by a hedge. Darius went to ring the doorbell, then stopped, making a decision that would haunt him for the rest of his life. He slipped behind the hedge and peered around the corner of the blinds into the bedroom, reasoning that if Eve had fallen asleep while studying, he didn't want to wake her.

In the candlelight he saw Eve sitting astride Viktor, both of them naked, Eve's eyes rolled towards the ceiling, mouth open in a soft oval of pleasure, hips rocking back and forth in a luxurious rhythm.

Darius's feet became twin blocks of cement. He stood as what felt like his entire youth slipped away, both titillated and appalled, watching in silence as his beloved made love to another man, his best friend, right before his eyes.

When they finished, covered in sweat and laughing in each other's arms, Darius slunk away from the hedge, abhorring himself and his pathetic frail body, feeling pain in places he never knew existed, unable to blame Eve but cursing the universe for allowing such a thing to happen. He cursed Viktor even more, and, most of all, he vowed never to be impotent again.

Darius forced himself to focus on the articles on-screen. He had long ago decided to embrace that memory, as a reminder of his former weakness. Yet he knew he could never truly embrace it until Viktor Radek was rotting beneath the earth.

He was pleased to find a short profile in *The New Yorker* discussing the Order of New Enlightenment. This was the best press he had received so far, and he read the best parts twice.

THE INTELLIGENT RELIGION: A NEW AGE OF ORDER

If there is one thing to expect from Simon Azar's burgeoning new religious movement, it is the unexpected. Though the baseline humanistic message is a familiar one, everything else about the Order of New Enlightenment feels as fresh and necessary as the Arab Spring. A religion a thinking person can grasp on to, it is a backlash against needless ritual, as well as against the watery agenda and vague promises of the New Age movement.

. . .

Mr. Azar's theology embraces, rather than denies, the human condition. It is an admission that we do not have all the answers and should conduct our search with science, reason, and self-awareness, rather than with fantastical claims and anachronistic ideals that serve only to retard the progress of the human race.

. . .

Exhibiting a rare adeptness with social media for a religious leader, he attracts followers from a cross-section of humanity. From Christians to Jews, agnostics to atheists, biker gangs to boardrooms, scientists to Scientologists, it seems half the world is listening to Mr. Azar and shaking their heads in agreement. Human nature is not evil, but complicated and evolutionary? Sexuality should be glorified rather than vilified? A church should have no puerile, dogmatic requirements of ritual?

More, please.

. . .

The only flaw is the all-too-familiar condition in cults—and Ponzi schemes—that adherents pass through certain "stages"

# THE DIABOLIST

before reaching the "inner circle" of "enlightenment." Yet Mr. Azar even has a clever explanation for this: Like any other form of knowledge, he says, religious or scientific or otherwise, comprehension comes in stages. A medical student would never perform brain surgery on day one, just as an attorney would never argue before the Supreme Court without years of training. Though it brings to mind unfortunate comparisons with the sort of veiled, cloak-and-dagger elitism found in Mormon hierarchy, the occluded halls of Scientology, or even the Catholic Church, Mr. Azar's gifted rhetoric softens the comparisons. Whether he is sincere remains to be seen.

. . .

His detractors have called him a greedy demagogue, a charlatan, even the Antichrist. Yet the exodus in recent years from traditional Western religions, combined with the unprecedented growth of the Order of New Enlightenment, is a wake-up call to religious leaders.

. . .

No longer are we cavemen huddled beneath the stars, peering in awe at the passage of the moon through the night sky. Nor are we medieval peasants purchasing indulgences for salvation, or New World pilgrims imposing puritanical mores on a delicate village ecosystem. The existential questions of mankind have not changed, and they likely never will. What has changed is our perspective.

As Mr. Azar preaches, we need a new religion for a new age, and at least for the moment, the Order of New Enlightenment is doing a better job than its more venerable counterparts at plugging that gaping and inexplicable hole in the human psyche—the one that must ask why.

Darius browsed the comments, then scanned a recent mention of the murders on a weird-crime news blog called *Shep's 911*.

*Has anyone else noticed that major Satanists are being offed like deer in Alabama? I don't know about you people, but this is the sort of thing that gives me the cold sweats at night. Either we've got Captain America of the fundamentalist world on our hands, or else we've got a power struggle going on that makes the Mafia wars seem like a game of blind dodgeball.*

*What's worse is no one's talking about it. Every time the Feds or the po-po get real quiet, you can bet something nasty's going down. Anyone out there have any 411 for the Shepster on the murders of Matthias Gregory and the Black Cleric? What're we dealing with here? Do I need to keep my children locked in a Swiss bank vault at night? Brush their teeth with holy water? I'm counting on all you freaks to help me on this one. Tell the Shepster!*

He closed the laptop in amusement, not failing to see the irony that the ridiculous blog entry was much closer to the truth than the *New Yorker* piece. The beauty of the Order of New Enlightenment's system was that the identity of the inner circle would always be kept secret, and no one would ever know what they were missing. They would study, they would strive, they would yearn, but unless they were ready for the truth, and very few would be, then they would swim in ignorance. Moreover, unwittingly and by their very membership, they would serve to further his secondary goal: the disintegration of traditional religion.

# THE DIABOLIST

Once the Unveiling occurred, that disintegration would accelerate, the world would look to Simon Azar for answers, and the secondary goal would open the door to the primary.

It would open the door to *Him*.

An unveiling: to remove a veil or covering. To expose what lies underneath. Darius's job was easy, because the reputation of the greatest religion the world had ever known had been in decline for some time, twitching on its bed of geriatric rituals and employee scandal.

And he was about to deliver the death blow.

# 24

The tunnel led right to the street, just underneath a sewer grate. Stone workman steps had been cut into the wall below the grate, and Grey climbed out. The night air had never tasted so sweet. He replaced the grate and melted into the darkness.

Grey was always a careful man, but as he returned to his hotel in the deep of night, twisting and turning through back alleys until stumbling into a cab on a more crowded street, he found himself looking over his shoulder with every step, heart still thumping.

He walked into his hotel room, taking the time only to bandage his wound with the small medical kit in his pack. The knife wound turned out to be not that deep, the hospital a risk he couldn't take. Then he grabbed his backpack and slipped through a side door, walked a few streets over, and jumped into a taxi. He had paid for two nights in advance, and didn't want anyone to know he had checked out.

He didn't know what was more disturbing: being helped by a beautiful girl who kept disappearing into thin air, being chased by a pack of bloodthirsty Satanists who knew his name, or taking a plane to London in pursuit of a mysterious figure who terrified both the bloodthirsty Satanists and the girl.

# THE DIABOLIST

Grey breathed a sigh of relief once he entered Charles de Gaulle Airport, but part of him, still shaking with horror and rage, wanted to stay in Paris and hunt down every last one of those bastards.

*Damn* them. The image of that girl, hanging upside down and bleeding into a bowl like a slaughtered animal, wouldn't leave his head. Preying on the weak and helpless, performing their ghastly rituals while their victims quivered in fear . . . he put a hand on the wall and breathed through his nose.

Four a.m.

Two hours to go before he could buy a one-way ticket to London. He slumped in a corner and devoured an energy bar from his backpack. The first call he made was to Jacques. Grey kept him on the phone for an hour, providing every last detail of his descent into the catacombs, knowing the French police would find nothing but empty, bloodstained tunnels.

The next call was to Viktor, who surprised him with a rare show of emotion, saying he had been unable to relax since Grey sent his cryptic text and the photo of Gustave. Viktor provided little feedback except despair at the fate of the girl and approval when Grey told him about London.

When Grey finished, Viktor was quiet for a moment. "I don't think I need remind you to be supremely careful in London."

"No," Grey said, "you don't."

"There's been another murder, two nights ago, though no letter has appeared. It was in London—oddly coincidental."

"You know what I think about coincidence," Grey said. "Who was murdered?"

"The reputed head of the Clerics of Whitehall."

"Who?" Grey said.

"The Clerics are the modern successor to the Monks of Medmenham, an infamous occult social club that started in eighteenth-century England. As a mockery of Christ's disciples, the Monks were comprised of twelve influential men—including a prime minister—who would meet in the ruins of Medmenham Abbey to perform debauched occult rituals. A risky target today, since the Clerics of Whitehall allegedly have deep connections in business and politics, as the name implies."

Grey kept a continual vigil for anyone or anything out of place, but the airport was still and quiet. "I wouldn't think they'd want a public investigation."

"No."

"So who was the guy?" Grey said.

"Earl Ian Stoke, a prominent businessman and former MP, found dead in his South Kensington townhome yesterday morning. The coroner reported time of death at roughly midnight, and the state of the body resembled Xavier's."

"Do we have those toxicology reports yet?"

"No," Viktor said.

"Get them."

"I suspect the English report will come before the French," Viktor said. "Deaths of former MPs tend to take priority over Satanic cult leaders."

Grey checked the time and stifled a yawn. Five-thirty a.m. "What's the next move?"

"I leave for York tomorrow. I'd like you to investigate Ian's death in London."

"Why the letter to the York magicians?" Grey said. "What's the link? Are they Diabolists?"

"There exists no society of Diabolists, as far as I'm aware. The York Circle, however, is one of the most well-organized groups of magicians in the Western world. My guess is this is a power play. Whoever's behind the murders—and I'm not ready to point the finger at Darius—is trying to extend his power base, from Satanists to practitioners of magic and the occult. Though if it is Darius"—Viktor hesitated, as if he were sharing the next piece of information grudgingly—"then the York letter is personal."

"Darius knows the recipient," Grey said.

"Yes."

Grey took a stab. "You, too?"

# THE DIABOLIST

"Yes, I know Gareth."

"I'm gonna guess Darius was kicked out of the York magic circle for not playing nice," Grey said.

"Your instincts are correct. Diabolists are not looked upon very kindly by modern magicians. Consider them the fundamentalists of the magical world."

Grey crouched in a squat as Viktor described his conversation with Zador, interrupting when Viktor mentioned the Ahriman Grimoire. "What's a grimoire?" Grey said.

"A grimoire is simply a transcribed collection of magical instruction, ritual, wisdom, or incantation. The form can vary wildly. Think of it as a textbook for practitioners of magic."

"You mean a spellbook."

"In the vernacular, yes," Viktor said. "Though while there have been countless books, scrolls, texts, and parchments reputed to contain magical knowledge, an extreme few have survived to become grimoires. Designation as a grimoire means that the knowledge has been . . . attested to . . . over time."

"What's so special about this one?" Grey said.

"I haven't seen it myself, but the book Zador lent me, *The Ahriman Heresy*, discusses the Ahriman Grimoire. It was a startling read."

"And there're only six copies of *that* book?" Grey said.

"*The Ahriman Heresy* is more akin to a historical pamphlet. It was written in the mid-sixteenth century and discusses a sect of Ahriman worshippers that proliferated rapidly among the remnants of the Gnostic sects and heresies. The text was unclear whether the cult had just formed or had existed for millennia and recently emerged. In any event, the Ahriman cult became a major problem for the Catholic Church, challenging the Church's views on theodicy."

Grey rose to stretch his legs, blinking to stave off exhaustion. "Why was it so dangerous?"

"According to the pamphlet," Viktor said, "the devotees of the heresy were advanced practitioners of black magic, and their leader possessed a book he claimed was the source of his power."

"The Ahriman Grimoire," Grey said.

"The heresy was a terrible one, believed responsible for all sorts of atrocities. It syncretized Lucifer with Ahriman, promoting him not as a doomed fallen angel, but as an equal adversary to God. Numerous people attested to the leader's powers, including the ability to appear in two places at once."

Grey thought back to the woman's strange appearances, as well as the claims of a robed figure manifesting out of nowhere behind Matthias. Instead of calm and sleepy, the airport now felt too quiet. He started walking towards the ticket area.

Viktor continued, "The Church moved more swiftly than it ever had, rounding up the followers of Ahriman in Templar style, torturing and burning every last one within a short time span."

"Can you actually make a group disappear from history like that, such that no one's even heard of them?"

"In that era," Viktor said, "with a fringe group that never gained historical traction, then yes. Who's to say how much of history has been spoon-fed to us, and how much remains to be discovered? I'm aware of hundreds of historical cults that no one outside of a few scholars has heard of."

"And the treatise is reputable?" Grey said.

"I found it to have the ring of authenticity."

Grey was walking through a deserted hallway, following signs to the ticket counter. "So this grimoire was their playbook, their bible of black magic."

"Grimoires run the gamut in size and scope. According to *The Ahriman Heresy*, the Ahriman Grimoire is not a compendium of occult knowledge, such as the Key of Solomon, but a thin codex made for a very specific purpose."

"I'm guessing it wasn't to discuss fertilization techniques in ancient Persia," Grey said.

"In classic medieval thought, the Devil possessed three principal powers he used to wreak havoc on earth. I never made this particular historical connection between Ahriman and Satan until now—I'm not sure anyone has—

but the Ahriman Grimoire is dedicated to unlocking three powers that Ahriman can choose to convey to his disciples: the power to influence the minds of men, mastery of the art of seduction, and the ability to move about the world unseen, like Ahriman himself. According to the treatise, the leader of the heresy claimed to have mastered the secrets of the Ahriman Grimoire."

"It sounds more like a fairy tale than history," Grey said, quickening his step and wondering how long this hallway would go on. His exhaustion and the events of the last few days were getting to him.

"So does the Bible, to nonbelievers. I believe Darius thinks the grimoire will grant him leverage with his worshippers, historical validation. Some movements rely on prophecies or revelations, some on golden plates found buried in a hill. It's always more potent for a cult leader to anchor himself with the weight of history."

"So what happened to it?" Grey said. "Did Crowley ever find it?"

"I have no idea. The leader of the heresy was burned alive, all mention of the grimoire lost. I hope to learn more of the story in York, as Crowley apparently had a copy of *The Ahriman Heresy*."

"I don't like the idea of you going off somewhere by yourself. I'm already a marked man, and we have to assume you are, too."

"I appreciate the concern," Viktor said.

Grey's voice was harsh. "You didn't see what I saw, and the person we're tracking just took out the leader of these fanatics. You hired me for a reason, dammit, and I don't think you should be investigating by yourself right now."

"I made a superb hire, but we don't have the luxury of time. I'll avoid dangerous situations and utilize local law enforcement if there's any trouble."

"Trouble chooses you," Grey said quietly, "not the other way around. And when it does, there's no time to call for help."

"Granted," Viktor said.

"You're set on this?"

"I am."

Grey waved his hand through the air, dismissive. "There's something else. I saw that girl again."

"The one from the plane?"

Grey saw movement up ahead and started. He realized it was just a janitor, crouched low over a mop, and Grey gripped the phone. "Yeah. She helped me escape from the catacombs, then disappeared again. My guess is she slipped into some hidden doorway, but I didn't have time to check."

"I have no idea who she might be," Viktor said, "but I do know Darius is an expert tactician, a game player extraordinaire."

"Somebody's playing games, that's for sure."

Grey finally reached the ticket area. It stirred with morning life: ticket counters opening, passengers pouring in, the smell of roasting coffee wafting in the air. A modicum of tension left his body. "Where's all of this going, Viktor? What's the endgame?"

"I don't yet know," he said, a rare hint of confusion in his voice.

# 25

Viktor didn't like keeping things from Grey that might impact an investigation. While nothing was certain, he was growing dangerously close to that line. Viktor was quite familiar with the collected works of Shakespeare and the tragic consequences of withholding truth, but what went unsaid by the Bard was that some things were so private, so painful, they were worth the risk to conceal.

It was true the Ahriman Grimoire and even the heresy were news to Viktor—startling news—but he had his own past with this ancient god of evil, this eldritch deity that had given birth to the Christian Devil.

He rose from the couch in his suite. Since he had read *The Ahriman Heresy* at Zador's shop earlier that day, he had been in that addled state that succeeds disturbing news, nerves jittery and mind spinning, his body moving as if wading through a sea of oil.

He uncorked another bottle of vintage absinthe, his second of the day. Viktor knew this was unhealthy, that consuming this much thujone was a risk to his health and his sanity. And it could put him in a dangerous place, unable to distinguish between reality and fantasy, when he most needed to be lucid.

The truth was that he had to finish the story, he needed to return to Darius and Eve and remove the coffin lid of buried memories. He had to confront the demons of his past before they climbed out of their graves on their own, devouring him from within.

And he didn't want to do it sober.

His plane left for York at noon the next day, and the itch was upon him, whispering in the air and crawling up his skin, his sweet muse calling.

*Drink me, Viktor, take me to the dregs, forget your troubles and sink into my sweet embrace.*

And drink he did. Viktor loosened his shirt and cuffs and sank into the leather couch as the capricious imps of memory cavorted around his skull in a dark ritual of remembrance, taking him back to his final year at Oxford, shoving Viktor inside the ring of faerie.

*Are you ready,* Darius said.

Viktor finished inscribing the second and third layers of protection around the pentagram, inch-thick concentric circles of runes and sigils. This was no ordinary circle of protection: This was a sealed fortress of magic that had taken days to prepare and months to research. As he looked from the nervous face of Eve to Darius's eager eyes, both of them wearing Egyptian amulets of protection similar to Viktor's, he asked himself what he felt.

The problem was, he didn't feel very much. It was all very interesting, and he had thrown himself into the research and preparations with gusto. If Ahriman did, in fact, exist and paid them a visit that night, then Viktor was satisfied that every precaution had been taken, the laws of magic satisfied, the old masters and grimoires followed to the letter.

But Viktor still didn't believe.

Eve took his arm. *Shall we finish that brandy when this is over?*

Darius walked over to them, glowering. *This isn't a game, Eve. We're conjuring dark powers, perhaps the darkest, and none of us knows what will happen. If your mind isn't one hundred percent on task, you have to leave. The ritual can be satisfied by one person alone, in case either of you isn't up to the task.*

Viktor barely concealed his amusement, but Eve licked her lips and brushed a stray blond hair from her eyes. *Ready for a fag,* she mouthed. Viktor should have paid more attention to her mental state, the fear simmering just beneath the surface.

Lying open on the table in front of them was the ancient scroll they had procured from the Oxford library, hiding in an uncatalogued room in the rare books section. Darius's and Viktor's search for black magic had taken them deep into the guts of history. They had put aside their differences long enough to explore the range of Satanic cults, the Gnostic heresies, the devils of Greek, Roman, and Egyptian origin. They probed the gods of the Aztecs and the African tribes, they studied the witchcraft of the shamans and gypsies, they learned about the frightening gods on the fringes of Hinduism and Daoism. Then they looked harder and found the devil that was older than all the others, the one called Angra Mainyu.

Ahriman.

Though half-Persian with a Baha'i mother and a Protestant father, his parents did not raise Darius in a religious household. He knew of Zoroaster and Ahura Mazda, but Ahriman was not a name known to those outside the faith. But as Darius and Viktor explored the Persian origins of Solomon's knowledge of the black arts, Darius became convinced that occult secrets lay with the elusive followers of Ahriman, the black mages of Zoroastrianism that lurked deep in the barrows of history.

They searched far and near for information on the Ahriman priests, coming up shockingly short. As if all mention of them had been erased from history. Viktor knew enough about history to know that happened only when a greater historical force expended the effort to do so.

The scroll they had found was written in Avestan and contained an actual ritual designed to call upon Ahriman. They compared it to demon summoning rituals from various sources, and once satisfied of its authenticity, they spent weeks in preparation, gathering the required ingredients, memorizing the Avestan inscriptions, researching the protection spells, preparing themselves mentally. Viktor may not have been a believer, but he respected the potential of the unknown enough to proceed with caution.

Incense poured forth from charcoal braziers, rolling through the forgotten basement they had discovered beneath the college of religion. *Light the candles*, Darius said to Viktor, scroll in hand. *Eve, start the invocation.*

A cold breeze passed across Viktor's face, and he started. It was May in England, and the weather was still quite cool—but not that cool. Moreover, he knew he had shut the cellar door. Had he read one too many novels by Dennis Wheatley, imagined the breeze?

As practiced, they began to chant in unison, each of them reading from an exact copy of the scroll to ensure no missteps. Vials of mercury in hand, they stood on previously drawn extensions of the three greater points of the pentagram, forming a triangle just outside the protection spells, each extension inscribed with one of the three words of power—*Primeumatun, Anexhexeton, Tetragrammaton*. Resting on the two lesser extension points were human skulls they had stolen from the med school, each of the skulls bearing, like the three living souls in attendance, different markings symbolizing one of the five elements.

Darius took out the ritual knife he had prepared with the proper runes, actually using a soldering iron to carve the characters into the blade. Continuing to chant, Darius walked around the circle and made a shallow cut on each of their arms. They held their arms over the chalked pentagram for a count of three, infusing the circle with life. The pentagram was not to be crossed again, lest the summoned entity escape.

Viktor felt a mixture of annoyance and nostalgia. This was to be his last foray into black magic: He was graduating in three weeks, and for some time had been ready to move on from the practice of magic to the pursuit of greater truths, the search for other hidden doorways. Darius, he knew, was far from finished, still convinced that real power simmered in that mysterious nexus of magic and faith.

And Eve, his eccentric and beautiful Eve: For the first time, Viktor had moved away from the shallows of youthful romance and stepped into the deep and turbulent waters of love. Whenever he thought about leaving Eve for graduate school in Paris he felt as if one of those American mechanical bulls had been loosed in his stomach, twisting and kicking his insides. He had decided to ask for her hand after graduation, and he relished her surprise.

*Did anyone feel that breeze?* Eve asked.

*I did,* Viktor said. *There must be a crack somewhere.*

*Silence,* Darius hissed. *The forces are stirring. From this point forward there can be no more chatter, or we risk breaking concentration. And I needn't repeat that under no circumstance can anyone enter the circle. Eve, do you understand? I'm quite serious about this. No matter what you hear or see, or how he tempts you,* you must not break the circle.

*And just exactly what will happen,* she asked with her usual world-weary sarcasm, though the quiver in her voice belied her cool tone. Viktor knew Eve harbored religious beliefs ingrained in her from childhood, and that a sense of spiritual trespass into the realm of evil, more than any belief in ancient sorcery, was the source of her anxiety.

*You don't want to know,* Darius said, though without his typical smugness. The statement had been uttered with respect but also with a trace of fear, which surprised Viktor. He had never seen Darius afraid of magic.

The ritual began in earnest. As set forth in the scroll, the middle of the pentagram was stuffed with Persian inscriptions and numerology that comprised the bulk of the spell. Darius and Viktor had worked hard to translate the Avestan, even consulting experts at the college. They knew it was designed to call to Ahriman, but still did not understand the full meaning of the scroll. The symbology reminded Viktor of something out of the kabbalah, especially the use of the pentagram.

They had filled the other portions of the pentagram, the triangular tops of the five points, with the required ingredients, such as the clay golem and pillar of salt at Viktor's feet, representative of the element of earth. Darius stood on fire, Eve on spirit, and the two skulls guarded air and water.

All that remained was to chant and stay the course. They had no idea how long it would take, though Darius had suggested hours, perhaps the entire night. Nor did they know what to expect. Would Ahriman appear as a disembodied voice, a burning bush, a whirling djinn ready to grant their every desire?

Viktor, of course, expected nothing. If there were truth to magic, Viktor thought, then it did not involve three college kids summoning an antediluvian Persian god from a cellar.

As time dragged on and the minutes became hours, something happened they hadn't planned on: The incense smoke from the five braziers clouded the air, creating a dense and aromatic fog that made Viktor light-headed. He hadn't thought it possible for the braziers to put out that much smoke, but the lack of ventilation added to the effect.

After another hour Viktor could see Eve shifting back and forth, and he knew she was weakening. How long would this nonsense go on before they put a stop to it? He knew Darius would continue until he dropped, but Eve was nearing her limit.

*I feel something.*

Eve's words so startled Viktor that he took a step backwards. He saw her slap at her arm, and then her leg. *Something's pricking me. There must be an insect in here.*

*There's no insect,* Darius said evenly. *Ahriman is coming forth, and he will test us to see if we're worthy. He'll concentrate on the weakest link.*

*Thanks for telling me that beforehand.*

*There's no cause for alarm. You're strong.*

*I'm tired.*

*Eve! Continue chanting, or we risk disruption of the ritual. Remember, under no circumstances do you break the circle. Quit or leave if you must, but don't cross the barrier.*

Eve resumed chanting. The cadence of their combined voices returned, a steady current of words in a forgotten language. In rituals such as these, Viktor knew the alleged power of magical incantation lay not just in the content of the words but with the repetition, the continuous beseeching to the astral plane that was supposed to unlock or awaken certain forces. He would later learn, from studying various religions around the world, that the effect of such a ritual was to induce the participants into a somnolent state, thus producing the reputedly magical effects or visions. But standing in that smoke-occluded room without the benefit of years of phenomenological study, feet standing at the point of a pentagram filled with occult symbology from an Avestan scroll, mind numbed by the unceasing chanting, Viktor found himself fully in the moment. With a sense of increasing dread, he had to keep reminding himself his fear was a product of his imagination.

Viktor had been staring off to the side, and his head jerked up when Eve screamed. His eyes focused on her across the obscured pentagram. She was hugging herself with her arms, eyes locked in the center of the circle as if she could see something inside the chalked barrier.

She screamed again, and Darius's voice rose in volume, his chanting cutting through her scream.

*Eve,* Viktor said. *What's wrong?*

She started rubbing her arms, and her voice cracked when she spoke. *Make it stop, Viktor. I can't bear it.*

Viktor could feel Darius seething at the interruption. *What is it?*

*The things in the circle, they're terrible.*

*I don't see a thing,* he said. When she screamed again he said, *Just step back. Shut if off.*

*I can't.*

*Eve!* Darius's voice rang loud and clear. No one was chanting now, and Viktor was surprised Darius would risk disrupting the ritual, knowing he would have done so only for Eve.

*You must be strong,* Darius said. *We're at the endgame. We have Him.*

Her hands went to the sides of her head, her screams becoming little bursts of jagged sound. Viktor felt nothing, could see nothing. At first he thought she might be mocking Darius, but her voice held genuine terror. Had the incense and the uninterrupted chanting gotten inside her mind, had she taken one too many pharmaceutical concoctions?

Darius was no longer looking at Eve, his fierce gaze trained on the circle, his frail body somehow commanding as he stood with raised arms, now shouting the words of the ritual.

The incense obscured the air, Eve's svelte frame barely visible in the gloom. Her screams turned to whimpers, and she put a hand towards the circle, as if reaching in supplication.

Darius's voice grew louder still, ringing off the walls, enunciating each syllable with his powerful will. Viktor saw Eve wobbling as if she were going to faint, and both outstretched arms reached towards the circle.

*Enough!* Viktor roared, and started towards Eve. She wobbled and started to tumble forward into the circle. He lunged for her.

His hands just missed her as she fell, her feet scuffing the chalk. She landed in a crumpled heap in the middle of the pentagram. Viktor scooped her in his arms, holding her and stroking her hair.

*It's over,* he said. *It's over for good, my love. No more rituals, no more magic. Just you and me.*

Darius approached through the fog of incense, staring in shock at the broken circle. He looked to Viktor and then to Eve, then slowly backed away from the circle, eyes wide.

Viktor carried Eve out of the basement in his arms, and she peered up at him with a tired smile. It was then when he noticed that her irises, once as blue as the glacial lake beside his parents' house in the Alps, had turned black as oil.

A voice whispered his name. *"Viktor."*

At first he thought he was still in the past, but then he realized he was on the couch in his suite in San Francisco, the lights from the city a neon glare outside the window. The voice came to him again, two mocking, drawn out syllables that cut through the fog in his brain. "Vik-tor."

He knew he was very drunk, and of course he knew about the hallucinogenic effects of drinking too much absinthe. He did not feel like he was hallucinating, but then again, one never did.

# THE DIABOLIST

"Viktor . . . Viktor . . . Viktor. . . ."

Darius's voice.

Viktor lowered his head in his hands, uncaring if Darius was somehow whispering his name or if he was imagining it, because in his mind, after what had happened next, the terrible thing, he deserved the torture.

He deserved it all.

He reached for the bottle. "Come, then," he bellowed, shaking the bottle at the air. "Convince me, spirits. Convince me you exist, reveal yourselves, torture me if you can."

He sank to his knees, swigging the rest of the bottle and letting it clang to the floor. "Come if you will, but leave my memories be."

Viktor woke the next morning on the floor, slumped in a sticky mess of spilled absinthe and drool, the dawn light bruising his temples. He pushed to his knees, feeling sick from drink for the first time in twenty years.

He stumbled to the same coffee shop and had a double espresso before his customary cappuccino. With sobriety came shame. Viktor could barely remember the end of the evening, except for the whispers lingering in his mind. He blamed it on the wormwood.

He thought again of the events of the day before, trying to see an angle with the Crowley information. Drumming his thumbs on his cup, he forced his thoughts into focus.

During the First World War, after living in New York for a time, Crowley had also made trips to New Orleans and San Francisco. The three best places in America to search for an ancient occult text. But according to Zador, Crowley already *had* the rare treatise when he had arrived in San Francisco.

Perhaps Viktor was taking the wrong approach. He checked his watch: He had about an hour to spare before heading to the airport. As he pushed away from the table, he noticed, in the corner of the coffee shop, the same dark-haired man he had seen in Zador's bookstore the other day, the last customer to leave before Zador had locked the door. The man was absorbed in a magazine, but when Viktor stood he had glanced his way. Or at least Viktor thought he had.

Viktor feigned a trip to the restroom and concealed his cell phone with his suit jacket, managing to take a photo of the side of the man's face. He texted the photo to Grey and Jacques.

After walking a few streets over to ensure the man wasn't following him, which he didn't appear to be, Viktor hailed a taxi and strode into Zador's shop. Viktor rang the bell, and Zador emerged from the stacks.

"We're back, I see," Zador said.

"You said there were only six copies of *The Ahriman Heresy* in existence," Viktor said. "Do you know where Crowley obtained his copy?"

"Ah, a clever question at last."

"Do you?" Viktor said.

"No."

Viktor clenched his hands. "Do you know where it is now?"

"I thought you might never ask."

Viktor took a step forward, eyes sparking with an intense light. "And?"

"The York Circle of Magicians is known to possess select rare items from Crowley's estate."

Viktor dashed to the airport, on his way to the walled city of York to investigate both the delivery of the newest letter, as well as Crowley's copy of *The Ahriman Heresy*. As he pondered these developments, just after seeing the same man twice in twenty-four hours in a city of a million souls, he thought of Grey and his scorn for coincidence.

Viktor felt the same.

# 26

## LONDON

**G**rey spent the flight to London staring out the window, struggling to force away the image of the girl in the cavern, feeling the greasy residue of the violence. It didn't matter how necessary or right his actions had been. The violence still affected him, chipped away a little more of his soul. That was the price.

After landing he took the Tube to Notting Hill. Viktor had given him the address for Alec Lister, one of the Clerics of Whitehall as well as a barrister with an office on High Street Kensington. Grey had no idea how Viktor had gotten the name.

Grey had lived in London when he was twenty after drifting out of Southeast Asia, a coiled spring of restless energy. He worked the odd nightclub security gig, fought when he had to, and spent his days taking the Tube to random parts of the city or walking the city's parks, pondering life amid the throng of foreign faces.

London had been everything Grey thought it would be: immense, chaotic, sodden, diverse, a city bolstered by the grandeur of its past and pulsating with the swagger of its present. A megalopolis could be the loneliest of places, but Grey was used to being alone, and at least in London he felt alive.

Notting Hill looked the same to Grey as it had a decade ago, vibrant sidewalk cafés sandwiched between antiques and vintage shops, pubs so quaint they seemed fake, the pastel facades of the townhomes on Portobello. He found an Internet café, caffeinated, and did some quick research.

He didn't find a word on the Clerics of Whitehall. What he found on the Monks of Medmenham, however, affirmed the sordid story Viktor had hinted at: gentlemen with too much money and time on their hands whose idea of a good time was orgiastic rituals and debasing religious icons.

Lovely men, these pillars of society.

Realizing how hungry he was, he stopped for lunch at a sushi bar in Notting Hill lined with black wood and neon-blue lighting. After lunch he walked a few streets over to a more commercial area, entering a four-story office building and taking the lift to the barrister's address. The secretary, an East Indian woman with her hair in a bun, sniffed as Grey approached.

"I'm here to see Alec Lister," Grey said.

"And you are . . . ?"

Grey took out his Interpol badge. "Dominic Grey. I have a few questions for Alec about Ian Stoke."

The secretary's eyes registered nothing. She rose, opened a solid oak door, and disappeared inside, emerging seconds later. "I'm afraid Mr. Lister is engaged with conference calls the rest of the morning, and then he's due in court. He wants to know if you could call back later in the week?"

"I'm afraid not." He thought for a moment, then said, "Tell him Sir David Naughton sends his regards from Harare."

Grey had neither the time nor the inclination to go through local law enforcement to get Lister's attention, so he took a gamble. Sir David Naughton was a British diplomat Grey had met during the Juju investigation in Harare, and he had a proclivity for poking his nose into dark and secret places. Grey thought him an exceptional candidate for membership in the Clerics of Whitehall.

The secretary disappeared, then reappeared and flicked her wrist. "He'll see you now."

She closed the door behind Grey. A plush office sprawled before him, with a window overlooking the bustle of Kensington. A lean older man with wispy gray hair, large ears, and tufted silver eyebrows sat behind a desk, an arrogant lilt to his mouth.

"I'm afraid I've no idea who you are," Alec said. "You say Naughton sent you?"

"I knew Naughton in Zimbabwe, when I was looking into the disappearance of an American diplomat at a Juju ceremony. I thought you might know the name."

The silver eyebrows angled upward.

"Right now I'm investigating the death of Ian Stoke," Grey said.

"Who?"

"Don't."

"I'm afraid I've no idea—"

Grey slammed his hands down on the desk, and Alec jumped. "You're a member of the Clerics of Whitehall, as was Stoke."

Alec said nothing. Grey let him stew. The best interrogation technique, especially when Grey had as little actual information as he did, was to let Alec's mind run wild with possibilities. Was Grey here to bust him? Did the authorities know about the secret ceremonies and the underage attendees? Grey was sure Alec Lister had plenty to think about.

When he started fidgeting Grey doled out a little more information. "Ian got a letter a week ago, didn't he? A letter giving him six days to step aside as leader of the Clerics."

Alec swallowed but managed to keep his superior tone. "How do you know about the letter?"

"Because you're not the only lowlifes on the hit list. Who's in charge of the Clerics now?"

No answer.

"Is it you?" Grey said. "Or Dante?"

This time Grey got a reaction. Alec shrunk into his seat as if deflating. "God, you know about Dante? Who *are* you?"

"Is Dante in charge now?"

"If you think we're the criminals"—he gave a short, hysterical laugh—"then you haven't met Dante. He's an animal, that one. A very cunning, vicious animal. Dante and his ilk are a sorry lot."

"Your predecessors sounded pretty sorry themselves," Grey said.

"The Monks? Christ, we're nothing like them," he said with a snort, though Grey could tell by the shifting of his eyes that they, in fact, were. "What is it you want, then? No one was present when Ian died, and I don't know anything about it other than the letter."

"Were you with him the night he died?"

"I talked to him on the mobile," Alec said. "There's a night guard on his street, and he retired to his room. He thought it was an idle threat, some kook. The maid found him at sunrise the next morning, on his bedroom floor."

Grey felt like he was plugging a dam with his thumb. It took far longer than a few days to investigate something like this properly, the forensic report hadn't even come in, and by the time he found a clue the next letter would be delivered and another victim found dead.

"I'll need to see the house," Grey said.

"I don't have a key, so I don't see how—"

"Just take me. Now."

Grey kept his hand on Alec's elbow as they walked down the busy street. Ian's residence was only a few blocks away on Ladbroke Mews, a quiet cul-de-sac just inside Holland Park. Grey's eyebrows rose as they entered the tree-lined, cobblestone scythe of a street; it was stocked with immaculate, stand-alone brick homes with ground-floor garages. This was the center of London, and those properties would cost millions.

Ian's three-story home had an iron entrance gate, and the white brick facade was trimmed in black wood and draped with climbing roses. Grey inspected the front door. Solid and likely dead-bolted. Grey would need cover of darkness for that job. He led Alec to the rear of the house, inspecting as he went. High windows and fairly secure.

Any half-trained professional could break into a house. It was the alarm system Grey saw, the wires and the cameras, that raised questions about the night of Ian's death.

"Did the alarm go off that night?" Grey said.

"No."

No alarm meant one of three things. Either a master thief was involved, someone Ian knew assisted with the murder, or the Magus teleported himself inside and administered poison gas. Grey was going with option number two.

"Have the police talked to the guards and checked the cameras?" Grey said. "Did anyone go inside that night?"

"Not a soul, other than Ian."

"He drove in?" Grey said.

"I assume so. Bollocks, I don't know."

Grey rubbed at his stubble. "The cameras probably don't reach inside the car."

"Anyway, Ian has tinted windows."

"I'm sure he does. Was he seeing anyone?"

"Just the same young filly he'd been seeing for a few months. But you must understand," he said with a creepy smile, "Ian always had a young filly, the younger the better."

Grey's voice hardened. "Do you know her name?"

"Why would I?"

Grey took him by the elbow again, exerting pressure on the ulnar nerve. Alec yelped in pain. "This isn't a courtroom," Grey said. "I ask the questions, and you answer."

"Isabella."

Grey knew he was getting straight answers; the man didn't have the stomach for interrogation. "Isabella what?"

"He never said."

"Where can I find her?" Grey said.

"No idea."

"Did Ian videotape?"

Alec didn't answer, and Grey pressed harder on the nerve. "Yes! But not here, as far as I know. Only with the group."

"When was the last . . . meeting . . . that was taped?" Grey said.

"Ten days ago."

"Where's the tape?"

"With his lawyers," Alec said.

*Damn.*

"I'll need to see it," Grey said.

Alec laughed, harshly. "I wouldn't be so sure about that."

They moved to the rear of the property, a narrow courtyard filled with plants and a gurgling fountain. It smelled of lavender. Grey shoved Alec against the wall of the house and told him to wait. He spotted the camera covering the back door halfway up the house, and he shimmied up a trellis to redirect it, using a waterspout for support. He jumped back down, pulled a thorn out of his leg, and went to work on the back door with his iron filings. If the alarm was still active, and Grey doubted it would be, he could just leave if he tripped it.

He had the door open within minutes, with Alec watching in sullen silence. Grey took him with him as he walked through the house.

Either everything of interest had been stripped, or Ian kept his goody bags elsewhere. Like Xavier's abode, the house was unassuming, full of expensive furniture and bric-a-brac from around the world. Maybe Grey was expecting too much, trying to impose too much abnormality on to these people. Then he remembered the catacombs and the girl hanging upside down, blood spilling into a silver bowl. No, there was nothing normal about this place. Ian and Xavier just knew, like other sociopaths, how to wear the mask of civility, how to construct a quotidian existence that would divert prying eyes.

He inspected the bedroom last, finding a king-size bed, a double-vanity bathroom, and a full entertainment system behind wood cabinets. He also found a closet full of sex toys, an empty camcorder, a bathroom full of lubricants and scented lotions, a bottle of cologne and an oversize copy of the Kama Sutra on the nightstand, and stacks of German pornography inside a chest at the foot of the bed.

He could go for the videotape, but there was no time for a legal battle. Talking to this Isabella was another option, but he would have to track her down, and if she had been with Ian the night of the murder, the guard would have seen her leave, if not enter.

After ushering Alec out through the back door, Grey left him standing in the rear garden. He called out as Grey walked away. "Where're you going?"

Grey felt no need to reply.

# 27

Dante lay on the chair at the tattoo parlor, listening to the prick of sharpened bone as it worked down his spine, the thin skin and nerves making it one of the most painful places on the body to apply a tattoo. Dante had decided to work the name of Ahriman into the intertwined snakes running down his spine, though he knew that half the reason for the decision was that he enjoyed the sting. Dante's entire body was covered in piercings and tattoos, from the pentagram on his scalp to the crosses on the soles of his feet.

Though the parlor was cool, beads of sweat formed on the artist's brow as Dante observed in the mirror. The artist was one of the best in the business, and one of the few who knew the traditional Hawaiian method of tattooing, far more painful than vibrating needles. He was also one of the few who could work on Dante without his fingers trembling.

The pricking bone released a rush of warmth that spread through Dante, lightening his limbs, releasing some of the terrible pressure that had built within him since his sister's death.

His cell vibrated from a table in the corner, and Dante tilted his head towards the phone. The artist scrambled to retrieve it, and Dante checked the number. A London exchange.

"Yes?" Dante said.

"Sorry to bother you, but something's come up."

Dante recognized Alec Lister's posh English accent. A particularly cruel and depraved man, of which Dante approved, but also a cowardly one, of which he did not. He could hear the fear seeping through the phone. "The gent you told us to watch out for just paid me a visit."

Dante straightened in the chair. "Dominic Grey? In London?"

"Just left me outside Ian's flat ten minutes ago. He came to my *office*. I'd like to know what you have planned for the little bugger, because I'd like to—"

"Where is he?"

"I've no idea, he left on foot. Didn't say a word about his plans, just wanted to know about Ian. What do you think—"

Dante hung up on the buffoon and rose from the chair. The rest of the tattoo would have to wait. He donned his shirt and strode out of the parlor without a word, walking down the underground corridor in the depths of the East End that housed a row of unsavory establishments.

After what happened in Paris, even Dante had to admit Dominic Grey was someone to take seriously, though the next time Grey would be dealing with Dante himself, and the outcome would not be so fortunate. Dante made a call of his own, to Dickie Jones, a Japanese-Irish gangster who ran an underground fighting ring that used to fund the IRA. Now it funded an assortment of unsavory people, Dante included.

"Yep?"

"Have you found what I asked for?" Dante said.

Dante knew Dickie had not paid attention to the number, because it took him a few seconds to process who was speaking. After a pause he blubbered into the phone. "Dante, sorry, didn't make it for you. Yeah, yeah, I looked into that. Was gonna ring you later."

"And?"

"I didn't need to look into anything, I know the bloke from way back. I ran fights for Dominic Grey. He's not one to feck with. Ex-Recon and a jujitsu expert, a real killer. Use to obliterate guys twice his size in the ring."

"Do you fear him?" Dante said softly.

"Jujitsu isn't much good against a Glock, and I'll take my laddies against a Marine, on my streets, any day of the week."

"He's in London," Dante said.

Dante heard the hesitation in Dickie's voice. "You want me to have a talk with him?" Dickie said.

"I do," Dante said. "We have things to discuss."

"I'll put the word out. Anything else?"

Dante reached the end of the hallway, the sickly light filtering down the staircase illuminating decades of grime and neglect. He whispered into the phone. "Do you fear him more than you fear me?"

There was another brief silence, then Dickie spoke in a subdued voice. "I'm not soft in the head."

This time Dante heard no equivocation, and he hung up the phone.

Since Viktor was en route to York, Grey decided to try a different angle. He made a few phone calls and then took the Tube to Lewisham, following Google directions to the only listed temple of Zoroaster in Greater London. Lewisham was a calm suburb, full of weathered townhomes and a flurry of low-end shops and restaurants surrounding the Tube station. Grey walked a mile or so southwest, then down a street lined with plane trees rustling in the breeze.

The address was a two-story brick house, one of the nicer residences in the area. A short iron gate surrounded the property, and a plaque on the gate confirmed the location of the temple.

Grey wasn't sure what he expected from a Zoroastrian place of worship, perhaps something akin to a Hindu temple, complete with beehive towers and exotic frescoes. What he hadn't expected was the home of the local dentist.

He rang the bell. A sallow East Indian man in jeans, a tailored sweater, and a white turban opened the door and walked to the gate. "Dominic Grey?"

"Yes."

"Thank you for making an appointment, though as you can see, we're in no danger of overbooking."

# THE DIABOLIST

"My pleasure," Grey murmured.

"I'm Ervad Kasraavi; we spoke on the phone. Do come inside."

"Thank you," Grey said.

"Chai?"

"Please."

He led Grey into a study redolent with the sweet smell of sandalwood. Grey took a seat in a leather armchair while tea was served with a plate of chickpea flour cookies.

"The place of worship is in the rear of the house, though unfortunately, we don't have the resources to be a full-fledged *agiary*, or fire temple. I must say, this is quite an unusual request. For a thousand years Zoroastrianism was the religion of three empires, but today we number less than the population of Brighton. After you called I would have guessed a graduate study thesis, but you . . . don't look like a student."

"I'm a private investigator," Grey said. "Something has come up during an investigation that might have to do with Zoroastrianism."

His eyebrows lifted as he sipped his tea. "I can't imagine what that might be."

"There's a specific subject I'm looking for information on," Grey said. "I assume you're familiar with Ahriman?"

He stopped sipping. "Your investigation involves Angra Mainyu?"

"Something like that," Grey said.

"This temple doesn't concern itself with that aspect of the Prophet's teachings. What is it you wish to know?"

Grey covered his mouth with his hand, tapping two fingers against his lips. "I'd like to know more about the worshippers of Ahriman, if any still exist. If not, then maybe something about the mythology surrounding Ahriman."

"I'm afraid," he said slowly, "you're talking to the wrong person. As far as I know, no worshippers of Ahriman exist today, thank goodness. But I'm simply not educated on the subject."

Grey sat back. Ervad Kasraavi cocked his head, thoughtful. "I do know someone who might be able to help."

"I'd appreciate a referral," Grey said. "Is he in London?"

"Cambridge. Dastur Zaveri. He's a Parsi high priest, perhaps the foremost historian of our religion outside Mumbai. I can't speak to his availability, but I've heard the topic of Angra Mainyu is a specialty of his."

# 28

## YORK

Upon arrival in York, Viktor took up residence at a luxury hotel on the northern edge of the city center. The hotel sat just outside Bootham Bar, one of the four gatehouses that provided access through the enormous wall encircling the medieval old town.

After a shower in the marble bathroom of his suite, Viktor put on a fresh suit and headed to the dining area, where he enjoyed foie gras and a peppercorn filet alongside a glass of vintage Bordeaux.

An hour remained before Viktor's seven p.m. meeting with Gareth Witherspoon, chief thaumaturge of the York Circle. Gareth had been a few years ahead of Viktor and Darius at Oxford, and Viktor knew him to be a fair and intelligent, if misguided, man. Viktor was interested to find out what Gareth knew about Darius's activities over the years.

Viktor left the hotel, walking through Bootham Bar and then alongside the Gothic bulk of the Minster, cake-like spires and crenellated towers rippling across the top of the block-long cathedral, statues and gargoyles looming from every angle. He wound through the old city, a place full of worn stone and magic, enclosed by an ancient wall and steeped in history.

Like his beloved Prague, York felt lost in time to Viktor, as if half the city were obscured not just by the omnipresent mist, but hidden in some ethereal dimension more connected to the swirling vapors of myth than to the technological and geopolitical complexities of the modern world. One could wander the twisted cobblestone alleys and forget what century it was, lost in the corridors of imagination, soaking in the spirits rumored to roam the streets at night.

York's old town was not large, but it was a maze, and Viktor realized he had ventured too far east. He found his way back to Stonegate, a handsome street which housed the headquarters of the York Circle.

The entrance was deceptive: An iron gate gave access to a brick-walled alley, but further in he realized the end of the alley opened into a large court-yard and an even larger mansion that had been built within the surrounding blocks, such that it was unnoticeable from the street. Two stone sphinxes flanked a set of double doors, and a weathervane in the shape of a dragon pierced the sky from atop the four-story building. Viktor guessed the entire structure had been planned and built by the Freemasons who had lived in York for centuries.

Viktor rolled his eyes as he performed the secret knock Gareth had given him. A young mage in white robes opened the door and led Viktor down a hallway covered with tapestries, through an oak door and then up a staircase to the fourth floor. Down another hallway to a rune-covered wooden door that was reinforced with iron hinges and cross-braces. The mage performed a different knock, and the door swung open to reveal a domed room with walls covered in more arcane scrawl. A room whose purpose Viktor recognized from his own days as a magician.

A room designed to protect its occupants from magical attack.

The mage bowed and left, and moments later Gareth Witherspoon entered from a concealed door opposite Viktor. He was wearing the white robes and golden sash of the Magister Templi, the highest grade of magician awarded by the Circle, requiring decades of study and demonstrations of power during secret rituals. Though it was alleged that different planes of existence were tapped at the higher levels of initiation, Viktor had not witnessed these rituals and had his doubts as to just what in fact occurred.

Viktor studied Gareth's appearance as he approached: a short and compact body more suited to an aging footballer than a magician, a tight silver beard adding gravitas to his burly appearance. Viktor had not seen Gareth in years, but he had aged well.

"Viktor," Gareth said, clasping Viktor's hand. "A shame we have to meet under such circumstances. Thank you for coming."

"Of course," Viktor said.

"How's your work?" Gareth said.

"At the moment, quite interesting."

Gareth's mouth tightened, and he withdrew a folded letter from his robes and handed it to Viktor. "This was delivered on Saturday." Viktor opened the letter as Gareth said, his voice laced with sarcasm, "It appears I have two days left to resign my position as chief mage."

Viktor read aloud. "'You will renounce your false beliefs and declare yourself a HERETIC, or you will die at the hand of the one true God on the sixth midnight hence.'"

He returned the letter to Gareth. "Almost identical to the others," Viktor said. "Ludicrous as it may seem, you need to take this letter seriously. At least three people have been murdered after receiving such a letter."

"And you have no idea who the sender might be?"

Viktor folded his arms. "I believe the man behind the letters might be Darius Ghassomian."

Gareth's hawkish eyes flared at the news. "I can't say I ever believed Darius's—or shall I say Simon's—recent conversion was genuine, but genuine or not, why send me a letter?"

"I don't think Darius has abandoned his beliefs," Viktor said. "I suspect his popular cult is a front, a vehicle to mask his true intentions and make them more palatable to the public. In cult vernacular it's known as cloaking: instilling the subversive belief system gradually, corrupting slowly and from within."

"And the letters, the murders?"

"He's weakening his competitors, putting his people in positions of power among the occult vanguards. Though I've no evidence, I have the feeling he might soon target other, more mainstream, competitors."

"Traditional religion?" Gareth said.

"History has never seen a movement dedicated to a malefic power that approaches the influence of the major religions. I believe Darius has such ambitions."

"But why?"

Viktor scoffed. "Because there will always be human beings who wish to dominate others, whether through government or religion, in the boardroom, or on the playground. Lust for power is simply narcissism, and cult leaders tend to be the most narcissistic of all. In the worst cases, true conviction is involved."

Gareth took in Viktor's answer with a slow nod. "Darius was always the most determined among us. And the timing, the grand scheme?"

"I'm unsure, and it's irrelevant to your situation."

"I once taught him, you know," Gareth said. "He was an extraordinary magician, but from what you've told me about these murders . . . this is far beyond his power."

Viktor flicked a wrist. "Don't be foolish. Neither Darius nor anyone else is using magical powers to carry out these murders. We're awaiting toxicology reports, but the victims who died alone exhibited signs of asphyxiation by poison gas. I'm sure the fires have a logical explanation as well."

"Darius was always interested in fire and its magical properties," Gareth said.

"He was just as interested in its physical properties. He read chemistry at Oxford."

"But how could he start the fire if he was never there?" Gareth said.

"With inside help from the organizations."

"And the appearing and disappearing at will?"

"You know as well as I," Viktor said, "that Darius, like most magicians, started off as a master of sleight of hand and illusionist technique. There's no evidence that he has actually *had* a corporeal presence in the places in which he's appeared."

"So what do you propose?" Gareth said.

# THE DIABOLIST

"I propose you step aside as chief mage until I bring him to justice."

"Out of the question."

"You need to take this threat seriously," Viktor said.

Gareth's lips curled. "I won't step aside for that egomaniac."

Viktor stepped close to Gareth, towering over him. "Don't be a fool," he said, his voice heavy. "Your hand waving and incantations in dead languages won't protect you from a common murderer."

"Maybe not," Gareth said. "But it will protect me from a practitioner of magic. I'll be in this very room two nights hence, under the protection of the entire Circle."

Viktor balled his fists in frustration. "*He's not using magic.* At least let me stay with you, and a police escort."

Gareth considered the proposition. "I'll allow you and no one else. I won't have the other magicians see me cowering behind the police. And I refuse to make this building a public spectacle."

Viktor shook his head. "You're a fool," he said again.

Gareth's face reddened. "You of all people shouldn't scoff at what you don't understand. Words and paraphernalia are irrelevant, a way to channel the will. Magic is self-realization, unlocking the powers of the cosmos and the abilities that lie dormant within us all. If you never saw the results, then you weren't paying attention."

"*Do prdele!*" Viktor said, then stalked back and forth as Gareth watched with flashing eyes. "I can't make you leave," Viktor said, "but in the meantime, I need your help."

"With what?"

"Access to Crowley's possessions. Specifically, a book entitled *The Ahriman Heresy.*"

"We keep what we have of Crowley's in our museum in Whitby," Gareth said. "I'll grant you access."

"Whitby?"

Gareth gave an embarrassed shrug. "We have a magic shop next to the Bram Stoker museum."

"I see," Viktor said.

"I'm unfamiliar with *The Ahriman Heresy*," Gareth said.

Viktor gave a brief account of his search for the Ahriman Grimoire, and Gareth plucked at his beard. "There were always rumors that Crowley was seeking something significant. And the possibility of a new grimoire . . ."

"What do you know of Darius's recent past?" Viktor said.

"He left us fifteen years ago when we wouldn't promote him directly to Magister Templi. No one's heard from him since. There were rumors that he went east, following in the footsteps of Blavatsky and Crowley, and one adept claimed to have met him in Tehran as Darius was enroute to the Kurdish regions of Iraq and Syria. The adept said Darius was searching for the Yazidi."

"There's basis for believing the early followers of Ahriman borrowed elements of Yazidi devil worship," Viktor said.

"There were also rumors that Darius reached the level of Ipsissimus."

Viktor waved a hand at the mention of the near-mythical society of advanced magical adepts. "Is that all?"

"Yes, Viktor, that is all. You know, despite your personal convictions, you might be wise to open your mind."

"I assure you no one has a more open mind than I. It's your universe that is limited, Gareth. You see only one piece of the puzzle, and even that is obscured by pageantry."

Gareth straightened, his voice cold. "When would you like to arrange to see the book?"

"Now."

# 29

Grey reclined in his seat as the train pulled out of King's Cross. If this were pleasure travel he would have had a Hesse or Vonnegut novel on hand, perhaps Murakami or Thomas Mann. Grey, realist though he was, believed deeply in the beauty and truth of literature, and all art. The world was a depressing place, full of the triteness and tragedy of the human race, governed by the selfish decisions of whoever had clawed their way to power. The best works of art were cathartic, the very act of self reflection a spark of hope for humanity.

But this was a far cry from pleasure travel. The sordid details of the case cluttered his mind as the train escaped the endless grays and browns of greater London, morphing into a bucolic landscape that was a blur of lime-green squares divided by low stone walls.

Grey grabbed a coffee from the dining car, then stood near the restroom to stretch his legs. When he pushed through the door that led to his compartment he stopped, his coffee sloshing against the rim.

She was in the seat next to his, watching him as the train rocked back and forth, full lips pressed together, eyes uneasy, hair loose and framing her face.

He approached slowly, his eyes both searching the train for danger and keeping her in his line of sight, afraid she might not be there when he looked back. She was dressed in designer jeans and a white suede jacket, her exquisite face reeling him in. He saw no sign of trouble and slid in beside her, resisting the urge to reach out and touch her, ensure that she was real.

"Let's start over," he said. "I'm Dominic Grey. My friends call me Grey."

She put her hands in her lap and expelled a long breath, as if gathering her courage. "I'm Anka."

"Just Anka?"

"I'm an orphan. The state gave me the name Georgescu. I didn't like it."

*Romanian, then.* "How do you keep finding me?" Grey said. "I didn't tell anyone where I was going today."

She bit her lip and her eyes slid to the side. Grey spread his hands. "Why don't I start with thank you. I'm not sure what would've happened in Paris if you hadn't shown me that passage, but it wouldn't have been pretty."

She blinked and didn't answer.

"That was you, wasn't it?" Grey said.

"Yes."

"Look, you're obviously here for a reason, so why don't you just tell me what you have to say? And I'd like it if you stayed longer than two minutes."

"It's very dangerous for me to be here," she said. "If he realizes I'm gone he'll find us."

"Who? Simon?"

She put a finger to his lips as he said the name, and his first thought was that she was corporeal. His next thought was that the contact, the smoothness of her skin, almost made him dizzy. He scoffed at himself. He knew nothing about this woman except that she had helped him once, disappeared twice, and he had no reason to believe a word that came out of her mouth.

"I need your help," she said in her throaty accent.

"Then why didn't you stick around in Paris? And where'd you go?"

Grey was guessing she hadn't wanted to risk being seen with him and had slipped into a different passage. But he wanted to hear her explanation.

"I couldn't stay," she said.

"You couldn't?"

She shifted. "I was . . . never there." It was Grey's turn for silence, and she said, "I know how insane this must seem, but I need you to trust me."

# THE DIABOLIST

"Trust is gained, not asked for," he said. "And you didn't come to me for trust, you came for help. I can't help you if I don't know anything about you."

She wrung her hands. "I'm not sure I can be helped."

"Why don't you let me be the judge of that? Let's start with the obvious: Where is he?"

"I don't know," she said.

Grey frowned, and she laid her hand on his arm. "I'm not trying to be difficult," she said. "But he can find me whenever he wants. If he discovers I'm gone and wants to find me, he'll come and . . . it won't be good."

Grey put a hand up. "Slow down. What do you mean, he can find you whenever he wants? I don't understand. Does he have people everywhere?"

"I thought you understood," she said.

"Apparently I don't."

Her eyes clouded. "He read the grimoire."

Grey stared at her. "You mean he has the three powers of the Devil? What are they, the powers to charm, seduce, and move about the world, or something like that?"

"Yes."

He continued examining her face for signs of deceit. Her liquid eyes were unblinking, without a shred of subterfuge or forced calm. Which meant either she was a very good actress, or she believed what she had just said.

"Forgive me if I'm not a believer," he said. "Though for the sake of argument, why wouldn't I think that you can do the same thing, given our last few meetings?"

Her face morphed so rapidly, shrinking as if she had been slapped, that Grey knew it wasn't faked. *"Never."*

He put his hands up. "Okay."

She looked out the window, then back at him. "I understand your confusion. And you're right that trust is earned." She took a deep breath, as if what she was about to say pained her. "I was raised in a Romanian orphanage in Brasov. When I was sixteen, my . . . ability . . . manifested."

"Ability?"

"Astral projection."

Grey gave her a frank, disbelieving stare. She flinched. "I've been facing that look my entire life."

"So you're telling me that on the plane, and in the catacombs, you were only there in spirit?"

"Not just in spirit," she said, "but not fully there."

"You seemed fully there to me."

"It's hard to explain," she said. "There're plenty of documented cases in the world, though mine is an extreme case. I can't control it. It usually happens when I'm under great duress, and on rare occasions when someone I know is."

"But how'd you know I'd be on the plane?" Grey said.

"I didn't. I've been so afraid lately, and after a particularly frightening visit from him, I passed out. When I woke . . . I was on the plane beside you, and he was on the monitor. I knew I'd been sent to you for some reason."

Grey shook his head and looked away.

"I know it's hard to believe," she said. "Astral projection, psychic powers—they work on a level or in a place we don't understand. Science has shown us that distance is irrelevant at the quantum level, that we're all inter-connected in ways no one understands. I have to believe our subconscious somehow brought us together."

"And Paris?" Grey said.

"He tells me things sometimes, to torture me. He told me about you and Viktor, and I knew what was waiting for you in Paris. That time I was able to appear and help. It's not easy, you know. It takes great concentration and it almost never works when I want it to."

"How'd you know about the passage?"

She tugged at the collar of her jacket. "I have a different sort of vision when I'm . . . there. I can't explain it."

"So you're telling me you saw through the walls?" Grey saw the hurt in her eyes at the sarcasm he knew was dripping from his voice, so he said, "Let's set this aside for now," he said. "How'd you get hooked up with Simon, or Darius, or whoever he is?"

# THE DIABOLIST

She seemed relieved to be switching topics. "I was thrown out of the orphanage when my abilities first manifested, because in Romania the Devil is given credit for such a thing. I lived on the streets of Bucharest, selling trinkets to tourists, but that's a dangerous life and there was only one other choice of employment. I made my way to a remote village and started a new life, as a librarian of all things, doing everything in my power to suppress my abilities. But one night I manifested in the village square, scaring a group of old men half to death. I was called a witch and thrown out of the house where I was staying. Word spread to the other villages, and I was forced to live outside like a dog. Not even the gypsies would have me." She looked Grey in the eye, any emotion at her past long since spent. "One day Simon found me and took me in."

Grey couldn't imagine this beautiful creature forced to live on the streets of anywhere. Romanian superstitions must be strong indeed. "How'd he find you?"

"He heard about me, I'm not sure how. I thought he was being kind, so of course I went with him. Winter was coming. But I later learned he just wanted to use me, find out why I was able to do what I did. He, too, believed it was a power of the Devil, though he had a different agenda than my countrymen."

"How is it that you speak English so well?" Grey said.

"You don't trust me at all, do you? The nuns in my orphanage were English. It's quite common in Romania. Only outsiders help the street children."

"And did Simon learn your secrets?"

"Once I arrived in London," she said, "we studied day and night, but there's no rhyme or reason to psychic powers. I have no idea how it works, and neither does science."

"And Simon? Assuming for the sake of conversation he can just show up whenever he wants, what will he do when he gets here?"

"He'll burn you," she said simply.

Grey again searched her face for signs of pretense. Not only did he fail to find any, but her lack of emotion lent an eerie ring of truth to her words.

"So you tried to leave," Grey said, "but he wouldn't let you?"

"He's in love with me."

"And you're not with him?"

She hesitated. "Do you really want to hear all of this? Or are you just humoring me?"

He glanced around the train, opening his palms. "I'm kind of trapped here." She laughed lightly, and he said, "I very much want to hear your story."

"You're a good listener," she said.

She relaxed in her seat, laying her hand on the armrest next to his. The light touch sent a tingle of warmth arcing up his arm.

She faced the seat in front of her as she spoke, curled into her seat. "When he found me he took me to the nicest hotel in Bucharest and gave me my own suite. We discussed literature and history for hours. He was very charming and, yes, even handsome. I was never in love with him, but he was my savior."

She turned her head towards him again. "You must understand, in the beginning he kept who he really was from me. When he asked me to come to London I had to tell him I wasn't interested in him romantically, but he demurred and said he would help me find a job and start a new life, that there were no strings attached. I agreed. I know it was foolish. I've always wanted to be a doctor, and in Romania I had no money, no family, and no future. I was an outcast, penniless, *homeless*. Sometimes we hear what we want to hear, and believe what we want to believe."

"That we do," Grey said.

"This was more than a year ago. Of course I knew about the Order of New Enlightenment, and that was fine. I'm not religious—or at least I wasn't then—but I didn't mind that he was. It was quite thrilling to be with someone so admired. But then I saw . . . some terrible things."

"Such as?"

"A month ago we had a wonderful day of shopping and dining in the West End. I felt like a princess, felt that perhaps one day I might even develop real feelings for him. That night when he left my apartment I looked out the window and saw him talking on the street to a man with a terrible tattoo on his head. Even from that distance there was something about his face that frightened me, an absence of humanity. They walked down the street and in that moment I asked myself why I trusted Simon so much, when I really knew nothing about him. I know on some level I never trusted him, but didn't care. I followed them to a townhome and waited outside until they exited with an older man. All three left in a black sedan. I followed them again, in a taxi, to a mansion in North London."

One thing apparent to Grey was that Anka was relaying her story in a very fluid, natural manner. Either it was true, or she had practiced it over and over. He said, "Weren't you afraid he'd see you?"

"My curiosity overpowered my fear, and I was a street orphan—a survivor. Besides, he would never harm me."

"Then why're you so worried about him coming here?" Grey said.

"I'm afraid for *you*."

"You don't need to worry about me."

"You don't understand," she said. "You can't fight him."

Grey gave her a tight-lipped smile. "So what happened when you followed him? Do you know where you were?"

"I wish I'd paid better attention to the street names. Somewhere in North London." Her eyes slipped downward. "They disappeared inside the house, but there was a huge walled cemetery behind the grounds, and I slipped over the wall. It was late, the cemetery was deserted. I could hear strange sounds coming from the grounds of the mansion, some kind of chanting. There was a huge oak twenty feet behind the wall, and I climbed until I had a good vantage point. I was terrified someone would see me, but it was dark, and the tree provided good cover."

She wrapped herself in her arms. "A rock waterfall drowned most of the noise. Everyone was dressed in black cassocks and wearing some type of animal mask. There were people chanting, and in the middle of the property, right on the grass, there were at least ten people . . . copulating." Her face twisted in disgust. "Everyone else was watching."

"Did you see Simon?" Grey said.

"Everyone had a mask on, even the people on the ground. But there's more, Grey. The people chanting were all holding a black book they were reading from, and there were large crosses lying on the ground. People were urinating on the crosses." She shuddered, her eyes downcast. "There were also animals. A large dog and a goat."

"Sacrifices?"

"They were . . . they were using them," she said.

"Jesus."

"I don't know for sure," she said, "but I think I witnessed a Black Mass. Whatever it was, it was barbaric, evil, and Simon was part of it."

"So why didn't you leave him?"

She looked up. "I raced home that very second, flung my clothes into a bag, and took a train to Exeter. I didn't have the money to leave England. The next night he knocked on my door at the hotel. I didn't open it. I was shocked he'd found me so quickly, and I told him I never wanted to see him again. Then he was . . . standing in the room with me."

"As in, he didn't use the door."

"He claimed he was the most powerful magician in the world," she said. "It was as if he was this new person, this thing full of ego and power. He told me he knew I'd watched the ceremony and that I didn't understand yet. That he wanted to tell me everything but was waiting on the right time, was sorry for lying but wanted to ease me into the truth. He also said the people in that ceremony were misguided, and he was helping them change their ways."

"I bet he was. What I saw in Paris was worse."

She took a deep breath. "I told him I was going back to Romania. He told me that wasn't possible. He said he couldn't make me love him but that I could never leave him."

Grey balled his fists, his temper boiling to the surface. Despite the incredible nature of her story, he could see the fear of Simon smothering her.

"Did you try to leave again?" he said.

"Of course. Each time he appeared and took me back. He can find me whenever he wants." She took Grey's hand and squeezed it, her lissome body shifting into his, eyes pleading. "I'm so afraid, Grey. I just want to be away from him."

"Why haven't you gone to the police?"

"Because I haven't a single piece of proof. And because I know what he can do. The police can't help me."

"Did he murder the cult leaders?"

"I think so," she said. "Him or Dante—the man with the tattoo."

"Do you know what Simon's plans are, his ultimate goal?"

"I've no idea."

"Why did you choose to help me?" he said.

"I don't know. You're strong." She put a hand against her forehead. "I know it's selfish of me to involve you."

"Let me worry about that," he said.

Grey saw the spires of Cambridge approaching in the distance, piercing the sky above a lingering morning fog. Grey was not a trusting person to begin with, and he didn't know what to believe. True honesty was a myth anyway, he mused. No one revealed the entirety of self.

"So what now?" he said.

"I have to return to London."

"You're free to do as you please, within reason?"

"He knows there's nowhere I can go. But they're looking for you, I overheard them talking. You're investigating him, aren't you?"

"It looks that way," he said.

She squeezed her eyes shut, searching for his when she opened them. "Please be careful."

The train pulled into the station, the Gothic backdrop of the town a fitting setting for the story Grey had just heard. The passengers rose, and Grey walked Anka to the next track over for her return trip. "Stay," he said.

She gave the spires a longing glance, then lowered her gaze. "I can't."

"Then meet me later. Tell him you need to get out of London and you're coming here for the afternoon, for the night if possible."

"I'll try," she whispered.

"Do more than try."

She squeezed his hand, and he made her repeat his cell number until she memorized it.

# 30

## WHITBY, ENGLAND

**V**iktor hired a black cab to take him through the Yorkshire Moors to Whitby. They drove north through the craggy countryside, past a line of villages hunched together in tight stone clusters, turned inward against the forbidding weather. An hour later they entered the coastal town of Whitby on the cusp of an approaching storm, the skies gunmetal gray, the howling winds from the moors a horde of barbarians flailing at the gates.

The taxi descended towards the harbor. Port of call to both Captain Cook and Bram Stoker's fictional count, Viktor understood why Stoker, student of the occult himself, chose this setting for the arrival of his undead liege. The ruined archways of an abandoned abbey, set on a cliff high above the harbor, loomed over the town with subtle menace as waves crashed on the rocks below. From a distance, the gulls circling the darkening sky above the abbey looked suspiciously like bats.

The driver let Viktor off at the entrance to the pedestrian-only old town. Though an atmospheric collection of quaint pubs and historic buildings, Whitby had become a caricature, Goths flitting about in vampire costumes, entire shops devoted to Dracula curios, tourists and haggard local fisherman sitting side by side in the bars, swigging Captain Cook's namesake ale.

Viktor made his way to the Circle's combination magic shop and museum, a narrow facade of black-painted wood situated at the base of the long stone stairway leading to the abbey. Pushing through a velvet curtain, he regarded the contents of the shop with amusement.

An array of potted herbs sat in the windowsills, warding off everything from halitosis to leprechauns. Painted sigils covered the door and ceiling, and the walls were lined with shelves overflowing with an impressive collection of magical arcana: One shelf contained jars of animal parts, rare plants, and fungi; another sparkled with an array of exotic crystals; yet another was stacked with more versions of tarot decks than Viktor had known existed. Goblets and staves, daggers and animal skulls, rings and amulets, books on everything from magical theory to rune systems: It was a treasure trove of occult esoterica.

Viktor strode to the counter, manned by a tall man with a sharp chin, a ponytail, and a receding hairline. He wore black leather pants and a frilly white dress shirt, unbuttoned low enough to showcase a ruby-studded Celtic cross hanging from a chain. A different ring adorned each finger, and black disk earrings elongated his earlobes. Viktor made sure the distinctive ring of L'église de la Bête was not part of the costume.

The attendant peered at Viktor's nearly seven-foot frame and black trench coat with arched eyebrows.

"I'm Viktor Radek."

"Ah, right, Gareth said you'd be calling." He spoke briskly and with an educated British accent. He called over a pimply girl in fishnet stockings to watch the counter, and led Viktor through a beaded doorway in the rear, up a flight of stairs and through a locked door at the end of the hallway. "This is where we house our private Crowley collection. Invitation only. The Mags in this town would start a siege if they knew this stuff was back here."

"Mags?" Viktor said.

"Street magicians. Magpies."

"Ah."

"You know, the wannabes who start with *Harry Potter* and D&D, revere Crowley as a god, and think that dressing in black and owning the Necronomicon will get them shagged. Which it might, but it won't make them magicians."

Viktor didn't reply.

# THE DIABOLIST

"I'm rather guessing you're not a Mag," the clerk said.

"Correct."

"They should be prancing about in York instead of Whitby, if they knew any better. York has an amazing psychogeography, though I'm sure you know that. The Masons have been there since the Dark Ages. I'd be there myself if it weren't for the shop."

The clerk started flipping through a thin ledger. "What level are you? Third Order? Fourth?"

Viktor snorted.

"Higher, aren't you? You have the look. Can't fake true magical wisdom. Did you study with Gareth? I've never actually met him. What's he like? Are any of the rumors true?"

"All of them," Viktor said. "The book, please?"

"Right, right. Apologies."

The attendant unlocked a cabinet and extracted a familiar thin volume, though Crowley's copy of *The Ahriman Heresy* was even more worn than the one in Zador's shop, the edges yellowed, a water stain splotched across half the cover. He laid the book on a desk.

"What's your opinion of Crowley? Brilliant bloke and a master magician, but a bit of a cad if you ask me. Can't deny his contributions, but he couldn't keep his mouth shut. He was sort of like Jesus: Either you believe Crowley's mumbo jumbo about Aiwass speaking to him, or he was a liar or insane. None of that chuckle chuckle, he's-just-a-misguided-bloke middle ground for those kinds of claims. By the way, you ever read his fiction? It's rather undervalued."

Viktor's lips compressed. "No."

The clerk put his hands up. "Hey, I get it. The room's all yours. Just pull the cord by the door if you need to ring me."

He started to leave the room, and Viktor called out to him. "There is one thing. Do you know where Aleister acquired this book?"

"Not for certain, no, but he had it when he returned from the East."

"I see," Viktor said. "Thank you."

The clerk gave his chin a thoughtful tug. "You don't know Scarlet Alexander, do you?"

"Who?" Viktor said.

"Magister Templi of the Thelema Lodge in Cefalù. Scary good magician. If it's information on Crowley you're after, I'd look her up."

"Thank you," Viktor said.

"Gareth knows her, I believe."

"*Thank* you."

He left the room, and Viktor sat at the desk, his nose twitching not from the musty smell of aging parchment but from the enigma surrounding Crowley's copy of *The Ahriman Heresy*. Cad he might have been, but Crowley had spent his life in pursuit of hidden knowledge.

Viktor felt a flutter of excitement as he opened the book. He turned the pages slowly, searching for variations in the text. There were a few notes in the margins, circled words and phrases, but nothing of importance. As far as Viktor could tell, the copy was identical.

His hopes dwindled the longer he read. He would have to conduct more research he didn't have time for, try to retrace Crowley's steps and decipher which ones, if any, were related to *The Ahriman Heresy*.

On the last page something caught his eye. Just beneath the text, written in the same tightened scrawl he recognized from past experience as Crowley's handwriting, was a word, circled and underlined.

Viktor rubbed at his chin and copied the word into his notepad. In both Latin and Italian, the phrase meant roughly "the guardians," or "the defenders." The emphases signified importance, though what that might be, Viktor had no idea. Since as far as he could tell it was the only difference in the two copies, it was worth noting.

He could hear the rain starting to clack against the building as he flipped through the final pages of blank parchment, included in ancient texts just like in today's books, and then a series of chills coursed through him when he turned the last page, leaving him clutching the book in trembling hands.

A short note had been taped to the inside of the back cover. The note was penned in a different hand than Crowley's, a neater and loopier handwriting that Viktor also thought he recognized, a thought confirmed by the note itself.

*Dearest Viktor,*
*I never doubted you would come.*

*Darius*

# 31

# CAMBRIDGE, ENGLAND

Grey watched from the platform as the train carrying Anka back to London rumbled to life. She was small in her seat, staring out the window, arms crossed and hugging her chest.

He stepped off the platform in a fog, the skin on his arm still tingling from where she had touched him, his mind enwrapped in the mysteries hovering around her. Why claim she needed his help if it wasn't true? What possible motive lay beneath that striking veneer?

He approached the pretty center of Cambridge, feeling the pang of being on the other side of the glass in this town of grassy lawns and bourgeois charm, surrounded by laughing students and families strolling arm in arm, the graceful spires of the university rising in the distance.

The Zoroastrian scholar lived outside town, and Grey decided to walk, tired of being cooped up on planes and trains. He skirted the university, pausing when he saw a sign for the Cambridge University Library.

He had to know. If he was going to help Anka, if he had even the hope of trusting her, he had to verify some part of her story.

He entered the intimidating building, and a shy librarian with a Scottish accent led him to the area housing the collection on paranormal research. Grey couldn't believe the size of the stacks.

Three hours later he had his answers, and he felt a little bit lighter than when he had entered. Astral projection, he learned, was a fancy name for an out-of-body experience, and human beings had been claiming to have them since the beginning of time. Recent studies in the United States evidenced that at least 8 percent of people, and perhaps more than 20, believed they had undergone an out-of-body experience at one time or another. The conventional wisdom, at least among those who accepted the phenomenon, was that the spiritual or "astral" body was separate from the physical body—the concept of the soul—and, at least with certain people and at certain times, was capable of traveling outside it. No one claimed to understand it, except for the mystics and the quacks. The phenomenon had been called by many names in many different cultures, appeared to occur both in conscious and unconscious states, and was associated with near-death experiences, dream and meditative states, hallucinations, religious experience, and a plethora of other phenomena.

Most often, Grey learned, the astral traveler had no control over the event, and found him- or herself floating above or away from the corporeal self, or rising in a tunnel of light after heart failure. There were occasional reports of people who could control the phenomenon, though these were unverified and largely ignored by the scientific community, or at least the Western one.

However, and Grey's pulse increased when he read this part, out-of-body cases existed where people appeared to observers in physical form far from their actual locations, sometimes thousands of miles away. This phenomenon was known as bilocation, and there was ample literature documenting purported cases over the years, across a multitude of cultures and belief systems. There were even a few extremely rare cases of a reported doppelgänger—the actual corporeal appearance of the same person in two different locations, at the same time. Though such reports had been scoffed at in the past, and attributed to the Devil in earlier times, recent developments in quantum physics had scientists rethinking astral projection and bilocation, and even the appearance of a doppelgänger, as within the realm of possibility and perhaps even—according to some theoretical physicists—probability.

Grey left the library deep in thought. He was far from convinced, but at least the phenomenon existed, or was thought to exist.

Powers of the mind, Viktor always preached. Grey had worked with Viktor long enough to know there were plenty of things in this world that no one understood.

Plenty.

Grey went a step further. He contacted Rick Laskin, an old acquaintance in Diplomatic Security, now posted at the Romanian embassy in Bucharest. Rick had been a Navy SEAL before joining DS, and when he and Grey had undergone DS training together they had bonded over their respective stints in Special Forces. Grey wasn't sure if Rick could dig up the information Grey sought, but Rick was a solid all-American kind of guy and would do his best.

It was worth a shot.

Grey hailed a cab. A mile past the university the driver turned onto one of those tiny lanes that wound through the English countryside, originally built for the horse and buggy and for some perverse reason never expanded. Following Grey's Google directions, twenty minutes into the maze of hedge the driver stopped in front of a wooden gate bearing the address of Dastur Zaveri, the Zoroaster priest and historian whom Ervad Kasraavi had recommended in London. There was no buzzer or sign of a house, just a pebbled path that disappeared into the woods.

The gate was unlocked. Once past the tree line Grey spied a cottage in the clearing, complete with a thatch roof, chimney, and a rock garden. A stream gurgled through the woods to the left, a bench beckoned from underneath an apple tree, chirping birds darted through the forest.

A wisp of a man appeared in the doorway, crinkled eyes hidden within a beard that swarmed over his face and down his white tunic. Age lines etched his swarthy skin, and he smiled at Grey through tea-stained teeth.

"Please, come in."

Grey removed his boots and followed the old man to a sitting room. Despite the relative warmth of the day, a gas stove poured heat into the room. Grey took a seat and waited until, just like Ervad Kasraavi, Dastur Zaveri returned with tea and a platter of light snacks, this time dates and pistachios.

Dastur Zaveri eased into the chair across from him. Grey felt a strong vibe of peaceful energy emanating from his eyes. "I'm Dominic Grey. I assume Ervad Kasraavi informed you I'd be stopping by?"

"Sorry, no. I don't keep a cell or computer here. I have an apartment in town with more modern amenities."

Grey eyed the platter of food. "How'd you know I was coming?"

"I didn't."

He saw Grey's confusion and said, "Our faith strongly encourages kindness to visitors. You looked as if you needed tea."

Grey felt for a minute as though he were back in Japan, in a village outside Kyoto, having tea with some kind soul who had invited him in from the rain. "Thank you."

"Not at all."

"I went to Ervad Kasraavi in London, seeking information on your faith, and he suggested I see you. I'm looking for information on Ahriman."

The priest's head bobbed, lips parting in interest, as if Grey had just asked him to recommend a good walk through the woods. "He told you I'm a historian and that Ahriman is one of my spheres of interest?"

"He did," Grey said.

"You probably have the opinion of most, which is why concern oneself with something considered taboo by nearly every society?" Grey didn't dispute the statement, and Dastur Zaveri said, "I think it's best if we know and understand our adversaries, or at least those whom we perceive our adversaries to be. I believe in combating ignorance with knowledge, and hopefully wisdom."

"I couldn't agree more," Grey said. "I'm a private investigator, working on a case believed to involve a priest of Ahriman."

Wrinkles appeared like a bundle of twigs on his forehead. "A case? Involving a priest of Ahriman? That's certainly fascinating, but as far as I know there've been no worshippers of Ahriman for quite some time."

Grey rolled up his sleeves, his forearms damp from the heat. "Exactly. No one seems to know much of anything about Ahriman."

Dastur Zaveri fussed over the platter, finally selecting a pistachio. "Are you aware the plateaus of modern-day Iran have been continually inhabited for at least thirty-five thousand years, making it the oldest developed civilization in the world?"

"That's a long time for a religion to develop," Grey said.

"As well as the perfect place for a deity to make itself known."

"I suppose." Grey leaned forward. "Have you heard of the Ahriman Heresy?"

"Of course. There's a historical treatise by the same name."

His eyes flicked into the next room over, which Grey could see was filled with ceiling-high bookshelves. "I have a copy," he said. "It's quite rare, I believe."

That rocked Grey back in his seat. "I don't suppose you have a copy of the grimoire?"

"The legendary Ahriman Grimoire?" Dastur Zaveri said. "I'm afraid not. As I understand it, there are no copies."

"What's your opinion on it?" Grey said. "Is there anything to it?"

The old man took a long sip of tea. "Let me ask you a question, if I may."

"Sure."

"What's your definition of evil?"

"I don't know," Grey said, "the evening news?"

He chuckled. "Granted. But if you had to choose a concrete example?"

Grey cupped his tea in his hands. "Molesting a child."

"Intriguing answer," he said, cocking his head. "Pure hedonism as the highest form of evil, the antithesis of selflessness. And from where do you believe the impetus for such behavior derives?"

"I'm sure not going to blame God or the Devil or Ahriman for my or anyone else's actions, if that's what you're getting at," Grey said.

"I understand. But I sense that you're a philosopher, so if you had to speculate?"

# THE DIABOLIST

Grey shrugged. "I'd like to say nature, but I'm not sure I believe that. Plenty of evil acts serve no biological or evolutionary function. But nurture just begs the same question, since it started somewhere. Looking at this world, it's a hell of a lot easier for me to throw my hands up in ignorance than to try and believe that some guiding force is behind all this misery."

"The easiest path most often leads down the wrong trail," the priest said gently.

Grey spread his hands. "Consider me lost. Not to be rude, but where exactly are we going with this?"

His eyes were kind, understanding. "Bear with me a moment longer. So if asked to choose, do you believe in an invisible God whose ways we cannot hope to understand as the source of all evil? Or rather that no God exists, and instead we have an unthinking multiverse that somehow created itself, in contravention of the principles of science?"

"Those are both pretty hard to believe," Grey said.

"But if you had to choose?"

"I suppose the first," Grey said slowly.

"If I may, then: You believe that certain acts, such as the abomination you proffered, are indeed evil. Yet you also find it impossible to conceive that God would allow such evil to exist in this world, if He has any shred of humanity or compassion as we understand it."

"Something like that," Grey said.

"Then you would make a good Zoroastrian. We Parsi don't try to fit God within a complicated and ultimately indefensible moral scheme, but rather believe there are two competing forces in the universe, one good, one evil."

Grey didn't have a response to that.

"Some question whether true evil exists at all. Is existence not reality, good and evil but a different viewpoint? Perhaps our gods are a race of beings to which humanity is a parasite, much like the tick or mosquito is to us. Perhaps Ahriman and Satan view the human conception of God as a belief gone terribly wrong."

"I can't speak for them," Grey said.

Dastur Zaveri bit into another pistachio, acknowledging Grey's point with a small nod. "While there may be two competing forces in the universe, nothing is black-and-white, and those forces are by definition more complex than we can ever possibly understand."

"Yeah, I get it. If the forces in the universe are by definition more complex than we can possibly understand, then maybe you and I and every other compassionate human being have got it all wrong. Sorry, I can't subscribe to that."

"But we must allow for the fact that perhaps this man you pursue, this follower of Ahriman, is correct. That Ahriman and his dominion of this world is the path of good, rather than evil. That the *ashavan* is filled with endless darkness and the *drgevant* the endless light."

Grey saw heat waves shimmering from the gas stove. His wrists had dampened with sweat. "I suppose anything's possible. And I never told you it was a man."

Dastur Zaveri opened his palms. "Forgive me. In the Zoroaster tradition women do not become priests, as archaic as that may sound." He leaned forward, an intense light pooled in the depths of his eyes. "To understand a priest of Ahriman, the question you must answer is not from where does evil derive, but what does it *mean?*"

Grey started to retort that after what he had seen in the catacombs, he understood that part just fine. But he could hear Viktor in his ear, telling him: *It's not about what you believe, Grey, but about what* they *believe.* Like Viktor had said, no one believes he or she is evil.

Then again, some people were just blind.

"You asked me to help you understand Ahriman and his followers," the priest said softly. "I could point you to a few dry historical texts or discuss the evolution of Zoroastrian cosmogony, but would such things really help?"

"The man's name is Simon Azar," Grey said. "Have you heard of him?"

"I would have to live under a rock not to have heard of him." He gave a rueful grin. "Though I do come close. Azar is a name of Parsi origin. Do you know the meaning?"

# THE DIABOLIST

"No," Grey said.

"Fire."

Grey wiped a bead of sweat from his brow, ready for the crisp night air. "Does anything you've read or heard about this man lead you to believe he's a follower of Ahriman?" Grey said.

"I approach Ahriman from the philosophical and theological angle. I wouldn't know any more than Ervad Kasraavi about the practices of a modern-day follower of Ahriman."

"What about an ancient one?" Grey said.

He ran his thumb and forefinger along his beard. "Records are almost nonexistent. The only rituals mentioned in the histories were similar to those of the medieval worshippers of the Christian Devil. As you're probably aware, many of the concepts later attributed to Satan or Lucifer originated with Ahriman."

"Yes," Grey said, frustrated with the lack of progress. Maybe he should leave the phenomenological research to Viktor.

"There is one thing," Dastur Zaveri said. "Though my research has never verified it, I assume the priests of Ahriman also utilize the fire temple, the eternal flame. You might be able to identify a shrine that way. Though I wouldn't expect it to be . . . the same."

"I'll keep that in mind. I've read about the Zoroastrian fire temples."

"The thing to understand about the followers of Ahriman is that they viewed Ahura Mazda—God—as unimaginably remote and uncaring, and Ahriman as more concerned with the trials and tribulations of this world." Dastur Zaveri took Grey's hands in his own, and Grey felt a trembling in the age-spotted grip. "Understand that I believe deeply in the Gathas and in the light of my Creator, just as I believe in Ahriman and the existence of evil. What I must question is the demarcation of human knowledge. Zoroastrianism is about devotion to truth, having the courage to cast off comfort and see reality for that which it truly is."

Grey squeezed the old man's hands in return, then rose. It was time to move on. Just before he left, he thought of one final question and hesitated in the doorway. He felt silly asking this learned man such a question, but he did, after all, specialize in Ahriman.

"Have you heard of the three powers of the Devil—of Ahriman?" Grey said. "The power to influence the minds of men, seduce, and move about the world unseen?"

"Indeed. Why do you ask?"

"During the investigation there've been reports of some . . . remarkable . . . occurrences," Grey said. "I was just wondering if, to the followers of Ahriman, there's any truth to the myth? In their minds, I mean."

"Do the followers of Christianity consider the miracles of Jesus a myth?" Dastur Zaveri said mildly. "The abilities of the saints, the power of prayer? Do they doubt the power of a Supreme Being to affect the world in mysterious ways?"

Grey pursed his lips and gave a slow nod. "Thank you for the tea," he said, and eased the door shut.

# 32

As her return train to London slowed during its approach to the station, grinding on the track, Anka rose to disembark, peering out the window at the passengers lined up to board.

Then she dropped low into her seat, forgetting to breathe, pulse spiking with fear. In the line of passengers she saw an image she could never mistake, the top of a man's head ink-stained with a terrifying image.

*Why send Dante?* she thought in a panic. *Does Darius know about her and Grey?*

Her questions sparked in her mind and then faded, ceding to her survival instinct, an instinct honed from years of homelessness as a street urchin in Bucharest. Her world shrank to one finite problem: *How do I get away from the psychopath waiting outside this train?*

As the passengers disembarked, she grew more and more desperate. She couldn't stay on the train, or she would be too easy to spot. No, she had to get off the train. But to where? She couldn't outrun him, and he surely had other men with him, watching both ends of the train.

*Why does it never work when I want it to?*

She saw a filthy knit cap on the ground under the luggage rack, and she grabbed it and pulled it low on her head, stuffing her hair inside. It smelled like stale milk and body odor. An old couple were struggling to exit with their bags, and she hurried to help them, hunching as she slipped between them.

It got her off the train, but the old couple stopped to rest, and Anka panicked. She saw movement out of the corner of her eye, and caught a glimpse of a long black cloak swishing her way.

*Oh God.*

A group of teenagers ambled from the rear of the platform towards the station, paralleling the tracks. She joined them, trying to blend long enough to merge into the crowded station. Dante must have noticed and signaled, because she saw a man in a brown bomber jacket snap to attention and start towards her. She looked over her shoulder and saw Dante behind her, closing in.

She would never make it to the station. To her left, there were at least a dozen more tracks. To her right, only two tracks remained before the far end of the station, but a train was approaching on the next track over, seconds away.

Without further thought, she jumped down into the track on her right, gasping as she landed with a thud. Someone behind her shouted as Anka jumped over the electric rail tracks, made a desperate grab for the top of the next platform over, and scrabbled to climb up as the train approached, horn blaring and brakes screeching. She pulled, but wasn't strong enough to lift her body up.

She hung there in horror as the train drew closer, almost stopped but still fast enough to crush her. She twisted and flung a leg up, trying for the top of the platform.

Her leg only reached halfway. She couldn't do it.

The train was almost on her, and she screamed. Then she felt herself lifted up by her arms and set down on the platform as if she were weightless. She cringed as she looked up, but it was some random giant of a man in a Dallas Cowboys sweatshirt, helping her to the top.

Before she had a chance to thank him, she saw that Dante had pulled himself out of the same tracks, ten feet behind the man who had saved her, just ahead of the train. She screamed again, and her savior turned and saw Dante approaching. Dante's hand reached inside his duster.

# THE DIABOLIST

"Hey, pal," the towheaded man said to Dante, "why don't you—"

His next words gurgled out of his mouth as Dante whipped out a knife and gutted him. The American slumped against the train, and the crowded platform devolved into chaos. Anka swallowed her terror and took advantage. She darted into the crowd, her small size now a boon.

She could *feel* Dante behind her as she wove in and out of the mass of people, knocking over a magazine stand as she raced into the cavernous station.

She knew she wouldn't make it to the surface. She had to think of something else, somewhere to hide, but her mind could focus only on not letting Dante catch her. She careened around a corner and entered a tubular tunnel.

Bad choice. The tunnel extended as far as she could see. Her heart slammed against her chest, her body electric from fear-laced adrenaline. She risked a backwards glance and saw him thirty feet behind her, knife in hand, people melting to the sides as if he were parting the Red Sea. Dante knew about the hidden places underneath London, and he would take her and disappear down a tunnel before the police could help her.

She didn't have another option, and she ran with everything she had. Pushing and dodging through the crowd, she regressed to her time on the street when she would run from the police, stolen pretzel or jam-filled pancake in her tiny hands, eyes cast downward for someplace to hide. Though she couldn't risk another backwards glance, she could hear footsteps thumping behind her, the shouts of alarmed pedestrians.

She came to a convergence of tunnels filled with people and food stands, the crowd of people giving her one last chance. She dove into the crowd, then slipped down one of the emptier side tunnels, knowing she had seconds before Dante figured out which one she had chosen.

Just beside a kebab stand she noticed a square, two-foot high metal door set into the base of the tunnel wall. She had seen these before, storage units for the businesses in London's crowded subterranean complexes. The proprietor eyed her as she stopped right in front of his stand and said, "Please help me. You never saw me."

Anka folded her hands in the prayer position, put a finger to her lips, then dropped to the ground. The tiny door was unlocked, and she squeezed herself feetfirst inside the claustrophobic space, not risking a glance to see if Dante was watching, pulling the door shut and stuffing herself into the musty darkness.

She scrunched past the boxes and containers of foodstuffs and then stilled, nauseous with fear, her skin prickling as cockroaches and other unseen things skittered across her hands and face.

# 33

Viktor's mind burned on the way back to York. He would not have thought Darius capable of murder, but Viktor had witnessed countless cult members commit murder and other acts considered abhorrent outside of the cult setting. And he knew from long experience that ambition, personal tragedy, and insecurity were gateway drugs.

All three of which Darius had in spades.

Still, Darius was part of Viktor's past, and people in one's own past did not murder Satanic cult leaders and use a manipulative pseudo cult to strive for religious hegemony.

"I'd like to make a detour," Viktor said to the driver, as the rain lashed the windshield. "Are you familiar with Glaisdale?"

"It's just over the moor. There's a good pub if that's what you're after. You fancy a drink for the journey back to York?"

"Not tonight," Viktor said.

"Where to, then?"

"I'll show you."

The driver took the next turn into the foothills. Though it was dark, Viktor imagined the brown smudge of moor in the distance, and knew they were passing through a land of moist dales and peat bogs and long sloping ridges, stunning when the purple heather was in bloom and beautiful in a stark and lonely way the rest of the year. Just before they entered the village of Glaisdale, Viktor instructed the driver to make a few more turns, bringing them to the top of a low hill.

Viktor pointed at a gravel pullover. "Here."

The driver did as Viktor said, then craned his neck towards Viktor. "Mate? There's nothing around but this dodgy weather."

"I need fifteen minutes," Viktor said. "Keep the meter running."

"Fine by me."

The rain had slackened, but the wind had turned into a gale, whipping up leaves and whistling through the trees. Enough light from the moon seeped through the clouds to illuminate a stone path just off the road. Viktor hunched and headed down the path under a canopy of gnarled yew, crossing a brook on stepping stones and then following the path up a short hill.

Shoes soaked and caked with mud, he emerged from the trees at the crown of the hill. A stone archway greeted him, flanked by the remains of a wall. Through the archway he saw the ancient chapel, a mass of granite capped by a bell tower. Tombstones littered the courtyard around the chapel, stained green by hardened moss, tilted and sunken into the earth.

Viktor picked a wild rose from a vine snaking up the archway, then walked towards the chapel, memories stirring at the smell of damp earth and old stone. The wind was worse on the hill, a constant rush and whoosh, slamming into Viktor as he left the pathway and tramped through the knee-high grass. He wove in and out of the headstones, stopping when he came to a moss-covered stone engraved with a Celtic cross. It was part of a forlorn trio of family graves.

Spurts of rain splashed onto Viktor's head and face, the sky a leaky faucet. As Viktor laid the rose on Eve's grave the memories rushed forth, no longer a repressed whisper, spinning in his gut like a tornado as his finger traced his beloved's name on the headstone.

Eve's visions had started the morning after the ritual. Her eyes had returned to their normal robin's-egg blue, and Viktor chalked up the sudden dilation to extreme stress or fear, both of which Viktor's quick research confirmed as a possible culprit.

When Viktor woke in her apartment, he found her whimpering on the floor, clutching her pillow to her chest. She was staring at the wall, eyes wild, rocking slowly back and forth.

*Eve! What's wrong?*

He went to her, bringing her into his arms on the edge of the bed.

*He came, Viktor.*

*Who, love?*

Her voice barely cracked a whisper. *Ahriman.*

Prickles of gooseflesh ran up and down Viktor's arms. *There's no one here, Eve. It's all in your head. We didn't finish the ritual.*

*We didn't have to. I disrupted it, and he's terribly angry with me. He's been here all night. He's like nothing we could ever imagine, so beautiful and terrifying.*

Viktor threw back the blinds, flooding the room with sunshine. *Let's find someplace nice to go today, perhaps that walk by the river you love. You'll forget all of this by noon.*

A small, saddened smile crept to her lips. *Viktor, my Viktor. I love you more than I thought I was capable of loving. But we shouldn't have done that. I never cared for the occult at all, you know. I only cared for you.*

Viktor dressed both of them, slipping her into slacks and a sweater. The daylight seemed to help, though she barely said another word. He felt as if she were only half present, lost in a dreamworld that only she could see. By nightfall she wouldn't let Viktor leave her alone.

*Help me, Viktor. Make him go away.*

*It's in your mind,* Viktor said gently. *It's not real, Eve. What'd you take this morning?*

*Nothing. I'm afraid to make it worse.*

*Maybe a sample would help steady your mind?*

*No.*

Viktor was taken aback. Eve never refused pills.

It was the worst week of Viktor's life. Eve barely slept, and when she did she would awake screaming within an hour, claiming the nightmares were so visceral they made her physically ill.

Darius tried to see her, and Viktor told him what was happening. Darius grew very pale. *We have to reverse the ritual,* Darius said. *I can do it.*

*That's hardly what she needs.*

Darius reached up to take Viktor by the shoulders. *This isn't a game. We botched the ritual. She entered the circle. Where is she?*

*She doesn't want to see you.*

*I don't care what she wants! This isn't about me and you, it's about Eve and Ahriman.*

*There's no Ahriman, you fool!*

Darius struck him across the face. *Just because you don't have faith doesn't mean that other people don't, or that it isn't real. Ahriman exists whether you like it or not, and he'll tear her to pieces.*

Viktor stood in front of Darius for a long time, his hand on his cheek where Darius had slapped him. He knew his friend was in love with Eve and that he deserved that slap. *I'll grant you,* Viktor said finally, *that Eve's beliefs are the ones that matter, not mine.*

*You have to let me do this,* Darius said. *We have to reverse the ritual.*

Eve wouldn't entertain the idea. She wanted nothing more to do with rituals or magic, and Viktor didn't blame her. But the visions continued, and Viktor grew more desperate. He took Eve to three different psychiatrists, Oxford professors with PhDs from the best universities in the world. Each prescribed a different drug, telling Viktor the same thing: that Eve was schizophrenic and needed help.

Eve's family had a history of mental illness, and Viktor believed the ritual had triggered something in Eve's mind. She began a regimen of Haldol and then Stelazine, but she still grew worse, afraid to be alone or in the dark, sleeping during the day with the blinds thrown wide. Her family came and talked to the psychologists, and she was dangerously close to being sent away.

# THE DIABOLIST

Near the end of summer Viktor woke to find Eve naked in the street outside her apartment, brandishing a knife and screaming at the top of her lungs as she moved in circles, as if stalked by a predator. When Viktor approached she tried to stab him. It took him the rest of the night to calm her.

Viktor decided to try one last course of action. He would take her to London and hope against hope the bright lights of the great city would take her mind off what was happening, shake her back to normalcy. If that didn't work, he would take her to the ends of the earth, to a sun-drenched beach in the South Pacific or to America, as far from this sodden island as possible.

The doctors agreed a short trip might be a good idea, as long as she took her meds. Her mother had been in and out of a mental hospital for years, and her father, ashen at the prospect of institutionalizing another family member, also agreed.

Eve was excited. She may have been rapidly decompensating, but the one thing that remained constant was her love for Viktor. He took her to the Savoy in London, taking the suite with the most natural light. Eve managed a small smile when she saw the room, though her eyes kept darting to the corners, searching for the things only she could see.

They took a walk in the steep hills and swaying grass of Hampstead Heath. After a light lunch they ended up strolling down Swain's Lane, passing a walled cemetery with an elaborate, fortress-like entrance. Viktor knew the place: Highgate Cemetery, an infamous Victorian-era burial ground full of elaborate tombs. Neglected by the city, it was now a decrepit, overgrown eyesore. There were rumors about strange sights and sounds coming from the cemetery, though these were likely due to the criminals and occultists known to frequent the place at night.

A weird brightness came into Eve's eyes, and she pulled him towards the cemetery. *Let's go in there.*

*I don't think that's a good idea,* Viktor said.

*It's so beautiful and gothic. Take me.*

*It's closed, Eve. I couldn't even if I wanted to.*

Viktor pulled her away, and after dinner at a fancy Italian restaurant in Knightsbridge they saw *Oliver!* on the West End. She clapped after the show, her face bright, and Viktor felt a glimmer of hope. If one day in London produced these kinds of results, what would a week in Paris do? A month? A year?

They returned to the room and made love for the first time since the ritual. When they finished, Viktor brushed a hand down her cheek. He had one more card to play. *Wait here.*

She gripped his hand with such force he was taken aback. *Don't leave me.*

*I'll never leave you, love. I'm just going to the restroom. I'll be right back.*

Viktor went into the bathroom, disturbed at the fear in her eyes. The thought of losing her to a barbaric mental hospital nauseated him. He splashed water on his face and took out the diamond ring from his travel bag.

When he reentered the room he got down on one knee beside the bed. Eve's eyes filled with tears, and she took his face in her hands.

*Will you be mine?* he asked, his voice catching.

*Oh, Viktor, I was yours before you knew me. And, yes, I'll be yours forever. He can't change that.*

Viktor swallowed. *There's no he, Eve. Things are going to be different now.*

*He hates that you make me happy. Just know that no matter what happens, I'll always be with you.*

*Eve! Stop talking like that.*

*I love you, Viktor Radek.*

They made love again, and Viktor fell asleep with his fiancée in his arms, more content than he had ever been, despite the tragic circumstances.

He awoke in the middle of the night to her screams. She stopped screaming when she hyperventilated, pointing at the corner by the window. *He's in here,* she gasped.

*Did you take your meds?* Viktor already knew the answer. He always watched her take them.

*Yes.*

*Did you take more than your dosage?*

# THE DIABOLIST

*No.*

He finally calmed her, and she lay quietly in his massive arms, her head on his chest, eyes wide and staring into the corners of the room. Sometime deep into the night he dozed, and when he woke she was gone.

He at once berated himself for falling asleep. She had seemed calm, but he knew better than to trust her moods. He gave the suite a frantic sweep, then rushed downstairs. No one knew where she had gone. Later that morning, when the hotel received a call from the police, Viktor was in the lobby. The concierge handed him the phone.

*You should come right away,* the officer said. *Do you know Highgate Cemetery?*

Viktor let the phone drop and rushed to a cab. When he saw the police officers surrounding Eve's body in the middle of the cemetery, one of the hotel's bedsheets still hanging from the branch of a cedar tree ten feet above the prone form, he swooned for the first and last time in his life.

Memory merged with the present, and Viktor laid the flowers on the grave, the wind pressing the petals against the headstone. Then he knelt beside his beloved and wept.

# 34

It was dusk when Grey returned to Cambridge. As he passed through a court-yard surrounded by ivy-covered walls, purple lights dancing in an attractive little fountain, he debated whether to take a room in town or return to London.

He put a foot on the edge of the fountain and started to call Viktor, then canceled the call. Anka was walking towards him from the south side of the square, still in her leather jacket, jeans tucked into knee-high lambskin boots, now wearing a soft white hat.

He met her halfway and she peered up at him, huge eyes swimming within her hair and rimmed with fear.

"Your jacket's dirty," he said.

"Dante was waiting for me at the train station."

"Dante? Why?"

"To send me a message, or worse. I managed to hide until he left. We shouldn't be doing this, Grey. He could show up any minute."

Grey saw the trembling of her hands and heard the flutter in her voice. "I'd like nothing more," he said.

They walked in silence, drifting over the winding lanes. He waited until she calmed before he spoke again. "What will you do now?"

"I don't know."

"You can't go back," he said.

# THE DIABOLIST

She pressed her lips together. "Why don't we talk about something else for a while? I can't think about that right now." She looped an arm through his as they resumed walking. "Who are you? Where do you live, what do you do?"

"I assumed someone who can appear in a catacomb in Paris would be able to divine who I am."

She looked at him as if trying to judge his intentions, but even Grey wasn't sure what they were. "It doesn't work that way," she said.

Grey felt guilty when he heard the hurt in her voice. "I'm sorry."

"It's fine."

They walked a bit farther, and he said, "I live in New York for now. I'm not really from anywhere."

"Why not?"

"I guess it just worked out that way," he said.

"You have the look of someone who's never at rest."

"Yeah. Thanks."

"I didn't mean it that way," she said. "Just that you're pensive, like you understand how sad life is."

"It's sad all right."

"But beautiful, too," she said. "And I can tell you see that as well, or you'd just be angry all the time, not pensive."

Grey didn't respond.

"You don't have a family?" she said.

"No."

"Then I guess we're both orphans."

They had wandered to the edge of town, where a line of cozy restaurants dotted the river. "Hungry?" she asked.

"Starved," he said.

"I like the look of the small one near the end."

She led him to a cottage tucked against the river, a tiny establishment with a sign that read BABETTE'S. Inside he saw a smattering of tables, a few more on a covered patio overlooking the river. A chalkboard menu covered half of the wall to Grey's left, and he felt a pang of sadness for Nya, deeper and sharper than he had felt in some time. She was the girl he had loved most and then lost, the closest he had ever come to a soul mate. He had met her while posted in Zimbabwe, during his first case with Viktor.

He realized that pangs such as those would never go away, they would just become buried deeper over time, brought to the surface in dreams or by rare moments of association.

And that was okay.

Anka removed her jacket as they sat on the patio. Grey let her order a bottle of wine, though he would have preferred a cold beer. He never went to intimate French restaurants with beautiful women, so he thought he might as well have some wine.

As they waited for the food she said, "You never told me what you do. I assume you're in law enforcement?"

His eyes found the curve of her neck, following it to the cheekbones that provided just the right arch to her oval face. "I used to be with Diplomatic Security. Now I investigate pathological cults."

Her eyebrows lifted. "That's quite a transition."

"My employer, Viktor Radek, is a professor of religious phenomenology— the study of the effect of alleged religious phenomena on practitioners. We worked on a case together when I was posted in Zimbabwe. Diplomatic Security didn't work out. Viktor did."

"Religious phenomenology—Hegel and La Saussaye, more recently Van der Leeuw and Duméry? Analyzing the subjective nature of the religious experience?"

"That's right," Grey said, surprised.

"I used to work in a library, remember. Viktor must be an interesting man."

"Interesting and accomplished," he said. "He's the world's foremost expert on cults, or at least the violent ones."

# THE DIABOLIST

"Are you an expert, too?"

"Hardly," he said. "My knowledge is a drop in the ocean compared to his. A very deep ocean."

"What does he think about Darius?"

"What do you think?" he said.

She swallowed and fingered her wineglass. "Why were they chasing you in the catacombs?"

Grey watched her. "You really don't know?"

"I just know he sent them to find you and that you were in danger."

He told her about the ceremony, and her face paled. She set her fork down, staring at her half-eaten trout almondine.

When they finished eating, the waiter filled their glasses with the last of the wine. After the chocolate mousse arrived Anka said, "Why'd you leave Diplomatic Security?"

"The government and I were never a good fit. I don't take orders very well."

"The world needs more people like that," she said.

"It's my one redeeming trait."

She eyed him as she raised a spoonful of chocolate mousse to her mouth. "Other than witty, attractive, and dangerous?"

Grey mumbled his thanks. After dessert Anka moved her chair next to his and laid her head on his shoulder. "I almost feel safe with you."

They were alone on the patio, the only sound the clink of dishes from inside. Grey's eyes found the ripple of the current in the darkness, and after a moment he felt the warmth of Anka's breath on his neck. When he turned, her hair was brushing his cheek, lips an inch away, her scent enveloping him. He remembered his dream about her and pushed the memory away.

She moved forward until their lips brushed, and he tasted the sensual residue of wine on her tongue, her lips so soft they seemed to engulf his. He put a hand on her waist and cradled her neck, drawing her in. She ran her fingers through the cowlicks in his hair, pressed her body tighter.

When she pulled away they both glanced inside the restaurant with sheepish eyes. She traced a finger along his lips, her eyes flicking nervously to her watch. "I should leave."

"Stay with me until this is over," he said.

"It's too dangerous. We've been together too long already."

"Protecting people is what I do," he said.

She reached up and stroked his cheek. "And I'm sure you're very good at it. But you still don't understand. You can't fight him like that."

"Stay."

She rose, and he stood with her. She placed her hands on his chest. "I refuse to put you in danger any longer. He could show up any second."

"Anka—"

"I'll see you again soon. I promise."

He sat back in frustration. "Where're you going?"

"I don't know. Away. I'll be in touch soon, I swear. And please don't follow me."

Her good-bye kiss rocked him on his heels. Then she hurried away, head down and arms crossed against her chest. Grey felt foolish letting her leave, but she flagged a taxi and sped away, and he didn't know what else to do.

# 35

When the rain came harder Viktor rose, eyes lingering on the tragic dates on Eve's headstone. The pang in his gut was not quite as sharp, but even more bitter, than when he had stood in this cemetery many years ago, on the day of Eve's funeral. He put two fingers to his lips, then pressed them into the engraving on the headstone. "Until next time, my love."

Viktor returned through the cemetery as rain poured down his face, his suit clinging to his flesh. Viktor did not make excuses for the things he had done, the paths he had explored in his quest for truth. Yet his one regret was this: that he had agreed to perform that last ritual, that he and Darius had introduced Eve to the monster that was Ahriman.

Oh, Viktor did not believe that Ahriman himself had come into the basement that night, entered the broken circle, and tormented Eve until she took her own life. What Viktor did believe was that an idea had burrowed into Eve's head that evening, then mutated like a virus inside her, filling every facet of her being with a terrible insinuation. An idea so powerful that, to someone as mentally unstable as Eve, it had proven fatal.

The three of them had stared into the abyss that night, and none of them, in their different ways, had ever escaped.

Viktor had begged Darius to tell Eve that none of it was real, and to Darius's credit, he had tried. But Eve had seen in Darius's eyes that he believed, and that knowledge only reinforced her own belief.

Yet another poor decision by Viktor.

Darius had never forgiven Viktor, both for failing to convince Eve to try to reverse the ritual, and for taking her to London and allowing her to slip away on the night of her death.

Viktor had never forgiven himself, either.

As he exited the cemetery he stopped to grasp the rusty iron bars on the gate, loath to leave his beloved alone again, lost and vulnerable, in that place of no return.

Viktor trudged into the hotel well after midnight, falling asleep with a bottle of absinthe in the crook of his arm, images of Eve crowding the edges of his vision. The next morning his cell rang, and he recognized Jacques's number in Paris. He let the phone ring as he shuddered to his feet, then returned the call.

"Viktor, *bonjour*. Have there been any developments?"

*None I'm going to tell you about.* "I'm in York with Gareth. He believes this is a game, a war between magicians. These childish men and their foolish magic—I say let them destroy one another with their meaningless charades!"

There was silence on the other end. Viktor's hand shook as he reached for the slotted absinthe spoon.

Jacques's voice was quiet. "Is everything okay?"

"I apologize," Viktor said evenly. "It's difficult to help those who refuse to help themselves."

"Three people are dead, all after receiving the same letter. One would think Gareth would take this seriously."

"One would think," Viktor said.

"Do you have any theories?"

Viktor watched the cube of sugar slowly dissolve into the absinthe. "My theory is that someone is performing some very elaborate magic tricks, and not of the supernatural variety. Do you have the toxicology reports yet?"

"It's one of the reasons I called," Jacques said. "According to the autopsies, the gas that killed both Xavier and Ian Stoke was Vikane."

"I'm unfamiliar with that gas," Viktor said.

# THE DIABOLIST

"It's odorless and tasteless, virtually undetectable by humans. Quite toxic. The Americans use it for pest control, to fumigate termites."

"I see," Viktor said. "And how was it administered?"

"We have no idea. The gas dissipates quickly and is almost impossible to detect after a few days. As far as we know, both victims were alone the night of their deaths, so I suspect the gas was pumped in through a hole or an open window."

"Any chemist could figure something out," Viktor said with a tired wave. *And Darius was a brilliant chemist.* "And the fires? Any news?"

"The San Francisco arson experts inform me that for the fire to burn that hot and that quickly, a highly flammable starting agent with a high heat-release rate had to have been used. An accelerant, in layman's terms. Using megawatts rather than kilowatts."

"Do we have any idea what that might have been?" Viktor said.

"The accelerant could vary, but the delivery device itself was likely something akin to a flamethrower. Which is rather hard to conceal, *oui.* But they also tell me that if the clothing was soaked or sprayed with an odorless accelerant beforehand, that would speed the process and require a simpler delivery device."

Viktor grunted. "It's starting to make sense. You might want to do some checking on Douglas Oakenfeld, Matthias's right-hand man."

"Your theory, then, is that the murderer is using inside help from the cults?"

"Of course," Viktor said.

"And your thoughts on the perpetrator?"

"As soon as I have hard evidence to discuss, you'll be the first to know."

"Wouldn't someone in the room have noticed an ignition device?" Jacques said.

Viktor twirled the spoon between his fingers. "Magic is all about sleight of hand, illusion. The robed figure is a diversion. The same person who soaks the clothing of the victim provides the spark for the fire, while the rest of the room is watching the illusory robed figure."

"It is the plausible theory."

"It's the only theory," Viktor said. "I plan to find out more tomorrow night."

"What precautions will you take?"

"I'll be alone in the room with Gareth, so there'll be no chance for someone else to start the fire. I have a few other ideas as well. Let's just say that I, too, know some tricks of the trade."

"And if Vikane is used?" Jacques said.

"The gas has to enter from somewhere. I'll ensure the room is sealed and the vents are closed, and I'll have a protective mask on hand. How long does the gas take to affect human beings?"

"Not instantaneous, though not long. I'm told a better option is a device that can measure levels of sulfuryl fluoride, the active ingredient in Vikane."

"I'll try and obtain one," Viktor said. He remembered the man from Zador's and the coffee shop. "Did you run the photo I sent?"

"There's no facial match with Interpol, though the quality of the photo doesn't help. Viktor, you needn't do this."

The absinthe reached the perfect milky color, and Viktor hovered over the glass. "Darius knows Gareth is too proud to use the police for what appears to be a question of magic. I need to be there."

"Inform Gareth that this is the twenty-first century," Jacques said.

# 36

Grey spent the night in a hostel on the outskirts of Cambridge. He woke early and took a long run by the river to clear his head and tame the nervous energy coursing through him.

When he finished, he showered and had breakfast at a café. At ten a.m. his cell rang. Viktor. The café was quiet, and Grey took the call with coffee in hand. He listened as Viktor relayed his recent finds and the conversation with Jacques.

After Viktor told him about the note in the back of Crowley's copy of *The Ahriman Heresy*, Grey said, "And you didn't tell Jacques that Simon is really Darius because we don't have a shred of real proof, and telling him would only hamper our own investigation."

"Jacques knows enough to help as needed," Viktor said.

"I doubt Satanic cult leaders sleep very well at night, knowing their own people could turn on them on a dime."

"Unless measures were taken to ensure compliance," Viktor said.

"Like convincing your followers you have the ability to murder someone whenever and wherever you want."

"Precisely."

Grey's eyes swept the empty café. "I assume you want me in York by tonight?"

"No. We have to find out where he's operating from, and the only way I know how to do that is penetrate his cult. I need you to start from the bottom, in London, and work your way up. Attend a meeting, find out how the leader became involved. Move to the next level and do the same. Wade through until you come to Darius. It won't be easy, but the cult is relatively young."

"That sounds like it could take weeks," Grey said.

"It needs to take days. I don't know his endgame, but I assure you we won't want to find out."

"Do you think he'll ever join the two? The Order of New Enlightenment with what's he really doing?"

"Perhaps one day," Viktor said, "though he doesn't need to. Worshippers of cults and religions worldwide have no idea what really occurs behind the veil. Darius will use L'église la Bête and others like it to do his dirty work, while extending his power and influence with New Order."

"We can expose his name change. He's got a record in the occult, people know him. Why would anyone follow him after that?"

Viktor gave a bitter laugh. "So he had a change of heart. Saint Paul once persecuted Christians, Joseph Smith was a convicted con man, countless religious and world leaders have checkered pasts and worse. People who want to believe in something will do so at all costs, especially when it comes to political or religious dogma. They hear what they want to hear."

"There's got to be a link to his current crimes somewhere," Grey said, "even if it's buried deep within the Order of New Enlightenment."

"Yes, and he'll go to any lengths to protect it."

"Which is why I should be there tomorrow night," Grey said.

"We don't have that luxury."

"It's your call," Grey said. "You've heard my vote. Before you go, there's something I need to tell you about."

Grey relayed the events of the previous evening to Viktor. "Astral projection's an interesting angle," Viktor said, "though I'd turn my research to misdirection and sleight of hand, if I were you."

"If she's a liar, she's a very good one."

"It's Darius I don't trust," Viktor said.

"She's genuinely frightened, and what's her motive?"

"Motive doesn't apply to those embedded in a cult," Viktor said. "Either way, she could be our path to Darius."

Grey blew out a breath. "I had the same thought."

It didn't take Grey long to find a meeting. On the Tube ride into town from the airport he saw a flyer for a gathering of the Order of New Enlightenment, that evening at six p.m. at Speakers' Corner. He figured that was as good a place to start as any.

Planning to stay in London for a few days, he dropped his backpack in one of the threadbare, cramped hotels that circled Victoria station like vultures. He slipped inside, paid cash, and gave a false name.

At five p.m. he was stepping out of the Tube at Oxford Circus, grandiose gray buildings curving away in every direction, shops and chic cafés buzzing at street-level. London rushed at Grey as he walked, a blur of black cabs and double-decker buses, street vendors selling their red and blue trinkets, the babble of a hundred languages.

Just past Marble Arch, Speakers' Corner was pretty much as he remembered: a nutcase in a beanie cap standing on a makeshift platform and shouting conspiracy theories in a Cockney accent at an amused crowd, the regal calm of Hyde Park mocking his efforts in the background. Grey arrived thirty minutes early, hoping to catch the New Enlightenment representative before the event began.

The current speaker was talking about New Age Nazis in California, linking the Fourth Reich to McDonald's. When he left, the crowd swelled to an impressive size. No one arrived at the podium until five minutes after six, when a bulky, red-faced Scot stepped up and greeted the crowd with a booming hello.

Though pleasant enough, his voice possessed the myopic tone of conviction that immediately turned Grey off. To Grey, anyone who saw the world in black-and-white wasn't taking a hard enough look.

The speaker announced himself as Alan Lancaster and proceeded to give the crowd a similar spiel Grey had heard from Simon Azar, though with less eloquence. How the old ways of thinking about the world had failed, yet everyone in power was clinging to the old ways because, well, why wouldn't they? Some cheered, some jeered, most listened with hands in their pockets for a few minutes and then returned to their tourist maps.

Was this how all movements started, Grey wondered? Spread from street corners by simple-minded blusterers, scorned by most, gobbled up by the gullible few?

Was this how his mother had succumbed?

Grey felt eyes on him during the speech, and he saw various men sprinkled in the crowd, subtly scanning the onlookers. After the speech a line formed to talk to the speaker. Grey joined in. When he reached the front, Alan Lancaster's eyes locked on to his, hand extended in greeting.

He gave Grey his full attention, one thing at which zealots excelled. "Welcome, friend. Can I give ye this pamphlet?"

Grey took a loose-leaf pamphlet with a picture of the cosmos on the front, people of varying skin colors standing hand in hand beneath a starry sky.

"I'd like to invite ye to one of our Saturday services. Yer an American on holiday?"

Grey had to work to understand his accent. "This is home for now."

"Well, then. Let me suggest the Kensington and Chelsea Chapter House, in Earls Court. Services are Saturday mornings at ten. We'd love to have ye. Bring a guest or two."

"Appreciated," Grey said. "Who's the pastor there—or do you have pastors?"

"We have directors, and we just use names, no better or worse than ye. Just call me Alan, and the Earls Court director is Thomas Greene. He brought me into the Order."

"Is that right?" Grey said. "How long ago did you join?"

"Been a couple of months now."

"And you're already a speaker? Impressive."

# THE DIABOLIST

"The training only takes a few weeks," Alan said. "Might ye be interested?"

"I liked what you had to say," Grey said. "Let me sleep on it."

"It's a new way of thinking. No more false prophets or cryptic prophecies or silly codes of conduct, just human beings helping each other around the world."

"Sounds pretty good to me," Grey said.

"Aye, why don't ye talk to Thomas? He's at the chapter house most mornings, ye can tell him I sent ye."

Grey had what he needed, and he felt multiple stares on his back. "Sure. Looks like you've got plenty of people to talk to, so thanks again."

Grey stepped past him and kept walking. Step one had been easy, but he wondered how many starry-eyed handshakers he'd have to wade through to find someone who knew what was going on behind closed doors at the Order of New Enlightenment.

He debated trying to isolate one of the three flint-eyed men now following him through the park, all of whom looked like ex-convicts who had put on a nice shirt for the gathering. He decided they didn't look like decision makers, and there were too many people around. After exiting the park he turned left on Piccadilly, skirting Green Park on his right. He let them follow him for a while, so when he gave them the slip it would look natural, and so whoever sent them would keep searching for him in the West End. When he reached Leicester Square he kept on slipping, and out of the corner of his eye he saw them trying to keep up, unshaven faces walking a step too quickly, inexperienced with the subtle art of following someone in a crowd.

Grey wove in and out of the narrow lanes between Leicester and Piccadilly, then doubled back to the labyrinthine streets of Soho. By the time he reached Charing Cross he was sure no one was still following him, but he scanned the crowds down the long escalator to the Underground just in case, disappearing into the bowels of the city as he pondered how to approach Thomas Greene in the morning.

# 37

## YORK

By the time Viktor cleaned up and had brunch in his suite, it was nearly noon. Thirty-six hours before the alleged hour of Gareth's execution.

Viktor had a few things to do.

First he searched for a pest-control company that used Vikane. Fortunately for the citizens of York and unfortunately for Viktor, termites were not a problem in northeast England. Viktor had to persuade a London company that manufactured devices measuring sulfuryl fluoride to overnight one to his hotel. The company balked at the request until Viktor suggested a four-figure delivery fee. There was silence, and then acquiescence.

The sulfuryl fluoride device would let him know instantly if Vikane was present in the room, but just to be safe, he procured two gas masks from a local military supply store. Gareth agreed to seal off all ventilation to the room, and to check the walls and windows for cracks. Viktor was guessing that poison gas would be the weapon of choice, since Gareth would not be in a public place and there was less opportunity for deception.

Still, Viktor urged Gareth to install a fire extinguisher, to avoid wearing any clothing that might have been tampered with, and not to let anyone enter the room besides the two of them. There would be other members of the Circle nearby, armed and ready, and Gareth had agreed to install a camera and make his chamber off-limits to anyone but himself before the next night.

Viktor felt prepared.

# THE DIABOLIST

Of course, there was the black-magic angle, but Viktor did not believe for a second there was anything behind these murders other than the devious mind and barren soul of a human being he once called friend.

Defenses in place, Viktor turned to the task of finding Darius. To the clue he had uncovered in Crowley's copy of *The Ahriman Heresy*.

*Tutori*.

Viktor spoke Italian and knew Latin, and while he found plenty of references to *tutori* on the Internet, he found nothing that intrigued him as a possible link to Crowley. He spent the rest of the afternoon sifting through books at the library and making calls to various sources in academia. Still coming up empty, he decided to mull over the problem over a late afternoon lunch at a gastro pub on Goodramgate.

While working on his braised ox cheek with red onion chutney, he realized there was one place in town he had yet to try. He couldn't put his finger on why, perhaps because he just had a feel for this sort of thing after decades of experience, but *tutori* seemed to have a religious ring. York was slathered with churches, but none as grandiose as the York Minster, built in the thirteenth century to rival the grandeur of Canterbury. The York diocese was a hugely important one for the Church of England and would have learned priests. It was worth a try.

He made the short walk up Goodramgate to the Minster, the limestone of the Gothic cathedral casting a silver glow in the failing evening light. Despite the beauty of the town, Viktor couldn't believe the atrocity of the late September weather, the sky thick as gravy with clouds, a perpetual drizzle, temperature close to freezing, and a biting wind that lashed at Viktor like a vengeful pugilist.

The Minster imposed its will on the town, the cathedral itself comprising most of a city block, its parklike grounds stretching over several. His hand caught the door to the main entrance just as a red-faced man in a sweater was locking up.

Viktor flashed his Interpol ID. "Is there a priest still on hand? I apologize for the hour."

The man's eyes lingered on the badge. "I'm one of the vicars."

"I have a few quick questions," Viktor said, "if you have a moment."

"I suppose I do."

"I'm investigating a matter with some rather . . . arcane . . . elements. My research has produced a term with which I'm unfamiliar, and I was wondering if someone at the church might help."

"What is it?" the vicar said.

"*Tutori.*"

He ushered Viktor inside but didn't close the door. "Latin?"

"Probably," Viktor said. "It translates roughly to 'the guardians.' Have you heard of an organization with this name associated with the church?"

His jowls bounced as he shook his head. "Can't say that I have."

"Do you have a library?" Viktor said.

"The largest cathedral library in the country." He sighed. "I don't suppose this can wait until tomorrow? We have a church historian on hand during the day."

"Not unless it has to," Viktor said. "If you have a catalog, that could expedite the process."

"It's digital now. Typically you find the book you want online, reserve the book, and claim it the next day."

"But if the book is there," Viktor said, "you could help me now."

"I suppose."

"Interpol sincerely appreciates your cooperation."

The vicar muttered a reply, locked the huge door and led Viktor down a hallway to the cramped administrative portion of the Minster, then into a carpeted office. "The library's in another building, but we can check the catalog from here."

Viktor waited with folded arms as the computer warmed up. If the York Minster had the largest cathedral library in England, then outside of the

Vatican this should be one of the best places in the world to find a reference to the *tutori*.

The online catalog filled the screen. The vicar entered his registration information, confirmed the spelling of the word with Viktor, and typed the word into the title database.

Nothing.

"Let's try a broader search," the vicar said, "for text within the documents."

The search produced a few results in Italian, which Viktor scanned and disregarded as irrelevant. Viktor's weight shifted to his heels. He had gotten his hopes up. "That's unfortunate."

"Is there anything else I can do?"

"Are there any books that haven't been cataloged," Viktor said, "perhaps a storeroom or a rare records room?"

"I'm afraid not."

It was late, and Viktor decided to stop in for a pint at one of York's countless pubs. His emerald potion awaited him at his suite, and he knew at some point in the evening he would not be able to resist. But for the first time in a very long time, he feared what the absinthe would drag to the surface more than he feared the clarity of his thoughts without it.

A velvety darkness cloaked the town. Viktor bypassed bar after bar, each more beguiling and full of character than the last, with names like the Gimcrack, the Hansom Cab, the Three-Legged Mare, and the House of the Trembling Madness.

He continued down Petergate to the Shambles, a stone lane once littered with blood and offal from its many butcher shops, now lined with contiguous timber-framed houses and specialty shops, the tops of which jutted drunkenly over the constricted street. Viktor decided on the Golden Fleece, a somber pub with an entrance just off the Shambles.

A somewhat ominous effigy of a golden sheep hung from twin wires crossed above the door, but the darkened interior looked inviting, and Viktor didn't see the usual crowd of inebriated patrons spilling out the door. He made his way down a hallway lined with newspaper clippings of alleged hauntings in York, to a small room in the rear where a fire blazed in a stone hearth and a few patrons kept to themselves at candlelit wooden tables. Viktor sat at the bar and ordered a local ale.

The bartender set a mug in front of Viktor. Her graying hair was tied in a severe bun that made her drawn face look even tighter. "First time at the Fleece?"

"Yes," Viktor said.

"You here to see the Lady?"

"Sorry?"

"You've got the look of one of the ghost hunters, they come round about once a week."

"I take it the Lady is no longer in the realm of the living?" Viktor said.

"Not since 1700 or so. You do know the Fleece's haunted?"

Viktor smirked. "Is that so?"

"York's the most haunted town in England, and the Fleece here's our most haunted pub. A journalist from one of the fancy London stations stayed here for a night a few years back, doing a documentary on the hauntings. Ran out screaming before midnight. Psychics won't touch the place."

"I see," Viktor said.

"Enjoy your pint."

He raised his glass. "Cheers."

Viktor started thinking about Crowley again. He supposed he would have to dig deeper into the occultist's past, though Viktor had studied Crowley extensively and had never read or heard of a mention of Ahriman. Crowley had apparently kept his search for the Ahriman Grimoire under a strict code of secrecy, unusual for a man prone to public outburst. But magicians were notoriously secretive when it came to their research.

# THE DIABOLIST

Viktor's eyes wandered the bar, returning to a patron he had seen on the way in, an older man with a gaunt, pleasant face sipping his beer in the corner. He was wearing a faded crimson smoking jacket with a white rose embroidered on the front. The jacket looked vaguely official, and it triggered something in Viktor's memory, though he couldn't remember what. Some esoteric fact to do with the Church of England, he thought.

The bartender returned with another pint. "So what's your business in York? Just a look-see?"

"Something like that." He nudged his head towards the table in the corner. Bartenders were a wonderful source of information. "Do you know that man?"

She peered over his shoulder. "Red jacket?"

"Yes."

"Sure. Philip Lackle, captain of the Minster Guard."

Viktor snapped his fingers. "Of course."

He remembered now: The rose was the White Rose of York, and the jacket was issued to members of the Minster Guard, a tiny police force responsible for guarding the Minster since Norman times. He knew this because there were only two churches in the world with their own police force, the Vatican and the York Minster. Unlike the Swiss Guard, the Minster Guard had been relegated to mere functionaries.

The bartender looked surprised. "You've 'eard of 'em?"

"I'm a professor of religious phenomenology."

"What?"

Viktor waved a hand. "I'm interested in church history."

"The Guard aren't much these days, they carry a gob full of keys around and point tourists in the right direction. Philip's a good man, comes in here four nights a week and drinks his bitters in the corner. Go on over, he's nice as Yorkshire pudding. He's a crack for anything to do with the church."

"I just might do that." He took a few more sips, then rose and walked towards Philip, who peered up at him.

"Sorry to bother you," Viktor said. "Could I buy you a pint?"

"I, well, of course I can't say no to that." He motioned for Viktor to sit. "I'm sorry, do I know you?"

Viktor held up two fingers to the bartender, then sat across from Philip. "I'm a professor of religious phenomenology at Charles University in Prague, and I have a question about a rather obscure piece of church trivia. The bartender suggested you might be able to help."

Philip's eyes lit up as he wiped foam from his mouth. "We'll see what we can do, won't we?"

"I don't suppose you've ever heard of an organization called the *tutori*?" Viktor said. "I suspect it's an organization, though I'm not sure."

Philip thought for a minute, until the fresh round arrived. "You don't mean the Tutori Electus, do you? That *is* obscure."

"You'll have to educate me," Viktor said.

"The Tutori Electus were a select—thus the name—team of priests sent by the Vatican in the fifteenth and sixteenth centuries to help combat the rising tide of heresies."

Viktor didn't react, but his heart started to beat faster.

Philip continued, "A bit similar in training to the Knights of Malta or the Templars, though far smaller and more focused on the occult threat to the Church, witches and devil worshippers and the like. I read about them during a training course on church military."

"Can you be more specific?" Viktor said.

"They worked in small groups, and each faction was assigned a particular heresy. They led Inquisitions, as well as church troops where necessary."

"Do you know if any of the Tutori were dedicated to the Ahriman Heresy?"

Philip's face balled in thought. "Can't say I've ever heard of that one." He snapped his fingers. "Though I believe there's a book on the Tutori."

"I've already checked the Minster's catalog," Viktor said.

"Not in the Minster library, in the Guard's library. It's tiny in comparison but has a few books you won't find many places."

# THE DIABOLIST

Viktor leaned back and crossed his arms. "I'd love to see that book."

"We used to lend books to the public, but we stopped about a decade ago. I don't think anyone has borrowed a book in twenty years." From the inside of his jacket, Philip withdrew the largest set of keys Viktor had ever seen. "But why don't we finish these pints and take a walk over there?"

Grey needed sustenance, and decided to exit the Tube at King's Cross. He shoved his hands in his pockets and walked past the austere pillars of the British Museum, down a street populated with closed offices and a few cafés geared towards the lunch set, then emerged into a more lively and scraggly section of the city.

He ducked into a pub called the Kingfisher and ordered fish and chips at the bar. The rock music was loud, the crowd louder. A group of rugby players still dirty from the night's match were holding each other's shoulders and singing in a corner.

He was halfway through his meal when he noticed stares from a group of punks in a corner booth by the door. All four had Mohawks, leather jackets, and sneers, and they reeked of trouble. Their eyes flicked from Grey to a piece of paper on the table.

When the bartender swung by, Grey asked for the check and said, "You know anything about the Mohawks in the corner?"

He scowled in their direction. "They're part of a Newcastle gang that runs around the council housing in Euston, all of 'em on the dole. I've 'ad to kick the buggers out before, though they won't start trouble while the boys are here." The bartender glanced over at the rugby players, then back at the Mohawks. "They're looking your way; you 'ave words with one of 'em?"

"Not yet," Grey said.

"They're bothering you, I can call the boys over."

# THE DIABOLIST

Grey glanced at the rugby players again, now swaying and moving in a circle, heads tilted back as they sang. "Thanks, but no need."

"You a copper?"

"No."

The bartender looked Grey up and down, trying to figure out his angle. Then he reached for the stereo and cranked the music even louder, gave Grey a knowing look, and started washing a glass.

Grey left a huge tip, pushed away from the bar, and walked to the booth shoved against a window. All four punks watched him approach, and the one nearest Grey stood when Grey reached the table. Grey shoved him back in the booth and squeezed in beside him, trapping the two on his side against the window. His eyes flicked to the piece of paper on the table; it was a photocopied picture of himself, taken on the street outside Oak's house.

The one he had shoved had multiple piercings on his face, and a chain running from lip to nose. He started to stand again. "What the fook—"

Grey grabbed his nose chain and pulled him back down, hard enough to cause the punk's eyes to water, but not hard enough to rip it out. The nose was one of the most sensitive parts on the human body, and Grey marveled that anyone with tough guy aspirations would offer such an easy handle.

Grey shouted as he increased the pressure, the music muffling everything. "Stay down or I'll rip it out."

The kid seethed but stayed in his seat. The punk opposite Grey pulled a knife and started to rise. Grey already had one foot wrapped behind his ankle, and he kicked the side of his knee with his other foot, not hard enough to shatter the patella but hard enough to cause severe pain. He screamed and dropped the knife. Grey swept up the knife in his left hand, then slammed it on top of the photo, point-down in the wooden table.

"Where'd you get this?" Grey said.

All four gave him sullen looks. No one answered. Grey pulled harder on the nose ring.

"Okay, shite! Look, some guy passed it to us. Who the fook are you?"

"I'm asking the questions."

"We were just told to find you—"

"I know what you were told," Grey said. "I want to know who told you."

Grey extracted the knife, twirled it in his fingers, and slammed it down again, this time hilt first. All four jumped. "If I don't hear a name, I'm going to break a kneecap and rip out a nose chain."

He increased the pressure on the chain to the ripping point, the punk next to him bent double to relieve the pressure. "Dickie, man," he screamed. "It came from Dickie."

"Who the hell is Dickie?" Grey said.

"Dickie Jones."

Grey blinked, then pulled him around until he was looking Grey in the eye. "The fight organizer? If you're lying to me I'll come back and rip out every piercing in your body."

"Yeah, fook, that's him. For Christ's sake don't tell him we told you."

"Where is he now?" Grey said.

"He runs shite outta his gym in Tower Hamlets, down by Spitalfields. No shite man, you can't tell him."

Grey released his hold and stood, and the punk sank in relief. The one across from him was still holding his knee, hunched in pain, and the other two were pressed as far against the wall as they could go. Grey snatched the photocopy off the table and left.

At first Grey couldn't believe what he had heard, but on second thought he supposed he could. Most people never changed, and apparently Daisuke "Dickie" Jones, a half-Japanese IRA crony and organizer on the underground fighting circuit when Grey had lived in London more than a decade ago, hadn't either.

After a careful return journey to his hotel, Grey wedged a chair under the door handle and collapsed into bed. The next day he was shocked when he stepped off the bus near Spitalfields Market, at the western edge of the East End.

# THE DIABOLIST

Once a place for the working class to pick up cheap goods and have a pint in a gritty pub, the cavernous Spitalfields Market was now surrounded by organic grocery stores, gastro pubs, and yuppies patrolling the streets with double strollers and lattes. The Spitalfields Grey knew had barely been civilized, let alone gentrified. He walked a few streets over to Dickie's place, now a plush, air-conditioned gym with signs advertising Pilates and yoga classes.

Grey entered and asked for Dickie at the front desk, still shaking his head. The last time Grey had been here a boxing ring had dominated the room, surrounded by free weights, heavy bags, and a legion of local toughs.

The perky front-desk clerk led him to an office in back, where Dickie himself sat in a leather chair, reading a paper with his feet kicked up on the desk. It was the same bald head, swarthy skin, and short but powerful body Grey remembered. Instead of a stained tank top, however, Dickie now wore a pair of sleek jeans, a tight black shirt, and diamond studs in his ears.

He didn't look up as Grey and the desk clerk entered. "All right?"

"Dickie, someone's here to see you. Says he knows you."

Dickie lowered the tabloid, his curved eyes widening and then sinking into a guarded stare. "Thanks, love," he said, without taking his eyes off Grey. The attendant left and closed the door.

"Dominic Grey? Are you fucking kidding me?"

"Been a long time, Dickie," Grey said.

"Can't say you've changed much, still scruffy and frail as a baby bird." His voice possessed a touch of both warmth and nervousness. "Rather a grown-up Ollie Twist, aren't you?"

"You look good," Grey said.

Dickie ran a hand over his bald head, muscles rippling along his forearm. "Sorta easy staying in shape when you run a gym." He patted his belly, which was still hard, though Grey remembered it being much less rounded. "Now it's more like a leisure center."

"The neighborhood's doing well for itself," Grey said.

He spread his arms. "Can you believe this shite? Used to be people were afraid of the East End, now we've got Starbucks and wine shops. But go a few

223

blocks down and you'll see the same depressing shite as twenty years ago. The West London poofters like to stick their foot in Spitalfields, tell their pale-arsed friends they hang out in the East End. A few of them even buy condos here, then wonder why their wives get mugged walking the dog. Anyway. Last I heard you joined the goon squad."

"That didn't work out too well," Grey said.

"Didn't figure it would. And after that? Haven't heard a word about you in a decade."

"Is that right?" Grey said softly.

Neither spoke, and Dickie swallowed. An aerobics instructor chirped instructions in the background.

Grey took a step forward, and Dickie shifted in his seat. "Grey—"

"I know you put the word out. Just tell me who it came from, and we're all good here."

"Can't do that," Dickie said.

Grey took another step forward, and Dickie's hand moved under the desk. "I've got an alarm. Cops'll swarm this place in five minutes."

Dickie flinched as Grey spun the metal chair in front of him around, then sat. "I'm not going to hurt you, Dickie. That's what the people you work for do. And we both know you're not calling the cops. You may have upgraded, but the Dickie I know always has a hand in the cookie jar."

"I've changed, mate. Gone straight. No more tracksuits and paychecks in paper bags."

"Is that why you're cozying up to a bunch of militant Satanists?"

This time Dickie paled, and his fingers started tapping a nervous staccato on his desk. "You remember that time we tossed those Jamaicans who were putting twelve-year-old boys from Hackney in the ring? You, me, and Willie went right to Brixton and gave it to the lot of them."

"We go back, Dickie, you know we do. So talk to me. Why're half the lowlifes in London on the lookout for me? Who put out the word, and from where?"

# THE DIABOLIST

"I always liked you," Dickie said, "and I never saw anyone fight like you. You were an angry pup, but you had the gift. We coulda made a lot of quid, if you'd listened to me. But that's not one of your strong suits, is it? Take some advice from an old chum: Go home. I've seen a lot of ugly shite in my day, but someone bad has it out for you. *Real* bad."

"Someone?" Grey said. "You mean Dante?"

Dickie pursed his lips, the finger tapping more insistent. Grey could see the affirmation in his eyes, the slither of fear across his brow, and it surprised him. Dickie was a hard man.

Grey said, "What do they have on you? Surely the people you work for could step in?"

"It's not like that anymore," he muttered. "I freelance now. Dante and his people, they're like ghosts." He shuddered. "They come and get you in the middle of the night and there're only pieces of you left in the morning. Get out of East End, Grey. Get out of London."

"Where can I find him?" Grey said.

"I truly can't help you, mate. He calls me, not the other way around. He came around once, and made it clear the only way I'd see him again was if I wasn't waking up the next morning." He turned his forearm over, exposing two half-healed, deep slashes that formed a crude upside down cross, the longer slash running from wrist to elbow. "He left me with a parting gift."

Grey clenched the back of the chair when he saw Dickie's arm, his knuckles whitening as he stared at Dante's handiwork. Grey pulled out a business card and left it on the desk. "Call me if anything changes." He started to leave, then paused with a hand on the door. "Or if you need me."

# 39

Viktor returned with Philip Lackle, the captain of the Minster Guard, to the sprawling and now deserted grounds of the Minster. They traversed Dean's Park on the north side of the complex, then approached an elegant limestone building with an arched roof and columns. After unlocking a door in the rear, Philip took him past a series of sitting rooms, up a flight of stairs and to a door at the end of the hallway. He unlocked that door, revealing a handsome room filled with floor-to-ceiling bookshelves.

Philip pointed out a card catalog in the corner, and Viktor flipped through the letter *T* until he found the single subject entry for the Tutori Electus, a book printed in York in 1872, and entitled *History of Special Commissions from the Vatican.*

Viktor tracked down the section with the book as Philip puttered about the room. It took Viktor some time to root through the stacks, but he found the title, engraved with faded red lettering on the spine.

The section on the Tutori was short, and Viktor read it while he stood.

> *In response to the threat of certain heresies endemic to occultism and magick in Europe, the Vatican did theretofore assign the Tutori Electus to extinguish those heresies considered most dire. Having been tasked in groups of twenty, the priests of the Tutori were trained to withstand the severe physical and mental assaults fostered by the heresies. Much of the activities of the Tutori Electus were maintained in secrecy by the*

# THE DIABOLIST

*Vatican as these Commissions, ordained by the Pope himself, bore utmost importance to the health of the Catholic Church.*

Viktor skimmed a few sections discussing other heresies in which the Tutori were involved. He then felt a frisson of excitement when he read the next to last paragraph in the section.

*The Heresy of Ahriman, seeded in the late fifteenth century, was of particular concern to the Catholic Church for its Gnostic genesis and mass appeal. The origins of the Heresy remain unclear, but the involvement of the Tutori Electus in the year 1533 is certain, acknowledged by various sources of the time, and this particular Commission was augmented by a sizeable regiment, and tasked with the swift annihilation of the threat. Written records of the Commission are nonexistent outside the Vatican, but it is known that after a successful campaign the remaining Tutori Electus were honored for their valour by the Knights Hospitaller in a ceremony in the Palazzo dei Normanni in Palermo, then of the Kingdom of Sicily.*

Viktor closed the book, remembering Rudolf Steiner's bizarre reference to an Ahrimanic influence occurring during the middle of the fifteenth century.

During the time of the Ahriman Heresy, the Maltese Islands were still part of the Kingdom of Sicily. Viktor knew that Charles V had given Malta to the Knights Hospitaller—an order similar to the Templars—in 1530 to help protect the Holy Roman Empire from the Ottomans. In exchange, the Knights had paid the eclectic yearly tribute of one Maltese Falcon to both the Holy Roman Emperor and the Viceroy of Sicily.

All interesting historical facts, but it didn't answer the question of why the Tutori Electus had been in Sicily.

Viktor flipped through the rest of the book, finding nothing else useful. Attached to the inside of the back cover was a flap with a ledger containing the names of previous borrowers of the book, similar to that used by modern libraries.

He would have missed it had there been more names on the ledger, because the last name would have been hidden by the flap. But there were only two names, the latter with the date 1914 scrawled beside it, and the corner of Viktor's eye glimpsed the name of the second borrower just before he closed the book, his breath catching as he did.

The last person who had borrowed the book was listed as A. Crowley.

The name alone sent a tingle down Viktor's spine, but his next thought turned the tingle into an electric current of knowledge, swift and sure.

After his stint in America, Crowley left New York to establish his infamous Abbey of Thelema, purportedly a school of magical training for new adepts. The location he had chosen for the school had always been a bit of a mystery. It was a backwater, hard to reach and possessing no real spiritual or magical significance.

The site Crowley had chosen was Cefalù, a small village in Sicily.

Viktor thanked Philip as they left the library and passed through the fog-enshrouded grounds of the Minster, the tips of the spires floating disembodied in the moonlight. Just as Viktor was about to say good-bye and return to his hotel, he caught the flicker of a cloak in the fog behind them, in the direction of the Minster. Before he could catch a face, the cloak faded into the gloom.

Viktor didn't know who was stalking the grounds of the Minster at two in the morning, but he had a very good guess, and it left his mouth dry and his stomach churning.

The town was dark and still, the revelry dissipated, the buildings a stone tableau frozen by a Medusa in a time long past.

"Is your car close?" Viktor asked Philip, scanning the streets for signs of the cloaked figure.

"Just a couple of blocks past the Fleece."

# THE DIABOLIST

"I'm headed that way, too," Viktor lied, cursing to himself. The Golden Fleece was all the way across the center of town. His hand moved underneath his suit, finding the handle of his wavy-edged dagger. He couldn't let Philip walk the streets alone, and the chance of finding a taxi at that time of night was slim to none.

Viktor's eyes searched the streets for signs of movement. Had the cloaked figure been a chance sighting, or had Viktor glimpsed one of many hidden within the fog? He was no stranger to physical danger, but he knew that if L'église de la Bête had come for him, then this night might be his last.

He berated himself. He had been so absorbed in searching the library that he had forgotten the time and exposed them both. Images from his last investigation involving L'église de la Bête came to mind, the mutilated remains of the girls. He forced the fear away, knowing he had to keep a clear head to have a chance at staying alive.

As they turned onto Low Petergate, he took Philip by the arm. "Keep walking and don't show panic, but I think we're being followed."

Philip tensed, but he kept walking without looking back. "Who's there?" he said, his voice strained.

"Some very dangerous men. Do you know a faster way back to the Fleece?"

"We can try the snickelways," Philip said, "though we'll have to pop in and out of the streets."

"Lead on."

They hurried down the street to the entrance to the first snickelway, the narrow medieval footpaths that wove in and out of York's old town, connecting the larger streets or leading to hidden courtyards and back entrances.

After traversing the clandestine passageway, they popped out on Stonegate. They padded down the dull stones to another snickelway, hearing footsteps behind them just before they slipped into the stone-walled corridor.

"I think they saw us," Viktor said.

Philip took the cue, increasing the pace and leading them on a crisscrossing journey through the medieval alleys of the old town. The entrances to some of the snickelways were so cleverly hidden that Viktor never would have noticed them on his own. If it had been just one pursuer they might have been able to avoid them, but Viktor guessed a number of them lurked in the darkness, spread out among the old town.

They emerged into a courtyard Viktor recognized as Saint Helen's Square. The Golden Fleece was just a few blocks away, and they hurried out of the square. Just before they reached the next intersection, Viktor heard the patter of footsteps approaching from one of the other streets. *Do prdele.* The snickelway was too far behind to seek cover, and their pursuer was about to round the corner.

Viktor noticed a stone archway just past a closed jewelry shop, and he pulled Philip through the archway and into a darkened courtyard that dead-ended thirty feet away, at the iron-studded door to a cathedral. The courtyard was empty, its walls high and sheer.

The footsteps grew louder. Viktor spied two plastic trash cans in a corner and pulled Philip to them. They hunched behind the cans, praying the fog would help conceal them.

The footsteps manifested into a booted foot that appeared out of the fog. Viktor held his breath, knowing the trash can failed to conceal half his body, praying the fog and darkness concealed the rest. He could feel Philip trembling beside him.

Viktor had his knife in hand, but he knew the members of L'église de la Bête rarely worked alone. Even if Viktor managed to overcome their pursuer, the noise would carry into the night and betray their position.

As the figure peered into the courtyard, Viktor thought the pounding of his heart would announce their presence, like Poe's telltale organ. The way Viktor was positioned he could just see the side of the man's face, and Viktor gripped the hilt of his knife.

It was the same man he had seen twice in San Francisco, the customer from Zador's bookshop.

Viktor lost five years of his life as he waited, but the man scanned the courtyard without moving farther inside. When he turned to leave, Viktor sagged with relief, thinking it odd that L'église de la Bête would send someone halfway across the world when they had local chapters. He must be higher up in the hierarchy, perhaps an assassin sent for Viktor alone.

Whatever the reason, Viktor had no doubt there were more of them prowling within the fog, and his fear metastasized as they waited. They couldn't stay where they were.

He helped Philip to his feet. "Let's make a run for the Fleece," Viktor whispered. Philip nodded, his face ashen.

They emerged again near Saint Helen's Square, dashing down Parliament and turning left onto Pavement for the final few meters. The Golden Fleece was just ahead. Just as they reached the distinctive sign, a group of people emerged from the Shambles, led by a man in a black cloak.

Limbs rigid with panic, Viktor dug in his heels and twisted to sprint in the other direction. He yanked Philip by the sleeve, almost pulling Philip off his feet. There had to have been twenty people behind the lead man, and Viktor and Philip had walked right into their line of sight.

As they fled, he saw Philip look over his shoulder, then slow and stop. Viktor was about to shout at him when Philip said, "It's the bloody Devil's Hour, the three a.m. ghost tour. The Fleece is one of the stops."

When Viktor turned he saw the group with new eyes, this time not blinded by fear: the black-cloaked, unshaven figure smoking a cigarette and addressing the crowd, pointing at the Golden Fleece with a flourish as the crowd of tourists looked on with eager faces.

Philip pointed at his car just down the street. Viktor felt like a fool, but there was no time to relax. They hurried forward while the tour group was still within sight, the tension in Viktor's body not lessening until they were safely inside the vehicle, speeding into the night.

**G**rey left Dickie's gym and got on the Tube again. Though he didn't think Alan Lancaster, the speaker at Speakers' Corner, was clued in to the underbelly of the cult, Grey did expect Alan to have been questioned after their meeting.

Dangerous or not, paying a visit to the director of the Earls Court chapter house was Grey's only link to the upper hierarchy, so he had decided to don a disguise and hope for the best. The Earls Court chapter house was a two-story flat in a cramped row of brownstones near the Exhibition and Convention Centre. Grey showed up in clothes he had picked up in a secondhand store along the way: ripped jeans and a long-sleeved Rolling Stones concert tee, a ragged Union Jack scarf, clip-on earrings, and a long-haired wig. With his week's growth of scruff and his wiry frame, Grey thought he pulled off the starving artist look nicely.

He didn't notice anyone watching the entrance. He knocked on the front door, keeping a close eye on anyone and everything, seeing nothing out of place in the bustling commercial district.

A handsome, middle-aged man with a full head of blond hair opened the door. Behind the door Grey saw a sitting room slick with modern furniture.

The man's accent was posh. "Can I help you?"

"Hey, man," Grey said, "is this the Order of New Enlightenment?"

"Indeed it is. I'm Director Thomas Greene."

"Yeah?" Grey said. "I wasn't expecting a director."

"This isn't normal hours, but our door is always open."

"Yeah, man, I've been hearing good things about this New Order thing, saw the sign outside and thought I'd check it out."

"Let me get you a pamphlet." Thomas disappeared, and while he was gone Grey spied a stack of mail on a table just inside the door. He quickly flipped through the mail, seeing a copy of the *Times*, a few items that looked like bills, and an envelope addressed to Director Thomas Greene from a company called Central London Staffing Agency on Inner Ring Road. It was the end of the month, and Grey had a hunch about the contents of the envelope. He pocketed it just before Thomas returned to hand Grey the same pamphlet Alan had given him.

"Services are Saturdays at ten," Thomas said, "but they're held in our auditorium down the street, just behind the bus stop. This is the chapter house."

Grey ran a hand through his fake locks and gave Thomas a knowing look. "Where the bigwigs are."

Thomas chuckled and said, "I'm just a director. The, ah, 'bigwigs' are a few steps above me."

"I heard this was a regular-Joe kind of thing, no more rules and bishops and popes, if you know what I mean. How many steps are there?"

"I meant steps in a strictly intellectual sense. While we reject the frivolous hierarchy inherent to today's religions, we do believe the tenets of our system are best digested over time, with wisdom. You can think of it as learning algebra before you learn calculus."

Grey thought, *I've heard your analogy parroted before, and it sucked when the last guy said it.* "I've seen the head guy on YouTube and I gotta say," Grey said, "I like what he says. But I thought it was a universal kind of organization. No more secrets."

"I must be doing a poor job of conveying what we're about. We're not trying to keep people out, but advancing each person as they're ready." Thomas spread his hands. "Trust me, there're no secrets to be kept here."

Grey found that whenever someone asked to be trusted, he probably wasn't trustworthy. And what he wanted to say was, *I suppose that's why your leader's keeping the location of his headquarters secret and pretending he's not a Satanist?*

"You know," Grey said, "you remind me of the guy on TV, real polished. I bet you're on the fast track. Out of curiosity, how many levels are there between you and the big man? Are you like, say, a governor? Bishop? Prez?"

Thomas chuckled again, this time with a slight edge. "The people who report to the council contact me. I assume they report to Simon."

"What's he like in person?" Grey said.

"Simon?"

"Yeah."

"Couldn't say. I've never met him, though I hope to change that once the new headquarters are functional."

"I'm dying to see where these headquarters are going to be," Grey said.

"Me, too. No one knows outside of the council."

"You're pretty close, right?" Grey said. "A million followers, isn't that the goal?"

"We're within fifty thousand, if you can believe it."

"Hey, maybe I'll be the millionth! Is there a special prize or anything?"

Thomas brightened. "That's not a bad idea. Maybe I'll raise it at the next meeting."

Grey had already decided Thomas didn't know much of anything, and that he was going to have to find a way to jump a few levels.

His fingers closed around the envelope in his pocket. He might have just the thing.

"Why don't you come by on Saturday?" Thomas said. "I usually stay after the service and answer questions." He beamed a smile. "No dress code required."

"I like the sound of that already."

Thomas held the door for Grey. "Cheers, then."

"Cheers."

# THE DIABOLIST

After Grey merged into the chaos of Earls Court he opened the envelope he had lifted. When he saw the paycheck, confirming his suspicions, he beamed a grim smile of his own.

Paychecks were paper, and paper left trails.

Grey walked to Kensington High Street before finding a café tucked into a shopping center. He sat in a corner with a view of the street, knocked back an espresso, and took another look at the return address on the paycheck: Central London Staffing Company, Suite 550, Inner Ring Road, London, WC1X 8VH.

He knew Inner Ring Road was a major road encircling central London, thus the name, so that didn't narrow it down much. He entered the zip code into his smartphone and discovered the address was in King's Cross. King's Cross was the gateway to East London, and Grey was getting the feeling that East London played an important role in Darius's plans.

It made sense: East London was notorious for housing London's roughest neighborhoods, yet it was also home to revitalization projects, one of the few areas of the city where property was semiaffordable.

Of course, East London was about the size of Houston.

After his coffee, Grey took a taxi to King's Cross and then to the address on Ring Road, which turned out to be a mailing store. Grey stepped inside the store, his suspicions confirmed as soon as he saw the wall lined with numbered metal containers.

Suite 550 was a PO box.

"Central London Staffing Agency" was clearly a front, and Grey had to hope someone made daily pick-ups. The Order of New Enlightenment was a large organization now, so it was a possibility, and could short-circuit his search. On the other hand, the Order might use the PO box only as a return address for paychecks.

He supposed there was only one way to find out.

Luckily, a street window afforded a view of PO box 550. Unluckily, there was no café or bar across the street, just a ragged park. Grey found a bench with a view of the window, concealed enough that no one would spot him unless they entered the park.

It was almost noon, and the store closed at eight. Masses of charcoal cloud banks governed the sky, and by four p.m. no one had approached the PO box. Grey rose to shake out his legs. At four thirty p.m. his cell rang.

His forehead wrinkled when he saw the long exchange, coming from somewhere outside England. Then he picked out Romania's country code, and realized Rick Laskin must be returning Grey's voice mail asking him to look into Anka's background.

He rose to take the call. "Rick?"

"It's been a while, buddy. How the hell are you?"

"Older," Grey said.

"I hear that. You know you're a bit of a legend around the DS water cooler."

"I'm guessing of the infamous variety," Grey said.

"Depends on who you talk to. The top brass use you as an example of what not to do, Harris and his middle-management cronies hate your guts, but most of the grunts like me, especially the old SF types, respect the hell out of you. Of course it helps you're a badass, or else you'd just be a whiny dissident."

"I don't think that counts for much of anything."

"You wouldn't," Rick said.

"How's the posting?" Grey said.

"Romania's beautiful. Bucharest, on the other hand, is dirty, poor, corrupt, and full of stray dogs and prostitutes. A real shame what Ceaușescu did to this place, Commie asshole. They say it used to look like Paris."

"How much you have left on your rotation?"

"Year and a half," Rick said. "I'm hoping for ASPAC next, or even a banana republic, to be honest with you. I'm sick of being cold."

"I'm not that partial to it, either," Grey said.

# THE DIABOLIST

"So what're you up to these days? Rumor is you're hooked up with some international PI outfit, investigating cults or something like that? That true?"

"Pretty much," Grey said.

"Gotta say, I never figured you for that sort of thing."

"Me, either."

"Probably doubled your pay, didn't you?" Rick said.

"Pretty much."

"Slick bastard. For double the pay, I'd investigate gypsy carnies for a living."

"You're a patriot with a family, Rick. Stay where you are. The pension alone's worth it."

He grunted. "Yeah, probably right. Carnie healthcare might suck. I do miss the action, though."

"You miss it until it kills you," Grey said.

"Yeah, well, I miss you, too, buddy. Our own little Buddha. So listen, I checked out that girl."

Grey felt a fluttering in his chest. "I appreciate that."

"It took a few phone calls, but I found her. I hope this helps you in one of your cases, because I gotta tell you, it was a bit creepy."

Grey uncrossed his legs and held the phone tighter. "What do you mean?"

"I called the British-run convents in Bucharest—there aren't that many—and found one that knew what I was talking about. Your girl's roughly twenty-eight years old now. She was picked up off the street as a child by one of their nuns, like the rest of them." He paused. "You failed to mention she was kicked out of the convent for worshipping the Devil."

Grey grimaced but didn't respond.

"The nun said every now and then she appeared in different places around the convent from where her body was, called it astral projecting or something and said it was a power of the Devil. You know anything about that?"

"Not much," Grey mumbled. He felt a mixture of emotion at the news, sadness at the petty ignorance of mankind and for Anka's terrible childhood, relief her story had checked out, and unease at the fact that she might not have been physically present when she appeared to him on the plane and in the catacombs.

"As you can imagine, the Church looked on that very poorly," Rick said. "I was raised Baptist, so I can't say I disagree all that much."

"Did the nun say anything else?"

"Not really, except that Anka brought it on herself."

"What?" Grey said.

"Said she was into the occult before this astral projecting started happening. And that when you invite the Devil in, he usually comes."

# 41

Viktor spent the next day pacing the hotel. The air outside, pregnant with an approaching front, crackled with energy. The impending midnight rendezvous with Gareth was a tangible thing, present with Viktor no matter where he went, swirling in his morning cappuccino, hovering behind him as he paced.

Viktor begged Gareth to let him spend the day with him and help prepare the chamber. Like most magicians of his stature, Gareth was bright but arrogant, stuffed full of perceived power. Letting a nonbeliever such as Viktor assist with the magical defenses was unthinkable. He did, however, consent to Viktor's practical suggestions.

The day passed without event, and at ten thirty p.m. Viktor taxied the few blocks to Stonegate. The mood was grim as Viktor made his way to Gareth's chambers, the magicians in the building clad in full defensive regalia, busy in preparation. Freshly painted runes filled the doors and passageways, a fine golden powder covered the steps of the winding staircase. At least the powder had a sensible purpose, Viktor thought, noticing the imprint of his shoes as he passed.

Viktor wanted to throttle these people, these poor souls who were so desperate to believe in magic that they dressed like fools and behaved like jesters. And tonight, unless Viktor could do something about it, their misguided beliefs were going to result in a very non-magical death.

At the other end of the hallway, Viktor was pleased to see an armed security guard standing beside the door to Gareth's suite. At least the old fool had a modicum of sense.

"Professor Radek," the guard said, inclining his head as he opened the door. Gareth strode to clasp Viktor's hand, white robes rustling. Viktor set down the square black box he was carrying, then extracted two gas masks from his duffel bag, handing one to Gareth.

"You did as I asked?" Viktor said.

Gareth pointed to a fire extinguisher in the far corner and to a small video camera attached to the wall above the extinguisher. "The vents are sealed, I handled my robe myself, and no one else is to enter the room. We have an armed guard and everyone is on high alert, watching all possible entrances and ready to assist as needed. And *no one* is powerful enough to avoid our magical defenses."

Viktor gave Gareth a withering look, then set the controls on the black box as instructed by the vendor. "This device detects sulfuryl fluoride, in case Vikane gas is the weapon of choice. Regardless, to be safe we should leave the room within minutes of midnight."

"He won't use gas tonight," Gareth said. "He'll come himself. Or try."

"We shall see."

Viktor folded his arms and checked his watch. Fifteen minutes until midnight. He felt the hilt of his knife resting in a special pocket of his coat, and in another pocket was a Taser, adjusted to the most powerful setting.

Gareth closed the door, then extracted a jar from his robe and splashed the door with the contents. He performed a series of hand movements Viktor didn't recognize, took out an ornamental dagger, and carved a seven-pointed star into the wooden door. He pricked his arm, and with the bloody knife carved a circle connecting the tips of the heptagram. "It's sealed."

Viktor was busy inspecting the room, probing the floor for loose boards, checking the spherical walls for cracks, uneven surfaces, and secret entrances. Satisfied the room was secure, he joined Gareth in tense silence for the remaining minutes. Gareth rested his hands on his golden sash as Viktor's eyes continued roaming the chamber.

Viktor had to admit he was satisfied. They had the poison gas angle covered, the defenses against fire in place. He didn't think Darius himself had been present for any of the murders, but regardless, as far as Viktor could tell, there was no way to enter the room undetected. And Viktor and an armed guard stood between Gareth and the only entrance.

From Viktor's vantage point, a last-minute entrance by Darius was an impossibility.

The alarm on Viktor's phone chimed at midnight, startling them both. Nothing happened, and Viktor congratulated himself on a job well done. Apparently Darius had decided that tonight was not a good night for murder after all. The case was far from solved, but tonight, at least, a life had been spared.

It was amazing, Viktor thought, how easily the veil of superstition could be cast aside with logic and attention to detail. His eyes moved to the ceiling and then the door, satisfied nothing was going to happen. When his gaze returned to the center of the room a black-clad figure was standing behind Gareth.

It happened so fast that Viktor reared in shock. The figure was just as witnesses had described, cloaked in a black robe, face enshrouded by a voluminous cowl. There was nothing shadowlike about the figure: It looked tangible, as present as Viktor or Gareth. Just as John Sebastian had claimed, silver stars adorned the robe. The hood obscured the face, but the figure was the same height as Darius, about six feet tall.

"Gareth," Viktor said evenly, "step forward and turn around."

Gareth spun, and a number of things happened at once. Gareth shouted and raised his hands in defense when he saw the figure. When he cried out, the door behind Viktor swung open, and Viktor turned to see the security guard rushing inside, both hands clutching his gun. As the guard rushed past Viktor to get an angle for his shot, Gareth burst into flames.

Viktor roared and moved to help Gareth, but the heat was so intense he had to back away, hands shielding his face. Gareth's compact body became a pillar of flame, blazing as if soaked in lighter fluid and set alight with a blowtorch.

Viktor ran for the fire extinguisher as Gareth screamed and struggled to remove his robes. As Viktor jerked the fire extinguisher off the wall, he smelled the nauseating stench of burning flesh and saw bits of Gareth's hair and beard falling to the ground in charred clumps. Flames licked at the security guard's clothing as well. He dropped the gun and rolled to smother the flames.

"Ah, Viktor," the figure said, and all doubt in Viktor's mind as to his identity was erased as Darius's once-familiar voice resonated from underneath the hood. "Still the nonbeliever, I see."

Viktor ran towards Gareth with the fire extinguisher. "What have you done?"

"I'll see you soon, old friend," the figure said.

Out of the corner of his eye Viktor noticed the security guard scrambling to his feet. A shot rang out as the figure disappeared, winking out of existence as abruptly as it had arrived. The shot shattered the wall right behind where the figure had been. The whole exchange had taken seconds.

"Call for emergency!" Viktor shouted. He sprayed Gareth until the flames died, though a terrible amount of damage had been done. He could only watch in horror as Gareth's skin continued to crackle and bubble off his body, his crumpled form convulsing in shock until the paramedics rushed him away.

Viktor rode with a caravan of Gareth's followers to the hospital, waiting with folded arms as the families of the other patients tried to avert their eyes from the group of oddly garbed magicians swarming the lobby. Hours later a solemn-faced doctor informed them that Gareth had died from organ failure.

# THE DIABOLIST

Viktor escaped the constable's questioning by invoking his Interpol status, promising to report to the station in the morning. He returned to his hotel in a state of shock, trying to sort through his muddled thoughts, unsure if the absinthe would hurt or help that cause, and not giving a damn either way.

He prepared the emerald liquid with shaky hands, still processing Gareth's death and the appearance of the figure with the voice of Darius Ghassomian, both of those events far more troubling to Viktor than the details of whatever slick illusion Darius had used to deceive him.

The confirmed involvement of Darius magnified everything, gave the crimes a personal connection, a gravitas of familiarity that rattled him more than any of the previous atrocities he had witnessed during the course of his career. The psychotics, lunatics, and cult leaders he investigated were always a thing apart, their freakish genesis in society someone else's cross to bear.

Until now.

The first glass was finished before he left the suite's mini-kitchen, the second prepared and in hand as he entered the sitting room. He shrugged out of his suit coat, took off his tie and unbuttoned his collar, then rolled up the sleeves on his starched dress shirt. He sank into the leather couch and moved to set his glass on the coffee table.

Then he saw it.

He had the sensation of the hair on the back on his neck rising, as if he had hackles. His hand stopped halfway to the table, glass in midair. A sight came to him unbidden, Gareth's body on the stretcher as it entered the hospital, bandages swaddling the ruined body.

Before he reached for the thing on the table, he forced himself to remember who he was and where he had been, the hundreds of investigations that had preceded this one. It was just another case, another violent megalomaniac to be put behind bars.

Lips compressed, he reached for the envelope sealed with red wax, his eyes fixated on the single word handwritten in black ink on the envelope.

*NONBELIEVER*

Like he imagined Gareth and the others had done, Viktor extracted the single piece of paper and read the words, also scrawled in black ink, below his own name.

*Viktor Radek,*

*You, NONBELIEVER, shall acknowledge the power of Ahriman in a public forum, or you will die at the hand of the one true God on the third midnight hence.*

By eight p.m., Grey was beginning to question the wisdom of his decision to wait for a courier to visit PO Box 550. By midnight, he was questioning his decision, despondent, and freezing.

Although the mail store closed at eight, Grey discovered that key holders had twenty-four-hour access to the section by the front door. He knew the second he left his post he would miss someone who could lead him to the next step in the puzzle. So he could put up with the lack of sleep, the incessant drizzle, the gnawing hunger.

What bothered him was that he might be wrong. He had already lost too much time. He hunched under the umbrella he had bought off a passing street vendor, resolving to wait it out until noon the next day.

The minutes crept by. When Grey checked his watch again it was three a.m. The Devil's Hour, according to Viktor, so named because it was a mockery of three p.m., the hour when Jesus was supposed to have died on the cross. Despite himself, Grey shivered in the frigid damp, and not just from the rain and fog smoldering in the neon streetlights.

While Grey's rational mind might propound that the Devil didn't exist, the concept of an evil entity that had been with him from his earliest memories, a force of darkness at odds with God and humanity, was tough to shake.

Especially when huddled on a bench at three a.m. on a deserted street in East London, thinking of a beautiful girl with paranormal abilities who had rescued him in the catacombs beneath Paris from a bloodthirsty pack of Satanists and their demonic magus leader.

The Devil's Hour passed without incident, as did the two that followed. At six a.m. Grey's cell rang. Numb from cold, he rubbed his hands together before taking Viktor's call. He had been waiting anxiously to hear what happened with Gareth, having tried to call Viktor numerous times since midnight.

"I've been worried," Grey said.

"With good cause. Brace yourself, because the news isn't pleasant."

Viktor sounded rattled, which at once put Grey on his guard. Viktor didn't rattle. Grey could also tell, though Viktor hid it well, that he had drunk too much absinthe.

Viktor's addiction had never been a problem with Grey, as he always kept it under control, or at least appeared to. Some men could handle addiction, some couldn't. Grey wasn't one to interfere with another man's demons, but it was six in the morning.

Grey said, "I take it you haven't slept?"

Viktor was quiet for a moment, and Grey knew that he got the hint. Viktor was his friend, and Grey would spend as much time as needed talking through his issues when the time was right. But at the moment, if they were to have a chance to get through this case, he needed Viktor clear-headed and at the top of his game.

"Not yet," Viktor said, his voice more in control.

"Me, either."

Grey listened to Viktor's recounting of the past two days, feeling the color drain from his face when Viktor told him of the appearance of the robed figure and of Gareth's immolation.

"Jesus," Grey said.

"It's not the Darius I once knew. I know that sounds clichéd, that we all change with time, but there was something in his voice . . . something different."

"It's harder to deal with when it's your old college buddy."

"Yes," Viktor said quietly. "He's more brazen than I would ever have imagined."

"What'd the video show?" Grey said.

"The camera showed the appearance of a black-robed figure, or the illusion thereof. Unfortunately the camera was positioned behind the figure, and Gareth isn't visible once the figure appears."

"They knew where the camera was," Grey said. "Then what?"

"The cause of the fire is impossible to determine from the angle of the camera, though it appeared to start at the cuffs of the robes, and explode from there. *Do prdele*, I should have insisted on another camera."

"The robes must have been tampered with, some accelerant applied. Can we rule out the security guard?"

"Absolutely not," Viktor said. "He disobeyed strict orders not to intervene."

"His boss was being burned alive and screaming for help. You can hardly blame the guy."

Viktor was quiet.

"If he caught some of the flames as well," Grey said, "but didn't burn like Gareth, that reinforces our theory of an accelerant."

"It's not a theory," Viktor said.

"Just take it easy," Grey said. "We'll get him."

"I don't understand . . . I canvassed that room. But Darius was brilliant, perhaps the most intelligent person I've ever known. And he's an illusionist as well as a chemist."

"You don't have to convince me it's some kind of trick," Grey said. "Even if you subscribe to this three powers of the Devil nonsense, fire isn't one of the three."

"Precisely."

"So what's next? Are you coming to London?"

"Not yet," Viktor said. "There have been other developments."

"Such as?"

"Two more letters have been delivered. One of them was to me."

Grey cursed and pushed away from the bench. "When?"

"In my hotel, when I returned from the emergency room. I've no idea how it got there."

"The same thing?" Grey said. "Six days?"

"Three. And there were other differences, principally that I was called a nonbeliever rather than a heretic."

"Three days," Grey said. "Come to London. He's here somewhere, I can feel it."

"I trust you, Grey. Keep working the angle you're investigating, knowing that time is even more of the essence. I spoke to Jacques, and he'll relay any information from the forthcoming investigation."

"And you?"

"We must understand where he went and why," Viktor said. "I know I'm getting closer."

"What does it matter, now that he has the grimoire?"

"We don't know that he has the grimoire, just that he was pursuing it. He might be pretending to have the grimoire to gain influence over L'église de la Bête. Devious and not unlike him. If I can find it first, it would destroy his reputation."

"And if he already has it?" Grey said.

"Whether or not he found the book, I firmly believe the details are paramount to stopping him: where he went, what happened along the way, what he plans to do with it. We must discern his motives and predict his next move before it occurs."

Grey frowned. That wasn't where he would have placed his chips. He thought Viktor would better serve their cause by coming to London. But Grey wasn't the boss, and Viktor was rarely wrong.

"So what's next?"

"I leave for Palermo at noon," Viktor said. "Regardless of what happens, you have my word I'll rejoin you in three days."

"Let's hope so," Grey said. "You mentioned a second letter. Who was it to?"

"The pope."

# 43

When the computer shut down, ending the live feed, Darius reached for a glass of water. His daily regimen of broadcasts and magical preparation had been exhausting, not to mention handling the day-to-day workings of both the Order and the various other organizations over which he now presided. He had barely slept in a week.

But the final push had been made. He checked the number, hoping his calculations had been correct.

They had. In the last hour, the Order of New Enlightenment had topped one million online followers. A rush of excitement coursed through his body, followed by one of pride.

He had done it. The new religion was thriving, or rather an old one that was three thousand years overdue, one that was going to turn the world on its head. The growth of subscribers had been exponential, far faster than he had anticipated.

And this was just the beginning, confirming what he already knew: The need was great; his God was real; the time had come.

He would show the world that everything they thought they knew about God, about religion, was out of balance, wrong. Backwards.

*Evil? Good?* How did those terms apply to this world? Had anyone bothered to look around? Had anyone read the Book of Job?

Tonight he would make the announcement that ten days hence, he would throw wide the doors to the Order of New Enlightenment.

Ten days: seven days after the Unveiling, seven being representative of the invisible center, the spirit of all things that would reside in his temple of power and spread throughout the world.

After all these years, the countless hours studying and planning and searching, his moment had come. When the biggest domino of them all fell, Simon Azar would emerge from the resultant vacuum as the voice of reason for the world. And once his place at the top of Babylon was secure, Darius would show the world what real power was, what a *concerned* God could do. His towers of silence would pierce the clouds, his corpse bearers would fling the nonbelievers into canyons, rattling the earth with their screams.

It was time for a new age.

As he lingered, Darius admired the media room. His Internet connection was secured by the highest technology money could buy. The Russian hacker Darius had bought, a wanted man in three countries, had proved his mettle by hacking into the U.S. Department of Defense.

After slipping into his robe, Darius entered the six-sided antechamber, where four of the five other members of the Inner Council awaited. Darius took his place in the ebony armchair on the raised dais. Dante and Luc Morel-Renard sat to his right, two men whose loyalty he would never have to question. Dante relished his work, and Luc owed his political future to Darius.

The seats to Darius's left caused him more grief. Oak was a necessary evil, critical to the North American power base. He didn't worry about Oak's straying from the path; he worried about his stupidity. When the time was right, and that time was soon, he would be replaced.

To the left of Oak sat Alec Lister, newly appointed leader of the Clerics of Whitehall, another key figure. Alec granted Darius access to an elite sector of British society, one full of depraved and cruel patriarchs. Darius knew Alec was the least loyal of the Inner Council, and so far Darius had kept him in check by appealing to his monstrous carnal appetite. Moreover, unbeknownst to Alec, Darius had gathered evidence of Alec's proclivity for underage consorts.

# THE DIABOLIST

Darius looked at the seat across the room, the empty chair, and his stomach contracted.

*Eve, oh my Eve. Will you watch from afar as Viktor becomes a blackened corpse at my feet, pride stripped before the fall, his soul shucked and left to roam the ether? A discarded spirit pleading in vain for help from the gods in whom he never believed?*

As Darius's eyes drifted among the illusory stars of the chamber, he felt as if were sitting atop the galaxy. He saw the mysteries of the universe, of which there were many, spiraling from above, beckoning to the lost souls trapped within.

His thoughts returned to terrestrial matters, to the tiered flooring and ample spacing the architect had left between the oversize chairs, such that two more circles of six could fit within the original circle. When the time was right, Darius would expand to the proper number. The rest would be chosen for their influence, geography, and devotion, and he already had a few in mind: the leader of a heretical group of Sunnis, a Chinese billionaire, a devoted priest of Kali who commanded vast influence in the Mumbai underworld.

His lieutenants had gathered this evening because they were about to sample the event that would precipitate the Unveiling. Each was on the edge of his seat, eager to see what Darius's genius would reveal.

Darius's index finger depressed a button on the side of his chair. A section of the wall retracted, and moments later the members of the Inner Council gasped, the images on the giant projector laid bare before them.

Soon, very soon indeed, the entire world would see.

# 44

**G**rey huddled on the bench, the cell phone cold on his ear. "He's raised the stakes."

"The letter was found this morning in the chambers of His Holiness," Viktor said. "Jacques informed me just before I called you."

"Killing Satanist leaders is one thing, the pope another," Grey said. "He'll have half of Western civilization hunting him."

"It might not be another murder. As with mine, the language was different. This one read: "'You will renounce your religion and acknowledge the power of Ahriman, or the hypocrisy of your Church will be revealed at the hand of the one true God on the third midnight hence.'"

"I assume the Vatican has extraordinary protective measures in place?"

"All of which I believe will be futile," Viktor said. "Not because Darius can reach the pope, but because he has something else planned."

"Something else what?"

"I've no idea. But Darius is a precise man, and he changed the language for a reason. A few things are beginning to make sense. How many victims are there in total?"

Grey ticked them off. "Matthias, Xavier, Ian, Gareth, and then the two potentials: the pope and you. That makes six."

"Numerology is very important to magicians, Satanists, and occultists. Six victims, four of whom were given six days to repent, two of whom were given three."

# THE DIABOLIST

"And?" Grey said.

"Six is important to occultists and magicians because it represents the soul of man. Six-six-six is of prime interest to Satanists for its mention in Revelations Thirteen as the number of the Beast, so named because it's the soul of man multiplied three times, acting outside the will of God, representative of mankind's pride."

"So why the three-day timeline for the final letters?"

"Generally," Viktor said, "the number six is emblematic of the forces of evil, the number three the forces of good. To name but a few of its symbological meanings, the number three represents the triangular third eye of Hindu origin, as well as the Trinity of Christendom and the three days that passed before the resurrection of Christ. Darius is speaking the language of his victims' followers."

Grey ran through the letters in his mind. "So he called out the four heretics on the dark side for not recognizing the 'one true God,' called you a nonbeliever, and told the pope to renounce his religion and acknowledge the power of Ahriman."

"I don't know how much of this Darius actually believes, and how much he uses for effect. What is clear is that with the involvement of the pope, the endgame is nigh. Darius nears a million followers, if not there already. He's consolidated his power base, and I assume he plans to unveil the location of his new church once he's provided a disruption to traditional religion, to maximize effect."

"Striking a blow against the most powerful church the world has ever known would classify as disruptive," Grey said.

Viktor let out a slow breath. "Indeed. Impacting the Catholic Church in a significant way could create a vacuum for the human soul not seen for centuries."

"It could also pave the way for a holy war, if the Ahriman ties get out."

"Perhaps," Viktor said, "though it need not be so dramatic. Darius could further his own agenda securely within the cloak of his feel-good religion."

"What I don't get is why he bothered with a letter to you," Grey said.

"Perhaps he thinks eliminating the world's foremost investigator of cults would be a nice touch, symbolic of his growing power. Or perhaps it's . . . merely personal. Or both."

"Maybe it's time you told me about these personal issues."

Viktor fell silent, and Grey didn't really expect an answer. He was surprised when, in a quiet voice, Viktor proceeded to tell Grey about Eve, their common past with Darius, the tragic ending. Though useful background information, Grey knew Viktor hadn't needed to tell him and sensed this was a catharsis of sorts.

"I'm sorry for your loss," Grey said softly.

"He blames me for what happened to Eve, and to be honest, so do I."

"Well, you're both wrong," Grey said.

When Viktor didn't respond Grey said, "You said you have no idea how he plans to 'reveal the hypocrisy of the church'?"

"Perhaps he's uncovered a text or an object in contradiction to scripture or church tradition, something that will shake the faith of millions. Whatever Darius plans to do, reactive measures will miss the mark. We must find him—and stop him—within the three-day deadline."

Grey returned the phone to his pocket as a halo of ashen morning light spread behind the clouds. With dawn came traffic and pedestrians, and his last gasp of hope for a courier. He performed a series of stretches and jujitsu techniques to loosen his stiff joints, keeping a close eye on anyone entering the mail store.

Grey felt the case slipping away. He sensed that not only were he and Viktor further than ever from finding answers but also that Darius was toying with them. Grey was standing in a cold London drizzle with a rapidly dwindling chance of finding a link to New Enlightenment headquarters, Viktor was about to trek to Sicily on what Grey considered a wild-goose chase, there was a hit out on Grey, and Viktor had just received a death threat giving him three days to live. Darius now controlled a vast network of Satanists and dangerous underworld types, the Order of New Enlightenment was growing leaps and bounds by the day, no one possessed a shred of evidence linking Darius to Simon or knew how to find him, they still had no idea how he managed to appear at the stroke of midnight and murder his victims, and their only potential lead was a terrified young woman with an incredible story.

Grey had a few other ideas on how to find the Order of New Enlightenment, namely tracking the money flow or trying to find a hacker to trace the Internet feeds. But those avenues would take time he didn't have, with no guarantee of success.

He could use himself as bait to try to find a member of Darius's organization who actually knew what the hell was going on, then do whatever it took to extract the information. That was a dangerous road, and one Grey didn't want to go down unless he had to. He was also realizing that Darius's inner circle was even smaller and tighter than suspected.

There was one person, however, who Grey thought might lead him to Darius, if he could find him.

Dante.

Grey had never met him, but he had the feeling the two of them were on a collision course that one of them would not survive.

Midmorning came and went. Grey slumped on the bench, staring at the window with heavy-lidded eyes. He could almost feel a hot shower, and would have given half his worldly possessions for a steaming cup of coffee and a full English breakfast.

He checked his watch yet again. Ten thirty a.m.

By ten forty-five he was performing breathing exercises to stay alert, and at eleven the rain picked up, turning a miserable wait into full-on torment. At eleven thirty a small East Indian man in a beige raincoat and a backpack entered the store and stood in front of PO box 550.

At first Grey thought he would open one of the adjacent boxes, but then he inserted the key into box 550, the exact position of which Grey had memorized.

Adrenaline jolted Grey awake. He watched the man hover over the PO box, extract a stack of envelopes, then stick a bundle of mail from his backpack into the box. After making his drop, the man exited the building and headed up the street, huddled under his raincoat.

Grey followed.

## 45

## SICILY

Viktor's plane landed amid the craggy parched hills outside Palermo. He thought it quite appropriate his journey had taken him to Sicily, a place whose constant exposure to the light hid the rot underneath, leaving the casual visitor with a taste of sun-kissed vineyards and bucolic mountain villages, rather than economic inequity, government corruption, and the bitter aftertaste of a culture ravaged by organized crime.

Just, he thought, like Darius's cult.

The driver he had organized before leaving York, an angular, gray-haired Sicilian with a lined but handsome face, met him at the gate. A rush of sweltering dry air blasted them as they walked to the black Mercedes. Viktor could hardly believe the drastic change in climate.

It had been some time since Viktor had visited Sicily. A decade ago he had investigated the ritual murder of a church official in Palermo, which turned out to be a Mafia cover-up. And as a child, his parents had taken him to Taormina, a beautiful seaside resort at the foot of Mount Etna. But that was another lifetime.

Soon they were racing through the hills outside the airport and then merging into the outskirts of Palermo, a chaotic sprawl of dilapidated apartment buildings and traffic-choked streets. Impromptu trash dumps lined the freeway into town.

As requested, the driver had left a small package for Viktor in the backseat. Viktor eyed the package greedily, eager for the shiny liquid within. He had caught a few hours sleep on the plane, but he was still exhausted and feeling the effects of the absinthe from the previous evening.

He knew he was walking a dangerous line, especially with a mere three days to accomplish impossible tasks. The call with Grey had shamed him. He respected Grey, and he knew Grey had heard the tremor in his voice, both from the absinthe and the specter of his past.

As they passed through the city center, Viktor lowered the window to clear his head and was assaulted by the sound of honking horns, shouting vendors, and the whine of mopeds speeding between lanes. He rolled up the window when the driver cut through an alley, the pleasant aromas from street vendors supplanted by the nauseating stench of cat urine.

When the traffic ground to a halt the driver jumped the curb and whipped through a maze of narrow streets filled with overhanging laundry and shirtless men leaning on balconies. They charged through a square defined by a gleaming *enoteca* built into the graffiti-strewn ruins of a castle, and then through block after block of cement high-rises, sooty with neglect.

On the other side of the city the SUV careened back on to the highway, climbing high into the hills and following the road east along the cliffs. As civilization faded and the dry sea air rushed in, Viktor felt as if he had stepped back in time, before machines and factories had gobbled up the world, lost in a perfect union of sunlight, water and rich brown earth.

Viktor imagined Aleister Crowley traveling this same road long ago, on his way to establish his infamous Abbey of Thelema. Viktor had debated stopping in the Palazzo dei Normanni in Palermo, as it was the last place the Tutori had been mentioned. Given the three-day timeline that hung with Viktor like a circling vulture, claws extended, he decided to press on to Cefalù, reasoning that Crowley had done the legwork in Palermo for him. And he had already inquired about the Tutori with various sources at the Palazzo dei Normanni. No one had heard of either the Tutori or the Ahriman Heresy.

They crested a slope and Viktor saw the famous rock of Cefalù glowering in the distance like a titan from Greek mythology, a mammoth block of limestone that Viktor thought a fitting testament to Crowley's ego.

# THE DIABOLIST

The rock, which the driver said was known simply as La Rocca, jutted high above the velvety sea, the sheer cliffs topped by the ruins of a Moorish castle. The medieval town of Cefalù nestled at the feet of La Rocca, capped by the twin sandstone towers of the Duomo, under a sky so deep blue it looked bruised.

A place of surreal and isolated beauty, set amid a notoriously tight-lipped and lawless society. Viktor could see why Crowley had chosen it.

The Abbey of Thelema: Crowley's very own school of magic, a cesspool of sex, drugs, and occult experimentation that gave rise to Crowley's dubbing as the Wickedest Man in the World. The infamous abbey lasted until 1923, when one of Crowley's adepts died after drinking cat's blood consumed during a sacrifice. After a public outcry Mussolini closed the abbey, forcing Crowley to leave the country.

Despite the location, had Crowley come halfway across the world to Cefalù, a virtual lost world in 1920, merely to establish his school? More likely, Viktor thought, Crowley had the dual objective of using Cefalù as a research base to pursue the mythical Ahriman Grimoire.

So where had the Tutori gone? Had they disbanded, returned to Rome, settled in Palermo? If they had acquired the Ahriman Grimoire, what had they done with it? The obvious choice was that they had sent it to the Vatican's secret archives, but if that were the case, then Viktor didn't see how Darius would have acquired it, if he indeed had.

And why lead Viktor down this path? Viktor knew he was being toyed with, but Viktor had learned to trust his instincts, and his instincts told him there was something on this journey he needed to find, some important piece of knowledge to be gained.

The problem was, not all of his instincts concerned solving cases.

Viktor had just enough time to drop his bags and make his two p.m. appointment with Scarlet Alexander, Magister Templi of the Cefalù chapter of the Thelema Lodge. The rise of occultism in the last few decades had ignited a recent interest in Crowley, and a modern-day derivation of the Order of Thelema had sprung up in Cefalù, to the consternation of the locals.

According to Gareth, who had arranged the appointment for Viktor in the hours before he was burned, Scarlet Alexander possessed more knowledge on Aleister Crowley than anyone else alive.

After a brisk stop in the villa Viktor had rented he made the short walk to the medieval town center, dodging scooters as sweat poured down his collar. He zigzagged through the constricted cobblestone streets, church bells clanging in the background, relishing the pungent smell of fresh sardines heaped onto the trays of street vendors, catching glimpses of the sea down alleyways thick with hanging laundry.

He found the designated trattoria on Corso Ruggiero, the main thoroughfare lined with gas lamps and wrought iron balconies, shade from the handsome marble and stone buildings providing relief from the sun.

The restaurant was a rustic gem in the Piazza del Duomo. A few courtyard tables and palm trees were sprinkled around a fountain, a grapevine thick as Viktor's forearm snaked across a trellis, and he had views of both the honey-colored Duomo and La Rocca looming overhead.

Viktor normally would have relished a seven-course lunch of Sicilian culinary perfection, but instead he ordered a glass of Nero D'Avola to calm his nerves, and a simple pasta *con le sarde* for fuel. Halfway through his meal, Scarlet Alexander arrived in a green silk dress, her brown wrists covered in bracelets, a necklace studded with multicolored crystals draping her slender neck.

Viktor's brief research had disclosed that Scarlet was an African-American woman from Los Angeles, a former professor of sociology at UCLA, and a member of the Thelema Lodge since the late seventies. She didn't look a day older than forty, but Viktor knew she must be nearing sixty.

Viktor rose to greet her after she addressed the host in flawless Italian. They sat, and Viktor pushed his plate to the side. "Forgive my manners. I'm rather pressed for time."

She waved a hand in dismissal. "I was going to apologize because I can't stay long." Her eyes clouded. "I assume you've heard about Gareth?"

"I was in the room."

A spasm of fear twitched her face. "Dear God. It must've been terrible."

"It was."

She took a moment to compose herself. "Gareth was my mentor for a brief period when I was an adept," she said. "A wise man. A good man."

"He said the same of you. He thought you might be able to help me with a bit of research on Aleister."

The waiter brought Scarlet a glass of sparkling water. "I can try," she said.

"How much do you know of Crowley's quest for the Ahriman Grimoire?"

She hesitated for the briefest of moments, a reaction that spoke volumes. "I don't believe I've ever heard of that grimoire."

"It's come to my attention that not only was Aleister in pursuit of this grimoire, but that he might have devoted a significant portion of his life in pursuit of it."

She scoffed. "I'm very familiar with his life. Where did you get this information?"

"From a number of sources, including Aleister's personal copy of *The Ahriman Heresy*, which I found among his possessions in Whitby."

She dabbed at her mouth with a napkin. "It appears your scholarship exceeds mine."

"I doubt that. Gareth mentioned you're the world's foremost expert on Crowley."

Her bracelets tinkled as she raised her wrist to check the time. "It appears not."

Viktor folded his arms and met her gaze, the gurgle of the fountain drowning out the street noise. She seemed a strong and intelligent woman, but she had been compromised. Viktor couldn't blame her for not talking, but more lives than their own depended on the information he needed.

"Are you familiar with the Tutori?"

She gave him a puzzled look. "It's Italian for—"

"I'm aware of the Italian meaning, as well as the Latin. The Tutori were also a small group of priests tasked by the Vatican with flushing out the members of the Ahriman Heresy."

"I'm truly sorry," she said, "I don't have any idea what you're talking about."

She started to push her chair back, and Viktor caught her wrist. "Please. Just another moment of your time."

She swallowed and sank back down. "A moment."

"Is there anyone in Cefalù who was intimate with the original Order?" Viktor said.

"That was ninety years ago."

"Perhaps a descendant of someone with personal knowledge of Crowley?"

"There was one," she said, "living in a retirement home outside Palermo. His mother was one of Crowley's adepts. We were friends."

"Was?"

"He died recently." She looked Viktor in the eye. "In a fire."

His lips compressed. "I see."

"To my knowledge, there's no one else in Sicily connected to the original Order. After Mussolini ordered them off the island, it wasn't very healthy to admit to an association with Thelema."

"I understand the Lodge still stands, now as a private villa."

"It's less than a mile from here," she said. "I can assure you the owner has no interest in magic, and no ties to the villa's past."

Viktor signaled for two espressos, then said, "Darius was here, wasn't he?"

The question caught her off guard. She recovered quickly, again asserting her ignorance, but Viktor knew he had hit a nerve.

"I understand your reluctance," he said. "He's a very dangerous individual. But he's corrupted your art and is a defiler of people."

"Magic corrupts, but cannot itself be corrupted. You'd be wise to remember that."

# THE DIABOLIST

Viktor leaned forward. "This has nothing to do with magic. He killed Gareth, he killed your friend, and he'll continue killing until someone stops him."

She downed her espresso, dropped her napkin on the table, and rose. "Then you should be talking to the Italian police, not me. A pleasure meeting you, Viktor."

She left the courtyard, and Viktor resisted the urge to bang his fist on the table. He asked for the check, acutely aware that his options were melting away like gelato in the midday sun. As he took the bill, his eyes caught the side of Scarlet's napkin, which she had dropped in the center of the table instead of in her chair.

She had written something in pencil on a fold of the napkin, in a tight feminine scrawl.

*84 Corso Montera, Sant'Ambroggio.*

Viktor wet his finger and smeared the address on the napkin. He paid double the bill, unwilling to wait for change.

# 46

**G**rey followed the courier to three more mail stores within walking distance, then sixteen more across east-central London. For the most part the small man kept his head down and did his job, and Grey had an easy time tracking him. But after twenty stops in just a few hours, Grey wondered how many were on the full route.

How far did the reach of the Order of New Enlightenment already extend?

Though he had kept his wig, Grey's larger worry was that one of Dante's hired thugs would spot him among the crowds. At least the incessant rain allowed him to shrink into his waterproof jacket.

Midday came and went without trouble, but as evening approached, a few things gave Grey cause for concern: The cessation of the rain left Grey more exposed, the courier had stopped delivering envelopes, and Grey was now following him on the London Overground deeper into the East End.

At Dalston Junction the courier picked up a bus heading southeast. Grey took a seat near the driver, where he could keep an eye on the courier in the rearview and not arouse suspicion. The courier had his head buried in a newspaper, and Grey kept one eye on the courier and one on his surroundings.

As the bus wound through Hackney Central, the streets reverted to the warren of brick alleys Grey remembered, damp and crowded. A swarm of downtrodden white faces filled the streets, mingling with hijab- and burka-clad immigrants. Pawn and kebab shops lined the larger thoroughfares, along with a shocking amount of drab public housing. The nonpublic housing consisted of decrepit Victorians with front doors set ten feet apart, crowding out the sunlight in true Dickensian fashion.

Fifteen minutes later Grey began to worry. The crowd on the bus had thinned considerably, and he knew the environs only got worse the farther south or east they went, until they hit Canary Wharf.

Before they reached the Docklands, the courier exited on a potholed street running alongside a canal lined with warehouses, most of them graffiti-covered and abandoned. Grey asked the driver to let him off a block down the road, then hurried back to find the courier, spying him at the end of the street.

Grey stayed half a block behind as they paralleled the swampy canal. The courier kept his head down and maintained a fast clip. Grey suspected he was returning home. If so, Grey would have to make a decision. He couldn't afford another half-day wait while the courier caught up on sleep.

A few high-rises appeared in the distance, and Grey guessed they were finally nearing the Docklands. Then he saw a strange sight: a beautiful cylindrical glass building, five stories high and capped by a crystal dome, surrounded by barbed wire and sandwiched between a pair of weed-filled lots. The building looked new, a gleaming anomaly in the gutted neighborhood. Grey noticed the courier's gaze lingering on the building as he passed.

At the next intersection, Grey could see the Millennium Dome in the distance, a gaudy bauble squatting above the brackish crawl of the Thames. A few blocks later the package stores and corner shops returned, and the courier entered a seedy two-story pub painted entirely in black, including the windows. Grey saw the name of the place scrawled in red on the front door.

BAR 666.

*Lovely.*

Before Grey had a chance to decide what to do, five patrons spilled out of the front door, just after the courier entered. All five were blocky young men with creased stares, three of them sucking on cigarettes, all wearing West Ham United hoodies or jackets.

Grey tensed, though none of them was looking at him. They were talking in thick Cockney accents, and they started down the street in Grey's direction. His only chance to avoid attention was to keep walking.

As they passed, Grey kept his head down, hands in his pockets, disappearing into his jacket. No one said a word, but then four more patrons spilled into the street, holding pints and smoking.

*Damn*. Five behind him, four in front, buildings on either side of the street. Grey did the only thing he could, which was to act natural and keep walking with his head down, hoping no one noticed him.

When he was twenty feet away he saw one of the men outside the bar pointing at him. The chatter ceased, and the man who had pointed, a rangy man with a shaved head, flicked his cigarette at Grey.

"Hey, mate!"

Grey kept walking, head down.

He stepped into the street ten feet from Grey, the other three behind him. "I said, *Hey, mate*. Are you Dominic Grey?"

"Sorry," Grey said. "Wrong guy."

Grey kept walking, but no one moved. One of the men in back whistled and waved at the men who had just passed Grey in the other direction. Grey knew his window had just closed.

The man with the shaved head dipped a hand into his coat and pulled out a two-foot piece of metal piping. "There's someone wants to have a chat with you."

Grey stopped two feet from the guy, far enough not to spook him, close enough to do damage. Grey looked him in the eye and let him understand that he was wary but not the least bit afraid. "I don't know what you're talking about. You have no idea who I am and where this is going, so you need to ask yourself if you really want to do this." Grey clasped his hands in front of him and said softly, "Let it go."

There was a moment of doubt in the man's eyes, then the cruel edge returned. Grey was inside the swing before it was half-finished. He wrapped the man's punching arm with his left hand, striking the underside of his jaw with his right palm. The man's head snapped up and back, but Grey continued forward, stepping behind the man and sweeping out his back legs. Grey changed the direction of his chin thrust, shoving the man's off-balanced head straight down, the body following as Grey completed the violent *Osoto-Gari*. The man's head thudded off the pavement.

Nine against one, with more inside, some of them with weapons, was a losing proposition. He had to cause maximum damage to those in his way, as fast as possible, and then run. He took the fight to the next guy, a squat goateed man with a bandanna, faking a snap kick to the knee to get in close, then leveling him with an uppercut.

Someone grabbed Grey in a bear hug from behind. Grey remained in constant motion, reaching for the man's groin while leaning his weight back and thrusting his hips forward, creating space. He found the testicles and squeezed. As the man bellowed and released his grip, Grey found a fistful of hair and yanked him to the ground, stomping on his face to finish him off.

The other five were steps away, and he saw more men pouring out of the bar, most of them holding makeshift weapons. The last man between Grey and freedom came in swinging a beer bottle. Grey slipped to the left and caught his lead wrist and elbow, then whipped the man in a circle and threw him into the next closest attacker.

Grey saw open pavement and started sprinting. With his first step he felt a tug on his ankle, and then he was pitching forward, throwing his forearms down to protect his face. Grey twisted as someone pulled on his leg from behind, and he saw the bleeding visage of the man whose face he had stomped on.

Instead of pulling away, Grey leveraged forward and swung his other knee at the man's head, catching him on the side of the face. He released Grey's ankle, blood spraying from his nose. Grey scrambled to get to his feet, but was driven to the ground again as someone dove into his waist. Then a pile of men collapsed on him, punching and kicking and cursing, the stench of unwashed bodies almost as bad as the blows.

Grey tried to curl into a ball, but he couldn't protect himself from the assault that came from all sides, over and over, until Grey's vision clouded and he stopped moving. At some point the blows ceased, and someone spat on him. When he tried to move, a wave of nausea poured over him from the head blows. Blood dripped from his nose and mouth.

A huge set of arms wrapped him and pulled him to his feet, another kept a knife to his throat. Grey's vision was still blurry, and he had to take deep breaths not to pass out. They dragged him backwards, towards the bar.

"Dante said you'd be trouble. You'll pay for Speck and Nicky, you piece of shit Yank."

"Fucking wanker broke my nose! Cut him up!"

"You know the rules. He'll wish we had once Dante's here. Call him."

"Fuck that, Nicky isn't moving."

"You want to tell Dante you disobeyed him?"

They took Grey inside the bar, a cement-floored dungeon with a few pool tables and upside-down pentagrams chalked on the walls. A soccer game blared from a television over the bar, and a slinky bartender dressed in Goth stared at Grey as they dragged him through. He caught her eye and gasped. "Call the police."

Someone struck Grey in the back of the head, leaving him teetering on the edge of consciousness. He was taken to a storage room, handcuffed, and strapped into a chair with a length of heavy rope.

They left him alone, and the lights went out.

# 47

Viktor's driver knew of Sant'Ambroggio, a sleepy hamlet twenty minutes along the coast from Cefalù, perched high on a cliff. Viktor had no idea why he had been given the address, but something about Scarlet Alexander told him she wasn't the sort of person who would lead him into a trap.

Then again, she didn't seem the sort to cover up the fact that she had met with Darius.

With La Rocca in the rearview, the road wound along the coast, taking a steep turn into the cacti-laden hills. Five minutes later they were needling through Sant'Ambroggio, a collection of whitewashed houses with red-tiled roofs clustered along a narrow avenue that paralleled the sea cliff on their left. Even narrower side alleys branched to their right off the avenue, leading into the hills.

They parked near the village center, a tight square perched high above the Tyrrhenian, La Rocca glowering in the distance. The driver stayed in the car at Viktor's request, pointing down the street as he gave walking directions.

It was near the end of siesta, and Viktor could hear the murmur of families inside walled courtyards, preparing to finish up the day's work before engaging in the languid *passeggiata*. The asphalt street simmered as he walked, the heat exacerbating the sour whiff of overripe tomatoes.

He passed a *tabacchi* and a butcher shop, both closed, then turned right onto a steep alley lined with plaster-walled apartments. Grapevines and clusters of honeysuckle draped the residences, rosemary and basil spilled out of planters. A satellite dish on one of the balconies was the only sign of modernity, the rest of the alley a collage of dusty stone, cracked plaster, and hanging laundry.

Viktor's thighs burned halfway up the hill. A woman folding clothes on a balcony stared openly as he trudged past her home in his black suit. By the time he reached the address Scarlet had given him, a tiny apartment near the top of the street, he was mopping his brow and trying not to gasp for breath.

An elderly man in a stained white tank top sat on the stoop of his apartment, chewing on something in slow motion, skin burnished a permanent copper from the sun. A walking stick lay at his side.

Viktor didn't have time for pleasantries. He flashed his Interpol badge and spoke in respectful, formal Italian. "Are you the owner of this apartment?"

"*Sì.*"

"I'm with Interpol," Viktor said, "and I'm investigating a series of murders. Nothing involving you. I need some information I was told you might possess."

The old man said nothing. The deep tan had hidden some of the wrinkles at first glance, but he was a bag of skin and bones, a new set of wrinkles appearing every time his mouth moved to chew.

"Scarlet Alexander sent me," Viktor said. "I'm looking for information on Aleister Crowley, and she referred me to you."

The old man spoke out of the side of his mouth, in a low voice, and it took all of Viktor's considerable ability in Italian to understand his thick dialect. "I was there."

"I'm sorry?"

"I was ten. I was a groundskeeper."

This took Viktor aback. That would make the old man a hundred years old. "You knew Aleister Crowley?"

"I saw him every day for three years. He never spoke to me."

"You were there the entire time he was there?" Viktor said.

"And fifty years after."

"Do you know a man named Darius?"

"No."

"Simon?" Viktor said.

"No."

"Have you ever studied magic?"

The old man spit.

"Did you ever go inside the lodge?" Viktor said.

"Not unless I had to. That was the Devil's house."

"Did you ever see a book called the Ahriman Grimoire?"

"I can't read."

"Have you ever heard of the Tutori, a group of priests commissioned by the Vatican?"

"No."

The old man was a rare find, but Viktor wasn't sure why Scarlet had sent Viktor to him. "How do you know Scarlet?" Viktor said.

"She wanted to talk to me. Like you."

"What did you discuss?"

"What the villa looked like," he said. "What I saw. Who was there."

"Has anyone else come to interview you in the past few years?" Viktor said.

"Never."

Viktor didn't know where Darius had received his information, perhaps from the man in the retirement home who had burned, perhaps from Scarlet, perhaps from some other source. But looking at this elderly man free of guile, Viktor felt sure Darius had not been here.

Was it possible Darius's journey had ended at Cefalù? Had he encountered the same dead end as Crowley? Was Darius indeed using the idea of the Ahriman Grimoire, perhaps even a fake, to impress and control his followers?

"Did Aleister ever leave the lodge to your knowledge?" Viktor said.

"Of course."

"Not just for the day, but someplace out of the ordinary?"

The wrinkles on his brow congealed in concentration. "*Si.* We talked about it."

"Who did?"

"The servants."

"Why?" Viktor said.

"It was strange. He didn't like to leave."

"Where did he go?"

"Geraci Siculo."

"Is that in Sicily?" Viktor said.

"Yes."

"Is it a town?"

"Village."

"Where in Geraci Siculo did he go?"

"I don't know," the man said.

"Who did he go with?"

"His two best people."

Viktor felt a tingle of excitement. "How long did they stay?"

"Not long, a few days."

"Did they bring anything back?" Viktor said.

"I don't know. We were servants."

"Do you know why he went?"

"No."

"There were no rumors," Viktor said, "nothing overheard, no speculation among the servants?"

"No."

"Did he return to this place, Geraci Siculo?"

"No."

"Is there anything special about this village?"

The old man shrugged. "I don't know."

"Is there anyone else who might know more about this?" Viktor said.

"Everyone is dead."

# THE DIABOLIST

Viktor relaxed his stiff posture, sensing there was nothing more to be gained. He offered him a stack of euros for his trouble, but the old man pushed his hand away.

Dusk approached as Viktor returned to the village square, the steep hills casting fingerlike shadows over the sea, the limestone cliffs of La Rocca fading to blue in the distance.

His driver told him that Geraci Siculo, a village in the Madonie Mountains, was at least an hour and a half drive from Cefalù. He argued against making a journey so late, as the road was treacherous and the village would be asleep. Viktor relented only because he was exhausted, and saw more value in getting some rest and setting out before dawn.

The driver didn't know much about Geraci Siculo except that it was remote, one of those Sicilian villages untouched by time, set on a mountaintop for defensive purposes in the Middle Ages and never quite arriving in the present. As far as he knew, there was nothing of historical significance in the village. Viktor's own research at an Internet café evidenced the same.

Viktor returned to his quarters, his villa part of a chicly rustic six-villa complex situated on the edge of old town, at the base of La Rocca. Though exhausted, his mind was a shortwave radio he could not shut off, switching channels and rising in volume every time he closed his eyes. He again turned to absinthe to relax, taking his glass and his spoon to the grapevine-smothered trellis, sitting in a wicker chair between potted palms, with the scent of rosemary drifting off the hill.

He dripped the water over the spoon, shivering in anticipation as the milky swathe of La Louche swirled within the emerald elixir. One glass became three, then another. The inebriation peculiar to absinthe washed over him, muscles relaxing, tension evaporating, his mind adrift yet strangely lucid. It was like being drunk on wine without the silliness, sharing the numbness and slight euphoria, a philosopher's drink, drowning out the banality of one's surroundings and opening the mind's eye to a mysterious realm.

He didn't know how many glasses he had quaffed when she came to him, a curtain of flaxen hair rippling in the breeze on the hillside, spilling over her cloak.

"Viktor," she whispered.

*Her* voice.

He told himself it couldn't be real, could not be her voice, but his senses told him otherwise. He squeezed his eyes shut, knowing he was intoxicated. When he opened them he listened to the tick of the clock, flexed his fingers, touched the glass to his lips.

She was gesturing to him now, still whispering, the voice unmistakable. He had to obey his muse, illusory or not.

"Eve," he said, leaving the patio and climbing the low stone wall that bordered the property. She was moving away from him, across the hillside, towards the stone staircase leading to the heights of La Rocca.

He hurried to catch up, peering through the darkness that had settled over the hill. His long legs took the stone steps two at a time, yet still the ghost of his beloved drifted ahead, the distance between them an ache he had endured for decades, impossible to ignore.

He swigged straight from the bottle as he climbed, the unprepared absinthe burning his throat. If this was a vision from the Green Fairy, then he didn't want it to end. The steps became a faint path worn into the rock, then dirt and scrub. She would appear out of the darkness to beckon, her face cloaked by the hood. "Help me, Viktor. He still has me."

"Who does?" Viktor said.

"You know who."

*Oh, my Eve, I promise not to fail you this time. Whatever you need I shall do, my love.*

In the back of his mind he wondered whether this was the proof of the beyond he had sought all his life, his beloved returned from the grave, a living wraith before his very eyes.

# THE DIABOLIST

She stopped and half turned, beckoning with her finger, tawny blond hair silken as starlight, just as it ever was.

"Eve!" he moaned, reaching for those pale hands whose warmth he had not felt for lifetimes, a shudder of emotion coursing through him. The ache to bury his face in her hair was more than he could bear.

Viktor took the final step towards her, and then he was falling through the night, his last step never reaching solid ground.

# 48

Grey woke to someone dabbing his forehead with a wet cloth. Long straight hair, dyed black, brushed his face. Underneath the hair he recognized the gaunt body of the barmaid, clad in black fishnets, knee-high leather boots, and a lacy top.

"I'm sorry they did that to you," she said in a low voice.

Grey's eyes flicked upward, to the pierced lip and brow. "Did you call the police?"

She averted her eyes. "I can't."

"Yeah, you can."

"He'll kill me and my Lizzie."

"I can help you," Grey said.

"It's not just him. It's all of 'em; they're everywhere now. The East End's infected."

"Just give me names and an address. I work in law enforcement. With Interpol."

She gave a short, hysterical peal of laughter. "You 'aven't seen him, 'ave you? That tattoo? Those eyes? I've never seen the boys afraid of anyone but 'im."

"I've been hearing that a lot."

She moved her head closer, dropped her voice even more. "He's not even the worst. There's another one, someone *he* reports to."

"Are they in that new building a few blocks away, the glass one?" Grey said.

She exchanged the blood-soaked rag for another. "Blowed if I know."

"Why didn't they kill me?"

"I'm just the bartender; they sent me to wake you. There's someone they're looking for, though. Some girl. Maybe you know 'er?"

Grey's hands tightened. "Who is it?"

"Supposed to be a real stunner. Never seen 'er meself." She dabbed gently at his forehead. "If you know 'er, could be the only thing that can help you."

"Why do they want her?" Grey said.

"Like I said, I'm just the help. You do know 'er, don't you?" Her voice dropped to a whisper, conspiratorial. "Tell me where she is and I'll make a deal for the both of us." She made an abbreviated sound somewhere between a hiccup and a giggle. "A deal with the Devil."

"Aren't there three?" Grey said.

"Wha'?"

"Three in the deal. Me, you, and your Lizzie."

She lowered her eyes. "Yeah, that's right."

"Get out of my face," Grey said.

Her face transformed into a mask of rage, eyes blazing with righteous fury. She raked her nails across his face. "Foul thing! Where is she?" Grey cringed from another swipe of her claws. "He'll cut you into pieces and eat your heart; we'll toast to your blood and toss your bones in a bucket!"

The door swung open. When she saw who was in the doorway, a lean man about Grey's age and height and wearing a black duster, she swallowed her words and shrank away from Grey.

"I tried, Dante," she said, bowing her head. "I tried, but he 'ad nothing to say—"

"Leave us," Dante rasped, and Grey detected both a lisp and a harsh French accent.

She scurried out of the room and closed the door. Dante regarded Grey from across the room, expressionless. His long face had a Mediterranean pallor, and Grey could see the bottom half of the tattoo covering Dante's scalp, the tips of the pentagram reaching downward like the grasping legs of a spider.

He moved forward, stopping a few feet away. "Dominic Grey."

It was said as a statement, and Grey didn't deny it. As Dante spoke, Grey noticed the points of his sharpened incisors. "I thank you for making my job easy."

"I thought your job was in Paris," Grey said, "butchering innocent victims in your little Hell caves."

"Where's Eve?"

"Who?" Grey said.

Dante flicked his tongue across his incisors. "We know she helped you in the catacombs."

Grey didn't show it, but his head was spinning. How did they know someone had helped him in the catacombs, and who was Eve? Was it someone else, or Anka by a different name? And why did she have the same name as the girl from Viktor's past?

"That was just me, pal. I'm sure your friends will vouch for that, the ones still alive."

Dante's mouth tightened. "You're still alive because we want her. I ask one more time: Where is she? He knows you've been with her."

"She's not his toy."

Dante just smiled, and Grey didn't like it. At all. "Do you mean Simon, or Darius? How many names does he have? You might want to know who you're working for before you kill for him."

"Why?" Dante said.

The nonchalant manner in which Dante answered unnerved Grey, crawled under his skin as would the detached response of any psychopath to someone with a rational mind.

"I know about you," Grey said. "I know what happened to your parents, to your sister." Grey inclined his head towards his own back, where the scars from his father's beatings and cigarette burns lay intertwined within the

*Irezumi*-style jujitsu tattoo that sprawled over and around his father's handiwork. "You're not the only one who knows about pain."

Dante stepped to Grey, eyes bulging. Grey could see his face twitching to keep control. "You know nothing of pain." He withdrew a foot-long blade, then snapped the flat of the blade across the left side of Grey's torso, smacking the ribs that had been bruised in the fight.

Grey drew a sharp breath and gritted his teeth. "What I know is that pain is mental. It only controls you if you're weak."

"It controls you whether you like it or not. It's just a matter of degree."

"Submission is different from control, Dante. Everyone submits to torture eventually, but that doesn't mean the pain has controlled you, it means your body has failed and your mind's in shock. You recover when it's over. I've never seen anyone as controlled by pain as you. You're as good as dead."

Dante took the blade in both hands and thrust forward as if to impale Grey, reversing the stroke at the last minute to strike him in the side of the face, again with the flat of the blade. Grey's head snapped to the side, blood running out of his mouth from shredded gums. Colored dots filled his vision.

"I'm dead already," Dante said, "and you'll be dead soon, too. But before that, you'll learn to respect the pain."

"If it's respect you're after, you're in the wrong room. Untie me, and we'll talk about respect."

Dante's wrist twitched, and the knife in his hand flew downward. Grey felt a sunburst of agony, and saw the knife sticking out of the top of his thigh. He balled his fists against the darts of fire shooting through his leg, and it took all of his willpower not to gasp.

"You know I would have killed you already, if that was my goal," Dante said. "You know we need you alive for a few more days, and you know I'll move you someplace more private and torture you when I have more time. You're fine with all of that—you're strong; you accept it. What you may not know is what we have planned for Viktor and for Eve. I'll make sure to allow you to watch. *Oui*, I can see in your eyes that this is your form of torture. I can see in your eyes you're already closer to me than you realize. No one as good with pain as you can be far from embracing it forever."

Grey spoke through tightened lips. "Remember when I told you I knew about you? You interrupted me. I wasn't going to say I sympathized with you; I was going to say I didn't give a damn. Life is hard for everyone, some more than others. But the damage you cause to other people, that's on you. Your pain has made you into a monster."

Dante's mouth curled. "We'll see who knows what about pain." He grasped the hilt of the knife stuck in Grey's thigh and twisted it, tearing deeper into flesh and muscle. Grey's vision blurred as waves of nauseating pain tore through his nerve endings. Only his training in pain management kept him from going into shock.

Dante yanked the knife free, another knife appearing in his hand as if by magic. He held the tips of both to Grey's eyes. "After you watch me kill your loved ones, I will take these next, so you can suffer in darkness. *À demain.*"

With a flick of his wrist he reversed the knife again, and swiped the hilt across Grey's temple.

 **49**

Viktor opened his eyes to tendrils of pink sunlight threading the hillside. He tasted dirt, and spat. After wiping his mouth he groaned to a sitting position.

Nothing felt broken, though everything hurt. His head throbbed the hardest, though from the fall or excessive absinthe, Viktor wasn't sure. He surveyed his surroundings and realized he was at the bottom of a long slope, at the base of the path to La Rocca. He could see his villa through a pine grove to his left. Looking up, he saw the five foot wall off which he must have stepped. He vaguely remembered tumbling down the hill and lying in a daze at the bottom.

Two early climbers gave him sidelong glances. Viktor stood and brushed himself, remembering Eve's voice, her hair, her lips. She had seemed so real. He cursed himself for his weakness and shuffled towards the villa.

His driver was taking coffee on the balcony next to Viktor's, eyes widening as Viktor approached from the hillside. "We leave for Geraci Siculo in fifteen minutes," Viktor said, his voice hoarse, his hands still shaking from the absinthe.

"I can help you?" the driver said.

"No."

Viktor showered, dressed, and made espresso in the moka pot. He tried to call Grey and got no answer. Just after the coffee bubbled upward, Jacques called.

"Yes?" Viktor said.

"Where are you?"

Viktor held the phone to his ear while he added a dollop of cream. "Investigating."

"I asked you to come to Rome."

"Not all requests are granted," Viktor said. "I will come to Rome in two days."

"That's the day after the deadline for His Holiness," Jacques said.

"Tell me what it is I can do to protect His Holiness that the entire Swiss Guard cannot?"

Jacques didn't answer.

"Trust I am doing what I consider best for the investigation," Viktor said. "My partner is doing the same, exploring leads in London."

"*Oui?* Such as?"

Viktor informed Jacques of his theory that Darius, Simon, and the man behind the murders were all the same man, leaving undisclosed that he had suspected this for days.

"If we can locate this man before tomorrow night," Jacques said, "we can at least observe or detain him until the threat to His Holiness has passed."

"My partner's working on finding him."

"Surely someone knows where he is?"

"His broadcasts from the Internet are from an undisclosed location," Viktor said. "You could try a trace, but he's far too clever not to have planned for that. We suspect he's in London, but London's a megalopolis. Alert the local police, but he won't appear in public before tomorrow night."

"And yourself? What precautions are you taking?"

"I'm not concerned with myself," Viktor said as he paced back and forth, eager to start the journey to Geraci Siculo. "Surely there's another purpose to your call? I assume you have the pope under close surveillance?"

"Of course, though your presence is always comforting in these situations, when dealing with these . . . how do you say in English . . . maniacs.

# THE DIABOLIST

*Bien sur*, I've been thinking about what you said, that it may not be a direct attack on His Holiness."

"And?" Viktor said.

"I admit the alternative, the unknown, frightens me just as much."

"It should," Viktor said. "Darius is a very devious man."

"We discovered that Gareth's bodyguard has connections to L'église de la Bête. We detained him and found their ring at his apartment. He's currently being interrogated, but has given us nothing."

"He fears his own church far more than prison," Viktor said. "That's helpful, though, and answers the question of who set Gareth on fire. *Do prdele*. I told him no one else was to be in the room."

"Your theory is the guard, and Douglas Oakenfeld in San Francisco, worked in tandem with Darius?" Jacques said.

"Of course. The black-robed figure is a clever illusion used to frighten his followers. The guard used a recording of his voice in Gareth's room, which the guard must have had on his person."

"Is there anything else you suggest we do?" Jacques said.

"Prepare for the worst."

Geraci Siculo was not far in kilometers, but it was a winding drive through the Madonie Mountains, Sicily's wildest and most remote region, full of switchbacks and cliff-hugging roads knifing through steep mountain passes. Viktor's driver took him deep into the interior, isolated villages replacing the towns, vultures and peregrines taking the place of cars and people.

More akin to enormous hills than mountains, the rugged Sicilian topography reminded Viktor of the Greek islands, though the brown slopes of Sicily possessed a more somber hue than the playful colors of Greece, as if life were lived more seriously here. They spotted Geraci Siculo on a distant hillside long before they arrived, a speck of white snuggled amid the craggy peaks like the pearl of a half-cracked oyster.

The village disappeared as they passed through a forest of stunted cork oaks, the exposed crimson of the half-harvested trees resembling flesh wounds. Viktor kept a constant vigil, but no other cars appeared ahead or in the rearview. After the forest they passed through a grove of wild olives, the short and twisted limbs a group of old crones cringing from the sun.

The vegetation lessened, the topography morphing to a vast moonlike plateau of peaks and ridges shadowed by taller mountains in the distance, the swaths of brown broken by clusters of ocher-colored grass. Geraci Siculo reappeared, the road ascending sharply towards the village, winding around the mountain like a coiled spring before narrowing into a cobblestone road that dead-ended at the village entrance.

Viktor felt a rush of warm air as they exited the car, and he left his jacket on the seat. The village was a chiseled block of stone on top of the mountain, the inaccessible location and tight architectural layout designed, he knew, to shield the villagers from medieval bandits roaming the countryside.

He told the driver to be ready to leave at a moment's notice, then extracted the photo of Darius from his coat pocket, prepared to walk around the village until someone recognized him. He had been here, Viktor was sure of it.

The village looked deserted, and in true Sicilian fashion, the few faces Viktor saw eyed him warily. How much of the legendary Sicilian Mafia still remained was a matter of fierce debate, but here in the timeworn hills and villages, with customs and appearances unchanged for centuries, the old rules held sway, the deep mistrust of outside influence that had to the rise of local enforcers in the first place.

Most of the villagers, especially the black-garbed older women, scurried away before Viktor got close enough to show the photo. The men who let him approach glanced at the photo and shook their heads.

Viktor was undaunted. He had no time for ancient custom or untrusting villagers, and he continued walking the absurdly steep streets, ducking through ancient passageways, popping into every tabacchi and café, even pestering the customers at the lone pizzeria. He came to a group of elderly men sitting in a line on a stone ledge outside a cathedral and went down the line one by one, the swarthy old men either giving him scathing looks or ignoring him outright. Viktor cursed and carried on.

At the edge of the village he entered a bar with a patio view of the surrounding mountains. After flashing the photo in vain to the patrons at the inside bar, Viktor ordered a bottle of water and sat on the patio in frustration, resting his legs.

Time was running out, and the showdown with Darius the midnight after next loomed like the rumble of an avalanche. Maybe Darius had only passed through the town, or sent someone else.

No, Viktor thought. If this was indeed the path to the grimoire, then Darius would not have entrusted this journey to anyone but himself.

He finished the water, thighs aching, the breeze on the patio chilling the dried sweat under his shirt. As he stood to leave, one of the patrons from the bar, a scruffy young man with weatherworn skin, looked up. Viktor eased back into his seat and indicated for the young man to join him. He came over, hesitant. Like the old man in Sant'Ambroggio, his thick Italian was peppered with the occasional incomprehensible dose of Sicilian.

He set his beer on the table and cradled it in both hands. "The man in the photo? I've seen him."

Viktor leaned forward. "Where?"

He glanced over his shoulder, towards the men in the bar, and lowered his voice. "There's no work in the village. I'm a guide in the Madonie, I have a wife and son and . . . there's not much work," he finished lamely.

"What's your name?" Viktor said.

"Antonio."

Viktor knew what Antonio couldn't bring himself to say, and he withdrew two hundred euro notes from his wallet. Excessive, but there was no time for delay. Viktor slid the bills across the table. "Would this help?"

Antonio pounced on the bills, then straightened in the chair, a proud Sicilian once again. "This man in the photo, he came to Geraci months ago, looking for a guide."

Viktor forced himself not to appear overeager. "And you complied?"

"He paid like you."

"Where did he want to go?"

"He asked if there were any monasteries or chapels in the mountains near Geraci," Antonio said.

"And?"

"I said there are four, maybe five. He asked if any of them had been there for a very long time, centuries. I said there is one. A monastery."

"Of what type?" Viktor said.

Antonio frowned. "This is Sicily."

"Catholic, then," Viktor murmured. He had assumed it was Catholic, and had been questioning the type of monastic order, many of which had been present in Sicily over the centuries. "Do you know if this monastery has ties to the Tutori?"

"What?"

"Do you know the history of this monastery?" Viktor said.

"Just that it's been here longer than anyone can remember, and the monks keep to themselves."

"Is no one curious?"

"In Sicily, these questions are not asked, especially of the Church. The Church has a reason for this monastery, and the Church will tell us what they want us to know."

If the Tutori had indeed selected this site, Viktor thought, then it had been well chosen.

"What do you know about this monastery?" Viktor asked.

"It is very small and hard to reach, just a tiny chapel on top of the mountain. Only a couple of monks live there. One of them comes to town a few times a year for supplies."

"Have you seen this monk recently?"

The young man rolled his Moretti between his palms. "It's been some time. Maybe last year?"

"I assume you took the man in the photo to the monastery?" Viktor said.

# THE DIABOLIST

"Yes."

"Has anyone else been to Geraci, asking about this place?"

"Not to me," Antonio said.

Viktor had a very bad feeling about the current state of this monastery. "Is Geraci the closest village to the monastery?"

He nodded. "This monastery is deep in the Madonie, on one of the most remote mountains in Sicily." He must have seen Viktor deflate, because he grinned and said, "Lucky for you, Geraci is one of Sicily's most remote villages. And this is not the Alps. It is a half-day journey, less on horseback. Would you like me to take you?"

Viktor extracted three more bills and pushed them forward. "Indeed. I'll require your services for at least the day."

"When do you wish to leave?" Antonio said.

"After you finish your beer."

Antonio tipped it back.

It took an hour for the guide to procure the horses and meet Viktor on the western edge of the village. They trotted off on a dirt trail, descending into the high valley.

They navigated the valley and climbed the next ridge over, cantering alongside a line of spindly windmills, hearing the tinkling of bells before they saw the sheep gnawing on a patch of yellow grass.

Viktor saw no other signs of civilization on the journey, amazed at how remote the small island could feel. The sun bore down on them, causing Viktor to keep a constant grip on his handkerchief. An hour later they topped another ridge. As far as Viktor could see, there was nothing but brown hillside, bulbous cacti, blue sky, and the pulsating sun. A few vultures circled lazily on the current. *What a glorious, tortured island,* he thought.

They descended a few hundred feet on an angle, then circled the hill until they came to a shallow, basin-like depression ringed by peaks. Antonio reined in his horse and pointed towards the top of the highest peak. "There."

Viktor saw a speck of white just below the peak, above a near-vertical cliff. It looked like a slight rock overhang. Antonio reached into his pack and withdrew a pair of binoculars. He focused on where he had pointed, then handed the binoculars to Viktor.

Viktor peered into the lens, realizing the rock overhang was a clever rampart, built into the side of the mountain like the aerie of some great prehistoric bird.

"The monastery," Viktor said.

"*Sì.*"

He led Viktor across the basin to the base of the peak. "This is where I left the man in the photo," Antonio said. "He requested I go no further. I didn't ask why."

*So you wouldn't witness whatever it was he was about to do,* Viktor thought. "How long is the climb from here?"

"I've never been to the monastery, but"—Antonio eyed the top of the huge rock—"that's a three-hundred-meter climb, maybe three hours on foot if we're lucky? It's not safe for the horses."

"I'll go alone," Viktor said.

The guide regarded Viktor's disheveled form, sweat already trickling down his face, skin reddening from the sun. "I should go with you."

"Thank you, but no."

Whatever waited at the top of the mountain was Viktor's cross to bear, and he wouldn't endanger the guide. He was dehydrated and suffering from the heat, but he could make this final push.

"Then I'll wait for you here."

Viktor eyed the exposed ground, then said, "Why don't you return to the top of the hill, and wait by that fig tree? If I'm not back by dusk, return to the village. I'll find my way back."

"It's not a good idea to walk the hills after dark." He unslung his pack and thrust it towards Viktor. "You'll need more water, and there's an emergency kit inside. Take the binoculars as well."

# THE DIABOLIST

Viktor objected, but Antonio moved his horse closer, reaching up to loop the pack around Viktor's neck. He pointed at a faint path worn into the rock. "When I was a boy I took this path halfway up the mountain before turning back. I believe it leads to the monastery. Be careful of loose rock."

Viktor clasped his hand. "Thank you."

The guide started to canter away, and Viktor called out, "Did you wait for him?"

Antonio twisted his torso to reply. "I waited, but he never returned."

# 50

Grey again woke to darkness and a dull ache in his side, now joined by a parched throat and an agonized throbbing in his thigh. Wincing, he raised his cheek off a cold concrete floor. A pair of handcuffs hampered his hand movement. He rose to a sitting position, felt and then heard the clinking of chains around his ankles. Unable to see his hands in front of his face, he reached down and probed.

His feet were manacled, attached by a three-foot chain to an iron ring in the floor. He was still clothed, though they had taken his backpack. They had not, however, taken his boots, and his mouth pursed in a grim smile.

Cracking a variety of locks and entranceways had been one of Grey's specialties in Force Recon. After his capture by Al-Miri's men in Egypt, and inspired by one of his companions on that journey, Grey had decided to perform a little surgery on the black combat boots he wore almost everywhere. He installed a hollow space in the left heel, where he now kept a miniscule tension wrench, a bobby pin, and a thin iron file that was curved at the end. Tools that could open most handcuffs and locks.

He had the cuffs off in seconds, the manacles around his feet a few minutes later. He stood gingerly, the pain in his thigh acute but manageable—barely. Dante's knife hadn't reached bone, and a torn muscle was painful as hell, but not incapacitating. A severed muscle was a different story, but the top of the thigh was a solid piece of anatomy, providing protection for the femoral artery underneath.

# THE DIABOLIST

Grey still had to contend with the lack of light and the small fact that he was imprisoned God knew where, likely surrounded by murderous cultists. On the other hand, those manacles and that chain had been pretty thick, and he was guessing no one expected to see him anytime soon.

When *did* they plan to see him? What was their endgame, and why hadn't Dante just killed him? It obviously had something to do with Anka, or Eve, or whatever her name was. Dante might be on his way right now to extract more information, or waiting outside Grey's prison.

But why? Grey had to assume she knew more than she should, and had threatened to go public. It was the only option that made sense. They knew about the meetings she had with Grey, and they thought Grey might know where she was.

Well, he didn't. For all he knew, she lived in Hong Kong and did the astral projection thing whenever they met up. He knew as much about this girl as he knew about the queen of Denmark, and torture wasn't going to change that. And the Eve angle disturbed him. Was Darius playing out some twisted fantasy through this girl? Was she telling him the whole story, or were there angles in this theater of the bizarre he wasn't seeing?

He could sort through all this once he got out of this hole. He had no idea how long he had been unconscious, but he knew time was running out. He moved about the room, testing the walls for a door, deflated when he found nothing but wood and concrete. No openings, no secret doors, no hollow walls as far as he could tell. He did the same thing to the floor, probing for a way out.

Nothing.

That left the ceiling. If it were out of reach, he was out of luck. He prepared himself for the worst and jumped off his right foot, pushing through the terrible throbbing in his left leg. His fingers touched plaster about a foot above his head. He moved about the room, probing the low ceiling at various points, until he found his exit: a wooden square that budged when he pushed on it. There must be a padlock on the other side, but Grey couldn't generate enough power to break through.

He stepped back three feet from the wooden trapdoor, jumped off one foot and punched the ceiling. The plaster cracked, and he did it again and again, until he was able to rip down enough plaster to expose a ceiling beam. He knew he was making way too much noise, but he had no choice. He ripped at the plaster until his fingers bled, face and hair covered in white dust.

He jumped and grabbed onto the exposed beam with both hands, then began to swing. It took him a few times to gain momentum, and then he kicked at the wooden square with his good foot. After a dozen or so kicks he heard a splintering sound, and on the next kick the wood separated from the metal hinge. Grey ripped down the wooden slats, then jumped and felt around the opening until his fingers closed on an aluminum ladder. After the searing pain in his thigh subsided, he pulled it down and climbed out of his makeshift cell.

He felt his way through stacks of boxes, finding an unlocked door. He cracked it open, and a glimmer of light emanated from the end of a hallway. Before he left he opened a few of the boxes. Pamphlets for the Order of New Enlightenment filled every one, the same pamphlet Grey had received from Thomas and Alan. Grey estimated a hundred boxes lined the walls of the room, each filled with thousands of pamphlets.

He left the storeroom and crept down the long hallway, understanding why no one had heard him kick through the trapdoor. The hallway stretched in both directions, with closed doors at either end. When he got to the first door he stopped to listen. A television blared on the other side, a British comedy. He waited, hands at the ready, but heard only laughter from a single voice.

Grey gently tried the doorknob. Unlocked.

Thinking through various scenarios in his head, knowing one could never plan for chaos, Grey cleared his head of thought and burst into the room.

Even limping, he was on top of the guard before he was out of his chair, the bag of chips in his hand spilling to the floor. His hand reached for a gun at his side, but Grey forced his arm behind his back before he could draw, twisting it until he felt the shoulder wrench out of socket. The guard swooned from the pain, and Grey removed the gun and helped him the rest of the way to dreamland with a blood choke, cutting off the oxygen on both sides of the carotid, forearms wrapped around the guard's head and neck.

As the guard slumped to the floor, Grey noticed the ring on his right index finger, the same ring Viktor had noticed on Oak's hand. A chill rippled through Grey. No doubt the building was infested.

He tore off the guard's shirt and made a crude bandage for his thigh, thankful the bleeding was muscular rather than arterial or venal. He also found a small bottle of ibuprofen. Adrenaline had carried him through the fight with the guard, but the pain from his cracked rib and thigh threatened to overwhelm him. It wasn't much, but he popped a handful and put the rest of the painkillers in his pocket.

He surveyed the room. Two rows of monitors showed various shots of the grounds, as well as a rotation of interior rooms. Dozens of people worked throughout the complex at a variety of tasks, most of them cleaning or setting up chairs and tables. Some of the rooms looked like offices or conference rooms, some worship centers or meditation rooms. He also noticed a kitchen, a dining hall, and a small gym.

There were no windows in the room, but on one of the monitors he saw a modest, well-kept lawn surrounded by a huge iron gate that looked familiar. Grey had a strong suspicion he was inside the cylindrical glass building he had seen close to Bar 666.

A clock on the wall showed seven p.m. He assumed, he prayed, he had only been unconscious since the previous evening. That left him a little over a day before the appointed hour of Viktor's death.

The alarm system was fairly sophisticated, but it was designed, as were most alarm systems, to keep people out. Judging from the lack of windows he had seen, he guessed this level was the basement.

Monitors marked floors one through five. On one of the monitors he saw the hallway from which he had just escaped, and he silently praised British comedy.

Searching the room, he found nothing of interest other than the guard's key ring, which he pocketed along with the guard's wallet and cell. He also took the gun, as well as a silencer he found in a drawer, then stripped and switched clothes with the guard, having to tighten the belt to the last notch. Grey dragged the guard back to the same hole in which Grey had been held, then handcuffed him, manacled his feet, and shoved a stack of boxes over the splintered trapdoor.

Before returning to the guard room he walked the length of the hallway, finding a door at the other end. It was locked, and he worked his way through the guard's keys until he found the right one. A small service elevator was on the other side of the locked door.

On his way back to the guard station he checked the other rooms, finding them stuffed with boxes. He opened a few, and found the same pamphlets translated into Spanish, Russian, Chinese, Arabic, and French.

He debated calling Jacques or the police, but discarded the idea. Grey had an opportunity to find real information, and scurrying away while the police arrived, likely without a warrant, wasn't going to help Viktor in the next twenty-four hours. From the look of things, a quick search by the cops would yield nothing, and Grey didn't want the lackeys arrested. He wanted Dante and Darius arrested.

He knew this building held secrets, but the longer he observed the monitors the less he saw, and he knew he was pushing his luck. Someone could contact or visit the guard station at any minute, and eventually they would.

Just past the guard room was the huge main elevator, a staircase right beside it. Even leaving was a dicey proposition: He was going to have to slip into the grounds, fumble with the iron gate, and hope no one noticed.

He disabled the silent alarm protecting the complex, then put his palms down on the counter beside the monitors and leaned forward.

What was he missing?

Two things came to him. The first was that the service elevator down the hall appeared on none of the monitors. The second was his discussion with

# THE DIABOLIST

Viktor about the importance of symbology and numerology to black magicians and occultists.

Why only five floors? Why not three, six, seven? Perhaps he was overthinking it, but Darius didn't seem like the type of man who left anything to chance. Or maybe the number five had some significance of which he was unaware.

Blowing out a breath, he hobbled to the service elevator and unlocked the door. He slipped into the small space and ran his eyes over the control panel. The basement was labeled as the first floor, the upper levels two through five. Just below the fire alarm was an access box. He tried the guard's keys, and none of them worked.

Grey frowned. The guard should have a key to the elevator's access box. Maybe it was on a separate key ring, but if so, then it wasn't kept in the guard room, which was also odd. Grey went to work on the lock, complicated but still a pin-and-tumbler. It took him a few minutes of exact pressure and careful listening, ear pressed to the panel, but he finally heard the click of success. When the panel swung down, Grey's jaw dropped along with it.

Two more buttons appeared, set into a hidden control panel. The bottom button was labeled *G*, the top one labeled with the next number in line.

The sixth floor.

Grey knew he might be walking into the lion's den. He shut and locked the elevator door, then pressed the button for the sixth floor.

When the elevator stopped ascending, Grey pulled the handgun and readied it at chest level, easing the door open. He found himself in an empty foyer, the walls draped in black cloth, illuminated by gaslit candelabra. No sound except the faint hiss of gas.

A door led from the foyer to a hexagonal room with six empty armchairs made of black wood. The walls and floor were made from the same material. A sigil-inscribed door loomed opposite where Grey was standing, and the rounded ceiling, painted to resemble a star-filled galaxy, lent an illusion of depth. A skylight in the middle of the ceiling allowed moonlight to filter inside. Grey let his eyes adjust to the low luminosity, then moved to the door in the far wall. He had to pick the lock again.

His eyes roamed the next room, taking in the cushion-strewn floor, the Persian carpet and silk netting, the velvet-covered walls and dozens of unlit candles placed about the room. A sizable triangle outlined in chalk covered the middle of the room, a variety of other sigils surrounding the chalk. Grey was getting the distinct impression that the entire level had been abandoned for the night.

Inside a walk-in closet Grey found a rack of silk robes, boxes of candles, and entire shelves full of massage oils and sex toys. A curtain next to the closet concealed a marble bathroom with a wall-length mirror, a walk-in shower, a giant bathtub with multiple jets, and a cabinet full of syringes and pharmaceuticals.

Grey went through another curtain leading to a bookshelf-lined study. The bookshelves were spilling over with books on magic and the occult, with an entire bookshelf devoted to manuals on sexual practices, both ancient and modern. A tapestry on one of the walls depicted a tree with roots growing out of a pile of rotting corpses, vultures perched on the branches and feeding on the bodies.

On a desk in the center of the room was a laptop docking station. The absence of the computer confirmed Grey's suspicion: Darius had already set in motion whatever he had planned for tomorrow night.

Grey searched the desk and took a stack of folders, full of receipts and papers. Another door led to a modest kitchen, and then Grey stopped in front of a black wooden door that gave him an uneasy feeling.

The door was unlocked. Grey eased it open.

A giant urn filled the center of the stone-walled square room, tongues of flame flicking upward from the mouth of the urn. From his research and his conversation with Dastur Zaveri, Grey knew this was the *atashkadeh*, the fire temple, representative to Zoroastrians of purification and marked by a cease-less flame tended by the priests. He also knew that dry sandalwood was most often used to fuel the sacred fire, but from the greasy smell of animal fat emanating from the urn, and the piles of knobby bones stacked along one of the walls, Grey made a wild guess that, to the followers of Ahriman, this fire represented something besides purification.

On the far wall, an enormous glass aquarium swarmed with snakes, spiders, and a variety of insects. Grey knew Zoroastrians considered crawling, slithering creatures abhorrent. This room was an abomination, a perversion of a fire temple.

He had found his priest of Ahriman.

Grey was no sociologist, but he was pretty sure the Order of New Enlightenment's starry-eyed worshippers might be put off by the drugs, sex, and black magic lurking on the top floor. How many other inner sanctums, Grey wondered, looked similar to this? Who knew what lay underneath the veils, inside the holy-of-holies, behind the proverbial and sometimes all-too-real curtains?

Grey left the room and swept the entire sixth floor, searching for hidden doors, safes, anything that might contain more information on tomorrow night. Finding nothing else, he stood in the middle of the room with the six throne-like chairs, staring at the skylight, shivering from the pain in his thigh.

If there was something that revealed Darius's hand, it was either long gone or buried among the folders Grey was holding. It was time to get the hell out of Crazytown.

He returned to the elevator and descended to the basement, planning to return to the guard station, trip a few alarms, and walk right out the front door, on the pretense of securing the perimeter. He'd have to do his best to mask his limp, but if he could get to the gate before anyone stopped him, he might have a chance. The bigger issue was escaping the neighborhood, as he had the feeling it was teeming with Satanists.

Grey could call the police with the guard's phone, but he still couldn't risk getting tied up in procedure, and he wasn't giving up those folders. Instead, he called information and found a taxi service, instructing the driver to meet him at an intersection two blocks away from Bar 666.

As he started down the hallway to the guard station, the door to the guard room burst open and a group of men brandishing guns spilled out. Grey cursed and scrambled backwards. They must have caught him on the monitor as soon as he left the service elevator.

Grey pulled his gun and shot the first man in the chest, causing mass confusion. They should have expected him to have the guard's weapon. He moved in a backwards crouch as he fired, trying to keep them unbalanced long enough to cover the ten feet to the elevator. He shot at least three more, but before he reached the elevator a bullet clipped his side, just below his injured rib.

He lurched inside, slamming and locking the door. No way he could last another round. He heard shouting and running, and he didn't waste any time. There was only one button left to press, and he did so furiously.

**51**

The heat was intense, the sense of isolation more so. The world stilled as Viktor climbed, his sense of time winding down and then ceasing altogether. By the time he had climbed a fourth of the way up the mountain, he felt as if he were moving in a bubble of shimmering heat and pain, sweat pouring down his body, every muscle throbbing, his mind screaming at him to do the sensible thing and stop.

Halfway up, Viktor rested in the limp shade of a desiccated pine. He gulped water from the canteen, forcing himself to save enough for the return. When he had regained his wind he rose and peered across the basin, to where he had left the guide.

No sign of Antonio. Viktor assumed he had wandered off for the moment or gone to relieve himself.

His gaze moved downward, and he saw a figure climbing near the bottom, following the same path as Viktor. Viktor whipped out the binoculars and focused.

He cursed. It was the man from Zador's shop, the same man who had followed him in York.

Viktor replaced the binoculars in the pack and started climbing, this time for his life. He scrabbled over loose rocks and long slabs of stone, slipping on the smooth surfaces, bracing himself with his hands when the climb became near-vertical. He alternated between admiring and despising whoever had built this monastery in such an absurd place. It was impregnable without an army of harpy eagles.

He tried not to think about the man below. Viktor knew he stood no chance against his pursuer. This man was much younger, most likely a trained killer, and Viktor was nearing the end of his endurance. His only hope was to reach the monastery and hope someone was left to help him.

He stopped to use the binoculars, realizing with a flagging spirit that the man was climbing at twice his speed. Viktor's legs hurt so much he debated moving off the trail and hiding among the droopy-leaved cacti or spiky palms. Then he realized the foolishness of a seven-foot-tall, sixty-year-old professor hiding behind a foot-wide cactus on an exposed Sicilian hillside, at the mercy of even the slightest glance to the side by his pursuer. Viktor said *do prdele* for the hundredth time and poured every ounce of his will into the remainder of the climb.

Somehow Viktor reached the top of the path first, though he knew the man was just behind him. The cliff wall rose fifty feet above him, impossible without gear. The path leveled off and continued around the side of a boulder.

Viktor was fighting for every breath, but he didn't dare rest. He risked a glance below, the long granite cliff a slab of shaved ice streaked with grime. No sign of his pursuer, and that worried Viktor even more.

Was he right below him, taking aim at Viktor from behind a shrub? Did he know another path to the top?

Viktor clambered around the boulder. The path ended at a narrow opening. He squeezed through, following the naturally cleft passage through the rock, his body sagging in despair when he rounded a corner and saw what lay at the end of the path.

An iron gate, fifteen feet tall and spanning the width of the passage, blocked his way. There was no handle, no lock, no possibility of ascent. Viktor heaved at the gate with all his might, but it didn't even rattle. The thing had been built to withstand a small army.

# THE DIABOLIST

Viktor heard a noise behind him, the scrabble of loose rocks below. He pounded on the gate and shouted in Italian, his voice weak from the strain of the climb. "Is anyone there?"

He took out his knife, debating fleeing back to the slope before his pursuer entered the narrow passage. At least he would have the advantage of higher ground, though he knew in his heart that wouldn't matter.

More sounds from below, and Viktor beat at the gate in frustration. "Anyone!"

"Who's there?"

Viktor jumped at the sound, already having decided no one still lived at the monastery. The voice had come from the other side of the gate, a man speaking Italian-accented English, an educated voice with the ring of authority.

A monastic voice.

"I'm a professor at Charles University in Prague," Viktor said. "Please hurry, I'm being followed. There's no time to explain."

"Why are you here?"

Viktor wanted to bellow in frustration, but he pushed his words out. "I'm a private investigator as well, working with Interpol. I'm trying to solve a series of murders, and there's about to be another one if you don't let me through."

"The last man I let through was a deceiver."

"I'm tracking that man," Viktor said. "It's why I'm here. I don't know how to convince you, except to swear that it's true."

There was a prolonged silence, each passing second a needle of compressed time piercing Viktor's spirit. Knife in hand, he kept his back against the gate, waiting for his pursuer to appear in the shade of the passage.

Again he heard the clatter of loose rock, this time on the other end of the cleft passage. Finally the monk said, in a voice as grim and stern as the mountain itself, "Renounce thrice the name of Ahriman, and I will open the gate."

Viktor didn't hesitate. "Ahriman, I renounce thee. Ahriman, I renounce thee. Ahriman, I renounce thee."

The gate creaked open. Viktor hurried through, the giant gate slamming shut behind him.

Grey knew where the other buttons led: either to one of the main floors smothered with cult members, or to a top floor with no exit. He worried the last button led to a dungeon, but he had no choice.

The elevator descended, and when the door opened he was looking at a small garage with four parking spaces. Three were empty, but in one of them the headlights of a black BMW X5 stared back at him like the eyes of a dark savior. Grey hurried to the SUV, expecting to waste precious time with a hotwire. Instead, he found the keys in the ignition, a rare gift from the capricious god of chance.

He roared down the only way out, a tunnel-like egress that ended at a wide steel door. Grey pushed the remote opener clipped to the driver's visor, and the door lifted. He sped down the driveway, noticing in the rearview that he had exited from what looked like an abandoned building.

He entered onto a street full of graffiti-covered warehouses. Grey guessed Darius had purchased the entire dilapidated block. Two blocks later he passed the gleaming glass building on his left, then entered the maze of East London.

No one followed, and Grey surmised that was because no one still left in that building had any clue about the service elevator, the sixth floor, the hidden garage, or whatever was going down tomorrow night.

When Grey had passed by the glass building, he had noticed an elongated space between the highest windows and the roof, a space that contained the windowless sixth floor. To the untrained eye it looked natural, part of the building's neo-modernist architecture. And the aesthetic capstone on the roof, a crystal dome in the middle of the structure, masked the rounded central chamber and the skylight.

Clever.

Grey worked his way back to Hackney Road, stopping at a pharmacy for supplies to treat and bandage his wounds. After stopping at a liquor store for a bottle of rum, he found a parking garage and went to work on his injuries.

Emergency medical care wasn't his forte, but he had enough training from the military to disinfect his wounds and stop the blood loss, stitch himself, apply bandages, and get through the next few days. Or so he hoped. The bruised ribs and the head injury would be fine, and the gunshot wound had only clipped his side, taking off a quarter-size piece of flesh. The leg needed a doctor. He knew he was risking infection and long-term damage by not seeking medical care. And if he lost too much blood, then he was no use to anyone.

He picked up a burner cell at a Vodafone store, having left the guard's phone in the garage, in case it had a tracer. He would ditch the SUV as soon as he reached central London.

He tried Viktor, but the call went straight to voice mail. Grey grimaced. He had to believe Viktor had been compromised. It didn't fit with the MO of the other murders, but Viktor didn't fit within the MO at all. Viktor was personal to Darius, and when something was personal, all bets were off.

Which made Grey think about Dante.

Made him think about his own torture, the people Dante had murdered, his carelessness for life and human dignity. Then Grey stopped thinking, consumed by an all-too-familiar rage that burned within him like a bottomless furnace, stoked by the injustice honeycombing the world.

Grey's temper had always flared at the slightest offense, and it was his greatest weakness. Not just because it could get him killed, but because of the easy violence that went with it.

Grey had been steeped in violence, beaten by his father from his earliest memory, alone on the streets as a teen. It shamed him. He knew he was part of an unfortunate cycle of violence that humankind had yet to overcome. Jesus and Gandhi and King, these were men who had changed the world with peace.

They were better men than he. He hated what the violence did to him, but he could only play the hand he was dealt, try to do good with it, and work to break the cycle the only way he knew how.

Dante had also been thrust into violence. Grey empathized with him, but he would never sympathize. Grey knew as well as anyone that violence was a choice, and Dante continued to choose poorly.

While Dante had to be stopped, Grey had to ensure that when they met again, Grey fought not out of rage, but out of necessity. Not only because Grey might lose the fight if he let the violence blind him, but also because if he lost control, then Grey and Dante would be no different, amoral slaves to their fury.

And *that* was what Dominic Grey feared most.

He checked his remote voice mail as he drove into central London. Still no word from Viktor. The one message he did have made him press the phone to his ear.

Anka.

She had called him less than thirty minutes ago, at nine p.m., asking him to meet her at a restaurant in the West End. She said she thought terrible things were about to happen, and that she would wait for him all night if need be.

Grey's first thought was that she had called him awfully close in time to his escape. His second thought was that she might be the only person who could help him find Darius and Viktor. His third thought was that the sound of her voice got under his skin, causing a tingling to spread throughout his body.

His fourth thought was that he was hungry beyond belief.

The monk in jeans and a worn shirt looked about Viktor's age. He was a robust man, short and stout. A trimmed gray beard covered the bottom half of a round face.

As the monk secured the gate with an iron bar as thick as Viktor's leg, Viktor eyed the top of the gate. "He might have climbing gear, though I didn't notice a pack."

The monk took a very modern pistol from the back of his jeans. "The gate is not the last line of defense."

Viktor eyed the pistol. "You're one of the Tutori. A warrior monk."

He didn't deny the statement, and Viktor took in his surroundings. He was on a hidden summit perched at the top of the mountain, a flat bed of rock-strewn grass perhaps a hundred yards square, dotted by a few hardy pine trees. On the other side of the summit he saw the stone rampart he had glimpsed from the valley. He realized it wasn't a rampart at all, but a small, fortresslike chapel made of granite and surrounded on three sides by another iron gate. A sheer drop protected the fourth side.

He stopped to consider the implications of the long climb, the gate at the end of the tunnel, the impregnable chapel, this entire medieval fortress stuck on top of a rock in the middle of nowhere.

*What are they protecting?*

A rectangular stone dwelling rested in the center of the plateau, topped by a barrel-tiled roof and a chimney. Viktor was not overly surprised by the isolated location. He had seen examples of asceticism from around the world, and the extreme lengths to which human beings would go in the name of religion or faith or enlightenment no longer surprised him. He had seen self-flagellating priests covered in puss-filled wounds, nuns who never slept more than an hour without rising to pray, Shaolin monks who meditated while lying under a two-ton rock, Tibetan lamas living in caves at twenty thousand feet with only a thin robe for protection.

In their quest for the divine, Viktor thought, some became more than human.

The monk led him to a chair outside the dwelling, facing the huge gate. "Wait."

He went inside and Viktor watched the gate, ready to call out if anyone appeared. Strangely, no sounds of attempted entry emanated from the rock passage. Viktor assumed the man on the other side was searching for another way through, but he felt secure with the monk and the centuries-old fortification, and was too exhausted to analyze further.

As night approached, the view of the valley changed from stunning to sublime, the pyramidal slopes rose-hued in the twilight. The monk returned with another chair in one hand, a glass of water in the other. "I'm Brother Pietro."

Viktor accepted the glass. "Thank you, Father. For this and for my life."

"Call me Brother, or just Pietro. I've taken the monastic vows, but I'm not ordained."

The monk sat in the chair beside Viktor, facing the gate, pistol in his lap. "Not many know of the Tutori outside these walls. Until last year, excepting a handful in the Vatican, I would have said none."

"I'm a student of history," Viktor said.

"Professors should be the best students," the monk replied. "What is it you teach that you're familiar with such an esoteric subject?"

"Religious phenomenology."

The monk turned to Viktor. "Interesting. And to what do you ascribe the religious phenomena you must have witnessed over the years?"

"A phenomenologist does not concern oneself with the question of ultimate origin," Viktor said.

"But a human being does."

Viktor took a long drink of water, soothing his parched throat. He was very much concerned with those questions.

"Who are you running from?" the monk said.

"A member of an organization called L'église de la Bête."

"I know them," the monk said quietly. One of his hands moved to the pistol. "How can I be assured this is not a clever ruse to gain access?"

"Because they wouldn't have sent an aging professor," Viktor said, "and because I believe that after recent events, no member of L'église de la Bête would dare renounce the name of Ahriman. I believe someone is reviving the heresy."

Brother Pietro returned to pointing the pistol at the gate, knuckles tensing. "I feared as much."

"I assume the Tutori settled here after defeating the original heresy, but why?"

The monk pursed his lips before he spoke, and Viktor sensed a tone of resignation, even loss, in his voice. "I'm a religious man by trade, but . . . let us just say that faith has never been my strong suit. I'm a man of duty, if nothing else."

Pietro turned his head towards the house, and this time a look of pain overcame his visage, his eyes flooding with such empathy and heartache that Viktor himself was moved.

"We defeated the Ahriman Heresy," the monk said, "but the threat of Ahriman remained alive and well. It is not so simple to defeat a god, or the idea of a god. The Vatican was terrified the heresy would spring up again, and it commissioned the Tutori to keep a perpetual vigil. It might sound extreme, but it's no different than any religious apparatus fulfilling Christ's commission over time, to keep the faith alive and well. Ours is just a more unusual task."

"But why here?" Viktor said.

"The leader of the heresy was possessed, according to the history, of supernatural beauty and charisma. It was also said that he could move about the world as did Ahriman, appearing at his whim."

"The legendary three powers of the Devil," Viktor said. "A myth originating with Ahriman."

"Nonsense, of course, at least to me. But it wasn't nonsense in the sixteenth century, and it was believed that this priest acquired his powers after reading a book, a certain occult tome."

A movement near the gate made Viktor's breath catch in his throat, but it was just a bird rustling through one of the pines. "The Ahriman Grimoire," Viktor said.

"You've read one of the surviving histories?"

"I have. Why didn't the Tutori simply burn the book?"

"The Vatican may destroy copies, or make a public show, but they always keep the original, to study and preserve the knowledge. Even if profane."

"But something as allegedly dangerous as this," Viktor said, "at least in those times . . ."

"That's why we have this absurd fortress in the middle of nowhere. The Vatican has a very hard time letting go of tradition, and two monks at a time are commissioned here to this day." The monk made a wry face, but Viktor saw a squandered life reflected in his eyes. "Though I think they've kept this place so long because of the excellent wine we cultivate from the hillside."

"How did Crowley find this place?"

Brother Pietro's gaze sharpened. "How do you know about Crowley's visit?"

"Once I learned the Tutori were decommissioned in Palermo, and given the location of Crowley's magical school in Cefalù, I made inquiries."

"I suppose the monastery is no secret to the villages in the area, though no one knows our true history. Aleister was a clever man and approached our predecessors."

"They turned him away, I assume," Viktor said.

# THE DIABOLIST

"Aleister threatened magical reprisal, and they threatened to send him home via the sheer cliff behind our fortress. He was forced out of the country soon after. A few others have found us over the centuries, with the same result." The monk's eyes again found the dwelling, fists clenched. "Until last year."

"Darius?"

The monk's head whipped around. "You know him?"

"I did, a very long time ago."

The monk looked through Viktor, his face tight and still.

"He took the book, didn't he?" Viktor said. "It's why you asked me to renounce the name of Ahriman. Not because of your beliefs, but because of his."

"I'd gone to the village for supplies. He must have known my schedule. My brother, the second monk commissioned, had not been . . . well . . . for some time."

"Your brother in the Tutori?"

"And by birth. He's my only family. After what was done to him, I begged him to return to Rome and let them send someone else. He refused."

Viktor's eyes slipped towards the dwelling. "You haven't told Rome what happened?"

"My brother chooses to live alone, not to be made a spectacle." Viktor didn't understand what he was talking about, but Brother Pietro stood with a world-weary sigh. "Come. He'll want to speak to you."

He led Viktor to a door in the rear of the dwelling, then gripped Viktor's arm. "His name is Father Angelo, and you should prepare yourself. Terrible things were done to my brother. Unlike me, he's a very holy man."

**53**

Anka had left no return number, and her call registered as unknown on Grey's voice mail. She wasn't giving him an option, he thought. She knew he would come.

Grey ditched the car in a parking garage and hit the Underground. He didn't know the Italian restaurant Anka had chosen, but he used to work as a bouncer at a club in Soho, and he knew the area well.

He exited at Piccadilly, riding the long escalator to the surface and stepping into a crush of people, neon billboards, and giant video screens. When he used to stand in Piccadilly Circus, he would get a mental picture of a traveler from a distant future stumbling upon the ruins of this place, the noise and lights gone, the monolithic remains the center of a dystopian Minotaur's maze. Now his old premonition felt eerily current, as if he were a lost warrior trying to unravel the secrets of the labyrinth before the monster devoured them all.

Grey left the chaos of Piccadilly, limped down theater-lined Shaftesbury and entered the twisting streets of Soho. After stopping at a hip secondhand store to ditch his bloody guard's uniform and change into a pair of jeans and a black sweater, he pressed through the crowd of pierced and tattooed Londoners, his rough appearance drawing stares. He popped a few more painkillers, then cut through an alley and spotted the brick eatery Anka had named on the phone.

# THE DIABOLIST

He noticed her at once. She was on the patio in her fitted leather jacket, blond hair spilling across her collarbone, sipping a glass of wine. In a café full of fashionably slim and beautiful European women, Anka still stood out like a flash of lightning in a moonless sky.

Grey eyeballed the restaurant and the street, saw nothing out of place, then strode to Anka's table. Her face sagged with relief as he approached, but he slapped a twenty-pound note on the table. "Does that cover it?"

"Yes, but—"

"Then let's go," he said.

"I just arrived, and no one knows I'm here."

"Now."

Her mouth puckered into an oval of hurt, but she grabbed her handbag and rose. "What happened to you? Why do you look like you were just . . ."

"Kidnapped and tortured? Because I was."

She grabbed his hands. "You can't think I had anything to do with that."

His flat stare never wavered. "I don't know what I think, when it comes to you."

They were standing in the middle of the street. She was looking him straight in the eye with no trace of subterfuge, no telltale body language. She reached up to stroke his cheek. "I can only imagine what happened. If Dante was involved, I'm sure it was terrible."

At least she hadn't given him empty promises, told him he could trust her. Regardless, he was out of options. He took her by the hand and led her down the street.

"Where're we going?" she said.

"To a different restaurant."

Grey led her across Regent Street and into a more residential section of the West End. It was a little risky, but he had to lose the crowds to make sure they were not being followed. And if they were, then he knew who to blame.

He wound in and out of the quiet streets and mews without a word, focused on the journey. Anka clenched his hand as they walked, peering nervously around each new corner. So far he had seen nothing out of the ordinary, and by the time they reached his destination, a hidden square with tiny streets branching in five directions, he felt sure they had not been followed.

He led her to a bistro in the middle of the square, flanked by a coffee shop and a tandoori restaurant. Grey had once dated a waitress who worked at this bistro, and they used to meet at an after-hours lounge across the street when their shifts ended.

Grey requested a table by one of the street-facing windows, with a view of all five streets spilling into the square. He also knew the back door of the restaurant opened to an alleyway. There were plenty of exits.

After they ordered, Anka said, "I've never noticed this square before. It's charming."

"It would be under different circumstances," he said. "So let me ask you: What's to stop Darius from doing his magic trick and popping in to greet us?"

"You're not asking because you think he might, are you?"

"No," he said.

She looked away. "You still don't believe me."

"Don't take it personally. I'm not much of a believer in anything of that sort."

"It means you don't trust me," she said.

"I think *you* believe it. But that doesn't make it real."

Her face sagged, and Grey reminded himself that she had saved his life. "It does beg the question as to why you're not worried," he said, "but let's move past that. Where have you been? Why'd you call me?"

"I've been in hiding, but something's happening. I think tomorrow night. And I *am* worried, just not about him showing up tonight. He's too preoccupied to worry about me right now."

"Then what're you worried about?"

She met his eyes. "You."

# THE DIABOLIST

"Judging by my pleasant little chat with Dante, you might need to be more worried about yourself. Most of his questions concerned your whereabouts." Her face paled, and Grey said, "It also makes me think Darius can't flit about the world as easily as you think he can."

She pursed her lips. "I've come to the same conclusion. I don't know if it requires a spell or a personal connection or proximity or what, but I do think there are limits. But regardless," she said hurriedly, noticing the glaze in Grey's eyes, "that's terrible what happened to you. Dante's pure evil."

"You don't need to convince me," he said.

"That's why you're limping?"

"Yes."

She covered her mouth with her hand. "Because of me."

"Dante's responsible for his own actions."

Her hand returned to her lap, and she looked to the side. "I saw him last night, with Darius. It's how I know something's happening."

"I thought you were in hiding?" he said.

"I . . . saw the conversation."

"Oh. You mean like that."

She bit her lip. "I wasn't present like I sometimes am. I was just sort of mentally . . . there."

Grey leaned back and crossed his arms. "Why didn't you tell me you were into the occult before you met Darius?"

"What?"

"Were you or were you not studying the occult before you met him?"

"Have you been researching me?" she said.

"Just answer the question, Anka."

Despair seeped into her eyes. "Without you, I'm truly alone in this madness. Of *course* I was researching the occult before I met Darius. Wouldn't you, if you suddenly found your spirit separating from your body and floating through walls? I'd never been so scared in my life. When everyone said I was possessed by the Devil, I started to believe them. I was looking for answers anywhere I could, long before Darius arrived."

She forced away a lump in her throat, and this time Grey put his hand on her arm. "I'm sorry, of course you would," he said. "I'd do the same. I checked up on you because I had to be sure I could trust you."

"And are you?"

"I'm not a very trusting person," he said. "And our relationship hasn't exactly been normal."

"I know," she whispered. "I guess I can't ask for more right now."

"If we get through tomorrow, maybe we can talk." Grey removed his hand from her arm. "There's one more thing I have to ask, though."

"I'm not afraid of questions."

"Why did Dante call you Eve?" he said.

"When I found out who Simon really was and confronted him," she said, "he told me we should start again, as new people. He asked if he could call me Eve. He said it was a good name for a new beginning. At that point I was terrified of him, so I agreed."

Part of Grey wanted to find a chink in Anka's armor, because that would restore the natural order of things, would let him know where they both stood. But try as he might, he failed to detect a flicker of deception.

He gave a very slow nod, and she squeezed his arm. "Thank you," she said.

He took a swallow of water. "Back to last night. Anything you can remember could help."

"I didn't get details, just that something will happen tomorrow night, something important."

"Do you know where they'll be?" he said.

"They didn't discuss leaving, so I assume somewhere in London. Darius asked Dante if all was ready for tomorrow night, and Dante said yes. I heard them mention a hacker as well."

"Like a computer hacker?"

She held her palms up. "I think so. I'm not sure."

"Curious," he said.

"The only other thing of substance I caught was that the Inner Council would be there to observe."

"Did you get any names, addresses, anything?"

"Nothing like that," she said. "I'm sorry. Whatever it is . . . I fear it's going to be terrible."

"I think that's a safe assumption. There's something else, isn't there?"

Her eyes moved downward. "Viktor's name came up."

Grey's lips compressed. "Another impression with no details?"

"I'm sorry again," she said, touching his arm.

Their meals came and Grey devoured his without pleasure, forcing it down for fuel. He asked for a double espresso and the check, paid in cash, and had to stop and grip the table as he rose, the throbbing in his thigh from the sudden movement almost unbearable.

He pushed away from the table. "Let's go."

# 54

**B**rother Pietro held the door as Viktor entered a tiny bedchamber reeking of decay. A cot lay against the far wall, a wooden bedside table at its head. On top of the table was an oil lamp, a basin of water, and a leather-bound Bible with a cover worn to a nub.

Despite his years in the field Viktor flinched when he saw the shell of a man lying on his back on the cot. A stained bandage covered his forehead. Empty, blood-encrusted sockets were all that remained of his eyes, and his pockmarked face looked ravaged by some terrible disease. Uncombed, wispy white hair spilled from his head onto the bedsheet.

Viktor couldn't guess his age. He looked far older than Pietro, but that might have been due to his deteriorating physical state.

"I apologize for my appearance." His voice was a controlled whisper that belied his appearance, and the opposite of his brother: the voice of a man completely at ease with the state of his soul, despite his terrible wounds. Viktor thought of his own aching body, and of various injuries he had sustained in the past, none of which he had borne this well, and none of which were in the same universe as the sufferings of this man.

Then Viktor noticed his wrists, lying face-up by his side. Ooze-encrusted sores covered the middle of each wrist, bleeding at the edges. On closer inspection he realized the sores possessed a circular shape, both in the same location. Viktor had seen similar wounds on one other occasion, when he had visited a Catholic priest in Uganda who was reportedly afflicted by the stigmata.

# THE DIABOLIST

Hundreds of verified cases of stigmata around the world no longer caused Viktor to doubt the occurrence of the phenomenon. He believed they were caused by auto-suggestion rather than faith, an extreme psychosomatic reaction. Theological placebo effect explained the relative limitation of the occurrence to Catholics, similar to the ability of Juju priests to cause spontaneous lesions and boils on the bodies of their worshippers. An unexplained wrinkle in the Uganda case was that the blood pouring from the priest's wound did not match his blood type. Fraud was suspected but never proven, and doctors investigating the case proffered no other explanation.

"Not all of this was done by my last visitor," the priest said. "I have been . . . afflicted . . . for some time."

"It's fine, Father. I'm not troubled by your appearance."

"You're Viktor Radek?"

"I am, but I never told your brother my name."

"It was told to me by my visitor." He grasped the iron cross attached to the rosary around his neck, fingers trembling. "The follower of Ahriman."

Viktor didn't say a word, but a nausea started building in his chest. Could Darius truly have done such a thing? He tried not to look at the priest's face, but his eyes kept sliding back to those empty sockets.

"You wonder why he left me alive. Why bother to pluck my eyes, to lay his hands on my body and scar me with his heresy?"

Like a baby's first struggling movements, the priest's hands moved to the top of the bedsheet, unfurling the white covering to reveal a chest covered with thickened red welts. At first Viktor didn't see it, but then he realized the scars formed a crude word written in Avestan.

*Ahriman.*

"Could you recognize his voice in a court of law?" Viktor said thickly. "Did he say anything you can remember?"

"He said to tell Viktor Radek he will always be a step behind."

Viktor's mouth opened, but then his face flushed and he clenched his jaw, an almost unbearable rage rising within him. Father Angelo replaced the bedsheet. "He's changed since you knew him, hasn't he?"

"Sorry?" Viktor said.

"Does he win the hearts and minds of men, has he mastered the art of the flesh, does he move about the world unseen? I've heard about the murders, even here."

"There's a plausible explanation, of that I assure you. Darius is a master magician, an illusionist."

"Do you understand the reason for the last power? It's a perversion of Jesus's appearance to his disciples after the resurrection. True bilocation. Are you familiar with the case of Padre Pio?"

"An Italian priest who witnesses claimed could bilocate," Viktor said. He looked at the priest's wrists and said quietly, "He also had wounds such as yours."

"Yes, he was united with the passion of Christ. Allowed to share in the tiniest portion of His pain."

"As do you, I presume," Viktor said.

"One never presumes such a thing. Christ would never *give* such a power, or *cause* an affliction such as the stigmata. They are gained through intimacy with Him, a physical manifestation of empathy with our Lord and Savior."

"What do you know about Ahriman, and about Darius's beliefs in this being? How do I find him?"

"Ahriman corrupts. He has defiled this man, and you cannot hope to overcome him now. His own faith alone can defeat him."

"This is about justice, not faith," Viktor said grimly.

"Faith is what connects us to God, drives the miracles of the saints. So, too, it allows Ahriman to work through this man. You must sever the tie."

Viktor tried to keep the impatience from his voice. "You mean the grimoire."

"The grimoire is an empty vessel, a tool used by Ahriman to strengthen the faith of his followers. A manipulation of the mind of man."

"You've read it?" Viktor said.

"How can we defend against that which we do not know?"

"Surely there's something inside that can help me. Is there a ritual he must perform, perhaps at a certain place?"

"Of course there's a ritual," the priest said. "Ritual is the first step towards faith, though ultimately unnecessary. True faith is rare in the extreme, and thus Ahriman must convince his servants that they are able to *gain* his favor. Terrible, terrible things are proffered within the grimoire, wicked deeds to be performed, unholy consumptions to be made."

"You're saying you believe anyone could gain these abilities if one's faith were strong enough?" Viktor said.

"'I tell you the truth, if you have faith as small as a mustard seed you can say to this mountain, "Move from here to there" and it will move. Nothing will be impossible for you.'"

Viktor stared in frustration at the sightless priest.

"But there is a limit, a constraint," the priest said. "To strengthen the faith of the servant, the grimoire claims there can be but a single favored disciple at any one time. Only one granting of the three powers."

"Forgive me, Father, but none of this helps me find Darius. I need something concrete. Do you have something his followers would fear? Perhaps another relic, from the days of the original heresy?"

"I told you, the relics mean nothing. It's not the letter of the law that concerns God but the faith it imparts. You must use faith as a weapon."

"And I told you that I'm not a man of faith," Viktor said.

"Not yours," he whispered, "his. Ahriman cannot be defeated, but his servant can. *Sever the tie.*"

"You'd make a good religious phenomenologist."

The monk's eyelids closed, and he folded his hands across his chest. Viktor had to move closer to hear his murmurings. "'And I beheld another beast coming up out of the earth, and he had two horns as a lamb, and he spake as a dragon. And he exerciseth all the power of the first beast before him, and causeth the earth and them which dwell therein to worship the first beast. And he doeth great wonders, so that he maketh fire come down from heaven in the sight of men, and deceiveth them that dwell on the earth by those miracles which he had power to do in the sight of the beast . . . and his number is six hundred threescore and six.'"

"Revelations Thirteen," Viktor said. "With all due respect, Father, quoting Revelations doesn't make sense. Darius is a Diabolist, a follower of Ahriman because he believes this being grants him power. Ahriman and Zoroastrianism have nothing to do with Christianity, except for a commonality of myth."

A convulsion lifted the priest's body off the cot, and it took him a moment to recover. "Do not be deceived. There is a singular evil force in this world, in this universe, and its name is irrelevant. Satan, Baal, Iblis, Mara, Kali, Tiamat, Ahriman: These denominations are human constructs. I quote the word of God as I know it to be, with the tools God has given me to humbly understand a portion of His design. Others do the same."

"I don't dispute the existence of evil," Viktor said. "What I dispute is the existence of a Devil with horns and a red pitchfork, tossing human beings into the nine circles of Hell. Or a mythological entity from Persian legend named Ahriman, who created a book that allows one of his worshippers to flit about the world causing murder and mayhem."

"Who knows why the Evil One chooses to act as he does?" the priest said softly. "Who knows why our Lord chose a Jewish carpenter to die on a cross for our sins? Why he created a universe as complex as the one we have? You may not be a man of faith, but I know that you search. I sense you at least allow for the possibility of a Creator God to whom you attribute the impossibility of existence, of a deity or life force or entity so apart from humanity, so *above*, that He is outside our ability to ever fully comprehend?"

Viktor didn't respond, and the priest said, "We can never hope to understand the mind of God. Of course He is not a white-bearded patriarch from the Middle East, enthroned in the firmament above. He is outside the scope of human imagination, he is God. But don't you see? *It is the same with the Evil One.*"

He let this statement sink in. In all of Viktor's years studying religions and cults, with their various beliefs and rationale concerning the presence of evil, he had never heard it put quite that way. It caused his skin to prickle, before he pushed away the priest's words as just another, albeit more complicated, superstition.

"I find these statements odd coming from a Catholic priest," Viktor said.

"Piety is not an absence of honest thought. To attempt to understand God is to attempt an impossible task, and to understand there might be other avenues to comprehension."

"Then why not attribute evil to God, rather than a second entity?" Viktor said. "Didn't Isaiah say, 'I am the Lord and there is no other. I form light and create darkness, I make weal and create woe'?"

"I'm Christian, not Zoroastrian. I do not believe in a separate but equal entity, but rather a Satan whose purpose as created by God I shall never understand. Then again, I also allow for the possibility that I might be wrong, or that the intertwining of the two is beyond my comprehension. Despite what some within the Church claim, the ontology of the Devil has never been resolved. I believe there is no striving towards the light without the dark, no love and free will without pain and suffering. But it's not our task to contemplate how evil sprang from God. It's our task to struggle against the Devil."

The priest beckoned Viktor closer. "Take my rosary."

Viktor hesitated, and the priest said, "Those of us at the extreme end of faith . . . such as myself and my visitor from Ahriman . . . we see this realm more clearly than do you. This rosary is the embodiment of *my* faith, my blood and spirit intertwined with that of my Savior."

He lifted his head ever so gently, removing the rosary from his neck. The movement seemed to take a lifetime, and Viktor stood there dumbly, a man always in control who was somehow indecisive in the presence of this priest. Though he had no desire to take the rosary, he couldn't bring himself to refuse.

Viktor bent to receive it, almost gagging at the putrescence of the priest's wounds. After slipping the rosary around Viktor's neck, Father Angelo lay back as if he had expended his last ounce of energy.

"Do you know where he is?" Viktor said.

"I do not."

"Do you have any idea what he plans to do?" Viktor said.

"He has renewed the heresy." His enfeebled fingers made the sign of the cross. "Go with God, my son." Then his hands returned to his chest, his eyelids sagging with the heaviness of sleep.

Viktor waited beside Father Angelo for a long moment, feeling as if this entire foolish journey had been in vain. He had learned nothing more about Darius except the knowledge that he had slipped further into madness than Viktor thought possible, that he had destroyed the body of this gentle man of God. For that alone there was no penalty too harsh.

He stepped out of the room and eased the door closed. He would leave for London in the morning, his appointment with Darius little more than twenty-four hours away.

Brother Pietro approached with a lantern. "You'll stay the night?"

"Thank you, but no."

He nodded as if expecting Viktor's answer. "Come with me."

"Has there been any sign of my pursuer?" Viktor said.

"No," he said, and Viktor didn't have time to worry about it further.

The monk led him across the summit to the iron gate surrounding the ancient chapel. Charcoal clouds smothered the top of the mountain, the valley below invisible in the darkness.

Pietro inserted a six-inch key into the gate, and it creaked open. Viktor saw no door, and the monk led him to the left of the chapel, putting his hands on a section of the wall that appeared as smooth and inaccessible as the rest of the granite mass. He pushed on the wall, and a block of stone swung inward.

"This is where you kept the grimoire," Viktor said.

"Yes."

The lantern illuminated a stone passage, which they followed deep into the church. They came to a three-way intersection, but instead of choosing another passage, Pietro again went to an indistinguishable section of the wall, pushing on another stone. This time Viktor heard a groaning sound, and the two-foot square block next to Pietro fell away, revealing a staircase descending into blackness.

Pietro shone the lantern down the staircase. Huge oak casks lined the passage. At the bottom of the staircase was an old motorcycle with knobby tires. The monk handed Viktor a set of keys.

"You didn't actually think we climbed down the path every time we left? This tunnel will take you through the mountain. When you exit, follow the dirt trail for the better part of an hour. Be careful, it is steep. This will merge into a road, which you will take to a village. After the village is a bridge, and a house with a flat roof just after the bridge. The man who lives there will recognize the motorcycle. He will take you where you wish to go, at any time of night."

"I can't thank you enough," Viktor said.

He grasped Viktor by the arm. "You can thank me by avenging my brother."

Viktor sped through the night, and everything was as Pietro had said: the drive through the tunnel with nothing but stone and silence and the mental image of Father Angelo's ruined eyes, riding for miles under a bloated moon beside cacti bent at fantastical angles, and the surreal rendezvous with Pietro's man in the village, who took Viktor to Cefalù without so much as a word or a backwards glance.

He dropped Viktor at Piazza Garibaldi. After another futile attempt to call Grey, which worried him immensely, Viktor began the climb to his villa, weary beyond belief, shaking from the need for absinthe.

His driver's villa lay just below his. When Viktor exited the mountain tunnel, he had called and told the driver to be ready to leave at first light, a mere three hours away.

He saw a light inside the driver's villa, casting a soft glow over the patio. He glanced inside, expecting to see the driver asleep on the couch in front of the television. Instead, he saw the driver in a pool of blood on the floor, his insides curled beside him like the glistening strands of a web, his face locked in a final expression of horror.

Before Viktor could react they surrounded him, at least a dozen figures in black masks. He caught the flash of a silver ring, and one of them injected him from behind with a needle, catching him as he fell.

A barrage of emotion coursed through him before he lost consciousness. Terror, rage, anguish at the fate of his driver, worry for Grey. The one emotion that did not register was surprise, because he knew, with awful certainty, why they had waited until now to take him, until after he had visited the monastery.

Darius had wanted him to see.

# 55

Grey took Anka to a hotel a few blocks away, paying in cash for the room and acting as nonchalant as possible, trying to hide his battered face from the clerk. Anka waited off to the side, face buried in a fashion magazine.

Their fourth-floor room was a typical Lilliputian affair, though it did have a small desk next to the bed. Grey went to the bathroom to change the blood-soaked dressing on his wounds. Anka helped, gingerly unwrapping his thigh. Her face expanded when she saw the wound.

"You shouldn't be walking," she said.

"No choice. It'll cause more scarring, but I have plenty of that already."

She removed his shirt to change his bandages without a word, revealing the halved tattoo on the backs of his upper arms that symbolized justice and balance, as well as the various scars on his body. Anka was only the second woman who hadn't reacted in surprise when she saw his back. Nya was the first.

She helped him rinse the wounds and apply the antiseptic, then sat cross-legged on the floor to help wrap the bandages. The pain from his thigh lanced through him. He shuddered and breathed deep through his nose.

When it was over Anka's arms encircled him from behind, fingers resting on his ridged stomach. He eased into her, and her hands moved upward to stroke his chest. Her fingernails sent little shivers of pleasure channeling through those same nerve endings, distracting him from the pain. He eased her away.

"I know," she said with a hungry look, helping him to his feet. "What're you going to do?"

"I'm not sure yet." Grey thought of the harem he had seen on the sixth floor. "I assume Darius doesn't live in the same place anymore?"

"I have no idea," she said. "As you can imagine there's not much trust between us."

"What's his old address? I'll check it as a last resort."

She wrote the address down on a piece of paper, a flat in South Kensington. He knew that would be a dead end. He moved to the desk, where he had placed the folder full of documents taken from the glass building.

"While I'm looking at these documents, I want you to think of everything he's ever said or done, every goal or dream he's mentioned, every name, every place. Anything that might help. Try to remember the location of the house you were at when you witnessed the ceremony."

"I will," she said, hovering behind him and kneading his neck muscles. "What're these papers?"

"After they kidnapped me," he said, "I was held in a building in East London which has to be their home base. Before I escaped I found these."

"Let's hope something's in there."

"We'll see," he said. "We're running out of options."

"Give me a second to freshen up," she said, "then I'll help."

She slipped into the bathroom, and Grey started poring through a stack of receipts pertaining to the procurement and build out of real estate in East London. Before he finished the first folder, Anka emerged and grabbed her handbag. "I'm going to the vending machine for a bottle of water."

"The one by reception? Don't let anyone see your face."

She kissed his forehead. "Sure, love. Be right back."

When she stepped out, Grey checked his remote voice mail again. He had a message from Viktor summarizing his visit with the priest, which Grey listened to with increasing dread. When Grey tried Viktor's cell and it went straight to voice mail again, his pulse thumped with worry.

# THE DIABOLIST

Viktor's cell should not be off. Grey knew in his gut they had found him, and that Viktor's only hope was Grey's intervention before midnight of the next night, little more than twenty-four hours away.

Grey eyed the stack of documents in front of him, praying they held a clue to Darius's whereabouts, knowing Viktor's life might be forfeit if they didn't. He ran a hand through his hair and rose to use the bathroom.

On the bathroom counter by the door he noticed a bottle of perfume. He thought nothing of it at first, but as he washed his hands a troubling thought entered his mind.

When Anka bent to kiss him before she left the room, he hadn't smelled any perfume.

Why remove a bottle of perfume from a handbag without using it? There was also something familiar about the bottle, which was shaped like an elongated pyramid.

Removing the bottle alone might not have been cause for alarm, but as he returned to the desk, he had another thought. Anka had left the bathroom door wide open, which was a strange thing for a woman to do, and the bottle had been placed on the counter as close to the door as possible, just out of Grey's line of sight.

Then it hit him, and he gripped the desk. His memory was hazy, and he was sure the label had changed, but he remembered the bottle of perfume he had found in Xavier Marcel's bedroom, also triangular in shape. And while he didn't remember seeing perfume in Ian Stoke's residence, there had been a bottle of cologne on the nightstand.

Both men had been seeing someone new. Both crime scenes contained perfume-size bottles placed in strategic locations.

He covered his mouth and nose with his arm, gathered the documents and fled the room. More conclusions, long harbored as possibilities in the back of his mind, crashed in like a series of punishing waves.

Darius burned his victims in one location while she killed them with poison gas in another, no doubt discharged from the perfume-size bottles, no doubt equipped with some ingenious release mechanism. Viktor had said Darius was a master chemist.

He took the stairs three at a time. She had seduced them, gained access to the bedroom and set the time release of the poison gas for midnight. Had she slept with them as well?

Of course she had.

His last flicker of doubt concerned the timing. She could have killed him, or at least left him to be killed, in the catacombs. Or she could have come with him to his room in Cambridge, knowing he wouldn't have protested, and released the gas.

So why now? He realized what he was carrying, and the last piece fell into place.

There was something about her in the documents.

He didn't know why she had waited, but he had forced her hand. He burst through the hotel door and onto the street, head straining to spy a glimpse of her. She had played him perfectly, easily, and without a shred of remorse.

He saw her at the end of the block, hurrying across the street as the light turned. He caught up with her, grabbed her by the wrist and pulled her around.

She gasped. "What're you doing? You're hurting me!"

"I'd wager death by poison gas hurts a hell of a lot worse than a bruised wrist."

"What are you talking about—how could you think I had something to do with that? Grey, it's *me*." She reached up to stroke his cheek, and he swatted her hand away. He had to admit she was the best liar he had ever encountered, flawless under duress, a scarily competent operative in the field.

"It's over, Anka. I saw the perfume bottle. I know what it is."

"You're wrong," she whispered. "I'll go back in the room if you don't believe me. You can shut the door and wait outside."

"Is that why're you hurrying down the street?"

"The vending machine was out of order." She pointed at a pharmacy just ahead on the street. "That's the closest place. I'm coming right back."

"You're unbelievable," he said.

"Go check the machine, if you don't believe me."

"Was a bottle of water that important?"

"I was already downstairs," she said with a helpless shrug. "I didn't think it would matter."

He patted the folders he was carrying. "You're mentioned in here, aren't you?"

"Why wouldn't I have betrayed you long before now? And why would they torture you to find me?"

Grey didn't answer her last question, because he hadn't figured that one out. But he was through with her duplicitous words and her poisonous touch, the narcotic honey in her eyes. Love might be dependent on trust, but attraction sure as hell wasn't.

Instead of pulling away she came closer, her face inches away. "You know this doesn't feel right. You know when I kissed you I meant it."

"I don't know anything when it comes to you," he said.

She took his hand. "Come back to the room. I'll stay in there as long as it takes for you to trust me."

He held her gaze, then said, "You've called them already, haven't you? Where are they, Anka? Where's Viktor?"

She sobbed and beat his chest. "Don't don't *don't*. You're the only man in my life who hasn't tried to take advantage of me, even though you had the most reason to do so. There's no one else I can trust. No one but you, Grey."

"No one else except Darius."

"I despise him with all of my being," she said.

"I'll ask you one more time. *Where are they?*"

She spoke between sobs, reaching for his face. "Don't do this."

Whatever she knew or didn't know, he knew he wouldn't uncover anything without tying her down and torturing her until she gave him what he wanted to know. If Viktor died he might never forgive himself, but neither could he torture this girl who would whisper her innocence as he destroyed her body.

And despite his conviction, he had to admit he did not have absolute proof. But it was enough, and he had to trust his instincts. He backed away from her. She collapsed while standing, face crumbling. "Please don't leave me."

"Good-bye, Anka. Don't get in my way."

He continued backing away, watching her wring her hands and then finally turn and walk away in the same direction she had been going.

Then he followed her.

## 56

Viktor woke to darkness and the musty smell of burlap. The rough fabric brushed against his face. When he tried to move he realized he was tied to a chair, his waist and feet bound with rope, wrists handcuffed behind him.

The back of his throat felt like sandpaper, and he felt lost in a fog. It took long minutes for his head to clear, but then he remembered the journey back to the villa, the grotesque body of the driver and the swarm of cult members, the painful injection.

He had no idea how long he waited under the hood, barely able to think through his thirst. At one point he heard a faint hum, then felt a whisper of warm air. He reasoned he had been taken to a cooler climate, kept indoors, and placed near a heating vent.

A rising intonation of voices, then footsteps creaking on wood. He heard a door open. Light flared as his hood was yanked away. Viktor blinked and saw a hardened man in a black cloak, about Grey's size and build, his scalp covered with a pentagram tattoo that spilled on to his forehead. Viktor's gaze traveled to the man's flat eyes, and Viktor knew at once there would be no quarter given.

The man stepped aside, revealing Darius standing behind him, hands clasped, his face calm and sure. He was different from the college student Viktor had known, almost unrecognizably so. This man was dignified, smooth, handsome—as if his previous incarnation had been the caterpillar, and he had emerged from a cocoon into this polished specimen. But the eyes were the same, and the way he stood with his left foot splayed at an angle, and the nickel-size birthmark on the back of his right hand.

A hand Viktor had once clasped in friendship.

"Free his hands and feet and leave us," Darius said to the other man. After the man complied Viktor flexed his limbs, still bound by the waist.

"It's been a very long time, Viktor. Or I suppose I should say Professor Radek. We've taken quite different paths."

"Indeed we have."

"Congratulations on your success," Darius said. "I hear you're the world's foremost expert on cults."

Viktor didn't answer, taking a moment to examine his prison, a plush bedroom exuding the sort of good taste to which Viktor had long grown accustomed. The creamy Persian rug, the original artwork on the walls, the period furniture and king-size bed: They all screamed wealth and privilege. The only difference was the ceiling, painted with baroque pornographic images.

Viktor realized he was wearing the same soiled suit, now reeking of sweat and urine. They had left him with the rosary the priest had given him.

"I hope you enjoy your accommodations," Darius said, "though I'm afraid they're only yours for the day. We have an appointment tonight."

"The one where you murder me."

"I view it as justice. Human tribunals are such arbitrary constructs. How is an execution by the state, ordered by an impartial judge and carried out by hourly workers, more just than a retribution killing by the father of a murdered son, or the mother of a raped daughter?"

"Or the negligent murderer of one's beloved," Viktor said.

Darius lifted his chin in agreement, the silver coif unmoving.

"Where's my partner?" Viktor said.

"Incapacitated and in the dark, like the rest of the world."

Viktor sneered. "And thus spoke Simon Azar. Where are we?"

"The house of a supporter." The flash of Darius's white teeth lingered on narrowed lips. "It's what's adjacent to this property that you'll recognize."

"Oh?" Viktor said.

# THE DIABOLIST

"I prefer it to be a surprise."

"What about the girl?" Viktor said.

"You mean Eve?"

"Don't, Darius. It happened thirty years ago. We were just children. No one regrets it more than I."

Darius took a few steps closer, his voice soft. "That's where you're wrong."

Viktor shook his head. "Was it so bad, Darius, that it's come to this? Did you need the power that badly?"

Viktor's question was rhetorical, because history, and his own cases, had proven to him time and again that people like Darius did, in fact, need power that badly. They would do anything to get it, and once they got it, it corrupted them even further.

"Spare me your needs, your wants, your contrived philosophy and morality," Darius said. "There are those who live, and take, and there are those who do not. After tonight, the Order of New Enlightenment will experience a meteoric rise, and I will take even more. It's been too long since we've had a new major religion, don't you think?"

Viktor laughed. "Your shallow little cult?"

"Even you must admit a million followers in less than a year is impressive. And don't they all start small, a band of twelve disciples, a man alone in a cave, a young prince on a pilgrimage of enlightenment?"

"Colossal hubris was not exactly a hallmark of those three men."

"Wasn't it? Did you know them? Did you oversee the chain of oral and written history that documents their exploits? And my cult, as you so loosely term it, has the weight of history behind it, as well as a very powerful sponsor. Someone you know quite well."

"Don't you see this is typical cult behavior, displacing guilt and logic and morality with the guise of faith?" Viktor said. "And if you believe as you say, then why blame me? Ahriman was responsible for Eve's death, not I."

Darius snarled. "It was Eve's fault for disrupting the ritual, and it was your fault for taking her from me, poisoning her mind with untruths, not allowing me to reverse the deed, and leaving her alone when she needed you most. Ahriman has rules, and we failed to follow them. I accept those conse-quences, and it doesn't impact my faith in the slightest."

"I can't believe this is all about your towering ego. After all these years, you still have to prove yourself to me."

"Don't flatter yourself," Darius said.

"Then why not just kill me ages ago? It's quite amazing the lengths to which you went, sending me around the world to witness your cleverness. Am I the only person who's ever challenged you, is that it?"

Darius took a step closer. "You're the most pompous, arrogant, conceited man I've ever known."

Viktor scoffed. "The truth hurts."

Darius backhanded Viktor across the face. "Then why is it you're sitting in this chair, awaiting your execution?"

Viktor gave a harsh laugh as his eyes watered. "Is that what you think? That you could possibly get the better of me? I have a secret for you, Darius. But I think I'll wait for you to find out. I'll wait until the time of my alleged death, with all of your followers watching."

"You've no idea who I am, what I've become. *No idea.*"

"Sorry," Viktor said, "did you mean a prankster, an illusionist, a parlor act performing tricks for a gullible audience of feeble-minded cultists?"

"You've seen my work."

"Oh, I've seen it. Using plants to help you start the fires, Vikane gas to asphyxiate the other victims."

Darius's smile, slow and sure, chilled Viktor. "In all your brilliance, Vik-tor, you still lack one quality that has always been your Achilles' heel."

"I assume you mean my faith? You don't know me as well as you think, Darius."

"Don't I?" He reached down and grasped the rosary around Viktor's neck with a mocking grin. "Are you a man of faith now, Viktor?"

Viktor produced a matching grin. "You'll see tonight."

"What're you talking about, old fool?"

"Don't you have things to do, preparations to make?"

Darius leaned down, until he was inches from Viktor's face. "You'll die tonight, by my hand and at the will of Ahriman. Eve's death shall be avenged, the broken circle repaired." He straightened. "Dante will return to untie you and bring food and wine. I assure you nothing has been tainted. You'll find the shower quite pleasant, the bed should you desire. Enjoy your last hours of life."

He opened the door, but just before he left the room he turned. "You shouldn't have taken her from me, Viktor. It was your gravest mistake. And yes, I've preparations to make."

As he spoke his last words, he looked Viktor in the eye, and Viktor searched deep for the touch of madness that characterized nearly every single cult leader he had faced. He saw nothing in Darius but a coldly rational mind, firm in his beliefs, and that unnerved him most of all.

Grey was going to see for himself what Anka was up to. After stumbling down the first block in apparent despair, he saw her gait straighten as she hastened down the street. She observed her surroundings like someone untrained in the art of espionage: furtive body language revealing her state of mind, head whipping back and forth for signs of pursuit. She was worried about someone or something, that much was clear. Grey trailed half a block behind, slipping in and out of parked cars, trees, storefronts, and the few people still on the street.

He followed her for five blocks, then saw her veer towards an entrance to the Underground. Just before she reached the station, a black Mercedes screeched to a stop next to her. Anka screamed as two men leapt out and stuffed her in the car, to the horror of a couple strolling arm in arm on the other side of the street.

Grey couldn't catch the vehicle's plate, cursing as his only lead slipped away. He thought about how they might have found her, and got a chill when he remembered her words that Darius could find her whenever he pleased.

He scoffed at himself. They might have a tracking device on her, one of their lookouts might have spotted her, or she might even have staged the capture knowing Grey would follow, though it sure looked as if she had gone into that Mercedes unwillingly.

Was it all a ruse, Grey a pawn in some elaborate scheme? Or was it something else altogether?

He wanted to check to see if the vending machine was out of service, but he couldn't risk returning to the hotel. Hurrying as best he could, dragging his foot behind him, Grey took the Tube to Islington and found another hotel, this one dirty and anonymous and close to the Underground. Islington was the gateway to East London, and offered a plethora of transportation possibilities.

Confident no one had followed him, Grey hunkered down in his boxcar of a room and resumed poring over the documents. They were his last link to Viktor. They had to produce.

Three hours later, deep into the night, he stopped to caffeinate again, his eyes crossing from not sleeping for two days straight, his only rest a few hours of forced unconsciousness. He read spreadsheet after spreadsheet, picked apart receipt after receipt. The goateed desk attendant knew him by now, the disheveled guy with the limp who kept asking for more coffee. Grey didn't care. Someone recognizing him was no longer his principal worry.

So far the documents had been useless. He had found stacks of receipts, loan documentation, payroll information, and other records that came with running a large business. Despite the mundane nature of the documents, he pored through them with painstaking care, knowing the answer might lie with an extra number here, a dab of Wite-out there.

The cult's reach stunned him. Darius, and whoever else was involved in the power structure of the cult, already owned a king's ransom of stocks and bonds, as well as properties in London, Tokyo, Shanghai, Paris, Mumbai, New York, Doha, Sydney, and San Francisco, together worth untold millions. Tithes and donations had been pouring in from around the world, and that was just the income on the books. Grey was quite sure a large portion of the transactions were illegitimate and unrecorded, and he was looking at the fiscal records that would satisfy the inevitable government inquiries.

# THE DIABOLIST

The cult business, Grey thought grimly, was booming.

By four a.m., Grey had gone through every single document, and he had but a single piece of information that he decided to pursue: O.N.E. Enterprises, the name of the company that had purchased the East London properties. A few other threads had potential, but not in the time frame in which he was working.

Though he could always push further, his eyes had almost gummed shut, his head so torpid from exhaustion it felt filled with glue. He needed to be alert for tomorrow, and he needed information he wasn't going to find in the middle of the night. He set a wake-up call for six a.m., asleep before the small hand on the clock completed a single revolution.

His last conscious thought was that he had not found a single mention of Anka.

# 57

**S**oon after Darius left, Dante entered the room carrying a tray full of caviar and paté. He handed Viktor a bottle of Bordeaux and a wineglass. He also left a white robe atop the bed and ordered Viktor to wear it when they returned for him before midnight. Seeing the way Dante fondled the long knife at his side, gleaming underneath the cloak, Viktor had no doubt he would be forced to comply.

Viktor didn't touch the food or drink, but he used the huge, glass-enclosed shower to wash away the grime. The steam and pounding water helped clear his head, and he sat on the marble bench inside the shower, thinking through his predicament.

Viktor knew he was probably going to die. He had no idea where he was, and he had no means of communication with the outside world. He feared for Grey's life, but even if he was still alive, Viktor had no hope that Grey would find him before midnight.

Viktor was no coward, but he did fear entering that looming abyss, that most occluded of passageways, without a shred of knowledge of what to expect. After a lifetime of searching, the only thing he could say for certain was that he was not convinced that death was the end of the line. He had seen far too much, experienced too many implausibilities, to know for sure.

Regardless, Viktor wasn't ready.

What did he know? He knew Darius had gained access to the Ahri-man Grimoire roughly a year ago, and had gone public with the Order of

# THE DIABOLIST

New Enlightenment shortly thereafter. Either Darius wanted his followers to believe this book granted him favor by Ahriman, or he did, in fact, believe such a thing, in which case Viktor had to give weight to the power of belief. The human mind was a powerful and barely understood tool—a weapon—that could, quite literally, accomplish miracles. He had witnessed the power of the mind time and again with his own fieldwork, including the extreme example with the Juju sorcerer in Zimbabwe, his first case with Grey. Just recently in the national news, a group of teenage girls in upstate New York had all contracted the same mysterious twitching disease for which no doctor could identify a cause, forcing the medical community to admit the disease was a collective physical manifestation of psychological symptoms.

Translation: It was all in their minds.

Viktor had a plan of attack to counter Darius's belief, which he had already implemented. Every word uttered by Viktor during their last conversation had been carefully chosen, and he believed he had accomplished his initial objective: He had planted the seeds of doubt.

Tenuous at best, the larger problem with Viktor's plan to undermine Darius's faith was that, even if successful, Viktor would still be surrounded by cult members in an unknown location, with no help on the way.

The needles of hot water slammed into his back, millions of droplets running off his body and swirling into the drain. He watched their inevitable journey, wondering how much fate played a part in the human lifespan, whether all was predetermined or random chance or whether, as with most things, the truth lay somewhere in between.

Before Viktor rose, he cupped a handful of water and tossed it on the bathroom floor. A perverse and ridiculous gesture, he knew. Maybe he had no say in the matter, and he knew his odds had never been worse, but if force of will counted for anything, then let it be known to the universe that Viktor Radek would not sail gently past those barrier islands.

He knew Darius had toyed with him from the beginning, had left clues along the way for Viktor to follow. And Viktor had to admit that he had bested him thus far, had used Viktor's insatiable curiosity and pride against him. The girl had been an ingenious addition.

He knew Darius had used artifice on some level to set up the fire-based murders, and he guessed that he had used an accomplice, probably the man with the knives, to administer the poison to the other victims. Or, Viktor mused, perhaps he had used the girl. Mind control within a cult was a powerful and well-documented precedent to murder, from the Manson family to the Jonestown massacre to the Aum doomsday cult.

Viktor was sure a tiny ignition device was used to start the fires, and surmised that the victims' robes had been soaked in an accelerant beforehand. He had already saturated his robe with water to counteract any accelerant. After hanging it on the towel rack, he wrung it out every few minutes, hoping it dried in time.

He knew about the Vikane, and thus the only remaining mystery was the strange appearances by the robed figure before the murders. Viktor had examined every inch of Gareth's chamber for a hidden device or recorder, and had found nothing. How was Darius doing it?

The water poured over him, not so much a final cleansing but a pounding reminder of the mistakes he had made in life, of the inevitable regrets from a life spent chasing the unknown, rather than home and hearth.

He reached for the fresh bar of soap in the ornate dish, every last detail of this bedchamber as carefully planned as Darius's rise to power. One thing bothered him: Soaking the robe seemed too easy, too obvious a solution. Darius had to have something else in mind.

*Every last detail.*

With sudden comprehension, his hand stopped in midair.

The clang of the wake-up call jolted Grey awake. He jumped out of bed and reached for his gun before remembering where he was.

Eyes gummy and wounds throbbing, he took another handful of ibuprofen, then scooped up the folders and hurried out of the cheap hotel room. It didn't take him long to find his next destination, an Internet café two blocks away. Before entering the café he called Jacques.

"Do you have word from Viktor?" Jacques said.

"He's compromised," Grey said. "I'm sure of it."

"We have all our resources dedicated to protecting the pope and the major archbishops. I'm not sure what I can do."

"I need two things: a piece of information, and your hand on your cell the rest of the day."

"*Oui*, of course. What is it that you need?"

"Have someone find out everything you can about O.N.E Enterprises," Grey said. "It's the holding company for the Order of New Enlightenment."

"Done."

He told Jacques about the glass headquarters in East London, though the London police would be no help to Viktor, because Grey didn't know what to tell them to do. His bitterness and frustration burned through him, and he fought against the rage that clawed at the edges of his vision.

He entered the café, ordered a triple-shot espresso, and slid into a chair with a view of the front entrance. The café was empty except for a bespectacled girl typing in a corner.

First he spent an hour scouring the Internet for mention of O.N.E. Enterprises. He found nothing, not even a listing on the Companies House website, the United Kingdom's registry of corporations.

He leaned back in his chair, drumming his fingertips on the mouse pad. He had a little more than fourteen hours to find Viktor. This company could be incorporated anywhere in the world, and it could take Grey days to find it.

Then again, he knew from his peripheral dealings with legal when he was a DSO that corporations in most countries had to keep a local registered agent, or the equivalent thereof, when doing business in a particular country. A few searches confirmed this was the case in the United Kingdom. Unfortunately, registered agents for foreign corporations were not public information in the U.K. He texted Jacques to try and acquire that information.

An idea came to him. Most companies used giant, specialized corporations as registered agents, but smaller companies, or companies who liked to keep their business under wraps, often used their own attorneys. It was a long shot, but Grey did know one attorney in England associated with Darius, and he was right here in London.

The more Grey thought about it, the more he liked the idea of seeing what else Solicitor Alec Lister knew about Darius, the Order of New Enlightenment, and O.N.E Enterprises. Grey hadn't trusted him then, he didn't trust him now, and he was betting Alec had a hand in the death of Ian Stoke and knew far more than he was letting on.

That, and Grey was out of options.

It was just after noon when he arrived at the fancy law office off Portobello Road. Grey was all too aware of the time, which at the moment seemed to be flowing like a barrel over Niagara Falls.

# THE DIABOLIST

Solicitor Alec Lister was the sole occupant of the fourth floor of the building. The office door was shut and locked. Grey didn't know many attorneys who closed up shop by noon on a weekday, unless they had someplace very important to be.

After knocking loudly and receiving no response, his fingers whisked the thin metal file in and out of the keyhole, releasing the dead bolt. No alarm sounded, and he saw no evidence of wires or cameras. He eased the door shut behind him, locked it, and swept his eyes around reception and the three closed doors. Then he went to work.

He moved as quickly as he could, aware this might be a red herring, trying not to think about the consequences if it were. He entered Lister's office and tried to access his computer, but it was secured, and Grey was no hacker. It took him far too long to search the desk, but he found nothing except innocuous papers.

After combing the rest of the office, still finding nothing, he tried the second door, which led to a conference room with boxes stacked along the wall. Before going through the boxes, he tried the third door, which revealed a file room filled with cabinets, shelves, and more boxes, all full of paper files.

He stood in the middle of the conference room, running both hands through his hair and holding them there. It was already well into the afternoon, and the files and boxes in the office could take the rest of the day to pore through. Should he return to the glass building and take his chances with the cadre of guards and cult members? The thing was, even if he gained access again, he didn't think he would find anyone of consequence in that building. And whatever was going down, Darius wouldn't risk exposing his headquarters, especially after Grey knew where it was. It just didn't feel right.

His burner cell rang, and Grey answered on the first ring. Jacques again.

"O.N.E. Enterprises is incorporated in Luxembourg," Jacques said. "The registered agent in the U.K. is Alec Lister, an attorney in Notting Hill."

"Yeah, I'm standing in his office. Anything else?"

"We investigated a few of the real estate purchases. As you said, it appears to be a holding company. Unfortunately, all of the transactions appear legitimate. Perhaps a full investigation would uncover irregularities, but I'm afraid there's nothing that will help us today."

Grey swallowed his disappointment. "Thanks."

He shoved the cell in his pocket and paced the file room. The information did help: It confirmed that instead of a giant international firm, Darius had chosen a solo attorney as registered agent. Alec Lister was important to O.N.E. Enterprises, which meant he was important to Darius. Alec Lister knew Ian Stoke and Sir David Naughton, he was a prominent member of the Clerics of Whitehall, perhaps even part of the inner circle of the Order of New Enlightenment.

Viktor and Darius were in London, Grey was sure of it. Dante was there; Anka was there; the power center was there. He wasn't sure if Darius had deliberately misled Interpol by sending that letter to the pope or if he had something else in mind, but whatever he had planned, Grey's gut told him it would take place in this city.

But where?

Grey tore into the boxes and files, determined to find something. But as afternoon faded to evening and Grey came up short, the doubts poured in and he questioned everything: his instincts, his judgment, his ability to save his friend.

He glanced at the clock on the wall, looking away as soon as he did.

Nine p.m.

The office now resembled a war zone, and Grey plowed ahead, slinging files on to the floor as soon as he scanned them. An hour later he found something, of course in the next to last file cabinet. Grey had started with the newest files because of the recent appearance of the Order of New Enlightenment, but what he had just found concerned one of Lister's oldest clients.

It was the slimmest of leads, perhaps nothing, a nugget of information that meshed with something in his recent memory. The client was Niles Widecombe, member of the House of Lords, another rich and powerful customer of Alec Lister. Perhaps the richest and most powerful of all, judging by his financial statements. The man seemed to own half of Devon, as well as a huge estate on Swain's Lane in North London.

What got Grey's attention was the North London address, combined with the fact that Niles Widecombe was a principal donor to Highgate Cemetery. Lister had set up an enormous trust in his name, the interest paid out to the cemetery in perpetuity.

It struck a nerve because of something Anka had told him about the night she had discovered Darius's identity. She said she had followed Darius to a mansion in North London that backed up to a cemetery. Grey couldn't get on to the computer, and his smartphone had been stripped, so he raced out of the office to an Internet café he had noticed down the street.

He did a quick Google maps search on the Widecombe address, and his grip on the mouse increased when he saw the large cemetery sprawling behind Swain's Lane.

He didn't trust Anka in the slightest, but at least some of what she had told him had been verified. And something about her story about that house had the ring of truth, though Grey suspected Anka had been a willing participant in the ceremony rather than an observer. Or maybe Darius had caught her and forced her to participate, and she had been compromised since that night.

What he did know was that Alec Lister's connection to this house, this fancy property of this powerful member of the House of Lords, a house that backed onto one of London's largest cemeteries, caused his internal radar to scream in alarm.

He gave the cemetery on the screen a final glance, then limped out of the café and onto Portobello Road, frantically signaling for a cab.

# 59

They came for him.

Darius looked pleased to see that Viktor had already donned the robe, and he ordered Dante to replace the burlap hood. They left his hands and feet unbound, but Dante kept the tip of his knife on Viktor's back, guiding him the entire time.

Viktor had no thought of attempting an escape: He knew he was no match for Dante, let alone the numerous voices joining the entourage once they left the bedroom. His mouth tightened when he heard Oak's belligerent growl.

Viktor heard a door open and felt a rush of cool outside air. He also heard the sound of falling water, guessing from the fragrant smell that they had entered a garden. The noise from the waterfall drew closer and then faded. He heard the creak of another door, and then Viktor became disoriented. They walked for a long time in what felt like the prescient silence of a wood. When they stopped, Viktor estimated the journey had taken twenty minutes.

The chatter ceased, and someone yanked his hood away. "Behold your place of execution," Darius said. "I think you'll find it quite appropriate."

Viktor's gaze swept his surroundings. He and Darius and a small entourage were standing on a wide, raised mound of earth encircled by a pathway ten feet below. Contiguous stone tombs and vaults crowded the pathway on both sides, the impressive architecture a mix of Gothic, classical, and Egyptian. He saw the spot of darkness heralding the entrance tunnel he knew was called Egyptian Avenue, with its obelisks and lotus-flower columns waiting on the other side. And in the darkness beyond the circle of tombs, he knew an enormous Victorian cemetery formed a sepulchral barrier between Viktor and the outside world. Finally, with him on the small hill, he saw the cedar tree that still haunted his dreams.

Yes, he knew at once where they were. It was a site he could never forget, not just because of the unique location but because this place had been forever scraped into the fabric of his soul, a festering wound that no medicine could heal.

He was standing in a spot called the Circle of Lebanon, a landmark in London's Highgate Cemetery.

The exact place where Eve had taken her own life.

Swain's Lane was all the way across London, north of Camden Town and just east of Hampstead Heath. Grey balled his fists in frustration at the clogged late-night traffic in central London. His cabdriver pulled onto Swain's Lane just after eleven p.m., and a few blocks later they arrived at the address for Niles Widecombe, an ivy-covered Italianate mansion with grounds that stretched into the darkness. By the light of the moon Grey could make out the tops of the twisted oaks dotting the cemetery grounds that backed onto the property. A large wall enclosed the sides and rear of the grounds, which rang true with Anka's story.

Grey had the cabbie drop him a few doors down the street. He hurried towards the side of the mansion, looking for a way to scale the wall and gain rear access. When he stepped onto the manicured lawn, a door opened and a man stepped out brandishing a large handgun. Grey dove behind a clump of trees and bushes, coming up behind a large elm, his own gun at the ready.

No shots were fired, which didn't surprise him. Grey flattened and then crawled forward to get a better view. Despite the fact that someone had a pistol pointed in his direction, he felt only the thrill of hope that an armed guard had been set. *They don't want anyone calling the police, and they don't want anyone snooping around this house.*

Before he could decide on a course of action or scan the grounds, a voice called out from the direction of the house. "Grey?"

Grey stilled. He knew that voice. "Dickie?"

"You're taking the mickey out of me. What the bloody hell're you doing?"

Grey peered beside the tree, still hidden from view by a line of bushes in the darkness. Dickie stood in the front door, now holding his handgun sideways, like an amateur gangster. "You know what," Grey said. "Drop the weapon."

"Can't do that."

Grey focused his weapon on Dickie, both hands gripping the hilt, thumbs forward, elbows steady. "You're not trained like that," Grey said, "and you know it."

No response. He had a clear shot at Dickie, and if he tried to reenter the house, Grey would take it. "My partner's about to be killed by these animals," Grey said. "That's not what you're about."

Dickie swung the gun around, trying to pinpoint Grey's voice. "Forget it."

Grey's index finger hovered over the trigger. "I won't ask again."

"Like I said, they scare me even more than you do."

"And you were wrong then, too," Grey said.

Grey saw Dickie pull a cell phone out of his pocket. Grey rose to a crouch and shot him in the shoulder, thankful he had picked up that silencer. Dickie dropped the gun and fell into the house, and Grey moved towards him as fast as his leg would allow, gun leveled at his chest. "Don't even think about it, Dickie. Just stay on the floor."

Dickie lay on his back, gasping in pain. Grey pocketed Dickie's cell and kicked the gun out of reach.

"Damn you, Grey."

"Where are they?"

"I'm just a driver."

"With a semiautomatic?" Grey said. "I'm going to ask you one more time before I shove this gun in your mouth and pull the trigger. I already told you the stakes." He took Dickie by the collar with one hand, holding the gun to his face with the other. "You know me, you know what I'm capable of, and you know I'm telling the truth."

"Fuck me." He started shaking in Grey's grasp, whether from pain or fear Grey was unsure. Nor did he care.

"Last chance, Dickie."

"You don't get it, the things I've seen them do. They won't just kill me for this."

"Then help me end it," Grey said.

Grey pried the gun into Dickie's mouth, cocking the trigger. Dickie mumbled, "The cemetery."

"How?"

"There's an entrance in the back, through the wall. I've no idea where they are or what they're doing."

"How many?" Grey said.

"Plenty, plus Dante. And he's enough." He pointed at Grey's lame leg. "You can't beat him like that."

"We'll see."

"Help me, Grey. Get me out of here before you go in."

"Close your eyes," Grey said.

"No, mate, don't—"

Grey struck him in the temple with the butt of his gun, leaving him sprawled on the ground. Then he sent a text to Jacques and stepped farther inside the mansion.

## 60

The tapestries, chandeliers, and high-end art floated at the periphery of Grey's vision as he moved through the Swain's Lane mansion. He was in a hyperaware state, eyes sweeping the minutia of his surroundings for signs of danger. Except for Dickie, the house appeared empty.

Grey hobbled through the dining hall and past an indoor swimming pool before entering a covered patio at the rear, wide French doors leading to the vast grounds in the back. On the far side the yard sloped uphill, topped by a rock garden with a waterfall spilling into a koi pond. Another detail corroborating Anka's story.

She had been to this house, whether in the way she told it or not.

The grounds were deserted, and Grey followed a path through the rock garden. Behind the waterfall he found a door set into the twelve-foot-high stone wall.

He took a few deep breaths to prepare himself mentally for the fight he knew was coming, readied the handgun at chest level, and opened the door.

A narrow cavity led through the wall, to another door a few feet away. The next door had no handle, so he pushed gently on it. It creaked as it swung open. Grey pushed harder and stepped through, finding himself three feet behind two startled guards, one in a black leather jacket, the other a wool overcoat. Grey didn't want to alert the entire cemetery if he could avoid it, so he reversed his grip on the handgun and pistol-whipped the first guard in the temple before he could react, dropping him. The next guard reached for his weapon, and Grey's blow glanced across his face. As the guard reeled, Grey dropped his gun and pounced, covering the man's mouth and driving his head back with one hand, holding the hand that might reach for the gun with his other. Grey spun him in a circle and then reversed his movement, striking him violently on the back of the neck with his stiffened forearm. The guard was unconscious before he hit the ground.

After making sure no one else was around, Grey pulled the guards behind a bush and surveyed his surroundings with a grimace of pain. His own leg had almost crumpled during that fight.

The moon hovered above like a swollen gray eye. He was standing in the middle of an unkempt wood, darkness pooled like blood, creepers and the spindly branches of moss-covered trees spreading throughout the gloom. Up ahead he could see a jumble of tombstones among the undergrowth, most leaning to one side or split by roots and vines. Behind him, the cemetery wall stretched in both directions.

The door must have swung shut and blended into the wall, because it was now invisible. Grey was going to bet that the other benefactors of the cemetery weren't using this entrance.

He took a flashlight from one of the guards, and risked pointing the light at the ground. A path of flattened grass led deeper into the undergrowth, past a huge oak tree—yet another tidbit from Anka's story—set twenty feet behind the wall.

Grey followed the path for a hundred yards until it intersected with a two-foot-wide stone path that curved deeper into the cemetery. Grey had no idea how big this place was, no idea if he was even moving in the right direction.

All he knew was that he had to hurry.

A few minutes later the presence of two more guards confirmed his route choice, and he wasted precious minutes slipping into the undergrowth and circling behind them. He was in no condition to try to surprise the guards, nor could he risk a shot being fired or a cry being raised.

After he rejoined the pathway his surroundings changed, the undergrowth on both sides becoming more manageable, most of the crypts and sarcophagi now free of vines and waist-high weeds. The tombs grew more frequent, fronted by mythological statues and carvings, some encased in marble vaults and mausoleums. The footpath wound among the atmospheric gravesites while the branches and undergrowth clutched at him from all sides, wraiths yearning for his warm flesh.

Twice more he had to waste precious minutes avoiding guards by stepping off the gauntlet of twisted pathways and into the undergrowth. The cemetery was enormous, and Grey cursed his maimed left leg and the man who had damaged it. It had to be close to midnight. He felt as if Viktor's life were an hourglass in Grey's hands, each second whisking away the remaining grains of sand.

He kept going until he saw a strange sight: an arched entranceway set into a high stone wall, next to a pair of obelisks disappearing into the gloom above. Ornate pillars flanked both sides of the entrance, and the iron gate had been left ajar. Grey couldn't see what lay on the other side of the archway, but he could hear the faint murmur of voices coming from the other end of what Grey assumed was a tunnel.

He moved forward. Just before the archway he caught a glimpse of movement out of the corner of his eye, from the top of the wall. Grey spun to the right, but a tornado of pain erupted along his left arm, and he saw the hilt of a knife sticking out of his arm below the shoulder. If he had not moved at the last second, it would have struck his heart.

Grey dove into the undergrowth, yanking out the knife as he rolled. It wasn't lodged into bone, but it had torn into the muscle, and deep shudders of agony rolled through him. He could hear his assailant jumping off the wall, and Grey willed his mind clear, knowing if he let the pain affect him he wouldn't live through the next minute. He might not anyway, since he had dropped the gun when the knife struck him.

He scrambled to his feet and saw Dante stalking him from ten feet away, searching for an opening to throw another knife he was balancing in his hand.

# THE DIABOLIST

Grey moved like a mix between a boxer and a cat, stalking forward to close the distance, bobbing and weaving to give Dante a moving target. Both knew that if Dante threw the knife and missed, or struck a glancing blow, then Grey would have a temporary advantage. As Grey drew closer Dante shifted his body from a throwing posture to an infighting stance and withdrew another knife. He held both knives in front of his body, weaving them through empty air as Grey closed the final few feet.

If Grey were healthy, Dante's knives would not have bothered him. Knives were an excellent choice of weapon for hand-to-hand combat, but for a jujitsu master, nothing equaled the versatility of a pair of human hands. From close range they could execute multiple strikes, manipulate and break digits and limbs, block and strip a knife or gun, stop a forward thrust at the wrist and continue on to scrape out an eye.

But Grey's wounds were serious, his ability to fight gravely compromised. He now had a useless leg and arm, and against an expert knife fighter like Dante, those two injuries would likely be his death knell.

As the gap between them closed to nothing, Dante grinned beneath the macabre tattoo. He knew of Grey's injuries, because he had inflicted them. And Grey knew that unless he somehow disarmed one of Dante's knives on the first clash, Dante would strike a fatal blow, and there would be no second round.

Dealing with two knives, especially from a trained wielder, centered on a strategy called defanging the snake: executing a well-placed strike that would either send the first weapon flying or immobilize the striking hand, quick enough to then deal with the second knife. The moves were extremely difficult to execute, requiring years of practice as well as perfect timing.

And they required two hands.

Grey would have one shot, and he didn't think it was enough. Dante came in with the first thrust, a diagonal overhand slash, and Grey could tell from tracking his movements that a second thrust from the other knife was on the way. Grey couldn't block both knives, and if he turned or retreated he was finished.

Grey had no other options, so he utilized the first principle of jujitsu. Cheat.

As the first knife swooped downward, Grey spit in Dante's face. Dante flinched, slowing him down a fraction, allowing Grey to slip to the side of the first knife. The second knife was already on the way, and Grey knew he couldn't avoid the strike. So he took it.

Defanging the snake entailed striking with both hands on opposite sides of the attacker's hand, crushing bones and sending the weapon flying. Since Grey had only one hand, he used his body instead, taking the knife with his injured shoulder.

The pain from Dante's strike almost ended the fight, but adrenaline and sheer force of will carried Grey through. He didn't waste time or words. He yanked the knife out of his shoulder and whipped it at Dante's face. It struck a glancing blow, but caused Dante to flinch again as Grey closed the gap. Dante recovered in time to execute a forward thrust at Grey's stomach, but his move was done in haste, and Grey again slipped to the side of the thrust, this time catching the wrist with his good hand. Had he had both hands free, the fight would have ended with Grey snapping Dante's extended elbow. Instead, he gripped Dante's wrist with the force of desperation, and took Dante to the one place Grey knew he didn't want to go.

Dante was a knife fighter, not a ground warrior. Grey executed a simple foot sweep and dragged him to the ground, keeping the hold on the wrist.

They ended up facing each other, side by side. Dante abandoned the knife in his trapped hand and reached into his overcoat. Grey saw a flash of silver, and he lunged to head butt Dante in the eye, thrusting with his hips as hard as he could. He heard the crack of bone, and Grey head butted him three more times in the face, at the same time moving his knee up to pin Dante's free arm to the ground, the one that had been reaching for the weapon.

Grey moved his other knee upward, now sitting astride Dante's chest and pinning his arms. Looking at Dante's destroyed face, Grey knew he had crushed the orbital bone structure around the eyes, broken his nose, sliced him up with his own piercings, and knocked him senseless. With a reserve of will that impressed Grey, Dante freed one hand enough to extract yet another knife, going for Grey's injured thigh, but Grey caught his wrist, prying the pinkie loose and bending it backwards until he heard the crackle of snapping phalanges. Grey took the knife off the ground, trapped the arm again with his knee, and held the knife to Dante's throat.

Dante whispered between flat and hardened lips, his face a balloon of blood and swelling. *"Maintenant."*

Grey wanted to take his time, to smash his bones and break his spirit, to leave him drowning in a lake of blood. He wanted to inflict the same pain on Dante that Dante had inflicted on Grey and countless others, many of them helpless innocents. But he knew it was not lack of pain or feeling that had made Dante who he was, but an abundance thereof. He also knew that to cross that narrowest of lines was to erode the distance between them.

He flipped the knife, twisted and drove it through the center of Dante's right foot. Dante jolted as if he were having a seizure, and Grey reversed the weapon and struck Dante in the temple, watching as his eyes dimmed and his face sagged against the earth. The wound to the foot was insurance in case Dante woke up too soon.

Plus a little bit of payback.

A cell phone had slipped out of Dante's pocket, lying next to Grey on the ground. Grey swooped it up and checked the time.

Midnight.

Grey lurched to his feet, dragging his crippled body towards the archway, blood seeping through his bandages and pouring from the new knife wounds on his arm. Three steps later he swooned and collapsed in a heap, his body depleted from loss of blood.

**61**

Someone kicked the back of Viktor's legs and pulled down on his shoulders. He fell to his knees. A noose was placed around his neck and tightened. Viktor looked up, following the length of rope to the branch of the giant cedar tree that stood on the mound.

The same tree Eve had used.

The rope had been looped over the branch, and three men behind Viktor held the other end. "Stand him up," Darius ordered.

They pulled on the rope and Viktor was dragged to his feet, the rough fibers cutting into his neck. As his feet left the ground, he felt an immense pressure constricting his windpipe, stealing his air.

Darius signaled by putting a hand out, and the men eased the pressure, allowing Viktor's toes to touch the ground. "She died alone in this place," Darius said. "Can you imagine? Walking in here at night, alone with the spirits that roam these grounds, driven here by *Him*, climbing this tree and looping a rope around this branch, casting herself into darkness with no one to bear witness."

"She was driven here by her madness."

Darius stepped closer. "No, Viktor," he said softly. "She was not."

"What is it you have planned for the pope?" Viktor said. "What's the all-powerful secret?"

"Rome will fall regardless of what happens to that silly man. Do you understand what's happening? Everyone longs for change, for something real, for something that speaks to their true needs and wants. They flock to me."

"They're flocking to a house of lies," Viktor said. "You're the flavor of the week."

Darius eyed a watch poking out from the sleeve of his robe, then waved his hand. "Bring her!"

From somewhere behind Viktor a man came towards them, dragging a young woman behind him. She was dressed in a white robe similar to Viktor's. When she turned Viktor's way he saw a mass of striking blond hair and gasped. It was, of course, not Eve, but the woman bore more resemblance to the girl he had once loved than anyone he had ever seen.

Darius addressed her. "Caught searching the temple like a rat digging through garbage. Most unbecoming, my dear."

She tried without success to wriggle free of her captor's arms. "Let me go."

"I'd prefer you by my side," Darius said, "alive and willing, rather than burning alive as you hang beside Viktor. But so be it. I do admit the scenario has a certain symmetry."

She took a step back, and the man holding her tightened his grip. "You wouldn't," she said.

"You betrayed me, love, and in my religion betrayal has consequences."

She shrank into her captor, and Viktor forced himself to peel his eyes away from this beautiful creature, this doppelgänger of his lost love. He laughed at Darius, pouring scorn into his voice. "So you're trying to conquer the world because you can't conquer love? Eve denies you now, as she did then."

Darius stared at the woman as he spoke. "Not even the Creator can force love."

"Let her go, Darius," Viktor said.

"You think she's an innocent? If you knew the deeds she had done, you'd kill her yourself." He stepped to Viktor, inches from his face, close enough for Viktor to catch his musky scent and observe the smoothness of his face. "You do understand you're going to burn before you hang? They say it's the worst way to die, painful beyond imagining. You'll beg for your neck to snap."

Viktor's lips curled upward. "Will I? Do you remember what I told you, that I had a secret for you?"

"There's one last thing I want you to see before you die," Darius said. "Perhaps we'll make a man of faith of you at last, a thief on the cross." Darius extended a robed arm to Viktor, the sleeve falling away from his manicured hand. "Touch my hand."

The men holding the rope eased the pressure by a fraction, and Viktor's heels touched the ground. He looked at the hand Darius had extended, palm downturned, fingers limp, as if he were an emperor waiting for a sign of allegiance. Viktor looked Darius in the eye and grabbed his hand. He felt the smooth skin merge with his own, then the hand, and the man it belonged to, simply ceased to be.

Viktor found himself looking at nothing but air.

The woman beside him gasped, and a murmur of awe rippled through the crowd. A voice called to Viktor from the darkness to his left. He swiveled his head and saw Darius sitting cross-legged atop one of the tombs.

"How's your faith now, Viktor?" Darius said. "Any improvements?"

He disappeared again, reappearing a foot from the cedar tree. He placed a hand on the tree, bowed his head, and whispered something Viktor couldn't hear. Then he approached Viktor and stood in front of him. "Shall we continue? I'll give you this, you maintain your composure well. After what you've witnessed, you should be groveling at my feet to spare your life and teach you my secrets."

Viktor ignored what he had just seen, forced away the thought of burning alive, and corralled his will into a hardened shell, coating his words with conviction. "That's because I know something you don't."

"Let me assure you there's nothing you could possibly know or say that can save you now," Darius said.

# THE DIABOLIST

"Your pride was always your Achilles' heel," Viktor said. "Why didn't you kill the priest in Sicily? We both know why: You left him to bear witness to what you had done. You wanted to see me lie prostrate before you in awe, and you still do. As they say, pride goeth before the fall."

Darius lifted his arms, and Viktor raised his voice. "Go ahead, Darius. Burn me. Everyone's here. Everyone's watching. Let's see these great powers you possess. But know this: Your time is done. Ahriman favors me now, and you're second-best once again." Viktor grasped the rosary at his neck. "Don't you recognize this?"

Darius stepped closer and squinted. "That dying fool's trinket?"

"Father Angelo read the grimoire," Viktor said. "He transcribed another copy."

"That's forbidden."

"It's forbidden to followers of *Ahriman*," Viktor said. "Father Angelo memorized the grimoire to learn how to fight you should the time come, but I used it for a different reason. Ahriman did make a believer of me, you know. Once long ago, and again in Gareth's chamber." Viktor pressed his face forward, the veins in his neck bulging. "I know what you've done for Ahriman, the consumptions you made. *I've made them, too.* I also know there can be but one disciple of the grimoire, and my will was always the stronger. Ahriman knows this. Why would He have you, when He can have me?"

"You're desperate," Darius said.

"Burn me, then, and we shall see who has His favor."

Viktor bellowed a phrase in Old Persian, and Darius's eyes widened. His handsome features contorted into a snarl, and he whipped his hands at Viktor. *"Then burn!"*

A huge flame sparked from Darius's outstretched hands, leaping to Viktor's robe. The flame sizzled and died, and another ripple of sound came from the crowd, this time one of confusion. Darius's face turned from rage to disbelief. "That's not possible." He flung his hands at Viktor a second and third time, each time the flame sparking but failing to ignite.

Viktor raised his arms and shouted, "Behold the power of Ahriman!"

The murmuring in the crowd swelled, and Viktor saw Darius close his eyes and then open them. Nothing happened.

"It can't be," Darius whispered.

Viktor gathered his will again, producing the most chilling smile he had ever mustered. "Your time with Ahriman is done."

Darius's scream shattered the silence of the stunned crowd. "Pull the rope! Hang him! *Hang him!*"

Viktor was jerked off his feet. He tried to work his fingers beneath the heavy rope to relieve the tension, but it was too tight, snapping his head backwards and blocking his air. Panic threatened to overwhelm him, and he forced himself not to flail his limbs, knowing that would only hasten his demise.

Darius walked underneath him. "Save yourself, then. If you're the favored one, save yourself."

The pressure on his neck was immense, and Viktor already felt light-headed. His eyes roved the cemetery in desperation. He had played his last card, and played it well, but the set, and the match, were going to Darius.

Viktor saw the light of confidence appear once again in Darius's eyes, and Viktor felt his last hope slipping away. It was appropriate, he thought, that he should die in this place, at Eve's side. He could think of no place better.

Viktor kicked his legs, praying the rope would snap or the tree limb would break. His movements only tightened the noose. He gurgled and choked as the oxygen seeped out of his body, and the conscious world began slipping away.

Darius's eyes regained their brightness, his face returned to that of a messiah. He raised his arms and then pitched forward, his back arching as he fell. Viktor saw the hilt of a knife protruding from between his shoulder blades.

Darius screamed again, this time in agony. He managed to rise to his elbows, his shrieks punctuating the moans of the crowd. With a final reserve of will, Viktor lifted his eyes to where the knife must have originated, and saw Grey atop the wall above the circle of crypts. As Viktor watched, Grey swayed and pitched forward, falling to the path below. He didn't get back up.

Viktor yanked on the rope, a final desperate act, but the rope held tight as the last ounce of air left Viktor's lungs.

Grey spat dirt, struggling to retain consciousness as colored spots swarmed his vision. He tried to push to his elbows and failed, his movements as feeble as a baby bird's. A cold sweat slicked his palms.

For a moment his vision cleared, and he saw Viktor hanging from the tree, convulsing at the end of the rope. Grey made another futile attempt to rise, then tried to croak out a plea for someone to help Viktor. No sound left his throat, and he could only watch in despair.

He saw Darius pulling himself along the ground as if he couldn't move his legs, he saw people whirling in confusion, he heard sirens and megaphones. The sirens and megaphones surprised him, and for a second he thought he was hearing trumpets at the gates of heaven. Then he saw a squadron of policemen rushing through the cemetery, towards the circle of tombs.

At the vanguard of the police force a man in a full-length wool coat was pointing at Viktor and shouting. Now Grey knew he was having a deathbed vision, because the man looked exactly like the assassin in the photo Viktor had texted Grey, the man who had pursued Viktor across the globe.

Grey felt utterly drained of energy, aching for water as if he had just crossed the Sahara on foot. He knew his dehydration was a very bad sign. He had lost far too much blood. With a torpid gathering of his will he focused on the scene atop the mound above him, watching his friend swaying back and forth under the tree branch, his fingers clinging to the rope around his neck, his face completely white.

Grey saw movement at Viktor's side. He shifted his gaze in time to see Anka slip out of her guard's grasp. Grey felt a moment of elation, thinking she would help free Viktor.

Instead, she ran past him without so much as a sideways glance, rushing straight to Darius. As she approached, Darius reached up to her with an outstretched hand, the bottom half of his torso dragging along the ground like a snake's. Grey's knife was still embedded in his spine.

Grey watched Anka lean down and rip the knife out of his back. Darius screamed. She raised the knife over her head, and Grey got a glimpse of her face, twisted beyond all recognition, a mask of rage and hate. She thrust the knife downward, first in Darius's back and then in his face, again and again and again, with so much abandon that a few of her thrusts missed him completely. Darius stopped moving, but she continued stabbing, her arm whipping up and down like a mechanized toy gone berserk, blood spattering her face.

Grey looked towards Viktor again. His fingers had dropped to his side, and his face looked empty, a marionette hanging limp above the ground. Grey moaned Viktor's name as the colored spots returned. Right before his vision blurred, he thought he saw men rushing to help Viktor, but they might have been with Darius.

He heard screams and shouts from the crowd, gunshots, more bellowing from the megaphone, and then the sounds merged into a roar of white noise. A shadow formed over Grey, coalescing into the figure of a man. Grey's vision cleared for a split second, and again he saw the face of the man who had pursued Viktor. Grey tried to move or yell for help, but his legs and voice failed him.

"I'm with the Swiss Guard," the man said, his voice thick and distant to Grey, as if traveling underwater. The man waved his hand above his head and said something about an ambulance and trying to stay conscious, but then colored spots faded to black, and Grey was falling down a long and sunless tunnel.

Grey woke to pressure on his face and the sound of concerned voices. He felt as if his mind were outside of his body. He thought he heard Anka's voice somewhere above him, and he had the hysterical thought that he was traveling to the astral plane to meet her.

As the fog cleared from his vision, he realized he was still lying where he had fallen. The odor of sulfur from spent gunpowder had settled on to the loamy smell of the cemetery. A medic placed an oxygen mask over his mouth, then multiple hands eased him onto a stretcher. He heard the medic tell someone to apply a tourniquet before they moved him. Looking up, he saw the tree and the rope, but there was no sign of Viktor.

He heard shouting and a woman shrieking to his right. Two policemen were forcing Anka down the narrow pathway in handcuffs, about to pass beside his stretcher.

Anka noticed him as they approached, and her screams turned to sobs. Despite her wild hair and blood-soaked face, her beauty was still in such contrast to the chaos around her that she made the cemetery look like a movie set, her sculpted features too perfect for the reality of the situation.

She dug in her heels and looked right at Grey, the madness and terror draining from her eyes. A tear streaked down her cheek, dripping over the petite curve of her nostrils.

"I didn't have a choice," she said. "I had to do it." A deep shudder rolled through her. "He found me that night, watching the ceremony from the oak tree. He made me do things, made me drink blood and eat . . ." her eyes slid downward. "He made me do them again and again, and I couldn't get away."

She was passing right beside him now. The officers squeezed her past Grey, and she twisted to keep him in her vision. "Don't you understand?" she said. "He read the grimoire. No cell could have held him. I had to do it."

Grey felt a chill at her words, a coldness settling inside him that had nothing to do with the temperature outside.

# THE DIABOLIST

Her eyes bored into his. "Bring me the book, Grey. I won't let it change me, I promise." She was almost to the entrance tunnel, her last words poisoned darts cutting through the floodlit cemetery. "We could be together."

Then she was gone. He closed his eyes as the medic finished wrapping his wounds and whisked him out of the circle of tombs.

# 63

The hospital door eased open, and Grey shifted in his bed to see Viktor enter the room carrying takeout from a Japanese restaurant, his broad neck covered by a swath of bandages. Grey had similar bandages on his thigh and arm, and was still attached to a bank of instruments monitoring his return from the precipice of severe blood loss. He knew if the police and medics had not arrived when they did, he would have entered hypovolemic shock. Instead of sneaking in sushi, Viktor would be lying six feet under in a grave next to Grey.

Though he had been told Viktor was alive, he had not yet seen him. Grey realized just how glad he was to see a friendly face, though even Viktor's impassive features looked wan, drained of emotion. Grey eased to a sitting position and eyed the bag of takeout with the kind of desperation that results from eating British hospital food for two days straight.

"You know me well," Grey said.

Viktor spread his hands. "You're a simple man."

"True."

"Not in the slightest." He helped Grey arrange the bedside tray. "But when it comes to the senses, we can all become simple."

Grey clacked the chopsticks. "Was that a jab at me for trusting Anka?"

"It was a jab at myself."

"For what?"

"For everything," Viktor said. "My apologies for the delay. After my release I debriefed Jacques and came straight here. Texting him was a smart move."

Grey worked the utensils with practiced flair, shoving sashimi into his mouth. "I figured an order from Interpol would be more effective than me trying to explain that insanity to a British cop over the phone."

"Indeed. But how did you find us in the first place?"

In between bites Grey summarized the events of the past few days. Viktor pursed his lips and listened. "Well reasoned," he said. "And my utmost gratitude."

Grey waved a hand. "Call us even for the sushi. So what was Darius's big surprise? A Mayan-inspired cataclysm? Jesus conspiracy theory?"

"According to Jacques, the police found a computer station in one of the tombs, manned by a hacker Jacques tells me is wanted for international cyber attacks."

"Those guys don't come cheap," Grey said. "But after the balance sheets I saw, that wouldn't have been a problem. What was he doing?"

"Preparing to broadcast a live feed on the Internet, via a virus that would hit the world's major news sites and interrupt their programming with a DVD prepared by Darius."

"I'm afraid to ask," Grey said.

"How familiar are you with the hierarchy of the Catholic Church?"

"I saw *Angels & Demons*."

Viktor cracked a smile. "Technically the hierarchy is quite flat: the pope, a couple of thousand bishops, and a few hundred thousand priests. But among the bishops there are powerful archbishops and cardinals, with a wide sphere of influence. The confiscated DVD exhibits sexual acts being performed by a number of the Western world's most powerful archbishops and cardinals."

Grey whistled. "How many?"

"Many."

"With who?"

"The faces of the other participants were digitally obscured," Viktor said, "and Jacques's people haven't been able to unscramble the images. But he tells me it was one man and one woman, sometimes alone with the priests, sometimes together. Occasionally a minor was also involved; it appears Darius was accounting for a variety of proclivities. Jacques tells me the images were . . . quite graphic."

"Did the woman have blond hair?" Grey said.

"She did."

Grey wiped his mouth. "Something like that could bring down the Church."

"So thought Darius."

"And you don't? Some of the highest-ranking members of a celibate order broadcast over the Internet performing threesomes with a minor?"

Viktor started to pace, stopping to look out the window. "Have the recent molestation scandals—evidence of which was found in the Vatican's own archives—brought down the Church? How many arrests at the higher levels have been made, how many parishes have been closed? No, this DVD would have made headlines worldwide, been discredited, a few reprimands made, and business at the world's wealthiest entity would have proceeded as normal."

"Perhaps," Grey said quietly. "Perhaps not. The DVD's already disappeared, hasn't it?"

"Faster than a Russian summer. There was a man with the police, the man I told you who'd been following me, and who I assumed was part of Darius's organization."

"I saw him at the end. He led the medics to me."

"He paid me a visit at the hospital," Viktor said. "His name is Farinata, and he's a ranking member of the Vatican's Swiss Guard. Somehow the Church discovered that a few of the cardinals had been compromised, and he was sent to control the damage."

"And he followed you because he knew you were investigating the murders, and he had no idea what else to do. He never approached you because he wanted to ensure all evidence was destroyed before involving anyone outside the Church."

"Presumably," Viktor said. "He didn't say. Curiously he himself had never heard of the Tutori. He told the Vatican where I had gone in Sicily, and connections were made."

"That must have caused a bit of heartburn in Rome. And Jacques called him after he got my text?"

"That, or he was in contact with the London police," Viktor said. "The Vatican has ways of keeping tabs on information it desires."

"So he showed up at the hospital with his tail between his legs, begging for silence."

"And asking whether we knew of any copies of the DVD," Viktor said. "The prospect of *that* will give them heartburn. He extended an apology on behalf of the Church and offered a reward for our troubles. I declined."

"Thanks for asking me," Grey said drily. He shoved a piece of tuna sashimi into his mouth. "Darius is dead, I assume."

"Anka stabbed him twenty-three times before they reached her."

Grey remembered the disturbing things Anka had told him at the end, the sight of her face just before she had killed Darius. He set down his chopsticks halfway to his mouth. "I suppose she hated him after all."

"Or she believed what the Sicilian priest told me," Viktor said with a smirk. "That Ahriman favors only one." He waved a hand in dismissal. "Whatever her reason, she's in custody. Something else: Jacques discovered there was a passenger on your San Francisco flight listed as Eve Summerfield, from Glaisdale. You can sleep better knowing Anka was booked on that flight."

Grey didn't think he would sleep better for a long time. Had Anka been insane all along, or had Darius tortured her to the point of mental instability? Had she, too, had a glimpse of that damnable book? Did something inside it have the power to warp, whether real or imagined?

Despite his bleak view of the world, Grey was at his core an optimist in the potential of the human spirit. He still wanted to help the woman whose touch had haunted his dreams, and whose life story, if at all to be believed, was a sad tale no matter what had later transpired. He wanted her to be spared the horror of those gray walls and bars.

Then his mind flashed, from her beckoning lips and sincere green eyes to the woman who had seduced and then placed poison-filled bottles in the rooms of multiple men, probably himself included; to the woman who had performed unspeakable acts in the video Viktor had described; to the woman who had stalked the Parisian catacombs with confidence and purpose, mingling with the members of L'église de la Bête, at home among the leering skulls and bones.

To the woman who had tried to use him even at the end.

Whoever she had once been, she had been made into someone else, her lost innocence warped by the power of evil into a weapon of unusual beauty and deceit.

"Farinata said the Ahriman Grimoire was never found," Viktor was saying, pulling Grey's thoughts back to the room. "Though Darius wouldn't have kept if far from his side. I've a strong suspicion it's now resting in a secret vault in the Vatican."

"What'd the media say?" Grey said.

"The Vatican orchestrated a cover-up, and since Niles Widecombe is a major MP, I suspect the British government didn't protest too much. A news release claimed Simon Azar has embarked on an undisclosed spiritual sabbatical. Some of his worshippers have already disbanded, some have formed splinter groups, some have proclaimed him the new messiah and await his return."

"Lovely."

"Jacques cleared up a few things as well," Viktor said. "As we suspected, they found a tiny ignition device in the sleeve of Darius's robe, a quite sophisticated mini-flamethrower."

"But how'd the flames spread so quickly on the victims? And how did you avoid being burned?"

"When Darius held me captive, he brought me into the bedroom filthy from my travels, allowing me a final cleansing before donning the ceremonial robe. Darius leaves nothing to chance, so I suspected an ulterior purpose. We already theorized the robes had been doctored, but when I saw the soap in the shower, it hit me. Darius was a chemist, not a tailor. Testing has already confirmed that the victims were literally coating their skin with a water-resistant chemical accelerant, and that's how they burned so fast and at such a high degree."

Grey whistled. "Clever. It fits with the poisoned perfume as well. Chemical concoctions in everyday products. How'd he manage the fire with the other two victims, if he wasn't actually there?"

"With an assistant and misdirection, I'm sure of it. When I was with Gareth it was chaotic, and the guard conveniently ran past Gareth right when the fire started. I'll bet my diplomas Oak and the guard were using mini-igniters."

"We still don't know how he managed the disappearing act." Grey said.

"The art of deception, in the rights hands, is a very powerful tool."

Grey looked Viktor in the eye. "When I climbed onto the tomb to throw the knife, it took me some time to gather my strength. I saw him touch you and disappear."

Viktor shrugged, but Grey saw a flicker of doubt buried deep in his eyes.

Grey continued, "At the cemetery I saw Oak, Alec Lister, and at least one member of the Beast Church I recognized from the catacombs. Did Jacques ask them about the disappearances?"

"To a person, they swore Darius had the power of the Devil. All of which reinforces the theory that for his greatest illusion, he confided in no one."

"Was there any evidence of hologram capability at the computer station?" Grey said.

"No."

"What about the research on bilocation?"

"Theoretically possible, I suppose. Though there are no verified cases of anyone being able to control such a phenomena to that degree."

"And you verify that how, exactly?" Grey said. "So your theory is an illusion of which we have no proof, and which you, an expert at debunking the supernatural, witnessed up close and personal."

"At night, in a cemetery, with ample time and opportunity to arrange an illusion beforehand."

"You touched his hand." Grey said.

"I *thought* I did."

Grey gave Viktor a long stare, then ticked off the choices on his fingers. "So it's an impossible illusion, astral projection or bilocation, some other arcane working of the universe of which we're unaware, or the power of the Devil."

"I can admit," Viktor said evenly, "that perhaps the power of Darius's belief allowed extraordinary psychosomatic acts to occur. This is uncharacteristic of you, Grey. Aren't you the Doubting Thomas?"

"Just seeing where you stand."

"I see," Viktor said. "And what did you learn?"

"That you're not convinced yourself of what happened."

Viktor's hand moved as if to straighten his tie, then he seemed to realize he wasn't wearing one. He folded his arms instead. "You can trust me when I say I don't believe that Darius gained the favor of a being named Ahriman, who made him handsome, charming, and afforded him the power of teleportation."

Grey said softly, "You almost died, Viktor, because you left me and went to Sicily to pursue the grimoire. And you still can't believe?"

"I went to Sicily to gain insight into Darius's actions. If I hadn't, I might not be alive."

"I'm afraid if something *is* out there," Grey said, "watching us from the spiritual realm or the astral plane or wherever the hell else, you can never prove it. And you might kill yourself trying to."

Viktor looked through Grey for a long moment. "Maybe there's nothing more than an unthinking and impossibly complex universe. Or maybe there's a personal God after all, or an unfathomable entity to whom we can never hope to relate, or something else entirely. All we can do is scrape at the truth and discredit anything false. What greater calling is there?"

"How about living life?"

"Why the third degree?" Viktor said. "Why does this matter so much to you?"

"Because what *I* care about is not seeing my partner killed."

Viktor seemed taken aback, then bent to clasp Grey's hand. "Thank you, my friend," he whispered.

"What'd you say to Darius at the end?" Grey said. "I heard you shout something, but I didn't recognize the language."

"It was Old Persian. Roughly translated, I said, 'In the name of Ahriman, the true God, thee I do swallow.'"

"Okay, that's chilling. Why exactly did you say that?"

"The priest I met in Sicily gave me the idea, as did my previous observances of Juju and other auto-suggestive mental phenomena. After the fire failed to burn me, I wanted to continue to erode Darius's faith, if for nothing else than to buy time."

"Let me get this straight—you hedged your bets by allowing for the possibility that Ahriman had granted Darius powers?"

"No," Viktor said, "I allowed for the possibility that Darius *believed* that Ahriman had granted him these powers."

"I thought you were a professor, not a lawyer." Grey ran a hand through his hair, leaving it cupped behind his neck. "I have a question for you, something that's been on my mind during this case for obvious reasons."

"Of course."

"Do you believe in evil?" Grey said.

Viktor chuckled.

"That wasn't supposed to be a joke."

"A student at a recent lecture asked me the same question," Viktor said.

"And has your answer changed?"

Viktor compressed his lips. "We're two generations away from Adolf Hitler, Rwanda and the Balkans are barely scabbed wounds. You yourself witnessed the depravity of L'église de la Bête. So no, I don't question the existence of evil. I just want to know where it comes from. And what's your opinion on the matter, my promising young student, after a year in the field?"

"Of course evil exists. And I don't give a damn where it comes from."

Viktor's eyes crinkled. "I suppose that's why we make a good team."

Grey noticed Viktor's hands had started to shake, whether from the lack of absinthe or from the weight of memory or from something else, Grey wasn't sure.

Viktor turned towards the door, and Grey said, "Heading back to Prague?"

Viktor kept his hands in front of him, out of Grey's line of sight. "Just stepping out for a bit of air."

"No need to stick around on my behalf. I've been in worse shape."

"It's not a need, Grey."

He left the room. Grey let his gaze linger on the closed door for a long time after Viktor left, then shifted to look out the window, at the afternoon light struggling to streak through the clouds.

Late that night, when Grey was alone with the beeping monitors, he found himself thinking, despite his strong words, about what had transpired. Though he saw no intrinsic value in it, maybe part of him, maybe part of everyone, yearned to know what this bottomless sea of atoms in which we swim was all about, this Ping-Pong game of quarks and quasars and dark energy, played out by forces unseen, wielding the paddles with such caprice.

And if a Supreme Being did exist, he had to admit he rather liked the idea of a more human concept of God, a God who was something less than perfect, and thus not accountable for evil. He knew the theologians would tell him how juvenile that was and that absolute free will was necessary and that our omnipotent God, with all his smiting, was like a father to a two-year-old because sometimes punishment just had to be given, and that, like two-year-olds, we humans become confused when we try to find rhyme or reason in God's actions, and the reality is that we just can't see clearly enough. And, so those theologians would argue, it was all okay because God knew exactly what He was doing when He created such flawed creatures and set the stage for a world where fathers beat their sons and men in white collars rape little boys and serial killers torture victims in dank holes and whole races are enslaved and whole cities are atomized and Jews are shoved into ovens and pink-skinned gurgling babies are born into crack houses.

Though he disagreed with those theologians, Grey could concede that maybe he just wasn't smart enough to understand the finer points of all the arguments. But he didn't really care, because he didn't think it mattered.

Grey thought in human terms, because that was the perspective he was given, and he thought the followers of all religions and cultures and creeds, people everywhere, knew the basic difference between right and wrong. That it was only when someone wanted something so badly that they began to justify their actions.

His eyes sought the window again, the dark. It was with us all, and he thought no one really needed to question the definition of evil. Because even if you didn't know why or understand how, you recognized it, and you knew.

You just knew.

# Acknowledgments

As they say, it takes a village, and I can't thank everyone enough who had a hand in this book. Special thanks to C-Money, J-Wall, Rusty, my wife, McLemore, and Mom for above and beyond support, assistance, and encouragement. Congrats again to Richard Marek for sending me into a tailspin of despair with his incisive comments—I wouldn't have it any other way. Andrea Hurst provided amazing editorial support. Mike Burke, M.D., made sure the book passed muster with the principles of medical science. A special nod to Scott Nicholson for his selfless support of a young author. Heartfelt thanks to Alan Turkus and the rest of the team at Thomas & Mercer for their mad publishing skills, enthusiasm, and for taking me on. And to Steve Axelrod, my scarily savvy agent: thanks for guiding me through.

Finally, a very grateful shout out to all the book bloggers and reviewers who helped get this series off the ground with their grassroots support. Thanks for what you do for books.

ROBIN SHETLER PHOTOGRAPHY

## ABOUT THE AUTHOR

LAYTON GREEN is the author of the Dominic Grey series and other works. Please visit him at www.laytongreen.com for additional information on Layton, his works, and more. He might also be spotted in the corner of a dark and smoky café in Bogotá, researching the next Dominic Grey novel.